Jim Waring
of Sonora-Town

Or, Tang of Life

by

Henry Herbert Knibbs

Double9
BOOKS

Jim Waring of Sonora-Town
Or, Tang of Life
by Henry Herbert Knibbs

ISBN: 978-93-62767-17-2

Published by

DOUBLE 9 BOOKS

2/13-B, Ansari Road
Daryaganj, New Delhi – 110002
info@double9books.com
www.double9books.com
Tel. 011-40042856

ABOUT THE AUTHOR

Henry Herbert Knibbs is a distinguished author renowned for his masterpiece "Jim Waring Of Sonora-Town: Or, Tang Of Life," a captivating tale that immerses readers in the rugged landscapes and untamed spirit of the American West. Set against the backdrop of Sonora-Town, Knibbs's evocative prose transports readers to a bygone era, where cowboys, outlaws, and pioneers collide in a whirlwind of adventure and intrigue. "Jim Waring Of Sonora-Town" follows the eponymous protagonist as he navigates the complexities of life on the frontier, grappling with love, loss, and the pursuit of justice. Through Knibbs's vivid descriptions and rich characterizations, readers are drawn into a world where honor is tested, and destinies are forged in the crucible of hardship and resilience. As a work of fiction deeply rooted in the traditions of Western literature, "Jim Waring Of Sonora-Town" stands as a testament to Knibbs's talent for capturing the raw beauty and rugged charm of the American West. With its timeless themes of courage, redemption, and the enduring bonds of friendship, Knibbs's masterpiece continues to captivate audiences and inspire generations of readers with its powerful portrayal of the human spirit.

CONTENTS

Chapter I
The Cañon

Waring picketed his horse in a dim angle of the Agua Fria Cañon, spread his saddle-blanket to dry in the afternoon sun, and, climbing to a narrow ledge, surveyed the cañon from end to end with a pair of high-power glasses. He knew the men he sought would ride south. He was reasonably certain that they would not ride through the cañon in daylight. The natural trail through the Agua Fria was along the western wall; a trail that he had avoided, working his toilsome way down the eastern side through a labyrinth of brush and rock that had concealed him from view. A few hundred yards below his hasty camp a sandy arroyo crossed the cañon's mouth.

He had planned to intercept the men where the trail crossed this arroyo, or, should the trail show pony tracks, to follow them into the desert beyond, where, sooner or later, he would overtake them. They had a start of twelve hours, but Waring reasoned that they would not do much riding in daylight. The trail at the northern end of the cañon had shown no fresh tracks that morning. His problem was simple. The answer would be definite. He returned to the shelter of the brush, dropped the glasses into a saddle-pocket, and stretched himself wearily.

A few yards below him, on a brush-dotted level, his horse, Dexter, slowly circled his picket and nibbled at the scant bunch-grass. The western sun trailed long shadows across the cañon; shadows that drifted imperceptibly farther and farther, spreading, commingling, softening the broken outlines of ledge and brush until the walled solitude was brimmed with dusk, save where a red shaft cleft the fast-fading twilight, burning like a great spotlight on a picketed horse and a man asleep, his head pillowed on a saddle.

As the dusk drew down, the horse ceased grazing, sniffed the coming night, and nickered softly. Waring rose and led the horse to water, and, returning, emptied half the grain in the morral on a blanket. Dex munched contentedly. When the horse had finished eating the grain, Waring picketed him in a fresh spot and climbed back to the ledge, where he sat watching the western wall of the cañon, occasionally glancing up as some dim star burned through the deepening dusk and bloomed to a silvery maturity.

Presently a faint pallor overspread the cañon till it lay like a ghostly sea dotted with strange islands of brush and rock; islands that seemed to waver and shift in a sort of vague restlessness, as though trying to evade the ever-brightening tide of moonlight that burned away their shrouds of dusk and fixed them in still, tangible shapes upon the cañon floor.

Across the cañon the farther trail ran past a broad, blank wall of rock. No horseman could cross that open space unseen. Waring, seated upon the ledge, leaned back against the wall, watching the angling shadows shorten as the moon drew overhead. Toward morning he became drowsy. As the white radiance paled to gray, he rose and paced back and forth upon the narrow ledge to keep himself awake. In a few minutes the moon would disappear behind the farther rim of the world; the cañon would sink back into its own night, all its moonlit imageries melting, vanishing. In the hour before dawn Waring would be unable to see anything of the farther wall save a wavering blur.

Just below him he could discern the outline of his horse, with head lowered, evidently dozing. Having in mind the keenness of desert-bred stock, he watched the horse. The minutes drifted by. The horse seemed more distinct. Waring thought he could discern the picket rope. He endeavored to trace it from horse to picket. Foot by foot his eyes followed its slack outline across the ground. The head of the metal picket glimmered faintly. Waring closed his eyes, nodded, and caught himself. This time he traced the rope from picket to horse. It seemed a childish thing to do, yet it kept him awake. Did he imagine it, or had the rope moved?

Dex had lifted his head. He was sniffing the cool morning air. Slowly the tawny-golden shape of the big buckskin turned, head up and nostrils rounded in tense rings. Waring glanced across the cañon. The farther wall was still dim in the half-light. In a few minutes the trail would become distinct. Dropping from the ledge, he stepped to his saddle. Dex evidently heard him, for he twitched back one ear, but maintained his attitude of keen interest in an invisible something—a something that had drawn him from drowsy inanition to a quietly tense statue of alertness. The ash gray of the farther wall, now visible, slowly changed to a faint rose tint that deepened and spread.

Waring stooped and straightened up, with his glasses held on the far trail. A tiny rider appeared in the clear blue circle of the binoculars, and another, who led two horses without saddles or packs. The men were headed south. Presently they disappeared behind a wall of brush. Waring saddled Dex, and, keeping close to the eastern wall, rode toward the arroyo.

The morning sun traced clean, black shadows of the chaparral on the sand. The bloom of cacti burned in red and yellow blotches of flame against its own dull background of grayish-green. At the mouth of the arroyo, Waring dismounted and dropped the reins. Dex nosed him inquiringly. He patted the horse, and, turning, strode swiftly down the dry river-bed. He walked upright, knowing that he could not be seen from the trail. He could even have ridden down the arroyo unseen, and perhaps it was a senseless risk to hunt men afoot in this land. The men he hunted were Mexicans of Sonora; fugitives. They would fight blindly, spurred by fear. Waring's very name terrorized them. And were they to come upon the gringo mounted, Waring knew that there was more than a chance his horse would be shot. He had a peculiar aversion to running such a risk when there was half a chance of doing his work on foot.

Moreover, certain Americans in Sonora who disliked Waring had said recently that no man was quick enough to get an even break with the gunman, which tentatively placed him as a "killer," whereas he had never given a thought to the hazard when going into a fight. He had always played the game to win, odds either way. The men he sought would be mounted. He would be on foot. This time the fugitives would have more than a fair chance. They would blunder down the pitch into the arroyo, perhaps glancing back, fearful of pursuit, but apprehending no ambushment.

Waring knew they would kill him if they could. He knew that not even a fighting chance would have been his were they in his place and he in theirs. He was deputized and paid to do just what he was doing. The men were bandits who had robbed the paymaster of the Ortez Mines. To Waring there was nothing complicated about the matter. It was his day's work. The morning sun would be in their faces, but that was not his fault.

As Waring waited in the arroyo the faint clatter of shod hoofs came from above. He drew close to a cutbank, leaning his shoulder against it easily. With a slither of sand, the first horse took the pitch, legs angled awkwardly as he worked down. The second rider followed, the led horses pulling back.

At the bottom of the arroyo, the Mexicans reined up. The elder, squat, broad of back, a black handkerchief tied round his thick neck, reached into his pocket and drew out tobacco and cigarette papers. The other, hardly more than a boy, urged that they hasten. Fear vibrated in his voice. The squat Mexican laughed and began to roll a cigarette.

> None had overtaken them, he said. And were they not now
> in the Land Where No Man Lived?

"Si!" said Waring softly.

The half-rolled cigarette fluttered to the ground. The Mexican's heavy lip sagged, showing broken teeth. His companion dropped the lead-rope and turned to gaze at Waring with eyes wide, wondering, curious. The led horses plunged up the back trail. Waring made no movement toward his gun, but he eyed the elder Mexican sharply, paying little attention to the youth. The horse of the squat Mexican grew restless, sidling toward the other.

Waring's lips tightened. The bandit was spurring his horse on the off side to get behind his companion. Evidently the numbness of surprise had given way to fear, and fear meant action. Waring knew that the elder Mexican would sacrifice his companion for the sake of a chance of killing the gringo.

Waring held out his left hand. "Give me your gun," he said to the youth "And hand it down butt first."

The youth, as though hypnotized, pulled out his gun and handed it to Waring. Waring knew that if the other Mexican meant to fight it would be at that instant. Even as the butt of the gun touched Waring's hand it jumped. Two shattering reports blended and died echoless in the close-walled arroyo.

The Mexican's gun slipped slowly from his fingers. He rocked in the saddle, grasped the horn, and slid to the ground. Waring saw him reach for the gun where it lay on the sand. He kicked it aside. The Mexican youth leaped from the saddle and stood between Waring and the fallen man. Waring stepped back. For an instant his eyes drew fine. He was tempted to make an end of it right there. The youth dropped to his knees. A drift of wind fluttered the bandanna at his throat. Waring saw a little silver crucifix gleaming against the smooth brown of his chest.

"If it is that I am to die, I am not afraid," said the youth. "I have this!" And his fingers touched the crucifix. "But you will not kill my uncle!"

Waring hesitated. He seemed to be listening. And as though in a dream, yet distinct—clear as though he had spoken himself came the words: "It is enough!"

"Not this journey," said Waring.

The Mexican youth gazed at him wonderingly. Was the gringo mad?

Waring holstered his gun with a jerk. "Get up on your hind legs and quit that glory stuff! We ride north," he growled.

Chapter II
José Vaca

The young Mexican's face was beaded with sweat as he rose and stared down at the wounded man. Clumsily he attempted to help Waring, who washed and bandaged the shattered shoulder. Waring had shot to kill, but the gun was not his own, and he had fired almost as it had touched his hand.

"Get your uncle on his horse," he told the youth. "Don't make a break We're due at Juan Armigo's ranchito about sundown."

So far as he was concerned, that was all there was to it for the time being. He had wounded and captured José Vaca, notorious in Sonora as leader in outlawry. That there were no others of Vaca's kind with him puzzled Waring. The young Ramon, Vaca's nephew, did not count.

Ramon helped his uncle to mount. They glanced at each other, Vaca's eyes blinking. The gringo was afoot. They were mounted. Waring, observing their attitude, smiled, and, crooking his finger, whistled shrilly. The young Ramon trembled. Other gringos were hidden in the arroyo; perhaps the very man that his uncle had robbed! Even now he could hear the click of hoofs on the gravel. The gunman had been merciful for the moment, only to turn his captives over to the merciless men of the mines; men who held a Mexican's life worth no more than a dog's. The wounded man, stiff in the saddle, turned his head. Round a bend in the dry river-bed, his neck held sideways that the reins might drag free, came Waring's big buckskin horse, Dexter. The horse stopped as he saw the group. Waring spoke to him. The big buckskin stepped forward and nosed Waring, who swung to the saddle and gestured toward the back trail.

They rode in silence, the Mexicans with bowed heads, dull-eyed, listless, resigned to their certain fate. For some strange reason the gringo had not killed them in the arroyo. He had had excuse enough.

Would he take them to Sonora—to the prison? Or would he wait until they were in some hidden fastness of the Agua Fria, and there kill them and leave them to the coyotes? The youth Ramon knew that the two little canvas sacks of gold were cleverly tied in the huge tapaderas of his uncle's saddle. Who would think to look for them there?

The gringo had said that they would ride to the ranchito of Juan Armigo. How easily the gringo had tricked them at the very moment when they thought they were safe! Yet he had not asked about the stolen money. The ways of this gringo were past comprehension.

Waring paid scant attention to the Mexicans, but he glanced continuously from side to side of the cañon, alert for a surprise. The wounded man, Vaca, was known to him. He was but one of the bandits. Ramon, Vaca's nephew, was not of their kind, but had been led into this journey by Vaca that the bandit might ride wide when approaching the ranchos and send his nephew in for supplies.

The pack on Ramon's saddle rode too lightly to contain anything heavier than food. There was nothing tied to Vaca's saddle but a frayed and faded blanket. Yet Waring was certain that they had not cached the gold; that they carried it with them.

At noon they watered the horses midway up the cañon. As they rode on again, Waring noticed that Vaca did not thrust his foot clear home in the stirrup, but he attributed this to the other's condition. The Mexican was a sick man. His swarthy face had gone yellow, and he leaned forward, clutching the horn. The heat was stagnant, unwavering. The pace was desperately slow.

Despite his vigilance, Waring's mind grew heavy with the monotony. He rolled a cigarette. The smoke tasted bitter. He flung the cigarette away. The hunting of men had lost its old-time thrill. A clean break and a hard fight; that was well enough. But the bowed figures riding ahead of him: ignorant, superstitious, brutal; numb to any sense of honor. Was the game worth while? Yet they were men—human in that they feared, hoped, felt hunger, thirst, pain, and even dreamed of vague successes to be attained how or when the Fates would decide. And was this squalid victory a recompense for the risks he ran and the hardships he endured?

Again Waring heard the Voice, as though from a distance, and yet the voice was his own: "You will turn back from the hunting of men."

"Like hell I will!" muttered Waring.

Ramon, who rode immediately ahead of him, turned in the saddle. Waring gestured to him to ride on.

The heat grew less intense as an occasional, vagrant breeze stirred in the brush and fluttered the handkerchief round Waring's throat. Ahead, the cañon broadened to the mesa lands, where the distant green of a line of trees marked the boundary of the Armigo rancho.

Presently Vaca began to sing; softly at first, then with insane vehemence as the fever mounted to his brain. Waring smiled with dry lips. The Mexican had stood the journey well. A white man in Vaca's condition would have gone to pieces hours ago. He called to Ramon, who gave Vaca water. The Mexican drank greedily, and threw the empty canteen into the bushes.

Waring listened for some hint, some crazy boast as to the whereabouts of the stolen money. But Vaca rode on, occasionally breaking into a wild song, half Yaqui, half Mexican. The youth Ramon trembled, fearing that the gringo would lose patience.

Across the northern end of the cañon the winnowing heat waves died to the level of the ground. Brown shadows shot from the western wall and spread across the widening outlet. The horses stepped briskly, knowing that they were near water.

Waring became more alert as they approached the adobe buildings of the rancho. Vaca had drifted into a dull silence. Gray with suffering and grim with hate for the gringo, he rode stolidly, praying incoherently that the gunman might be stricken dead as he rode.

The raw edge of the disappearing sun leveled a long flame of crimson across the mesa. The crimson melted to gold. The gold paled to a brief twilight. A faint star twinkled in the north.

Dogs crowded forward in the dusk, challenging the strange riders. A figure filled the lighted doorway of the Armigo ranch-house. The dogs drew back.

Ramon dismounted and helped his uncle down. Waring sat his horse until Juan Armigo stepped from the doorway and asked who came. Waring answered with his name.

"Si! Si!" exclaimed Armigo. "The señor is welcome."

Waring dismounted. "Juan, I have two of your friends here; José Vaca and Ramon Ortego."

Armigo seemed surprised. "José Vaca is wounded?" he queried hesitatingly.

Waring nodded.

"And the horses; they shall have feed, water, everything—I myself—"

"Thanks. But I'll look after the horses, Juan. I'm taking Vaca and Ramon to Sonora. See what you can do for Vaca. He's pretty sick."

"It shall be as the señor says. And the señor has made a fight?"

"With those hombres? Not this journey! José Vaca made a mistake; that's all."

Armigo, perturbed, shuffled to the house. Waring unsaddled the horses and turned them into the corral. As he lifted the saddle from Vaca's horse, he hesitated. It was a big stock saddle and heavy; yet it seemed too heavy. On his knees he turned it over, examining it. He smiled grimly as he untied the little canvas sacks and drew them from the tapaderas.

"Thought he showed too much boot for a hard-riding chola," muttered Waring.

He rose and threw some hay to the horses. He could hear Ramon and Armigo talking in the ranch-house. Taking his empty canteen from his own saddle, he untied the sacks and slipped the gold-pieces, one by one, into the canteen. He scooped up sand and filled the canteen half full. The gold no longer jingled as he shook it.

While Waring had no fear that either of the men would attempt to escape, he knew Mexicans too well to trust Armigo explicitly. A thousand dollars was a great temptation to a poor rancher. And while Armigo had always professed to be Waring's friend, sympathy of blood and the appeal of money easily come by might change the placid face of things considerably.

Waring strode to the house, washed and ate with Juan in the kitchen; then he invited the Mexican out to the corral.

"José and Ramon are your countrymen, Juan."

"Si, señor. I am sorry for Ramon. This thing was not of his doing. He is but a boy—"

Waring touched the other's arm. "There will be no trouble, Juan. Only keep better track of your horses while I ride this part of the country."

"But—señor—"

"I've had business with you before. Two of your cayuses are astray down the Agua Fria. One of them is dragging a maguey lead-rope."

"Señor, it is impossible!"

"No, it isn't! I know your brand. See here, Juan. You knew that Vaca was trying to get away. You knew I'd be sent to get him. Why did you let him take two spare horses?"

"But, señor, I swear I did not!"

"All right. Then when Ramon rode in here two days ago and asked you for two horses, why didn't you refuse him? Why did you tell him you would sell them, but that you would not lend them to him?"

"If Ramon says that, he lies. I told Ramon—"

"Thanks. That's all I want to know. I don't care what you told Ramon. You let him take the horses. Now, I'm going to tell you something that will be worth more to you than gold. Don't try to rope any stock grazing round here to-night. I might wake up quick and make a mistake. Men look alike in the moonlight—and we'll have a moon."

"It shall be as the señor says. It is fate."

"All right, amigo. But it isn't fate. It's making fool mistakes when you or your countrymen tackle a job like Vaca tackled. Just get me a couple of blankets. I'll sleep out here to-night."

Juan Armigo plodded to the adobe. The lamplight showed his face beaded with sweat. He shuffled to an inner room, and came out with blankets on his arm. Vaca lay on a bed-roll in the corner of the larger room, and near him stood Ramon.

"The señor sleeps with the horses," said Armigo significantly.

Ramon bent his head and muttered a prayer.

"And if you pray," said Armigo, shifting the blankets from one arm to the other, "pray then that the two horses that you borrowed may return. As for your Uncle José, he will not die."

"And we shall be taken to the prison," said Ramon."

"You should have killed the gringo." And Armigo's tone was matter-of-fact. "Or perhaps told him where you had hidden the gold. He might have let you go, then."

Ramon shook his head. Armigo's suggestion was too obviously a question as to the whereabouts of the stolen money.

The wounded man opened his eyes. "I have heard," he said faintly. "Tell the gringo that I will say where the money is hidden if he will let me go."

"It shall be as you wish," said Armigo, curious to learn more of the matter.

At the corral he delivered Vaca's message to Waring, who feigned delight at the other's information.

"If that is so, Tio Juan," he laughed, "you shall have your share—a hundred pesos. Leave the blankets there by my saddle. We will go to the house."

From the coolness of night, with its dim radiance of stars, to the accumulated heat of the interior of the adobe was an unpleasant change. The walls were whitewashed and clean enough, but the place smelled strongly of cooking. A lamp burned on the oilcloth-covered table. Ramon, wide-eyed with trepidation, stood by his uncle, who had braced himself on his elbow as Waring approached. Waring nodded pleasantly and rolled a cigarette. José Vaca glared up at him hungrily. The lower lip, pendulous, showed his broken teeth. Waring thought of a trapped wolf. Juan glanced from one to the other.

But the gringo seemed incurious, merely gazing at the pictures on the walls; a flaming print of the Madonna, one of the Christ, a cheap photograph of Juan and his señora taken on their wedding day, an abalone shell on which was painted something resembling a horse and rider—

"The gold is hidden in the house of Pedro Salazar, of Sonora. It is buried in the earth beneath his bed."

José Vaca had spoken, but Waring was watching Ramon's eyes.

"All right, hombre. Muchas gracias."

"And now you will let me go?" queried Vaca.

"I haven't said so." Waring's tone was pleasant, almost indifferent.

Ramon's face was troubled. Of what use was it to try and deceive the gringo? But Waring was smiling. Did he, then, believe such an obvious lie?

"Bueno!" Waring exclaimed. "That lets *you* out. Now, what about you, Ramon?"

"My uncle has spoken," said Ramon. "I have nothing to say."

"Then you will ride with me to Sonora."

"As you say, señor."

"All right. Don't sit up all night praying. That won't do any good. Get some sleep. And you, too, Juan." And Waring turned quickly to Armigo. "Sleep all you can. You'll feel better in the morning."

Waring turned and strode out. In the corral he spread his blankets. With his head on the saddle, he lay gazing up at the stars.

The horses, with the exception of Waring's buckskin Dex, huddled in one corner of the corral. That strange shape stretched quietly on the ground was new to them.

For a long time the horse Dex stood with head lowered and one hip sagged as he rested. Just before Waring slept he felt a gentle nosing of his blankets. The big horse sniffed curiously.

"Strange blankets, eh?" queried Waring drowsily. "But it's the same old partner, Dex."

The horse walked slowly away, nosing along the fence. Waring knew that he was well sentineled. The big buckskin would resent the approach of a stranger by snorting. Waring turned on his side and slept. His day's work was done.

Chapter III
Donovan's Hand

Waring was up with the first faint streak of dawn. He threw hay to the horses and strode briskly to the adobe. Juan Armigo was bending over the kitchen stove. Waring nodded to him and stepped to the next room. The Mexicans were asleep; young Ramon lying face down beneath the crucifix on the wall, where he had knelt in prayer most of the night.

Waring drew back quietly.

"Let them sleep," he told Juan in the kitchen.

After frijoles and coffee, the gunman rose and gestured to Juan to follow him.

Out near the corral, Waring turned suddenly. "You say that young Ramon is straight?"

"Si, señor. He is a good boy."

"Well, he's in dam' bad company. How about Vaca?"

Juan Armigo shrugged his shoulders.

"Are you afraid of him, Juan?"

"No. But if he were to ask me for anything, it would be well to let him have it."

"I see. So he sent young Ramon in here for two extra horses, and you were afraid to refuse. I had thought you were an honest man. After I have gone, go hunt up those horses in the cañon. And if any one from Sonora rides in here and asks about Ramon or Vaca or me, you don't know anything about us. Sabe? If your horses are found before you get to them, some one stole them. Do these things. I don't want to come back to see if you have done them."

Juan Armigo nodded, gazing at Waring with crafty eyes. So the gringo was tempted by the gold. He would ride back to Sonora, find the stolen money in the house of Pedro Salazar, and keep it. It would be a very simple thing to do. Young Ramon would be afraid to speak and José Vaca would have disappeared. The gringo could swear that he had not found the bandits or the gold. So reasoned Juan, his erstwhile respect for the gunman wavering as the idea became fixed. He grinned at Waring. It would be a good trick; to steal the gold from the stealers. Of a certainty the gringo was becoming almost as subtle as a Mexican.

Waring was not pleased as he read the other's eyes, but he said nothing. Turning abruptly, he entered the corral and saddled Ramon's horse and his own.

"Get José Vaca out of here as soon as he can travel," he told Armigo. "You may have to explain if he is found here." And Waring strode to the adobe.

Ramon was awake and talking with his uncle. Waring told him to get something to eat. Then he turned to Vaca.

"José," he began pleasantly, "you tried to get me yesterday, but you only spoiled a good Stetson. See? You shot high. When you go for a man again, start in at his belt-buckle and get him low. We'll let that go this time. When you can ride, take your cayuse and fan it anywhere—*but don't ride back to Sonora.* I'll be there. I'm going to herd young Ramon back home. He is isn't your kind. You are free. Don't jabber. Just tell all that to your saints. And if you get caught, don't say that you saw me. Sabe?"

The wounded man raised himself on his elbow, glaring up at Waring with feverish eyes. "You give me my life. I shall not speak."

"Bueno! And you said in the house of Pedro Salazar?"

"Si! Near the acequia."

"The Placeta Burro. I know the place. You'll find your horse and a saddle when you are able to ride."

The bandit's eyes glistened as he watched Waring depart. If the gringo entered the house of Pedro Salazar, he would not find the gold and he would not come out alive. The gringo gunman had killed the brother of Pedro Salazar down in the desert country years ago. And Salazar had had nothing to do with the Ortez Mine robbery. Vaca thought that the gold was still safe in his tapaderas. The gringo was a fool.

Waring led the two saddled horses to the house. Ramon, coming from the kitchen, blinked in the sunlight.

"It is my horse, but not my saddle, señor."

"You are an honest man," laughed Waring. "But we won't change saddles Come on!"

Ramon mounted and rode beside Waring until they were out of sight of the ranch-house, when Waring reined up.

"Where is that money?" he asked suddenly.

"I do not know, señor."

"Did you know where it was yesterday?"

Ramon hesitated. Was this a trap? Waring's level gaze held the young Mexican to a straight answer.

"Si, señor. I knew—yesterday."

"You knew; but you didn't talk up when your uncle tried to run me into Pedro Salazar."

"I—he is of my family."

"Well, I don't blame you. I see that you can keep from talking when you have to. And now is your chance to do a lot of keeping still. I'm going to ride into Sonora ahead of you. When you get in, go home and forget that you made this journey. If your folks ask where your uncle is, tell them that he rode south and that you turned back. Because you did didn't lie to me, and because you did didn't show yellow, I'm going to give you a chance to get out of this. I let your uncle go because he would have given you away to save himself the minute I jailed him in Sonora. It's up to you to keep out of trouble. You've had a scare that ought to last you. Take your time and hit Sonora about sundown. Adios."

"But—señor!"

Waring whirled his horse. "A good rider shoves his foot clear home," he called as he loped away.

Ramon sat his horse, gazing at the little puffs of dust that shot from the hoofs of the big buckskin. Surely the gringo was mad! Yet he was a man of big heart. Perplexed, stunned by the realization that he was alone and free, the young Mexican gazed about him. Waring was a tiny figure in the distance. Ramon dismounted and examined the empty tapaderas.

Heretofore he had considered subtlety, trickery, qualities to be desired, and not incompatible with honor. In a flash he realized the difference, the distinction between trickery and keenness of mind. He had been awed by his uncle's reputation and proud to name him of this family. Now he saw him for what he was. "My Uncle José is a bad man," he said to himself. "The other,—the gringo whom men call 'The Killer,'—he is a hard man, but assuredly he is not bad."

When Ramon spoke to his horse his voice trembled. His hand drifted up to the little silver crucifix on his breast. A vague glimmer of understanding, a sense of the real significance of the emblem heartened him to face the journey homeward and the questions of his kin. And, above all, he felt an admiration for the gringo that grew by degrees as he rode on. He could follow such a man to the end of the world, even across the border of the Great Unknown, for surely such a leader would not lose the way.

Three men sat in the office of the Ortez Mines, smoking and saying little. Donovan, the manager; the paymaster, Quigley; and the assistant manager, a young American fresh from the East. Waring's name was mentioned. Three days ago he had ridden south after the bandits. He might return. He might not.

"I'd like to see him ride in," said Donovan, turning to the paymaster.

"And you hate him at that," said Quigley.

"I don't say so. But if he was paymaster here, he'd put the fear of God into some of those greasers."

Quigley flushed. "You didn't hire me to chase greasers, Donovan. I'm no gunman."

"No," said Donovan slowly. "I had you sized up."

"Oh, cut out that stuff!" said the assistant manager, smiling. "That won't balance the pay-roll."

"No. But I'm going to cut down expenses." And Donovan eyed Quigley. "Jim Waring is too dam' high and mighty to suit me. Every time he tackles a job he is the big boss till it's done. If he comes back, all right. If he don't— we'll charge it up to profit and loss. But his name goes off the pay-roll to-day."

Quigley grinned. He knew that Donovan was afraid of Waring. Waring was the one man in Donovan's employ that he could not bully. Moreover, the big Irishman hated to pay Waring's price, which was stiff.

"How about a raise of twenty-five a month, then?" queried Quigley.

To his surprise, Donovan nodded genially. "You're on, Jack. And that goes the minute Waring shows up with the money. If he doesn't show up— why, that raise can wait."

"Then I'll just date the change to-day," said Quigley. "Take a look down the street."

Donovan rose heavily and stepped to the window. "By God, it's Waring, all right! He's afoot. What's that he's packing?"

"A canteen," said the assistant manager. "This is a dry country."

Donovan returned to his desk. "Get busy, at something. We don't want to sit here like a lot of stuffed buzzards. We're glad to see Waring back, of course. You two can drift out when I get to talking business with him."

Quigley nodded and took up his pen. The assistant manager studied a map.

Waring strode in briskly. The paymaster glanced up and nodded, expecting Donovan to speak. But Donovan sat with his back toward Waring, his head wreathed in tobacco smoke. He was apparently absorbed in a letter.

The gunman paused halfway across the office. Quigley fidgeted. The assistant superintendent stole a glance at Donovan's broad back and smiled. All three seemed waiting for Waring to speak. Quigley rather enjoyed the situation. The assistant superintendent's scalp prickled with restrained excitement.

He rose and stepped to Donovan. "Mr. Donovan, Mr. Waring is here."

"Thanks," said Waring, nodding to the assistant.

Donovan heaved himself round. "Why, hello, Jim! I didn't hear you come in."

Waring's cool gray eyes held Donovan with a mildly contemptuous gaze Still the gunman did not speak.

"Did you land 'em?" queried Donovan.

Waring shook his head.

"Hell!" exclaimed Donovan. "Then, what's the answer?"

"Bill, you can't bluff worth a damn!"

Quigley laughed. The assistant mopped his face with an immaculate handkerchief. The room was hot.

"Bill," and Waring's voice was softly insulting, "you can't bluff worth a damn."

Donovan's red face grew redder. "What are you driving at, anyway?"

Quigley stirred and rose. The assistant got to his feet.

"Just a minute," said Waring, gesturing to them to sit down. "Donovan's got something on his mind. I knew it the minute I came in. I want you fellows to hear it."

Donovan flung his half-smoked cigar to the floor and lighted a fresh one. Waring's attitude irritated him. Officially, Donovan was Waring's superior. Man to man, the Sonora gunman was Donovan's master, and the Irishman knew and resented it.

He tried a new tack. "Glad to see you back, Jim." And he rose and stuck out a sweating hand.

Waring swung the canteen from his shoulder and carefully hung the strap over Donovan's wrist. "There's your money, Bill. Count it—and give me a receipt."

Donovan, with the dusty canteen dangling from his arm, looked exceedingly foolish.

Waring turned to Quigley. "Bill's got a stroke," he said, smiling "Quigley, give me a receipt for a thousand dollars."

"Sure!" said Quigley, relieved. The money had been stolen from him.

Waring pulled up a chair and leaned his elbows on the table. Quigley unscrewed the cap of the canteen. A stream of sand shot across a map. The assistant started to his feet. Quigley shook the canteen and poured out a softly clinking pile of gold-pieces. One by one he sorted them from the sand and counted them.

"One thousand even. Where'd you overtake Vaca and his outfit?"

"Did I?" queried Waring.

"Well, you got the mazuma," said Quigley. "And that's good enough for me."

Donovan stepped to the table. "Williams, I won't need you any more to-day."

The assistant rose and left the office. Donovan pulled up a chair. "Never mind about that receipt, Quigley. You can witness that Waring returned the money. Jim, here, is not so dam' particular."

"No, or I wouldn't be on your pay-roll," said Waring.

Donovan laughed. "Let's get down to bed-rock, Jim. I'm paying you your own price for this work. The Eastern office thinks I pay too high. I got a letter yesterday telling me to cut down expenses. This last holdup will make them sore. Here's the proposition. I'll keep you on the pay-roll and charge this thousand up to profit and loss. Nobody knows you recovered this money except Williams, and he'll keep still. Quigley and you and I will split it—three hundred apiece."

"Suppose I stay out of the deal," said Waring.

"Why, that's all right. I guess we can get along."

Quigley glanced quickly at Waring. Donovan's proposal was an insult intended to provoke a quarrel that would lead to Waring's dismissal from the service of the Ortez Mines. Or if Waring were to agree to the suggestion, Donovan would have pulled Waring down to his own level.

Waring slowly rolled a cigarette. "Make out my check," he said, turning to Quigley.

Donovan sighed. Waring was going to quit. That was good. It had been easy enough.

Quigley drafted a check and handed it to Donovan to sign. As the paymaster began to gather up the money on the table, Waring pocketed the check and rose, watching Quigley's nervous hands.

As Quigley tied the sack and picked it up, Waring reached out his arm. "Give it to me," he said quietly. Quigley laughed. Waring's eyes were unreadable.

The smile faded from Quigley's face. Without knowing just why he did it, he relinquished the sack.

Waring turned to Donovan. "I'll take care of this, Bill. As I told you before, you can't bluff worth a damn."

Waring strode to the door. At Quigley's choked exclamation of protest, the gunman whirled round. Donovan stood by the desk, a gun weaving in his hand.

"You ought to know better than to pull a gun on me," said Waring. "Never throw down on a man unless you mean business, Bill."

The door clicked shut.

Donovan stood gazing stupidly at Quigley. "By cripes!" he flamed suddenly. "I'll put Jim Waring where he belongs. He can't run a whizzer like that on me!"

"I'd go slow," said Quigley. "You don't know what kind of a game Waring will play."

Donovan grabbed the telephone and called up the Sonora police.

Chapter IV
The Silver Crucifix

When in Sonora, Waring frequented the Plaza Hotel. He had arranged with the management that his room should always be ready for him, day or night. The location was advantageous. Nearly all the Americans visiting Sonora and many resident Americans stopped at the Plaza. Waring frequently picked up valuable bits of news as he lounged in the lobby. Quietly garbed when in town, he passed for a well-to-do rancher or mining man. His manner invited no confidences. He was left much to himself. Men who knew him deemed him unaccountable in that he never drank with them and seldom spoke unless spoken to. The employees of the hotel had grown accustomed to his comings and goings, though they seldom knew where he went or definitely when he would return. His mildness of manner was a source of comment among those who knew him for what he was. And his very mildness of manner was one of his greatest assets in gaining information. Essentially a man of action, silent as to his plans and surmises, yet he could talk well when occasion demanded.

It was rumored that he was in the employ of the American Government; that he had been disappointed in a love affair; that he had a wife and son living somewhere in the States; that for very good reasons he could not return to the States; that he was a dangerous man, well paid by the Mexican Government to handle political matters that would not bear public inspection. These rumors came to him from time to time, and because he paid no attention to them they were accepted as facts.

About an hour after he had left Donovan's office, Waring entered the Plaza Hotel, nodded to the clerk, and passed on down the hallway. He knocked at a door, and was answered by the appearance of a stout, smooth-shaven man in shirt-sleeves. They chatted for a minute or two. Waring stepped into the room. Presently he reappeared, smiling.

After dinner he strolled out and down the street. At a corner he edged through the crowd, and was striding on when some one touched his arm. He turned to confront the Mexican youth, Ramon. Waring gestured to Ramon to follow, and they passed on down the street until near the edge of the town. In the shadow of an adobe, Waring stopped.

Ramon glanced up and down the street. "The police—they have asked me where is my Uncle José. I have told them that I do not know. The police they asked me that."

"Well?"

"But it is not that why I come. They told me to go to my home. It was when I was in the prison that the policia talked in the telephone. He spoke your name and the name of Señor Bill Donovan of the Ortez Mine. I heard only your name and his, but I was afraid. You will not tell them that I was with my Uncle José?"

"No. And thanks, Ramon. I think I know what they were talking about. Go back home, pronto. If you were to be seen with me—"

"The señor is gracious. He has given me my life. I have nothing to give—but this." And Ramon drew the little silver crucifix from his shirt and pressed it in Waring's hand.

"Oh, here, muchacho—"

But Ramon was already hastening down a side street. Waring smiled and shook his head. For a moment he stood looking at the little crucifix shining on the palm of his hand. He slipped it into his pocket and strode back up the street. For an hour or more he walked about, listening casually to this or that bit of conversation. Occasionally he heard Mexicans discussing the Ortez robbery. Donovan's name, Waring's own name, Vaca's, and even Ramon's were mentioned. It seemed strange to him that news should breed so fast. Few knew that he had returned. Possibly Donovan had spread the report that the bandits had made their escape with the money. That would mean that Waring had been outwitted. And Donovan would like nothing better than to injure Waring's reputation.

Finding himself opposite the hotel, Waring glanced about and strode in. As he entered the hallway leading to his room three men rose from the leather chairs near the lobby window and followed him. Waring's door closed. He undressed and went to bed. He had been asleep but a few minutes when some one rapped on the door. He asked who it was. He was told to open in the name of the city of Sonora. He rose and dressed quickly.

When he opened the door two Sonora policemen told him to put up his hands. Donovan stood back of them, chewing a cigar. One of the policemen took Waring's gun. The other searched the room. Evidently he did not find what he sought.

"When you get through," said Waring, eyeing Donovan grimly, "you might tell me what you're after."

"I'm after that thousand," said Donovan.

"Oh! Well, why didn't you say so? Just call in Stanley, of the bank. His room is opposite."

Donovan hesitated. "Stanley's got nothing to do with this."

"Hasn't he?" queried Waring. "Call him in and see."

One of the police knocked at Stanley's door.

The bank cashier appeared, rubbing his eyes. "Hello, Bill! Hello, Jim! What's the fuss?"

"Stanley, did I deposit a thousand dollars in gold to the credit of the Ortez Mine this afternoon?"

"You did."

"Just show Donovan here the receipt I asked you to keep for me."

"All right. I'll get it."

Donovan glanced at the receipt. "Pretty smooth," he muttered.

Waring smiled. His silence enraged Donovan, who motioned to the police to leave the room.

Waring interrupted. "My gun?" he queried mildly.

One of the police handed the gun to Waring.

Their eyes met. "Why, hello, Pedro!" And Waring's voice expressed innocent surprise. "When did you enroll as a policeman?"

Donovan was about to interrupt when the policeman spoke: "That is my business."

"Which means Bill here has had you sworn in to-day. Knew you would like to get a crack at me, eh? You ought to know better, Salazar."

"Come on!" called Donovan.

The Mexicans followed him down the hallway.

Waring thanked Stanley. "It was a frame-up to get me, Frank," he concluded. "Pedro Salazar would like the chance, and as a policeman he could work it. You know that old game—resisting arrest."

"Doesn't seem to worry you," said Stanley.

"No. I'm leaving town. I'm through with this game."

"Getting too hot?"

"No. I'm getting cold feet," said Waring, laughing. "And say, Stanley, I may need a little money to-morrow."

"Any time, Jim."

Waring nodded. Back in his room he sat for a while on the edge of the bed, gazing at the curtained window. Life had gone stale. He was sick of hunting men and of being hunted. Pedro Salazar was now a member of the Sonora police through Donovan's efforts. Eventually Salazar would find an excuse to shoot Waring. And the gunman had made up his mind to do no more killing. For that reason he had spared Vaca and had befriended Ramon. He decided to leave Sonora.

Presently he rose and dressed in his desert clothes. As he went through his pockets he came upon the little silver crucifix and transferred it, with some loose change, to his riding-breeches. He turned out the light, locked the room from the outside, and strode out of the hotel.

At the livery-stable, he asked for his horse. The man in charge told him that Dex had been taken by the police. That the Señor Bill Donovan and Pedro Salazar had come and shown him a paper,—he could not read,—but he knew the big seal. It was Pedro Salazar who had ridden the horse.

The streets were still lighted, although the crowd was thinning. Waring turned a corner and drifted through the shadows toward the edge of town. As he passed open doorways he was greeted in Mexican, and returned each greeting pleasantly. The adobe at the end of the side street he was on was dark.

Waring paused. Pedro Salazar's house was the only unlighted house in the district. The circumstance hinted of an ambushment. Waring crossed to the deeper shadows and whistled. The call was peculiarly low and cajoling. He was answered by a muffled nickering. His horse Dex was evidently corralled at the back of the adobe.

Pedro Salazar knew that Waring would come for the horse sooner or later, so he waited, crouching behind the adobe wall of the enclosure.

Waring knocked loudly on Salazar's door and called his name. Then he turned and ran to the corner, dodged round it, and crept along the breast-high adobe wall. He whistled again. A rope snapped, and there came the sound of quick trampling. A rush and the great, tawny shape of Dexter reared in the moonlight and swept over the wall. With head up, the horse snorted a challenge. Waring called softly. The horse wheeled toward him. Waring caught the broken neck-rope and swung up. A flash cut the darkness behind him. Instinctively he turned and threw two shots. A figure crumpled to a dim blur in the corral.

Waring raced down the alley and out into the street. At the livery-stable he asked for his saddle and bridle. The Mexican, chattering, brought them. Waring tugged the cinchas tight and mounted. Far down the street some one called.

Waring rode to the hotel, dismounted, and strode in casually, pausing at Stanley's door. The cashier answered his knock.

"I'm off," said Waring. "And I'll need some money."

"All right, Jim. What's up? How much?"

"A couple of hundred. Charge it back to my account. Got it?"

"No. I'll get it at the desk."

"All right. Settle my bill for me to-morrow. Don't stop to dress Rustle!"

A belated lounger glanced up in surprise as Waring, booted and spurred, entered the lobby with a man in pajamas. They talked with the clerk a moment, shook hands, and Waring strode to the doorway.

"Any word for the Ortez people?" queried Stanley as Waring mounted.

"I left a little notice for Donovan—at Pedro Salazar's house," said Waring. "Donovan will understand." And Waring was gone.

The lounger accosted Stanley. "What's the row, Stanley?"

"I don't know. Jim Waring is in a hurry—first time since I've known him. Figure it out yourself."

Back in Pedro Salazar's corral a man lay huddled in a dim corner, his sightless eyes open to the soft radiance of the Sonora moon. A group of Mexicans stood about, jabbering. Among them was Ramon Ortego. Ramon listened and said nothing. Pedro Salazar was dead. No one knew who had killed him. And only that day he had become one of the police! It would go hard with the man who did this thing. There were many surmises. Pedro's brother had been killed by the gringo Waring down in the desert. As for Pedro, his name had been none too good. They shrugged their shoulders and crossed themselves.

Ramon slipped from the group and climbed the adobe wall. As he straightened up on the other side, he saw something gleaming in the moonlight. He stooped and picked up a little silver crucifix.

Chapter V
The Tang of Life

Waring rode until dawn, when he picketed Dex in a clump of chaparral and lay down to rest. He had purposely passed the water-hole, a half-mile south, after having watered the horse and refilled his canteen.

There was a distinction, even in Sonora, between Pedro Salazar, the citizen, and Pedro Salazar, of the Sonora police. The rurales might get busy. Nogales and the Arizona line were still a long ride ahead.

Slowly the desert sun drew overhead and swept the scant shadows from the brush-walled enclosure. Waring slept. Finally the big buckskin became restless, circling his picket and lifting his head to peer over the brush. Long before Waring could have been aware of it, had he been awake, the horse saw a moving something on the southern horizon. Trained to the game by years of association with his master, Dex walked to where Waring lay and nosed his arm. The gunman rolled to his side and peered through the chaparral.

Far in the south a moving dot wavered in the sun. Waring swept the southern arc with his glasses. The moving dot was a Mexican, a horseman riding alone. He rode fast. Waring could see the rise and fall of a quirt. "Some one killing a horse to get somewhere," he muttered, and he saddled Dex and waited. The tiny figure drew nearer. Dex grew restless. Waring quieted him with a word.

To the west of the chaparral lay the trail, paralleled at a distance of a half-mile by the railroad. The glasses discovered the lone horseman to be Ramon, of Sonora. The boy swayed in the saddle as the horse lunged on. Waring knew that something of grave import had sent the boy out into the noon desert. He was at first inclined to let him pass and then ride east toward the Sierra Madre. If the rurales were following, they would trail Dex to the water-hole. And if Ramon rode on north, some of them would trail the Mexican. This would split up the band—decrease the odds by perhaps one half.

But the idea faded from Waring's mind as he saw the boy fling past desperately. Waring swung to the saddle and rode out. Ramon's horse plunged to a stop, and stood trembling. The boy all but fell as he dismounted. Stumbling toward Waring, he held out both hands.

"Señor, the rurales!" he gasped.

"How far behind?"

"The railroad! They are ahead! They have shipped their horses to Magdalena, to Nogales!"

"How do you know that?"

"Pedro Salazar is dead. You were gone. They say it was you."

"So they shipped their horses ahead to cut me off, eh? You're a good boy, Ramon, but I don't know what in hell to do with you. Your cayuse is played out. You made a good ride."

"Si, señor. I have not stopped once."

"You look it. You can't go back now. They would shoot you."

"I will ride with the señor."

Waring shook his head.

Ramon's eyes grew desperate. "Señor," he pleaded, "take me with you! I cannot go back. I will be your man—follow you, even into the Great Beyond. You will not lose the way."

And as Ramon spoke he touched the little crucifix on his breast.

"Where did you find *that*?" asked Waring.

"In the Placeta Burro; near the house of Pedro Salazar."

Waring nodded. "Has your horse had water?"

"No, señor. I did not stop."

"Take him back to the water-hole. Or, here! Crawl in there and rest up You are all in. I'll take care of the cayuse."

When Waring returned to the chaparral, Ramon was asleep, flat on his back, his arms outspread and his mouth open. Waring touched him with his boot. Ramon muttered. Waring stooped and pulled him up.

Within the hour five rurales disembarked from a box-car and crossed to the water-hole, where one of them dismounted and searched for tracks. Alert for the appearance of the gringo, they rode slowly toward the chaparral. The enclosure was empty. After riding a wide circle round the brush, they turned and followed the tracks toward the eastern hills, rein-chains jingling and their silver-trimmed buckskin jackets shimmering in the sun.

"I will ride back," said Ramon. "My horse is too weak to follow. The señor rides slowly that I may keep up with him."

Waring turned in the saddle. Ahead lay the shadowy foothills of the mother range, vague masses in the starlight. Some thirty miles behind was the railroad and the trail north. There was no chance of picking up a fresh horse. The country was uninhabited. Alone, the gunman would have ridden swiftly to the hill country, where his trail would have been lost in the rocky ground of the ranges and where he would have had the advantage of an unobstructed outlook from the high trails.

Ramon had said the rurales had entrained; were ahead of him to intercept him. But Waring, wise in his craft, knew that the man-hunters would search for tracks at every water-hole on the long northern trail. And if they found his tracks they would follow him to the hills. They were as keen on the trail as Yaquis and as relentless as wolves. Their horses, raw-hide tough, could stand a forced ride that would kill an ordinary horse. And Ramon's wiry little cayuse, though willing to go on until he dropped, could not last much longer.

But to leave Ramon to the rurales was not in Waring's mind. "We'll keep on, amigo," he said, "and in a few hours we'll know whether it's to be a ride or a fight."

"I shall pray," whispered Ramon.

"For a fresh horse, then."

"No, señor. That would be of no use. I shall pray that you may escape As for me—"

"We'll hit the glory trail together, muchacho. If you get bumped off, it's your own funeral. You should have stayed in Sonora."

Ramon sighed. The señor was a strange man. Even now he hummed a song in the starlight. Was he, then, so unafraid of death that he could sing in the very shadow of its wings?

"You've got a hunch that the rurales are on our trail," said Waring, as they rode on.

"It is so, señor."

"How do you know?"

"I cannot say. But it is so. They have left the railroad and are following us."

Waring smiled in the dark. "Dex, here, has been trying to tell me that for an hour."

"And still the señor does not hasten!"

"I am giving your cayuse a chance to make the grade. We'll ride an hour longer."

Ramon bowed his head. The horses plodded on, working up the first gentle slope of the foothills. The brush loomed heavier. A hill star faded on the edge of the higher range. Ramon's lips moved and he crossed himself.

Waring hummed a song. He was not unhappy. The tang of life was his again. Again he followed a trail down which the light feet of Romance ran swiftly. The past, with its red flare of life, its keen memories and dulled regrets, was swept away by the promise of dawn and the unknown. "A clean break and a hard fight," he murmured, as he reined up to rest his horse. Turning, he could distinguish Ramon, who fingered the crucifix at his throat. Waring's face grew grim. He felt suddenly accountable for the boy's life.

The half-moon glowed against the edge of the world. About to ride on again, Waring saw a tiny group of horsemen silhouetted against the half-disk of burning silver. He spoke to his horse. Slowly they climbed the ridge, dropped down the eastern slope, and climbed again.

In a shallow valley, Waring reined up, unsaddled Dex, and turned him loose. Ramon questioned this. "Turn your horse loose," said Waring. "They'll keep together and find water."

Ramon shook his head, but did as he was told. Wearily he followed Waring as he climbed back to a rocky depression on the crest. Without a word Waring stretched behind a rock and was soon asleep. Ramon wondered at the other's indifference to danger, but fatigue finally overcame him and he slept.

Just before dawn Ramon awakened and touched

Waring. "They are coming!" he whispered.

Waring shook his head. "You hear our horses. The rurales won't ride into this pocket before daylight. Stay right here till I come back."

He rose and worked cautiously down the eastern slope, searching for Dex in the valley. In the gray gloom he saw the outline of his horse grazing alone. He stepped down to him. The big horse raised its head. Waring spoke. Reassured, Dex plodded to his master, who turned and tracked back to the pocket in the rocks. "I think your cayuse has drifted south," he told Ramon.

The young Mexican showed no surprise. He seemed resigned to the situation. "I knew when the señor said to turn my horse loose that he would seek the horses of his kind. He has gone back to the horses of those who follow us."

"You said it" said Waring. "And that's going to bother them. It tells me that the rurales are not far behind. They'll figure that I put you out of business to get rid of you. They'll look for a dead Mexican, and a live gringo riding north, alone. But they're too wise to ride up here. They'll trail up afoot and out of sight. That's your one chance."

"My chance, señor?"

"Yes. Here's some grub. You've got your gun. Drift down the slope, get back of the next ridge, and strike south. Locate their horses and wait till they leave them to come up here. Get a horse. Pick a good one. I'll keep them busy till you get back."

Ramon rose and climbed to the edge of the pocket. "I go," he said sadly "And I shall never see the señor again."

"Don't bet all you've got on that," said Waring.

When Ramon had disappeared, Waring led Dex back from the pocket, and, saddling him, left him concealed in the brush. Then the gunman crept back to the rim and lay waiting, a handful of rifle shells loose on a flat rock in front of him. He munched some dried meat and drank from the canteen.

The red dawn faded quickly to a keen white light. Heat waves ran over the rocks and danced down the hillside. Waring lighted a match and blackened the front sight of his carbine. The sun rolled up and struck at him, burning into the pocket of rock where he lay motionless gazing down the slope. Sweat beaded his forehead and trickled down his nose. Scattered boulders seemed to move gently. He closed his eyes for an instant. When he opened them he thought he saw a movement in the brush below. The heat burned into his back, and he shrugged his shoulders. A tiny bird flitted past and perched on the dry, dead stalk of a yucca. Again Waring thought he saw a movement in the brush.

Then, as if by magic, the figure of a rural stood clear and straight against the distant background of brownish-green. Waring smiled. He knew that if he were to fire, the rurales would rush him. They suspected some kind of a trap. Waring's one chance was to wait until they had given up every ruse to draw his fire. They were not certain of his whereabouts, but were suspicious of that natural fortress of rock. There was not a rural in Old Mexico who did not know him either personally or by reputation. The fact that one of them had offered himself as a possible target proved that they knew they had to deal with a man as crafty as themselves.

The standing figure, shimmering in the glare, drew back and disappeared.

Waring eased his tense muscles. "Now they'll go back for their horses," he said to himself. "They'll ride up to the next ridge, where they can look down on this pocket, but I won't be here."

Waring planned every move with that care and instinct which marks a good chess-player. And because he had to count upon possibilities far ahead he drew Ramon's saddle to him and cut the stirrup-leathers, cinchas, and latigos. If Ramon got one of their horses, his own jaded animal would be left. Eventually the rurales would find the saddle and Ramon's horse. And every rural out of the riding would be a factor in their escape.

The sun blazed down until the pocket of rock was a pit of stagnant heat. The silence seemed like an ocean rolling in soundless waves across the hills; a silence that became disturbed by a faint sound as of one approaching cautiously. Waring thought Ramon had shown cleverness in working up to him so quietly. He raised on his elbow and turned his head. On the eastern edge of the pocket stood a rural, and the rural smiled.

Chapter VI
Arizona

Waring, who had known the man in Sonora, called him by name. The other's smile faded, and his eyes narrowed. Waring thrust up his hands and jokingly offered to toss up a coin to decide the issue. He knew his man; knew that at the first false move the rural would kill him. He rose and turned sideways that the other might take his gun. "You win the throw," he said. The Mexican jerked Waring's gun from the holster and cocked it. Then he whistled.

From below came the faint clatter of hoofs. The rural seemed puzzled that his call should have been answered so promptly. He knew that his companions had gone for their horses, picketed some distance from the pocket. He had volunteered to surprise the gunman single-handed.

Waring, gazing beyond the rural, saw the head of a horse top the rise. In the saddle sat Ramon, hatless, his black hair flung back from his forehead, a gun in his hand. Waring drew a deep breath. Would Ramon bungle it by calling out, or would he have nerve enough to make an end of it on the instant?

Although Waring was unarmed, the rural dared not turn. The gringo had been known to slip out of as tight a place despite the threat of a gun almost against his chest. With a despondent shrug, Waring lowered his arms.

"You win the throw," he said hopelessly.

Still the Mexican dared not take his eyes from Waring. He would wait until his companions appeared.

A few yards behind the rural, Ramon reined up. Slowly he lowered the muzzle of his gun. The rural called the name of one of his fellows. The answer came in a blunt crash, which rippled its harsh echoes across the sounding hills. The rural flung up his arms and pitched forward, rolling to Waring's feet. The gunman leaped up, and, snatching his carbine from the rock, swung round and took his six-gun from the rural's limp fingers. Plunging to the brush beyond the pocket, he swung to the saddle and shot down the slope. Behind him he could hear Ramon's horse scattering the loose rock of the hillside. A bullet struck ahead of him and whined across the silence. A shrill call told him that the pursuers had discovered the body of their fellow.

Dex, with ears laid back, took the ragged grade in great, uneven leaps that shortened to a regular stride as they gained the level of the valley. Glancing back, Waring saw Ramon but a few yards behind. He signaled to him to ride closer. Together they swung down the valley, dodging the low brush—and leaping rocks at top speed.

Finally Waring reined in. "We'll make for that ridge,"—and he indicated the range west. Under cover of the brush they angled across the valley and began the ascent of the range which hid the western desert.

Halfway up, Waring dismounted. "Lead my horse on up," he told Ramon "I'll argue it out with 'em here."

"Señor, I have killed a man!" gasped Ramon.

Waring flung the reins to his companion. "All right! This isn't a fiesta, hombre; this is business."

Ramon turned and put his horse up the slope, Dex following. Waring curled behind a rock and swept the valley with his glass. The heads of several rurales were visible in the brush. They had halted and were looking for tracks. Finally one of them raised his arm and pointed toward the hill. They had caught sight of Ramon on the slope above. Presently three riders appeared at the foot of the grade. It was a long shot from where Waring lay. He centered on the leading rural, allowed for a chance of overshooting, and pressed the trigger. The carbine snarled. An echo ripped the shimmering heat. A horse reared and plunged up the valley, the saddle empty.

Waring rose, and plodded up the slope.

"Three would have trailed us. Two will ride back to the railroad and report. I wonder how many of them are bushed along the trail between here and Nogales?"

In the American custom-house at Nogales sat a lean, lank man gazing out of a window facing the south. His chair was tilted back, and his large feet were crossed on the desk in front of him. He was in his shirt-sleeves, and he puffed indolently at a cigar and blew smoke-rings toward the ceiling. Incidentally his name was known throughout the country and beyond its southern borders. But if this distinction affected him in any way it was not evident. He seemed submerged in a lassitude which he neither invited nor struggled against.

A group of riders appeared down the road. The lean man brushed a cloud of smoke away and gazed at them with indifference. They drew nearer. He saw that they were Mexicans—rurales. Without turning his head, he called to an invisible somebody in the next room.

"Jack, drift over to the cantina and get a drink."

A chair clumped to the floor, and a stocky, dark-faced man appeared, rubbing his eyes. "On who?" he queried, grinning.

"On old man Diaz," replied the lean man.

"All right, Pat. But mebby his credit ain't good on our side of the line."

The lean man said nothing. He continued to gaze out of the window. The white road ran south and south into the very haze of the beyond. His assistant picked up a hat and strolled out. A few doors down the street stood several excellent saddle animals tied to the hitching-rail in front of the cantina. He didn't need to be told that they were the picked horses of the rurales, and that for some strange reason his superior had sent him to find out just why these same rurales were in town.

He entered the cantina and called for a drink. The lithe, dark riders of the south, grouped round a table in one corner of the room, glanced up, answered his general nod of salutation indifferently, and turned to talk among themselves. Catering to authority, the Mexican proprietor proffered a second drink to the Americano. The assistant collector toyed with his glass, and began a lazy conversation about the weather. The proprietor, his fat, oily face in his hands and his elbows on the bar, grunted monosyllables, occasionally nodding as the Americano forced his acknowledgment of a highly obvious platitude.

And the assistant collector, listening for a chance word that would explain the presence of armed Mexico on American soil, knew that the proprietor was also listening for that same word that might explain their unprecedented visit. Presently the assistant collector of customs began a tirade against Nogales, its climate, institutions, and citizens collectively and singly. The proprietor awoke to argument. Their talk grew loud. The assistant collector thumped the bar with his fist, and ceased talking suddenly. A subdued buzz came from the corner where the rurales sat, and he caught the name "Waring."

"And the whole town ain't worth the matches to burn it up," he continued. "If it wasn't for Pat, I'd quit right now." And he emptied his glass and strode from the room.

Back in the office, he flung his hat on the table and rumpled his hair "Those coyotes," he said casually, "are after some one called Waring. Pablo's whiskey is rotten."

The collector's long legs unfolded, and he sat up, yawning. "Jim Waring isn't in town," he said as though to himself.

"Pat, you give me a pain," said the assistant, grinning.

"Got one myself," said the collector unsmilingly. "Cucumbers."

"You're the sweetest liar for a thousand miles either side of the line There isn't even the picture of a cucumber in this sun-blasted town."

"Isn't, eh? Look here!" And the lank man pulled open a drawer in the desk. The collector fumbled among some papers and drew out a bulky seed catalogue, illustrated in glowing tints.

"Oh, I'll buy," laughed the assistant. "I reckon if I asked for a picture of this man Waring that's wanted by those nickel-plated coyotes, you'd fish it up and never sweat a hair."

"I could," said the collector, closing the drawer.

"Here, smoke one of mine for a change. About that picture. I met Jim Waring in Las Cruces. He was a kid then, but a comer. Had kind of light, curly hair. His face was as smooth as a girl's. He wasn't what you'd call a dude, but his clothes always looked good on him. Wimmin kind of liked him, but he never paid much attention to them. He worked for me as deputy a spell, and I never hired a better man. But he wouldn't stay with one job long. When Las Cruces got quiet he pulled his freight. Next I heard of him he was married and living in Sonora. It didn't take Diaz long to find out that he could use him. Waring was a wizard with a gun—and he had the nerve back of it. But Waring quit Diaz, for Jim wasn't that kind of a killer. I guess he found plenty of work down there. He never was one to lay around living on his reputation and waiting for nothing to happen. He kept his reputation sprouting new shoots right along—and that ain't all joke, neither."

"Speakin' in general, could he beat you to it with a gun, Pat?"

"Speaking in general—I reckon he could."

"Them rurales are kind of careless—ridin' over the line and not stoppin' by to make a little explanation."

The lank man nodded. "There's a time coming when they'll do more than that. That old man down south is losing his grip. I don't say this for general information. And if Jim Waring happens to ride into town, just tell him who you are and pinch him for smuggling; unless I see him first."

"What did I ever do to you?"

Pat laughed silently. "Oh, he ain't a fool. It's only a fool that'll throw away a chance to play safe."

"You got me interested in that Waring hombre. I'll sure nail him like you said; but if he goes for his gun I don't want you plantin' no cucumber seed on my restin'-place. Guess I'll finish those reports."

The lank man yawned, and, rising, strode to the window. The assistant sauntered to the inner office and drew up to his desk. "Pablo's whiskey is rotten!" he called over his shoulder. The lank collector smiled.

The talk about Waring and Las Cruces had stirred slumbering memories; memories of night rides in New Mexico, of the cattle war, of blazing noons on the high mesas and black nights in huddled adobe towns; Las Cruces, Albuquerque, Caliente, Santa Fé—and weary ponies at the hitching-rails.

Once, on an afternoon like this, he had ridden into town with a prisoner beside him, a youth whose lightning-swift hand had snuffed out a score of lives to avenge the killing of a friend. The collector recalled that on that day he had ridden his favorite horse, a deep-chested buckskin, slender legged, and swift, with a strain of thoroughbred.

Beyond the little square of window through which he gazed lay the same kind of a road—dusty, sun-white, edged with low brush. And down the road, pace for pace with his thoughts, strode a buckskin horse, ridden by a man road-weary, gray with dust. Beside him rode a youth, his head bowed and his hands clasped on the saddle-horn as though manacled.

"Jack!"

The assistant shoved back his chair and came to the window.

"There's the rest of your picture," said the collector.

As the assistant gazed at the riders, the collector stepped to his desk and buckled on a gun.

"Want to meet Waring?" he queried.

"I'm on for the next dance, Pat."

The collector stepped out. Waring reined up. A stray breeze fluttered the flag above the custom-house. Waring gravely lifted his sombrero.

"You're under arrest," said the collector.

Waring gestured toward Ramon.

"You, too," nodded Pat. "Get the kid and his horse out of sight," he told the assistant.

Ramon, too weary to expostulate, followed the assistant to a corral back of the building.

The collector turned to Waring. "And now, Jim, what's the row?"

"Down the street—and coming," said Waring, as the rurales boiled from the cantina.

"We'll meet 'em halfway," said the collector.

And midway between the custom-house and the cantina the two cool-eyed, deliberate men of the North faced the hot-blooded Southern haste that demanded Waring as prisoner. The collector, addressing the leader of the rurales, suggested that they talk it over in the cantina. "And don't forget you're on the wrong side of the line," he added.

The Captain of rurales and one of his men dismounted and followed the Americans into the cantina. The leader of the rurales immediately exhibited a warrant for the arrest of Waring, signed by a high official and sealed with the great seal of Mexico. The collector returned the warrant to the captain.

"That's all right, amigo, but this man is already under arrest."

"By whose authority?"

"Mine—representing the United States."

"The warrant of the Presidente antedates your action," said the captain.

"Correct, Señor Capitan. But my action, being just about two jumps ahead of your warrant, wins the race, I reckon."

"It is a trick!"

"Si! You must have guessed it."

"I shall report to my Government. And I also demand that you surrender to me one Ramon Ortego, of Sonora, who aided this man to escape, and who is reported to have killed one of my men and stolen one of my horses."

"He ought to make a darned good rural, if that's so," said the collector. "But he is under arrest for smuggling. He rode a horse across the line without declaring valuation."

"Juan," said the captain, "seize the horse of the Americano."

"Juan," echoed Waring softly, "I have heard that Pedro Salazar seized the horse of an Americano—in Sonora."

The rural stopped short and turned as though awaiting further instructions from his chief. The collector of customs rose and sauntered to the doorway. Leaning against the lintel, he lighted a cigar and smoked, gazing at Waring's horse with an appreciative eye. The captain of rurales, seated opposite Waring, rolled a cigarette carefully; too carefully, thought Waring, for a Mexican who had been daring enough to ride across the line with armed men. Outside in the fading sunlight, the horses of the rurales stamped and fretted. The cantina was strangely silent. In the doorway stood the collector, smoking and toying with his watch-charm.

Presently the assistant collector appeared, glanced in, and grinned "The kid is asleep—in the office," he whispered to the collector.

Waring knew that the flicker of an eyelid, an intonation, a gesture, might precipitate trouble. He also knew that diplomacy was out of the question. He glanced round the room, pushed back his chair, and, rising, stepped to the bar. With his back against it, he faced the captain.

"Miguel," he said quietly, "you're too far over the line. Go home!"

The captain rose. "Your Government shall hear of this!"

"Yes. Wire 'em to-night. And where do you get off? You'll get turned back to the ranks."

"I?"

"Si, Señor Capitan, and because—*you didn't get your man.*"

The collector of customs stood with his cigar carefully poised in his left hand. The assistant pushed back his hat and rumpled his black hair.

All official significance set aside, Waring and the captain of rurales faced each other with the blunt challenge between them: "You didn't get your man!"

The captain glanced at the two quiet figures in the doorway. Beyond them were his own men, but between him and his command were two of the fastest guns in the Southwest. He was on alien ground. This gringo had insulted him.

Waring waited for the word that burned in the other's eyes.

The collector of customs drew a big silver watch from his waistband "It's about time—to go feed the horses," he said.

With the sound of his voice the tension relaxed. Waring eyed the captain as though waiting for him to depart. "You'll find that horse in the corral—back of the customs office," he said.

The Mexican swung round and strode out, followed by his man.

The rurales mounted and rode down the street. The three Americans followed a few paces behind. Opposite the office, they paused.

"Go along with 'em and see that they get the right horse," said the collector.

The assistant hesitated.

The collector laughed. "Shake hands with Jim Waring, Jack."

When the assistant had gone, the collector turned to Waring. "That's Jack every time. Stubborn as a tight boot, but good leather every time. Know why he wanted to shake hands? Well, that's his way of tellin' you he thinks you're some smooth for not pullin' a fight when it looked like nothing else was on the bill."

Waring smiled. "I've met you before, haven't I?"

Pat pretended to ignore the question. "Say, stranger," he began with slow emphasis, "you're makin' mighty free and familiar for a prisoner arrested for smuggling. Mebby you're all right personal, but officially I got a case against you. What do you know about raising cucumbers? I got a catalogue in the office, and me and Jack has been aiming to raise cucumbers from it for three months. I like 'em. Jack says you can't do it down here without water every day. Now—"

"Where have you planted them, Pat?"

"Oh, hell! They ain't *planted* yet. We're just figuring. Now, up Las Cruces way—"

"Let's go back to the cantina and talk it out. There goes Mexico leading a horse with an empty saddle. I guess the boy will be all right in the office."

"Was the kid mixed up in your getaway?"

"Yes. And he's a good boy."

"Well, he's in dam' bad company. Now, Jack says you got to plant 'em in hills and irrigate. I aim to just drill 'em in and let the A'mighty do the rest. What do you think?"

"I think you're getting worse as you grow older, Pat. Say, did you ever get track of that roan mare you lost up at Las Cruces?"

"Yes, I got her back."

"Speaking of horses, I saw a pinto down in Sonora—"

Just then the assistant joined them, and they sauntered to the cantina. Dex, tied at the rail, turned and gazed at them. Waring took the morral of grain from the saddle, and, slipping Dex's bridle, adjusted it.

The rugged, lean face of the collector beamed. "I wondered if you thought as much of 'em as you used to. I aimed to see if I could make you forget to feed that cayuse."

"How about those goats in your own corral?" laughed Waring.

"Kind of a complimentary cuss, ain't he?" queried Pat, turning to his assistant. "And he don't know a dam' thing about cucumbers."

"You old-timers give me a pain," said the assistant, grinning.

"That's right! Because you can't set down to a meal without both your hands and feet agoing and one ear laid back, you call us old because we chew slow. But you're right. Jim and I are getting kind of gray around the ears."

"Well, you fellas can fight it out. I came over to say that them rurales got their hoss. But one of 'em let it slip, in Mexican, that they weren't through yet."

"So?" said Pat. "Well, you go ahead and feed the stock. We'll be over to the house poco tiempo."

Waring and the collector entered the cantina. For a long time they sat in silence, gazing at the peculiar half-lights as the sun drew down. Finally the collector turned to Waring.

"Has the game gone stale, Jim?"

Waring nodded. "I'm through. I am going to settle down. I've had my share of trouble."

"Here, too," said the collector. "I've put by enough to get a little place up north—cattle—and take it easy. That's why I stuck it out down here. Had any word from your folks recent?"

"Not for ten years."

"And that boy trailing with you?"

"Oh, he's just a kid I picked up in Sonora. No, my own boy is straight American, if he's living now."

"You might stop by at Stacey, on the Santa Fé," said the collector casually. "There's some folks running a hotel up there that you used to know."

Waring thanked him with a glance. "We don't need a drink and the sun is down. Where do you eat?"

"We'll get Jack to rustle some grub. You and the boy can bunk in the office. I'll take care of your horse."

"Thanks, Pat. But you spoke of going north. I wouldn't if I were you They'll get you."

"I had thought of that. But I'm going to take that same chance. I'm plumb sick of the border."

"If they do—" And Waring rose.

The collector's hard-lined face softened for an instant. He thrust out his bony hand. "I'll leave that to you, Jim."

And that night, because each was a gunman unsurpassed in his grim profession, they laughed and talked about things trivial, leaving the deeper currents undisturbed. And the assistant collector, eating with them in the adobe back of the office, wondered that two such men found nothing more serious to talk about than the breeding of horses and the growing of garden truck.

Late that night the assistant awoke to find that the collector was not in bed. He rose and stalked to the window. Across from the adobe he saw the grim face of the collector framed in the office window. He was smoking a cigar and gazing toward the south, his long arm resting on the sill and his chin in his hand.

> "Ole fool!" muttered the assistant affectionately. "That there Jim Waring must sure be some hombre to make Pat lose any sleep."

Chapter VII
The Return of Waring

The interior of the little desert hotel at Stacey, Arizona, atoned for its bleached and weather-worn exterior by a refreshing neatness that was almost startling in contrast to the warped board front with its painted sign scaled by the sun.

The proprietress, Mrs. Adams, a rosy, dark-haired woman, had heard the Overland arrive and depart. Through habit she listened until the distant rumble of the train diminished to a faint purr. No guests had arrived on the Overland. Stacey was not much of a town, and tourists seldom stopped there. Mrs. Adams stepped from the small office to the dining-room and arranged some flowers in the center of the long table. She happened to be the only woman in the desert town who grew flowers.

The Overland had come and gone. Another day! Mrs. Adams sighed, patted her smooth black hair, and glanced down at her simple and neat attire.

She rearranged the flowers, and was stepping back to view the effect when something caused her to turn and glance toward the office. There had been no sound, yet in the doorway stood a man—evidently a rider. He was looking at the calendar on the office wall. Mrs. Adams stepped toward him. The man turned and smiled. She gazed with awakening astonishment at the dusty, khaki-clad figure, the cool gray eyes beneath the high-crowned sombrero, and last at the extended hand. Without meeting the man's eyes, she shook hands.

"Jim! How did you know?" she queried, her voice trembling.

"I heard of you at Nogales. I wasn't looking for you—then. You have a right pleasant place here. Yours?"

She nodded.

"I came to see the boy," he said. "I'm not here for long."

"Oh, Jim! Lorry is so big and strong—and—and he's working for the Starr outfit over west of here."

"Cattle, eh? Is he a good boy?"

"A nice question for you to ask! Lorry rides a straighter trail than his father did."

The man laughed and patted her shoulder affectionately. "You needn't have said that, Annie. You knew what I was when I married you. And no man ever said I wasn't straight. Just what made you leave Sonora without saying a word? Didn't I always treat you well?"

"I must say that you did, Jim. You never spoke a rough word to me in your life. I wish you had. You'd be away for weeks, and then come back and tell me it was all right, which meant that you'd 'got your man,' as they say down there. At first I was too happy to care. And when the baby came and I tried to get you to give up hiring out to men who wanted killing done,— for that's what it was,—you kept telling me that some day you would quit. Maybe they did pay big, but you could have been anything else you wanted to. You came of good folks and had education. But you couldn't live happy without that excitement. And you thought I was happy because you were. Why, even up here in Arizona they sing 'Waring of Sonora-Town.' Our boy sings it, and I have to listen, knowing that it is you he sings about. I was afraid of you, Jim, and afraid our boy would grow up to be like you."

Waring nodded. "I'm not blaming you, Annie. I asked why you left me—without a word or an address. Do you think that was square?"

Mrs. Adams, flushed, and the tears came to her eyes. "I didn't dare think about that part of it. I was afraid of you. I got so I couldn't sleep, worrying about what might happen to you when you were away. And you always came back, but you never said where you'd been or what you'd done. I couldn't stand it. If you had only told me—even about the men— that you were paid to kill, I might have stood it. But you never said a word. The wives of the American folks down there wouldn't speak to me. And the Mexican women hated me. I was the wife of Jim Waring, 'the killer.' I think I went crazy."

"Well, I never did believe in talking shop, Annie."

"That's just it. You were always polite—and calling what you did, 'shop'! I don't believe you ever cared for a single person on this earth!"

"You ought to know, Annie. But we won't argue that. Don't act as though you had to defend yourself. I am not blaming you—now. You have explained. I did miss the boy, though. Are you doing well here?"

"It was hard work at first. But I never did write to father to help me."

"You might have written to me. When did the boy go to work? He's eighteen, isn't he?"

Mrs. Adams smiled despite herself. "Yes, this fall. He started in with the Starr people at the spring round-up."

"Couldn't he help you here?"

"He did. But he's not the kind to hang round a hotel. He's all man—if I do say it." And Mrs. Adams glanced at her husband. In his lithe, well-set-up figure she saw what her son would be at forty. "Yes, Jim, he's man size—and I've raised him to go straight."

Waring laughed. "Of course you have! What name will I sign, Annie?"

"Folks here call me Mrs. Adams."

"So you're Annie Adams again! Well, here's your husband's name, if you don't mind." And he signed the register, "James Waring, Sonora, Mexico."

"Isn't that risky?" she queried.

"No one knows me up here. And I don't intend to stay long. I'd like to see the boy."

"Jim, you won't take him away!"

"You know me better than that. You quit me down there, and I won't say that I liked it. I wondered how you'd get along. You left no word. When I realized that you must have wanted to leave me, that settled it. Following you would have done no good, even if I had known where you had gone. I was free. And a gunman has no business with a family."

"You might have thought about that before you came courting me."

"I did. Didn't you?"

"You're hard, Jim. I was just a girl. Any woman would have been glad to marry you then. But when I got sense enough to see how you earned your money—I just had to leave. I was afraid to tell you—"

"There, now, Annie; we'll let that go. I won't say that I don't care, but I've been mighty busy since you left. I didn't know where you were until I hit Nogales. I wanted to see you and the boy. And I'm as hungry as a grizzly."

"Anita is getting supper. Some of the folks in town board here. They'll be coming in soon."

"All right. I'm a stranger. I rode over. I'd like to wash up."

"You *rode* over?"

"Yes. Why not? I know the country."

Mrs. Adams turned and gestured toward the stairway. She followed him and showed him to a room. So he hadn't come in on the Overland, but had ridden up from Sonora. Why had he undertaken such a long, weary ride? Surely he could have taken the train! She had never known him to be without money. But he had always been unaccountable, coming and going when he pleased, saying little, always serene. And now he had not said why he had ridden up from Sonora. "Why not?" was all that he had said in explanation.

He swung out of his coat and washed vigorously, thrusting his fingers through his short, curly hair and shaking his head in boyish enjoyment that was refreshing to watch. She noticed that he had not aged much. He seemed too cool, too self-possessed always, to show even the ordinary trace of years. She could not understand him; yet she was surprised by a glow of affection for him now that he had returned. As he dried his head she saw that his hair was tinged with gray, although his face was lined but little and his gray eyes were as keen and quick as ever. If he had only shared even that part of his life with her—down there!

"Jim!" she whispered.

He turned as he took up his coat. "Yes, Annie?"

"If you would only promise—"

He shook his head. "I won't do that. I didn't come to ask anything of you except to see the boy But if you need money—"

"No. Not that kind of money."

"All right, girl." And his voice was cheery. "I didn't come here to make you feel bad. And I won't be here long. Can't we be friends while I'm here? Of course the boy will know. But no one else need know. And—you better see to the folks downstairs. Some one just came in."

She turned and walked down the hall, wondering if he had ever cared for her, and wondering if her boy, Lorry, would ever come to possess that almost unhuman quality of intense alertness, that incomprehensible coolness that never allowed him to forget what he was for an instant.

When Waring came down she did not introduce him to the boarders, a fact that sheriff Buck Hardy, who dined at the hotel, noted with some interest. The men ate hastily, rose, and departed, leaving Hardy and Waring, who called for a second cup of coffee and rolled a cigarette while waiting.

Hardy had seen the stranger ride into town on the big buckskin. The horse bore a Mexican brand. The hotel register told Hardy who the stranger was. And the sheriff of Stacey County was curious to know just what the Sonora gunman was doing in town.

Waring sat with his unlighted cigarette between his fingers. The sheriff proffered a match. Their eyes met. Waring nodded his thanks and blew a smoke-ring.

"How are things down in Sonora?" queried Hardy.

"Quiet."

Mrs. Adams questioned Waring with her eyes. He nodded. "This is Mr Waring," she said, rising. "This is Mr. Hardy, our sheriff."

The men shook hands. "Mrs. Adams is a good cook," said Waring.

A clatter of hoofs and the sound of a cheery voice broke the silence.

A young cowboy jingled into the room. "Hello, Buck! Hello, mother!" And Lorry Adams strode up and kissed his mother heartily. "Got a runnin' chance to come to town and I came—runnin'. How's everything?"

Mrs. Adams murmured a reply. Buck Hardy was watching Waring as he glanced up at the boy. The sheriff pulled a cigar from his vest and lighted it. In the street he paused in his stride, gazing at the end of his cigar. Lorry Adams looked mighty like Jim Waring, of Sonora. Hardy had heard that Waring had been killed down in the southern country. Some one had made a mistake.

Waring had risen. He stood with one hand touching the table, the tips of his fingers drumming the rhythm of a song he hummed to himself. The boy's back was toward him. Waring's gaze traveled from his son's head to his boot-heel.

Lorry noticed that his mother seemed perturbed. He turned to Waring with a questioning challenge in his gray eyes.

Mrs. Adams touched the boy's arm. "This is your father, Lorry."

Lorry glanced from one to the other.

Waring made no movement, offered no greeting, but stood politely impassive.

Mrs. Adams spoke gently: "Lorry!"

"Why, hello, dad!" And the boy shook hands with his father.

Waring gestured toward a chair. Lorry sat down. His eyes were warm with mild astonishment.

"Smoke?" said Waring, proffering tobacco and papers.

Lorry's gaze never left his father's face as he rolled a cigarette and lighted it. Mrs. Adams realized that Waring's attitude of cool indifference appealed to the boy.

Lorry remembered his father dimly. He was curious to know just what kind of man he was. He didn't talk much; that was certain. The boy remembered that his mother had not said much about her husband, answering Lorry's childish questionings with a promise to tell him some day. He recalled a long journey on the train, their arrival at Stacey, and the taking over of the run-down hotel that his mother had refurnished and made a place of neatness and comfort. And his mother had told him that she would be known "Mrs. Adams." Lorry had been so filled with the newness of things that the changing of their name was accepted without question. Slowly his recollection of Sonora and the details of their life there came back to him. These things he had all but forgotten, as he had grown to love Arizona, its men, its horses, its wide ranges and magic hills.

Mrs. Adams remembered that her husband had once told her he could find out more about a man by watching his hands than by asking questions. She noticed that Waring was watching his son's hands with that old, deliberate coldness of attitude. He was trying to find out just what sort of a man his boy had grown to be.

Lorry suddenly straightened in his chair. Mrs. Adams, anticipating his question, nodded to Waring.

"Yes," said Waring; "I am the Waring of Sonora that you are thinking about."

Lorry flushed. "I—I guess you are," he stammered. "Mother, you never told me *that*."

"You were too young to understand, Lorry."

"And is that why you left him?"

"Yes."

"Well, maybe you were right. But dad sure looks like a pretty decent hombre to me."

They laughed in a kind of relief. The occasion had seemed rather strained.

"Ask your mother, Lorry. I am out of it." And, rising Waring strode to the doorway.

Lorry rose.

"I'll see you again," said Waring. And he stepped to the street, humming his song of "Sonora and the Silver Strings."

Mrs. Adams put her arm about her son's shoulders. "Your father is a hard man," she told him.

"Was he mean to you, mother?"

"No—never that."

"Well, I don't understand it. He looks like a real man to me. Why did he come back?"

"He said he came back to see you."

"Well, he's my father, anyway," said Lorry.

Chapter VIII
Lorry

In the low hills west of Stacey, Lorry was looking for strays. He worked alone, whistling as he rode, swinging his glasses on this and that arroyo and singling out the infrequent clumps of greasewood for a touch of brighter color in their shadows. He urged his pony from crest to crest, carelessly easy in the saddle, alive to his work, and quietly happy in the lone freedom of thought and action.

He felt a bit proud of himself that morning. Only last night he had learned that he was the son of Waring of Sonora; a name to live up to, if Western standards meant anything, and he thought they did.

The fact that he was the son of James Waring overcame for the time being the vague disquietude of mind attending his knowledge that his mother and father had become estranged. He thought he understood now why his mother had made him promise to go unarmed upon the range. His companions, to the last man, "packed a gun."

Heretofore their joshing had not bothered him. In fact, he had rather enjoyed the distinction of going unarmed, and he had added to this distinction by acquiring a skill with the rope that occasioned much natural jealousy among his fellows. To be top-hand with a rope among such men as Blaze Andrews, Slim Trivet, Red Bender, and High-Chin Bob, the foreman, was worth all the patient hours he had given to persistent practice with the reata.

But to-day he questioned himself. His mother had made him promise to go unarmed because she feared he would become like his father. Why hadn't she told him more about it all? He felt that she had taken a kind of mean advantage of his unwavering affection for her. He was a man, so far as earning his wage was concerned. And she was the best woman in the world—but then women didn't understand the unwritten customs of the range.

On a sandy ridge he reined up and gazed at the desert below. The bleak flats wavered in the white light of noon. The farthest hills to the south seemed but a few miles away.

For some time he focused his gaze at the Notch, from which the road sprang and flowed in slow undulations to a vanishing point in the blank spaces of the west. His pony, Gray Leg, head up and nostrils working, twitched back one ear as Lorry spoke: "You see it, too?"

Gray Leg continued to gaze into the distance, occasionally stamping an impatient forefoot, as though anxious to be off. Lorry lowered his glass and raised it again. In the circle of the binoculars he saw a tiny, distant figure dismount from a black horse and walk back and forth across the road directly below the Notch. Lorry wiped his glasses and centered them on the Notch again. The horseman had led his horse to a clump of brush. Presently the twinkling front of an automobile appeared—a miniature machine that wormed slowly through the Notch and descended the short pitch beyond. Suddenly the car swerved and stopped. Lorry saw a flutter of white near the machine. Then the concealed horseman appeared on foot. Lorry slipped the glass in his shirt.

"We'll just mosey over and get a closer look," he told his pony. "Things don't look just right over there."

Gray Leg, scenting a new interest, tucked himself together. The sand sprayed to little puffs of dust as he swung to a lope.

Lorry was curious—and a bit elated at the promise of a break in the monotony of hunting stray cattle. Probably some Eastern tourist had taken the grade below the Notch too fast and ditched his machine. Lorry would ride over and help him to right the car and set the pilgrim on his way rejoicing. He had helped to right cars before. Last month, for instance; that big car with the uniformed driver and the wonderfully gowned women. He recalled the fact that one of them had been absolutely beautiful, despite her strange mufflings. She had offered to pay him for his trouble. When he refused she had thanked him eloquently with her fine eyes and thrown him a kiss as he turned to go. She had thrown that kiss with two hands! There was nothing stingy about that lady!

But possibly the machine toward which he rode carried nothing more interesting than men; fat, well-dressed men who smoked fat cigars and had much to say about "high" and "low," but didn't seem to know a great deal about "Jack" and "The Game." If *they* offered to pay him for helping them— well, that was a different matter.

The pony loped toward the Notch, quite as eager as his rider to attend a performance that promised action. Within a half-mile of the Notch, Lorry pulled the pony to a walk. Just beyond the car he had seen the head and ears of a horse. The rider was afoot, talking to the folks in the car. This didn't look quite right.

He worked his pony through the shoulder-high brush until within a few yards of the other man, who was evidently unwelcome. One of the two women stood in front of the other as though to shield her.

Lorry took down his rope just as the younger of the two women saw his head above the brush. The strange horseman, noting her expression, turned quickly. Lorry's pony jumped at the thrust of the spurs. The rope circled like a swallow and settled lightly on the man's shoulders. The pony wheeled. The blunt report of a gun punctured the silence, followed by the long-drawn ripping of brush and the snorting of the pony.

The man was dragging and clutching at the brush. He had dropped his gun. Lorry dug the spurs into Gray Leg. The rope came taut with a jerk. The man rolled over, his hands snatching at the noose about his neck. Lorry dismounted and ran to him. He eased the loop, and swiftly slipped it over the man's feet.

Gray Leg, who knew how to keep a rope taut better than anything else, slowly circled the fallen man. Lorry picked up the gun and strode over to the car. One of the women was crouching on the running-board. In front of her, pale, straight, stiffly indignant, stood a young woman whose eyes challenged Lorry's approach.

"It's all right, miss. He won't bother you now."

"Is he dead?" queried the girl.

"I reckon not."

"I heard a shot. I thought you killed him."

"No, ma'am. He took a crack at me. I don't pack a gun."

"You're a cowboy?" And the girl laughed nervously, despite her effort to hold herself together.

"I aim to be," said Lorry, a trifle brusquely.

The elder woman peered through her fingers. "Another one!" she moaned.

"No, mother. This one is a cowboy. It's all right."

"It sure is. What was his game?"

"He told us to give him our money."

"Uh-uh. This is the second holdup here at the Notch this summer."

"He's trying to get up!" exclaimed the girl.

"My hoss'll take care of him."

"But your horse might drag him to death."

"Well, it's his own funeral, ain't it?"

The girl's eyes grew big. She stepped back. If she had only said something Lorry would have felt better. As it was he felt decidedly uncomfortable.

"If you'll say what is right, ma'am, I'll do it. You want me to turn him loose?"

"I—No. But can't you do something for him?"

Lorry laughed. "I reckon you don't sabe them kind, miss. And mebby you want to get that car on the road again."

"Yes," said the girl's mother. "I think this young man knows what he is about."

Lorry stepped to the car to examine it.

The girl followed him. "I think there is nothing broken. We just turned to come down that hill. We were coasting when I saw a rope stretched across the road. I didn't know what to do. I tried to stop. We slid off the edge."

"Uh-uh. He had it all ribbed up to stop you. Now if you had kept on goin'—"

"But I didn't know what the rope meant. I was frightened. And before I knew what had happened he stepped right on the running-board and told us to give him our money."

"Yes, ma'am. If you can start her up, I'll get my rope on the axle and help."

"But the man might get up!" said the girl.

Lorry grinned. A minute or two ago she had been afraid that the man wouldn't get up. Lorry slipped the rope from the man's ankles and tied it to the front axle. The girl got in the car. The pony buckled to his work. The machine stuttered and purred. With a lurch it swung back into the road. The girl's mother rose, brushed her skirt, and stepped to the car. Lorry unfastened the rope and reined to one side.

The car steered badly. The girl stopped it and beckoned to Lorry.

"There's something wrong with the steering-gear. Are the roads good from here to the next town?"

"Not too good. There's some heavy sand about a mile west."

She bit her lip. "Well, I suppose we'll have to turn back."

"You could get to Stacey, ma'am. You could get your car fixed, and my mother runs the hotel there. It's a good place to stop."

"How far?"

"About eight miles. Three miles back the road forks and the left-hand road goes to town. The regular automobile road don't go to Stacey."

"Well, I suppose there is nothing else to do. I'll try and turn around." And the girl backed the car and swung round in a wavering arc. When the car faced the east she stopped it.

Lorry rode alongside. She thanked him for his services. "And please don't do anything to that man," she pleaded. "He has been punished enough. You almost killed him. He looked so wretched. Can't you give him a good talking to and let him go?"

"I could, ma'am. But it ain't right. He'll try this here stunt again There's a reward out for him."

"But won't you—please!"

Lorry flushed. "You got a good heart all right, but you ain't been long in the West. Such as him steals hosses and holds up folks and robs trains—"

"But you're not an officer," she said, somewhat unkindly.

"I reckon any man is an officer when wimmin-folk is gettin' robbed. And I aim to put him where he belongs."

"Thank you for helping us," said the girl's mother.

"You're right welcome, ma'am." And, raising his hat, Lorry turned and rode to where the man lay.

The car crept up the slope. Lorry watched it until it had topped the ridge. Then he dismounted and turned the man over.

"What you got to say about my turnin' you loose?" he queried as the other sat up.

"Nothin'."

"All right. Get a movin'—and don't try to run. I got my rope handy."

Chapter IX
High-Chin Bob

The man's rusty black coat was torn and wrinkled. His cheap cotton shirt was faded and buttonless. His boots were split at the sole, showing part of a bare foot. He was grimy, unshaven, and puffed unhealthily beneath the eyes. Lorry knew that he was but an indifferent rider without seeing him on a horse. He was a typical railroad tramp, turned highwayman.

"Got another gun on you?" queried Lorry.

The man shook his head.

"Where'd you steal that horse?"

"Who says I stole him?"

"I do. He's a Starr horse. He was turned out account of goin' lame. Hop along. I'll take care of him."

The man plodded across the sand. Lorry followed on Gray Leg, and led the other horse. Flares of noon heat shot up from the reddish-gray levels. Lorry whistled, outwardly serene, but inwardly perturbed. That girl had asked him to let the man go and she had said "please." But, like all women, she didn't understand such things.

They approached a low ridge and worked up a winding cattle trail. On the crest Lorry reined up. The man sat down, breathing heavily.

"What you callin' yourself?" asked Lorry.

"A dam' fool."

"I knew that. Anything else?"

"Waco—mebby."

"Waco, eh? Well, that's an insult to Texas. What's your idea in holdin' up wimmin-folk, anyhow?"

"Mebby you'd hold up anybody if you hadn't et since yesterday morning."

"Think I believe that?"

"Suit yourself. You got me down."

"Well, you can get up and get movin'."

The man rose. He shuffled forward, limping heavily. Occasionally he stopped and turned to meet a level gaze that was impersonal; that promised nothing. Lorry would have liked to let the other ride. The man was suffering—and to ride would save time. But the black, a rangy, quick-stepping animal, was faster than Gray Leg. But what if the man did escape? No one need know about it. Yet Lorry knew that he was doing right in arresting him. In fact, he felt a kind of secret pride in making the capture. It would give him a name among his fellows. But was there any glory in arresting such a man?

Lorry recalled the other's wild shot as he was whirled through the brush. "He sure tried to get me!" Lorry argued. "And any man that'd hold up wimmin ought to be in the calaboose—"

The trail meandered down the hillside and out across a barren flat. Halfway across the flat the trail forked. Lorry had ceased to whistle. At the fork his pony stopped of its own accord. The man turned questioningly. Lorry gestured toward the right-hand trail. The man staggered on. The horses fretted at the slow pace. Keen to anticipate some trickery, Lorry hardened himself to the other's condition. Perhaps the man was hungry, sick, suffering. Well, a mile beyond was the water-hole. The left-hand trail led directly to Stacey, but there was no water along that trail.

They moved on across a stretch of higher land that swept in a gentle, sage-dotted slope to the far hills. Midway across the slope was a bare spot burning like white fire in the desert sun. It was the water-hole. The trail became paralleled by other trails, narrow and rutted by countless hoofs.

Within a hundred yards of the water-hole the prisoner collapsed. Lorry dismounted and went for water.

The man drank, and Lorry helped him up and across the sand to the rim of the water-hole. The man gazed at the shimmering pool with blurred eyes.

Lorry rolled a cigarette. "Roll one?" he queried.

The man Waco took the proffered tobacco and papers. His weariness seemed to vanish as he smoked. "That pill sure saved my life," he asserted.

"How much you reckon your life's worth?"

Waco blew a smoke-ring and nodded toward it as it dissolved. Lorry pondered. The keen edge of his interest in the capture had worn off, leaving a blunt purpose—a duty that was part of the day's work. As he realized how much the other was at his mercy a tinge of sympathy softened his gray eyes. Justice was undeniably a fine thing. Folks were entitled to the pursuit of happiness, to life and liberty he had read somewhere. He glanced up. Waco, seated opposite, had drifted back into a stupor, head sunk forward and arms relaxed. The stub of his cigarette lay smouldering between his feet. Lorry thought of the girl's appeal.

"Just what started you to workin' this holdup game?" he queried.

Waco's head came up. "You joshin' me?"

"Nope."

"You wouldn't believe a hard-luck story, so what's the use?"

"Ain't any. I was just askin' a question. Roll another?"

Waco stuck out his grimy paw. His fingers trembled as he fumbled the tobacco and papers.

Lorry proffered a match. "It makes me sick to see a husky like you all shot to pieces," said Lorry.

"Did you just get wise to that?"

"Nope. But I just took time to say it."

Waco breathed deep, inhaling the smoke. "I been crooked all my life," he asserted.

"I can believe that. 'Course you know I'm takin' you to Stacey."

"The left-hand trail was quicker," ventured the tramp.

"And no water."

"I could ride," suggested Waco.

Lorry shook his head. "If you was to make a break I'd just nacherally plug you. I got your gun. You're safer afoot."

"I'll promise—"

"Nope. You're too willin'."

"I'm all in," said Waco.

"I got to take you to Stacey just the same."

"And you're doin' it for the money—the reward."

"That's my business."

"Go ahead," said the tramp. "I hope you have a good time blowin' in the dough. Blood-money changes easy to booze-money when a lot of cow-chasers get their hooks on it."

"Don't get gay!" said Lorry. "I aim to use you white as long as you work gentle. If you don't—"

"That's the way with you guys that do nothin' but chase a cow's tail over the country. You handle folks the same as stock—rough stuff and to hell with their feelin's."

"You're feelin' better," said Lorry. "Stand up and get to goin'."

As Waco rose, Lorry's pony nickered. A rider was coming down the distant northern hillside. In the fluttering silken bandanna and the twinkle of silver-studded trappings Lorry recognized the foreman of the Starr Rancho; Bob Brewster, known for his arrogance as "High-Chin Bob."

"Guess we'll wait a minute," said Lorry.

Waco saw the rider, and asked who he was.

"It's High Chin, the foreman. You been ridin' one of his string of horses—the black there."

"He's your boss?"

"Yes. And I'm right sorry he's ridin' into this camp. You was talkin' of feelin's. Well, he ain't got any."

Brewster loped up and dismounted. "What's your tally, kid?"

Lorry shook his head. "Only this," he said jokingly.

Brewster glanced at Waco. "Maverick, all right. Where'd you rope *him*?"

"I run onto him holdin' up some tourists down by the Notch. I'm driftin' him over to Stacey."

High Chin's eyes narrowed. "Was he ridin' that horse?" And he pointed to the black.

Lorry admitted that he had found the horse tied in the brush near the Notch.

High Chin swung round. "You fork your bronc and get busy. There's eighty head and over strayin' in here, and the old man ain't payin' you to entertain hobos. I'll herd this hombre to camp."

With his arm outflung the tramp staggered up to the foreman. "I come back—to tell you—that I'm going to live to get you right. I got a hunch that all hell can't beat out. I'll get you!"

"We won't have any trouble," said Waring.

High Chin whirled his horse round. "What's it to you? Who are you, buttin' in on this?"

"My name is Waring. I used to mill around Sonora once."

High Chin blinked. He knew that name. Slowly he realized that the man on the big buckskin meant what he said when he asserted that there would be no trouble.

"Well, I'm foreman of the Starr, and you're fired!" he told Lorry.

"That's no news," said Lorry, grinning.

"And I'm goin' to herd this hoss-thief to camp," he continued, spurring toward Waco, who had started to walk away.

"Not this journey," said Waring, pushing his horse between them. "The boy don't pack a gun. I do."

"You talk big—knowin' I got no gun," said High Chin.

Lorry rode over to the foreman. "Here's your gun, High. I ain't no killer."

The foreman holstered the gun and reined round toward Waring. "Now do your talkin'," he challenged.

Waring made no movement, but sat quietly watching the other's gun hand. "You have your gun?" he said, as though asking a question. "If you mean business, go ahead. I'll let you get your gun out—and then I'll get you—and you know it!" And with insulting ease he flicked his burned-out cigarette in the foreman's face.

Without a word High Chin whirled his horse and rode toward the hills.

Waring sat watching him until Lorry spoke.

"They say he's put more than one man across the divide," he told his father.

"But not on an even break," said Waring. "Get that hombre on his horse He's in bad shape."

Lorry helped Waco to mount. They rode toward Stacey.

Waring rode with them until the trail forked. "I was on my way to the Starr Ranch," he told Lorry. "I think I can make it all right with Starr, if you say the word."

"Not me," said Lorry. "I stand by what I do."

to conceal the smile that crept to his lips. "All right, Lorry.
to explain to your mother. Better turn your man over to
)on as you get in town. Where did you pick him up?"

din' up some tourists over by the Notch. He changed his
___ along with me."

Waring rode down the west fork, and Lorry and the tramp continued
their journey to Stacey.

Chapter X
East and West

Mrs. Adams, ironing in the kitchen, was startled by a peremptory ringing of the bell on the office desk. The Overland had arrived and departed more than an hour ago. She patted her hair, smoothed her apron, and stepped through the dining-room to the office. A rather tired-looking, stylishly gowned woman immediately asked if there were comfortable accommodations for herself and her daughter. Mrs. Adams assured her that there were.

"We had an accident," continued the woman. "I am Mrs. Weston. This is my daughter."

"You are driving overland?"

"We were. We have had a terrible time. A man tried to rob us, and we almost wrecked our car."

"Goodness! Where did it happen?"

"At a place called 'The Notch,' I think," said Alice Weston, taking the pen Mrs. Adams proffered and registering.

"I can give you a front double room," said Mrs. Adams. "But the single rooms are cooler."

"Anything will do so long as it is clean," said Mrs. Weston.

Mrs. Adams's rosy face grew red. "My rooms are always clean. I attend to them myself."

"And a room with a bath would be preferable," said Mrs. Weston.

Her daughter Alice smiled. Mrs. Adams caught the twinkle in the girl's eyes and smiled in return.

"You can have the room next to the bathroom. This is a desert town, Mrs Weston. We don't have many tourists."

"I suppose it will have to do," sighed Mrs. Weston. "Of course we may have the exclusive use of the bath?"

"Mother," said Alice Weston, "you must remember that this isn't New York. I think we are fortunate to get a place as comfortable and neat as this. We're really in the desert. We will see the rooms, please."

Mrs. Weston could find no fault with the rooms. They were neat and clean, even to the window-panes. Alice Weston was delighted. From her window she could see miles of the western desert, and the far, mysterious ranges bulked against the blue of the north; ranges that seemed to whisper of romance, the unexplored, the alluring.

While Mrs. Adams was arranging things, Alice Weston gazed out of the window. Below in the street a cowboy passed jauntily. A stray burro crossed the street and nosed among some weeds. Then a stolid Indian stalked by.

"Why, that is a real Indian!" exclaimed the girl.

"A Navajo," said Mrs. Adams. "They come in quite often."

"Really? And—oh, I forgot—the young man who rescued us told us that he was your son."

"Lorry! Rescued you?"

"Yes." And the girl told Mrs. Adams about the accident and the tramp.

"I'm thankful that he didn't get killed," was Mrs. Adams's comment when the girl had finished.

Alone in her room, Alice Weston bared her round young arms and enjoyed a real, old-fashioned wash in a real, old-fashioned washbowl. Who could be unhappy in this glorious country? But mother seemed so unimpressed! "And I hope that steering-knuckle doesn't come for a month," the girl told a framed lithograph of "Custer's Last Fight," which, contrary to all precedent, was free from fly specks.

She recalled the scene at the Notch: the sickening sway of the car; the heavy, brutal features of the bandit, who seemed to have risen from the ground; the unexpected appearance of the young cowboy, the flash of his rope, and a struggling form whirling through the brush.

And she had said "please" when she had asked the young cowboy to let the man go. He had refused. She thought Western men more gallant. But what difference did that make? She would never see him again. The young cowboy had seemed rather nice, until just toward the last. As for the other man—she shivered as she wondered what would have happened if the cowboy had not arrived when he did.

It occurred to her that she had never been refused a request in her life until that afternoon. And the fact piqued her. The fate of the tramp was a secondary consideration now. She and her mother were safe. The car would have to be repaired; but that was unimportant. The fact that they were stranded in a real desert town, with Indians and cowboys in the streets, and vistas such as she had dreamed of shimmering in the afternoon sun, awakened an erstwhile slumbering desire for a draught of the real Romance of the West, heretofore only enjoyed in unsatisfying sips as she read of the West and its wonder trails.

A noise in the street attracted her attention. She stepped to the window. Just across the street a tall, heavy man was unlocking a door in a little adobe building. Near him stood the young cowboy whom she had not expected to see again. And there was the tramp, handcuffed and strangely white of face. The door swung open, and the tall man stepped back. The tramp shuffled through the low doorway, and the door was closed and locked. The cowboy and the tall man talked for a while. She stepped back as the men separated.

Presently she heard the cowboy's voice downstairs. She flushed, and gazed at herself in the glass.

"I am going to make him sorry he refused to let that man go," she told the mirror. "Oh, I shall be nice to him! So nice that—" She did not complete the thought. She was naturally gracious. When she set out to be exceptionally nice—"Oo, la, la!" she exclaimed. "And he's nothing but a cowboy!"

She heard Lorry clump upstairs and enter a room across the hall. She knew it was he. She could hear the clink of his spurs and the swish of his chaps. While she realized that he was Mrs. Adams's son and had a right to be there, she rather resented his proximity, possibly because she had not expected to see him again.

She had no idea that he had been discharged by his foreman, nor that he had earned the disapproval of his mother for having quarreled. Of course he had ridden to Stacey to bring the prisoner in, but he knew they were in Stacey, and Alice Weston liked to believe that he would make excuse to stay in town while they were there. It would be fun—for her.

After supper that evening Mrs. Weston and Alice were introduced to Waring, who came in late. Waring chatted with Mrs. Weston out on the veranda in the cool of the evening. Alice was surprised that her mother seemed interested in Waring. But after a while, as the girl listened, she admitted that the man was interesting.

The conversation drifted to mines and mining. Mrs. Weston declared that she had never seen a gold mine, but that her husband owned some stock in one of the richest mines in Old Mexico. Waring grew enthusiastic as he described mine operating in detail, touching the subject with the ease of experience, yet lightly enough to avoid wearisome technicalities. The girl listened, occasionally stealing a glance at the man's profile in the dusk. She thought the boy Lorry looked exceedingly like Mr. Waring.

And the person who looked exceedingly like Mr. Waring sat at the far end of the veranda, talking to Buck Hardy, the sheriff. And Lorry was not altogether happy. His interest in the capture and reward had waned. He had never dreamed that a girl could be so captivating as Alice Weston. At supper she had talked with him about the range, asking many questions; but she had not referred to that morning. Lorry had hoped that he might talk with her after supper. But somehow or other she had managed to evade his efforts. Just now she seemed to be mightily interested in his father.

Presently Lorry rose and strode across the street to the station. He talked with the agent, who showed him a telegraph duplicate for an order on Albuquerque covering a steering-knuckle for an automobile. When Lorry reappeared he was whistling. It would take some time for that steering-knuckle to arrive. Meanwhile, he was out of work, and the Westons would be at the hotel for several days at least.

There was some mighty fine scenery back in the Horseshoe Range, west. Perhaps the girl liked Western scenery. He wondered if she knew how to ride. He was rather inclined to think that her mother did not. He would suggest a trip to the Horseshoe Mountains, as it would be pretty dull at the hotel. Nothing but cowboys and Indians riding in and out of town. But there were some Hopi ruins over in the Horseshoe. Most Easterners were interested in ruins. He wished that the Hopis had left a ruin somewhat nearer town.

Yet withal, Lorry was proud to think that his father could be so interesting to real Easterners. If they only knew who his father was! Lorry's train of thought was making pretty good time when he checked it suddenly. Folks in town didn't know that Waring was his father. And "The whole dog-gone day had just been one gosh-awful mess!"

"Weston, you said?" Waring queried.

"Yes—John Archibald Weston, of New York." And Mrs. Weston nodded.

Waring smiled. J.A. Weston was one of the stockholders in the Ortez Mine, near Sonora.

"The principal stockholder," said Mrs. Weston.

"I met him down there," said Waring.

"Indeed! How interesting! You were connected with the mining industry, Mr. Waring?"

"In a way. I lived in Sonora several years."

"That accounts for your wonderful descriptions of the country. I never imagined it could be so charming."

"We have some hill country west of here worth looking at. If you intend to stay any length of time, I might arrange a trip."

"That's nice of you. But I don't ride. Perhaps Alice would like to go."

"Yes, indeed! But—"

"We might get Mrs. Adams to come. She used to ride."

"I'll ask her," said Alice Weston.

"But, Alice—" And Mrs. Weston smiled. Alice had already gone to look for Mrs. Adams.

Lorry, who had heard, scowled at a veranda post. He had thought of that trip to the Horseshoe Range long before it had been mentioned by his father. Wimmin made him tired, he told the unoffending post.

Shortly afterward Alice appeared. She had cajoled Mrs. Adams into promising that she would ride to the Hopi ruins with them, as the journey there and back could be made in a day. Alice Weston was aglow with excitement. Of course the young cowboy would be included in the invitation, and Alice premeditated a flirtation, either with that good-looking Mr. Waring or Mrs. Adams's son. It didn't matter much which one; it would be fun.

The Westons finally went to their rooms. Lorry, out of sorts with himself and the immediate world, was left alone on the veranda.

"She just acted so darned nice to me I forgot to eat," he told the post confidentially. "And then she forgot I was livin' in the same county—after supper. And she did it a-purpose. I reckon she's tryin' to even up with me for jailin' that hobo after she said 'please.' Well, two can play at that even-up game."

He rose and walked upstairs quietly. As he entered his room he heard the Westons talking. He had noticed that the door of one of their rooms was open.

"No, I think he went away with that tall man," he heard the girl say "Cowboys don't go to bed early when in town."

"Weren't you a little too nice to him at dinner?" Mrs. Weston said.

Lorry heard the girl laugh. "Oh, but he's only a boy, mother! And it's such fun to watch his eyes when he smiles. He is really good-looking and interesting, because he hasn't been tamed. I don't think he has any real feeling, though, or he wouldn't have brought that poor creature to Stacey and put him in jail. But Mr. Waring is different. He seems so quiet and kind—and rather distinguished."

Lorry closed his door. He had heard enough for one evening.

He did not want to go to bed. He felt anything but sleepy, so he tiptoed downstairs again and out into the night. He found Buck Hardy in a saloon up the street. Men in the saloon joked with Lorry about his capture. He seldom drank, but to-night he did not refuse Hardy's invitation to "have something." While they were chatting a rider from the Starr Rancho came in. Edging up to Lorry, he touched his arm. "Come on out a minute," he whispered.

Outside, he told Lorry that High Chin, with several of the men, was coming to town that night and "put one over" on the sheriff by stealing the prisoner.

"And you know what that means," said the Starr cowboy. "High Chin'll get tanked, and the hobo'll be lucky if the boys don't string him up. High Chin's awful sore about something."

Lorry's first idea was to report all this to Buck Hardy. But he feared ridicule. What if the Starr cowboys didn't come?

"Why don't you tell Buck yourself?" he queried.

His companion insisted that he dare not tell the sheriff. If High Chin heard that he had done so, he would be out of a job. And there was the reward. If the prisoner's identity was proven, Lorry would get the reward. The cowboy didn't want to see Lorry lose such easy money.

The subject seemed to require some liquidation, and Lorry finally decided that he himself was the only and legal custodian of the prisoner. As for the reward—shucks! He didn't want blood-money. But High Chin would never lay a hand on the hobo if he could help it.

Alice Weston, anticipating a real ride into the desert country and the hills, was too excited to sleep. She drew a chair to the window, and sat back where she could view the vague outline of the hills and a world filled with glowing stars. The town was silent, save for the occasional opening or closing of a door and the infrequent sound of feet on the sidewalk. She forgot the hazards of the day in dreaming of the West; no longer a picture out of books, but a reality. She scarcely noticed the quiet figure that came round the opposite corner and passed into the shadows of the jail across the street. She heard the clink of a chain and a sharp, tearing sound as of wood being rent asunder. She peered from her window, trying to see what was going on in the shadows.

Presently a figure appeared. The hat, the attitude, and manner seemed familiar. Then came another figure; that of the tramp. She grew tense with excitement. She heard Lorry's voice distinctly:—

"The best thing for you is to fan it. Don't try the train. They'll get you sure if you do. No, I don't explain anything. Just ramble—and keep a-ramblin'."

She saw one of the figures creep along the opposite wall and shuffle across the street. She felt like calling out. Instead she rose and opened her door. She would tell her mother. But what good would that do? She returned to the window. Lorry, standing on the street corner, seemed to be watching an invisible something far down the street. Alice Weston heard the sound of running horses. A group of cowboys galloped up. She heard the horses stop. Lorry had disappeared.

She went to bed. It seemed an age before she heard him come in.

Lorry undressed in the dark. As he went to bed he grinned. "And the worst of it is," he soliloquized, "she'll think I did it because she asked me to let him go. Guess I been steppin' on my foot the whole dog-gone day."

Chapter XI
Spring Lamb

Mrs. Adams had decided to have roast spring lamb for dinner that evening. Instead, her guests had to content themselves with canned salmon and hot biscuit. And because …

Lorry appeared at the breakfast table in overalls and jumper. He had purposely waited until the Westons had gone downstairs. He anticipated an invitation to ride to the hills with them. He would decline, and smile as he did so. If that girl thought he cared anything about *her*!

He answered their greeting with a cheery "Good-mornin'," and immediately turned his whole attention to bacon and eggs.

Alice Weston wondered that his eyes should be so clear and care-free, knowing what she did of last night's escapade.

Mrs. Adams was interested in the girl's riding-habit. It made her own plain riding-skirt and blouse appear rather countrified. And after breakfast Lorry watched the preparations for the ride with a critical eye. No one would know whether or not he cared to go. They seemed to have taken it for granted that he would. He whistled softly, and shook his head as his mother suggested that he get ready.

"Of course you're coming with us," said Alice Weston.

"I got to look after the hotel," he said with conclusive emphasis.

> Lorry disappeared, and in the bustle of preparation and departure Mrs Adams did not miss him until they were some distance out on the mesa.

"Where's Lorry?" she queried.

"He said he had to look after the hotel," said Alice Weston.

"Well, he didn't. I had everything arranged for. I don't know what's got into him lately."

Back at the hotel Lorry was leaning against the veranda rail, talking to Mrs. Weston. "I reckon it will be kind of tame for you, ma'am. I was wondering, now, if you would let me look over that machine. I've helped fix 'em up lots of times."

"Why, I don't know. It wouldn't do any harm to look, would it?"

"I guess not."

Mrs. Weston gazed at Lorry curiously. He had smiled, and he resembled Waring so closely that Mrs. Weston remarked it aloud.

Lorry flushed. "I think Mr. Waring is a right good-lookin' man, don't you?"

Mrs. Weston laughed. "Yes, I do."

"Yes, ma'am. But honest, Mrs. Weston, I never did see a finer-lookin' girl than your girl. I seen plenty of magazine pictures like her. I'd feel some proud if I was her mother."

The morning was not so dull, after all. Mrs. Weston was not used to such frankness, but she was not displeased. "I see you have on your working clothes. If you really think you can repair the car—"

"I got nothin' else to do. The sun is gettin' round to the front. If you would like to sit in the car and watch, I would look her over; there, in the shade."

"I'll get a hat," said Mrs. Weston, rising.

"Your hair is right pretty without a hat. And besides you would be in the shade of the top."

It had been some time since any one had complimented Mrs. Weston about her hair, and especially a man young enough to be her son. What was the cowboy going to say next?

Mrs. Weston stepped into the car, which was parked on the south side of the building. Lorry, whistling blithely, searched until he found a wrench in one of the forward-door pockets. He disappeared beneath the car. Mrs. Weston could hear him tinkering at something. She leaned back, breathing deep of the clean, thin air. She could not recall having felt so thoroughly content and keenly alive at the same time. She had no desire to say or do anything.

Presently Lorry appeared, his face grimy and his hands streaked with oil. "Nothin' busted," he reported cheerfully. "We got a car over to the ranch. She's been busted a-plenty. I fixed her up more times than I can remember.

Cars is like horses ma'am; no two just alike, but kind of generally the same. The steering-knuckle ain't broke. It's the left axle that's sprung. That won't take long to straighten."

Mrs. Weston smiled. Lorry thought she was actually pretty. She saw this in his eyes, and flushed slightly.

"And I'll just block her up and take off the wheel, and I reckon the blacksmith can straighten that axle easy."

"It's very nice of you. But I am wondering why you didn't go on the picnic—with the others."

"Well, who'd 'a' kept you company, ma'am? Anita, she's busy. Anyhow, I seen plenty of scenery. I'd rather be here."

"Talking to a woman old enough to be your mother?"

"Huh! I never thought of you like that. I'm only eighteen. Anyhow, what difference does it make how old a lady is, if she is pretty?"

Mrs. Weston's eyes twinkled. "Do you ever pay compliments to yourself when you are combing your hair or tying your scarf?"

"Me! Why, not so anybody could hear 'em. Now, I think my mother is right pretty, Mrs. Weston."

"So do I. And it was nice of you to say it."

"But I don't see anything wrong in sayin' what's so," he argued. "I seen you kind of raise your eyebrows, and I thought mebby I was bein' took as a joke."

"Oh, no, indeed!"

Lorry disappeared again. As he worked he wondered just how long it would be before Buck Hardy would look for him. Lorry knew that some one must have taken food and water to the prisoner by this time, or to where the prisoner was supposed to be. But he did not know that Hardy and his deputy had questioned Anita, and that she had told the sheriff the folks had all gone on a picnic to the hills. The car, at the back of the hotel, was not visible from the street.

With some pieces of timber Lorry jacked up the front of the machine and removed the damaged wheel and axle.

He took the bent axle to the blacksmith, and returned to the hotel. Nothing further offered just then, so he suggested that he clean the car. Mrs. Weston consented, deciding that she would not pay him until her daughter returned.

He attached the hose to a faucet, and suggested that Mrs. Weston take a chair, which he brought from the veranda. He hosed the car, and as he polished it, Mrs. Weston asked him about Waring.

"Why, he's a friend of ours," replied Lorry.

"Of course. But I was wondering what he did."

Lorry hesitated. "Didn't you ever hear that song about Waring of Sonora-Town? It's a whizzer. Well, that's him. All the cowboys sing that song."

"I have never heard it."

"Well, mebby dad wouldn't like that I sing it. He's kind of funny that way. Now you wouldn't think he was the fastest gunman in the Southwest, would you?"

"Gunman! Your father?"

Lorry straightened up from polishing the car. "I clean forgot what I was sayin'. I guess my foot slipped that time."

"I am sorry I asked," said Mrs. Weston. "It really doesn't matter."

"Oh, it ain't your fault. But I wasn't aimin' to tell. Dad he married my mother, and they went to live in Sonora, down in Mexico. Some of the minin' outfits down there hired him regular to—to protect their interests. I guess ma couldn't stand that kind of life, for after a few years she brought me up here. I was just a kid then. Ma she built up a good trade at this hotel. Folks call her Mrs. Adams. Her name was Adams afore she got married. We been here ten years. Dad didn't know where she was till last week he showed up here. I reckon she thought he got killed long ago. Folks would talk about it if they knowed he was her husband, so I guess she asked dad to say nothin' about that. He said he came up to see me. I guess he don't aim to stay long."

"I think I understand," said Mrs. Weston.

"Well, it ain't none of my business, long as ma is all right. Say, she shines like a new hack, eh?"

"You have cleaned the car beautifully."

"Oh, I dunno. Now, if it was a hoss—And say, I guess you'll be startin' to-morrow. That axle will be all right in about an hour."

Just then Anita came to call them to luncheon. She had heard them talking at the rear of the hotel shortly after Sheriff Hardy had inquired for Lorry. Several townsfolk came in, ate, and departed on their several ways.

After luncheon Mrs. Weston went to her room. She thought she would lie down and sleep for an hour or so, but the noon heat made the room rather close. She picked up a book and came down, where she found it comfortably cool on the veranda.

The town was quiet. A hand-car with its section crew of Mexicans clicked past, and hummed on down the glittering rails. A stray burro meandered about, and finally came to a stop in the middle of the street, where he stood, stoically enduring the sun, a veritable long-eared statue of dejection. Mrs. Weston turned a page, but the printed word was flat and insignificant.

She felt as though she were in a kind of twilight valley, midway between the hills of slumber and wakefulness. For the moment she forgot the name of the town itself. She knew that she could recall it if she tried. A dog lay asleep beneath the station platform opposite, one relaxed paw over his nose. Some one was calling to some one in the kitchen. A figure passed in the street; a young man who smiled and nodded. It was the boy, Lorry. He had been working on the car that morning. She had watched him work, rather enjoying his energy. A healthy young animal as unsophisticated as a kitten, and really innately kind and innocent of intent to flatter. He was not at all like the bright young savage who had roped and almost choked to death that awful man.

It was impossible to judge a person at first sight and especially under unusual circumstances. And he seemed not at all chagrined that he had not gone with the others to the hills. Alice had enjoyed reading about Westerners—rough, boisterous beings intolerable to Mrs. Weston even in print. And Mrs. Weston thought that proper environment and association might bring out their better qualities, even as the boy, Lorry, seemed to have improved—well, since yesterday morning. Perhaps he was on his good behavior because they were there.

It seemed past comprehension that anything startling could happen in that drowsy atmosphere.

The young cowboy was coming back down the street, some part of the car over his shoulder. Mrs. Weston anticipated his nod, and nodded lazily as he passed. She could hear him tinkering at the car.

A few blocks up the street, Buck Hardy was seated in his office talking with the undersheriff. The undersheriff twisted the end of his black mustache and looked wise.

"They told me at the hotel that he had gone riding with them Easterners," said Hardy. "And now you say he's been in town all day working on that automobile."

"Yep. He's been to the blacksmith twice to-day. I didn't say anything to him, seein' you was over to Larkins's, and said he was out of town. I'd hate to think he done anything like that."

"That hobo was gone when I went to talk to him this morning. The lock was busted. I can't figure it out. Young Lorry stood to win the reward, and he could use the money."

"Hear anything by wire?" queried the undersheriff.

"Nothing. The man didn't get by on any of the trains. I notified both stations. He's afoot and he's gone."

"Well, I guess the kid loses out, eh?"

"That ain't all. This county will jump me for letting that guy get away It won't help us any next election."

"Well, my idea is to have a talk with Adams," said the undersheriff.

"I'm going to do that. I like the kid, and then there's his mother—"

"And you'd hold him for lettin' the guy loose, eh?"

"I would. I'd hold my own brother for playing a trick like that."

"Well, I don't sabe it," asserted the undersheriff. "Lorry Adams always had a good name."

"We'll have a talk with him, Bill."

"Are you sure Adams did it, Buck?"

"No, not sure, but I'm going to find out. I'll throw a scare into him that'll make him talk."

"Mebby he won't scare."

"Then I'll run him in. He's some enterprising, if I do say it. He put High-Chin Bob out of business over by the water-hole yesterday."

"High Chin! The hell you say!"

"That's what I thought when I heard it. High was beating up the hobo, and Lorry claimed him as his prisoner. Jim Waring says the kid walloped High on the head and knocked him stiff."

"Whew! Bob will get his hide for that."

"I don't know. Jim Waring is riding the country just now."

"What's that got to do with it?"

"More than I'm going to tell you, Bill. But take it from me, he's interested in young Adams a whole lot."

When Hardy and his deputy rode over to the hotel there was a pause in the chatter. Alice Weston was describing their journey to her mother and calling upon Waring to substantiate her vivid assertions of the wonderful adventure. The saddle-horse still stood at the hitching-rail, and Hardy, who had an eye for a good horse, openly admired the big buckskin. Waring was talking with Lorry. Mrs. Adams had gone in. Hardy indicated that he wanted to speak to Lorry, and he included Waring in his gesture. Lorry rose and glanced quickly at Alice Weston. She was leaning forward in her chair, suddenly aware of a subtle undercurrent of seriousness. The undersheriff was patting the nose of the big buckskin.

The men stepped down from the veranda, and stood near the horses.

"That hobo got away," said the sheriff. "Do you know anything about it?"

"I turned him loose," said Lorry, without hesitation.

"What for?"

"I changed my mind. I didn't want any blood-money for arrestin' a tramp."

"That's all right. But you can't change the law so easy. That man was my prisoner. Why didn't you come to me?"

"Well, if you want to know, in company," said Lorry, "High Chin and the boys had it framed up to give that hobo a goin'-over for stealin' a Starr horse. They figured to bust in the jail, same as I did. I got that straight; I didn't aim to let High Chin get his hands on my prisoner."

"Well, Lorry, I don't like to do it, but I got to hold you till we get him."

"How do you figure that?"

"You've aided a prisoner to escape. You broke the law."

"What right had you to hold him?"

"Your own story. You brought him in yourself."

"I sure did. But supposin' I say I ain't got nothin' against him, and the folks over there won't appear against him, how could you prove anything?"

"He's under suspicion. You said yourself he was holding up them tourists."

"But you can't make me swear that in court."

Buck Hardy glared at the younger man. "See here, Lorry, I don't understand your game. Suppose the man ain't guilty. He was locked up — and by me, representing this county. You can't prove that the Starr boys would have done anything to him. And you can't monkey with the law to suit yourself as long as I'm sheriff. Am I right?" And Hardy turned to Waring.

"You're right, Hardy."

Lorry's gray eyes shone with a peculiar light. "What you goin' to do about it, Buck?"

"Two of my boys are out looking for the man. You're under arrest till he is brought in."

"You aim to lock me in that calaboose?"

"No. But, understand, you're under arrest. You can't leave town."

"Say, now, Buck, ain't you kind of crowdin' me into the fence?"

"I'd arrest my own brother for a trick like that."

Lorry gazed at the ground for a minute. He glanced up. Alice Weston sat watching them. She could not hear what they were saying, but their attitudes confirmed her apprehension.

"I'd like to speak to ma a minute," said Lorry.

"Go ahead. There's no hurry."

Waring, who had been watching his son closely, strolled to the veranda steps and sat down.

Hardy lighted a cigar. "I hate to do this, Waring," he told the other.

"That's all right, Hardy."

The sheriff leaned close. "I figured to bluff him into telling which way the hobo went. Mebby he'll talk later."

Waring smiled. "You have a free hand so far as I am concerned," he said.

Alice Weston was talking with her mother when she heard a cautious step on the stairway behind her. She turned her head slightly. Lorry, booted and spurred, stood just within the doorway. He had something in his hand; a peculiarly shaped bundle wrapped loosely in a newspaper. Hardy was talking to Waring. The undersheriff was standing close to Waring's horse. Alice Weston had seen the glint in Lorry's eyes. She held her breath.

Without a word of warning, and before the group on the veranda knew what was happening, Lorry shot from the doorway, leaped from the edge of the veranda rail, and alighted square in the saddle of Waring's horse, Dex. The buckskin whirled and dashed down the road, one rein dragging. Lorry reached down, and with a sinuous sweep of his body recovered the loose rein. As he swung round the first corner he waved something that looked strangely like a club in a kind of farewell salute.

Alice Weston had risen. The undersheriff grabbed the reins of the horse nearest him and mounted. Hardy ran to the other horse. Side by side they raced down the street and disappeared round a corner.

"What is it?" queried Alice Weston.

Waring still sat on the steps. He was laughing when he turned to answer the girl's question.

"Lorry and the sheriff had a little argument. Lorry didn't wait to finish it. It was something about that hobo that bothered you yesterday."

Alice crushed her handkerchief to her mouth. "I—shall we get ready for dinner?" she stammered.

Mrs. Weston rose. "It's nothing serious, I hope. Do you think your—Mr Adams will be back to-night?"

"Not this evening," replied Waring.

"You mean that he won't be back at all?"

"Not unless he changes his mind. He's riding my horse."

"He took your horse?"

"Yes. I think he made a mistake in leaving so suddenly, but he didn't make any mistake about the best horse."

"Aren't you worried about him?" queried Mrs. Weston.

"Why, no. The boy will take care of himself. Did you happen to notice what he had in his hand when he ran across the veranda?"

"No. It happened so suddenly. Was it a pistol?"

Waring grinned. "No. It was a shoulder of lamb. The next town is thirty miles south, and no restaurants on the way."

"But his mother—" began Alice Weston.

"Yes," said Waring. "I think that leg of lamb was for dinner to-night."

Alice Weston said nothing further, but as she got ready for dinner she confessed to herself that the event of Lorry's escape would have been much more thrilling, in retrospect at least, had he chosen to wave his hasty farewell with a silken bandanna, or even a pistol. To ride off like that, waving a leg of lamb!

Chapter XII
Bud Shoop and Bondsman

As a young man, Bud Shoop had punched cattle on the southern ranges, cooked for a surveying outfit, prospected in the Mogollons, and essayed homesteading on the Blue Mesa, served as cattle inspector, and held for many years the position of foreman on the great Gila Ranch, where, with diligence and honor, he had built up a reputation envied by many a lively cow-puncher and seldom tampered with even by Bud's most vindictive enemies. And he had enemies and many friends.

Meanwhile he had taken on weight until, as one of his friends remarked, "Most any hoss but a Percheron draft would shy the minute Bud tried to put his foot in the stirrup."

And when Bud came to that point in his career when he summed up his past and found that his chief asset was experience, garnished with a somewhat worn outfit of pack-saddles, tarps, bridles, chaps, and guns, he sighed heavily.

The old trails were changing to roads. The local freight intermittently disgorged tons of harvesting machinery. The sound of the Klaxton was heard in the land. Despite the times and the manners, Bud's girth increased insidiously. His hard-riding days were past. Progress marched steadily onward, leaving an after-guard of homesteaders intrenched behind miles of barbed-wire fence and mazes of irrigating-ditches. The once open range was now a chessboard of agricultural endeavor, with the pawns steadying ploughshares as they crept from square to square until the opposing cattle king suffered ignominious checkmate, his prerogative of free movement gone, his army scattered, his castles taken, and his glory surviving only in the annals of the game.

Incidentally, Bud Shoop had saved a little money, and his large popularity would have won for him a political sinecure; but he disliked politics quite as heartily as he detested indolence. He needed work not half so much as he wanted it.

He had failed as a rancher, but he still held his homestead on the Blue Mesa, some twenty miles from the town of Jason, an old Mormon settlement in the heart of the mesa country.

Friday morning at sunup Bud saddled his horse, closed the door of his cabin on the Blue Mesa, and, whistling to his old Airedale, Bondsman, rode across the mesa and down the mountain trail toward Jason. By sundown that night he was in town, his horse fed, and he and Bondsman sitting on the little hotel veranda, watching the villagers as they passed in the dusk of early evening.

Coatless and perspiring, Bud betook himself next morning to the office of the supervisor of that district of the Forest Service. Bondsman accompanied him, stalking seriously at his master's heels. The supervisor was busy. Bud filled a chair in the outer office, polished his bald spot with a blue bandanna, and waited.

Presently the supervisor called him in. Bud rose heavily and plodded to another chair in the private office. Torrance, the supervisor, knew Bud; knew that he was a solid man in the finer sense of the word from the shiny dome of his head to his dusty boot. And Torrance thought he knew why Bud had called. The Airedale sat in the outer office, watching his master. Occasionally the big dog rapped the floor with his stubby tail.

"He's just tellin' me to go ahead and say my piece, John, and that he'll wait till I get through. That there dog bosses me around somethin' scandalous."

"He's getting old and set in his ways," laughed Torrance.

"So be I, John. Kind of settin' in my own way mostly."

"Well, Bud, how are things up on the mesa?"

"Growin' and bloomin' and singin' and feedin' and keepin' still, same as always."

"What can I do for you?"

"Well, I ain't seen a doctor for so long I can't tell you; but I reckon I need more exercise and a little salary thrown in for luck."

"I'm glad you came in. You needn't say anything about it, but I'm scheduled to leave here next month."

"Then I reckon I'm left. Higher up, John?"

"Yes. I have this end of it pretty well whipped into shape. They seem to think they can use me at headquarters."

Bud frowned prodigiously. The situation did not seem to promise much. And naturally enough, being a Westerner, Bud disliked to come out flatfooted and ask for work.

His frown deepened as the supervisor asked another question: "Do you think you could hold down my job, Bud?"

"Say, John, I've stood for a lot in my time. But, honest, I was lookin' for a job as ranger. I can ride yet. And if I do say it I know every hill and cañon, every hogback and draw and flat from here to the Tonto Basin."

"I know it. I was coming to that. The grazing-leases are the most important items just now. You know cattle, and you know something about the Service. You have handled men. I am not joking."

"Well, this is like a hobo gettin' up his nerve to ask for a san'wich, and havin' the lady of the house come runnin' with a hot apple pie. I'll tackle anything."

"Well, the Department has confidence enough in me to suggest that I name a successor, subject to their approval. Do you think that you could hold down this job?"

"If settin' on it would hold it down, it would never get up alive, John. But I ain't no author."

"Author?"

"Uh-uh. When it comes to facts, I aim to brand 'em. But them reports to headquarters—"

The supervisor laughed. "You would be entitled to a clerk. The man I have would like to stay. And another thing. I have just had an application from young Adams, of Stacey. He wrote from St. Johns. He wants to get into the Service. While we are at it, what do you know about him?"

"Nothin'. But his mother runs a right comf'table eatin'-house over to Stacey. She's a right fine woman. I knew her when she was wearin' her hair in a braid."

"I have stopped there. It's a neat place. Would you take the boy on if you were in my place?"

Bud coughed and studied the ends of his blunt fingers. "Well, now, John, if I was in your place, I could tell you."

Torrance was amused and rather pleased. Bud's careful evasion was characteristic. He would do nothing hastily. Moreover, with Shoop as supervisor, it was safe to assume that the natives would hesitate to attempt their usual subterfuges in regard to grazing-leases. Bud was too well known for that. Torrance had had trouble with the cattlemen and sheepmen. He knew that Shoop's mere name would obviate much argument and bickering.

"The White Mountain Apaches are eating a lot of beef these days," he said suddenly.

Shoop grinned. "And it ain't all Gov'ment beef, neither. The line fence crost Still Cañon is down. They's been a fire up on the shoulder of Ole Baldy—nothin' much, though. Your telephone line to the lookout is saggin' bad over by Sheep Crossin'. Some steer'll come along and take it with him in a hurry one of these days. A grizzly killed a yearlin' over by the Milk Ranch about a week ago. I seen your ranger, young Winslow, day before yesterday. He says somebody has been grazin' sheep on the posted country, west. He was after 'em. The grass is pretty good on the Blue. The Apaches been killin' wild turkey on the wrong side of their line. I seen their tracks— and some feathers. They's some down timber along the north side of the creek over on the meadows. And a couple of wimmin was held up over by the Notch the other day. I ain't heard the partic'lars. Young Adams—"

"Where do you get it all, Bud? Only two of the things you mentioned have been reported in to this office."

"Who, me? Huh! Well, now, John, that's just the run of news that floats in when you're movin' around the country. If I was to set out to get info'mation—"

"You'd swamp the office. All right. I'll have my clerk draft a letter of application. You can sign it. I'll add my word. It will take some time to put this through, if it goes through. I don't promise anything. Come in at noon and sign the letter. Then you might drop in in about two weeks; say Saturday morning. We'll have heard something by then."

Bud beamed. "I'll do that. And while I'm waitin' I'll ride over some of that country up there and look around."

Torrance leaned forward. "There's one more thing, Bud. I know this job offers a temptation to a man to favor his friends. So far as this office is concerned, I don't want you to have any friends. I want things run straight. I've given the best of my life to the Service. I love it. I have dipped into my own pocket when Washington couldn't see the need for improvements. I have bought fire-fighting tools, built trails, and paid extra salaries at times. Now I will be where I can back you up. Keep things right up to the minute. If you get stuck, wire me. Here's your territory on this map. You know the country, but you will find this system of keeping track of the men a big help. The pins show where each man is working. We can go over the office detail after we have heard from headquarters."

Bud perspired, blinked, shuffled his feet. "I ain't goin' to say thanks, John. You know it."

"That's all right, Bud. Your thanks will be just what you make of this work when I leave. There has been a big shake-up in the Service. Some of us stayed on top."

"Congratulations, John. Saturday, come two weeks, then."

And Bud heaved himself up. The Airedale, Bondsman, thumped the floor with his tail. Bud turned a whimsical face to the supervisor. "Now listen to that! What does he say? Well, he's tellin' me he sabes I got a chanct at a job and that he'll keep his mouth shut about what you said, like me. And that it's about time I quit botherin' folks what's busy and went back to the hotel so he can watch things go by. That there dog bosses me around somethin' scandalous."

Torrance smiled, and waved his hand as Bud waddled from the office, with Bondsman at his heels.

About an hour later, as Torrance was dictating a letter, he glanced up. Bud Shoop, astride a big bay horse, passed down the street. For a moment Torrance forgot office detail in a general appreciation of the Western rider, who, once in the saddle, despite age or physical attributes, bears himself with a subconscious ease that is a delight to behold, be he lean Indian, lithe Mexican, or bed-rock American with a girth, say, of fifty-two inches and weighing perhaps not less than two hundred and twenty pounds.

"He'll make good," soliloquized the supervisor. "He likes horses and dogs, and he knows men. He's all human—and there's a lot of him. And they say that Bud Shoop used to be the last word in riding 'em straight up, and white lightning with a gun."

The supervisor shook his head. "Take a letter to Collins," he said.

The stenographer glanced up. "Senator Collins, Mr. Torrance?"

"Yes. And make an extra copy. Mark it confidential. You need not file the copy. I'll take care of it. And if Mr. Shoop is appointed to my place, he need know nothing about this letter."

"Yes, sir."

"Because, Evers," Said Torrance, relaxing from his official manner a bit, "it is going to be rather difficult to get Mr. Shoop appointed here. I want him. I can depend on him. We have had too many theorists in this field. And remember this; stay with Shoop through thick and thin and some day you may land a job as private secretary to a State Senator."

"All right, sir. I didn't know that you were going into politics, Mr Torrance."

"You're off the trail a little, Evers. I'll never run for Senator. I'm with the Service as long as it will have me. But if some clever politician happens to get hold of Shoop, there isn't a man in this mesa country that could win against him. He's just the type that the mesa people like. He is all human.— Dear Senator Collins—"

The stenographer bent over his book.

Later, as Torrance closed his desk, he thought of an incident in Shoop's life with which he had long been familiar. The Airedale, Bondsman, had once been shot wantonly by a stray Apache. Shoop had found the dog as it crawled along the corral fence, trying to get to the cabin. Bud had ridden fifty miles through a winter snowstorm with Bondsman across the saddle. An old Mormon veterinary in St. Johns had saved the dog's life. Shoop had come close to freezing to death during that tedious ride.

Bud Shoop's assets in the game of life amounted to a few acres of mesa land, a worn outfit of saddlery, and a small bank account. But his greatest asset, of which he was blissfully unconscious, was a big, homely love for things human and for animals; a love that set him apart from his fellows who looked upon men and horses and dogs as merely useful or otherwise.

Chapter XIII
The Horse Trade

The following day a young cowboy, mounted upon a singularly noticeable buckskin horse, rode down the main street of Jason and dismounted at the Forestry Office. Torrance was reading a letter when his clerk proffered the young man a chair and notified the supervisor that a Mr. Adams wished to see him.

A few minutes later, Lorry was shown in. The door closed.

Torrance surveyed the strong, young figure with inward approval. "I have your letter. Sit down. I see your letter is postmarked St. Johns."

"Yes, sir."

"Know anything about the Service?"

"No, sir."

"Why do you want to get into it?"

"I thought mebby I'd like the work."

"Have you any recommendations?"

"Nothin'—except what you're lookin' at."

Torrance smiled. "Could you get a letter from your last employer?"

"Not the kind of letter that would do any good. I had an argument with the foreman, and he fired me."

Torrance had heard something about the matter, and did not question further at the time.

"Do you drink?" queried Torrance.

"I never monkeyed with it much. I reckon I could if I wanted to."

Torrance drummed on the desk with his long, strong fingers. He reached in a drawer and drew out a letter.

"How about that?"

Lorry glanced at the heading. Evidently the sheriff knew of his general whereabouts. The letter stated that the sheriff would appreciate information leading to the apprehension of Lawrence Adams, wanted for aiding a prisoner to escape and for having in his possession a horse that did not belong to him.

"What he says is right," Lorry asserted cheerfully. "I busted into the jail and turned that hobo loose, and I borrowed the horse I'm riding. I aim to send him back. My own horse is in the corral back at Stacey."

"What was your idea in letting the man go after arresting him?"

Lorry's clear color deepened. "I wasn't figurin' on explainin' that."

"You don't have to explain. But you will admit that the charges in this letter are rather serious. We don't want men in the Service who are open to criticism. You're pretty young to have such a record. It's up to you to explain—or not, just as you like. But anything you tell me will be treated as absolutely confidential, Adams."

"All right. Well, everything I done that day went wrong. I caught the hobo tryin' to rob a couple of wimmin over by the Notch. I was takin' him to Stacey when Bob Brewster butted in. The hobo was sick, and I didn't aim to stand and see him kicked and beat up with a quirt, even if he did steal one of the Starr horses. I told High Chin to quit, but his hearin' wasn't good, so I had to show him. Then I got to thinkin' I wasn't so much—takin' a pore, busted tramp to jail. And it made me sick when everybody round town was callin' me some little hero. Then one of the Starr boys told me High Chin was cinchin' up to ride in and get the hobo, anyhow, so I busted the lock and told him to fan it."

"Why didn't you appeal to the sheriff?"

"Huh! Buck Hardy is all right. But I can tell you one thing; he's not the man to stand up to High Chin when High is drinkin'. Why, I see High shove a gun in Hardy's face once and tell him to go home and go to bed. And Hardy went. Anyhow, that hobo was my prisoner, and I didn't aim to let High Chin get his hands on him."

"I see. Well, you have a strange way of doing things, but I appreciate why you acted as you did. Of course, you know it is a grave offense to aid a prisoner to escape."

"Buck Hardy seems to think so."

"So do I. And how about that horse?"

"Well, next day I was fixin' up the machine and foolin' around—that machine belonged to them tourists that the fella stuck up—when along about sundown Buck Hardy comes swellin' up to me and tells me I'm under arrest. He couldn't prove a darned thing if I hadn't said I done the job. But, anyhow, he didn't see it my way, so I borrowed Waring's horse and come down this way. Everybody saw me take the horse. You can't call that stealin'."

"Did Hardy ride after you?"

"Yes, sir. But he was so far behind I couldn't hear what he wanted. That big buckskin is a wonder. I wish I owned him."

Torrance mentally patched the fragments of evidence together. He decided that a young man who could capture a holdup man, best the notorious High Chin in a fight, repair a broken automobile, turn a prisoner loose, and make his own escape all within the short compass of forty-eight hours was a rather capable person in a way. And Torrance knew by Lorry's appearance and manner that he was still on the verdant side of twenty. If such a youth chose to turn his abilities in the right direction he might accomplish much. Lorry's extreme frankness satisfied Torrance that the boy had told the truth. He would give him a chance.

"Do you know Bud Shoop?" queried the supervisor.

"No, sir. I know what he looks like. He's been to our hotel."

"Well, you might look him up. He may be out of town. Possibly he is up at his homestead on the Blue Mesa. Tell Mr. Shoop that I sent you to him. He will understand. But you will have to square yourself with the authorities before I can put you to work."

"Yes, sir. But I don't aim to ride back to Stacey just because I know where it is. If they want me, they can find me."

"That is your affair. When your slate is clear—"

"Mr. Waring to see you," said the clerk, poking his head through the doorway.

Torrance stepped out and greeted Waring heartily. Lorry was surprised; both to see his father and to learn that Torrance and he were old friends.

"I saw this horse as I rode up, and I took a fancy to him," said Waring, after having nodded to Lorry. "Sorry to bother you, Torrance."

"Here's the man you'll bother, I think," said Torrance, indicating Lorry. "He's riding that horse."

Lorry grinned. "Want to trade horses?"

"I don't know. Is that your horse?"

"Nope. I borrowed him. Is that your horse?" And he indicated Gray Leg.

"No. I borrowed him."

Torrance laughed. "The buckskin seems to be a pretty fair horse."

"Then I ought to get somethin' to boot," suggested Lorry.

"How much?" laughed Waring.

"Oh, I don't know. You'll find that buckskin a mighty likely rambler."

Waring turned to Torrance. "You'll witness that we made this trade, John?"

"All right. But remember; neither of you owns the horse you are trading."

"But we're goin' to," asserted Lorry.

Waring reached beneath his coat and unbuckled a heavy belt. From buckle to tongue it glittered with cartridges and a service-worn holster bulged with a short-barreled Colt's .45. He handed the belt to Lorry.

"It's a good gun," he said, "and I hope you'll never need to use it."

Lorry stammered his thanks, untied Dex, and gave the reins into Waring's hand. "The trade goes," he said. "But we change saddles."

"Correct," said Waring. "And here's a letter—from your mother."

Lorry slid the letter in his shirt. "How's the Weston folks?"

"They were to leave this morning. Mrs. Weston asked me to pay you for repairing their machine. She gave me the money."

"You can keep it. I wasn't workin' for pay."

"All right. Going to stay down here awhile?"

"I aim to. Did you see anything of Buck Hardy on the way down?"

"Hardy? Why, no. But I rode part way with his deputy. He's due here some time to-day."

"That bein' the case," said Lorry, swinging to the saddle, "I reckon I'll hunt up Bud Shoop. Thanks for my horse. Mebby I'll be back in this town in two, three days." And he was gone.

Waring dropped Dex's reins. "Got a minute to spare, Torrance?"

"Yes, indeed. You're looking well, Jim."

In the office they shook hands again.

"It's a long time," said Torrance, proffering a cigar. "You were punching cattle for the Box S and I was a forest ranger those days. Did Mexico get too hot?"

"Warm. What's the boy doing down here?"

"He seems to be keeping out of the way of the sheriff," laughed Torrance. "Incidentally he applied for a position as ranger."

"Did he? I'm glad of that. I was afraid he might get to riding the high trails. He's got it in him."

"You seem to know him pretty well."

"Not so well as I would like to. I'm his father."

"Why, I had no idea—but, come to think of it, he does resemble you. I didn't know that you were married."

"Yes. I married Annie Adams, of Las Cruces. He's our boy."

Torrance saw that Waring did not care to talk further on the subject of his married life. And Torrance recalled the fact that Mrs. Adams, who lived in Stacey, had been in Mexico.

"He's a live one," said Torrance. "I think I'll take him on."

"I don't ask you to, John. He's got to play the game for himself. He may not always do right, but he'll always do what he thinks is right, if I am any judge. And he won't waste time doing it. I told Hardy's deputy on the way down that he might as well give up running after the boy. Hardy is pretty sore. Did Lorry tell you?"

"Yes. And I can understand his side of it."

"I think that little Weston girl dazzled him," said Waring. "She's clever, and Lorry hasn't seen many of her kind. I think he would have stayed right in Stacey and faced the music if she hadn't been there when Hardy tried to arrest him. Lorry is only eighteen. He had to show off a little."

"Will Hardy follow it up?"

"Not too strong. The folks in Stacey are giving Hardy the laugh. He's not so popular as he might be."

"I can't say that I blame Hardy, either. The boy was wrong."

"Not a bit. Lorry was wrong."

"It will blow over," said Torrance. "I had no idea he was your son."

Waring leaned back in his chair. "John, I had two reasons for coming down here. One was to get my horse. That's settled. Now I want to talk about leasing a few thousand acres down this way, with water-rights. I'm through with the other game. I want to run a few cattle in here, under fence. I think it will pay."

Torrance shook his head. "The Mormons and the Apaches will keep you poor, Jim."

"They might, if I tried it alone. But I have a partner just up from the border. You remember Pat. He's been customs inspector at Nogales for some time."

"I should say I do remember him!"

"Well, he asked me to look around and write to him. I think we could do well enough here. What do you know about the land north of here, on up toward the Santa Fé?"

Torrance pondered the situation. The times were, indeed, changing when men like Waring and Pat ceased to ride the high trails and settled down to ranching under fence. The day of the gunman was past, but two such men as Pat and Waring would suppress by their mere presence in the country the petty rustling and law-breaking that had made Torrance's position difficult at times.

"I'll see what I can do," said he. "About how much land?"

"Ten or twenty thousand, to begin with."

"There's some Government land not on the reservation between here and the railroad. There are three or four families of squatters on it now. I don't know how they manage to live, but they always seem to have beef and bacon. You might have some trouble about getting them off—and about the water. I'll let you know some time next month just what I can do."

"We won't have any trouble," said Waring. "That's the last thing we want. I'll ride over next month. You can write to me at Stacey if anything turns up."

"I'll write to you. Do you ever get hungry? Come on over to the hotel I'm as hungry as a bear."

Chapter XIV
Bondsman's Decision

Bud Shoop's homestead on the Blue Mesa lay in a wide level of grassland, round which the spruce of the high country swept in a great, blue-edged circle. To the west the barren peak of Mount Baldy maintained a solitary vigil in sunshine and tempest. Away to the north the timbered plateaus dropped from level to level like a gigantic stair until they merged with the horizon-line of the plains. The air on the Blue Mesa was thin and keen; warm in the sun, yet instantly cool at dusk. A mountain stream, all but hidden by the grasses, meandered across the mesa to an emerald hollow of coarse marsh-grass. A few yards from this pool, and on its southern side, stood the mountain cabin of the Shoop homestead, a roomy building of logs, its wide, easy-sloping veranda roof covered with home-made shakes. Near the house was a small corral and stable of logs. Out on the mesa a thin crop of oats wavered in the itinerant breeze. Round the cabin was a garden plot that had suffered from want of attention. Above the gate to the door-yard was a weathered sign on which was lettered carefully:

"The rose is red; the violet blue;
Please shut this gate when you come through."

And on the other side of the sign, challenging the possible carelessness of the chance visitor, was the legend:—

"Now you've been in and had your chuck,
Please close this gate, just once, for luck."

Otherwise the place was like any mountain homestead of the better sort, viewed from without. The interior of the cabin, however, was unusual in that it boasted of being the only music-room within fifty miles in any direction.

When the genial Bud had been overtaken with the idea of homesteading, he had had visions of a modest success which would allow him to entertain his erstwhile cow-puncher companions when they should ride his way. To this end he had labored with more heart than judgment.

The main room was large and lighted by two unusually large windows. The dimensions of the room were ample enough to accommodate a fair number of dancers. Bud knew that if cowboys loved anything they loved to dance. The phonograph was so common that it offered no distinction in gracing Bud's camp; so with much labor and expense he had freighted an upright piano from the distant railroad, an innovation that at first had stunned and then literally taken the natives off their feet. Riders from all over the country heard of Bud's piano, questioned its reality, and finally made it a point to jog over and see for themselves.

For a time Bud's homestead was popular. A real piano, fifty miles from a settlement, was something worth riding far to see. But respect for the shining veneer of the case was not long-lived. In a moment of inspiration, a cowboy pulled out his jackknife and carved his home brand on the shining case. Bud could have said more than he did when he discovered it. Later another contingent, not to be outdone, followed this cowboy's incisive example and carved its brand on the piano. Naturally it became a custom. No visitor in boots and chaps left the cabin without first having carved some brand.

Bud suffered in silence, consoling himself with the thought that while there were many pianos in the lower country, there were none like his. And "As long as you don't monkey with her works or shoot her up," he told his friends, "I don't care how much you carve her; only leave enough sidin' and roof to hold her together."

Cowboys came, danced long and late as Bud pumped the mechanical player, and thrilled to the shuffle of high-heeled boots. Contingent after contingent came, danced, and departed joyously, leaving Bud short on rations, but happy that he could entertain so royally. Finally the novelty wore off, and Bud was left with his Airedale, his saddle-ponies, and the hand-carved piano.

But Bud had profited by the innovation. An Easterner sojourning with Bud for a season, had taught him to play two tunes—"Annie Laurie" and "Dixie." "Real hand-made music," Bud was wont to remark. And with these tunes at his disposal he was more than content. Many a long evening he sat with his huge bulk swaying in the light of the hanging lamp as he wandered around Maxwelton's braes in search of the true Annie Laurie; or hopped with heavy sprightliness across the sandy bottoms of Dixie, while Bondsman, the patient Airedale, sat on his haunches and accompanied Bud with dismal energy.

Bud was not a little proud of his accomplishment. The player was all right, but it lacked the human touch. Even when an occasional Apache strayed in and borrowed tobacco or hinted at a meal, Bud was not above entertaining the wondering red man with music. And Bud disliked Apaches.

And during these latter days Bud had had plenty of opportunity to indulge himself in music. For hours he would sit and gently strike the keys, finding unexpected harmonies that thrilled and puzzled him. The discords didn't count. And Bondsman would hunch up close with watchful eye and one ear cocked, waiting for the familiar strains of "Annie Laurie" or "Dixie." He seemed to consider these tunes a sort of accompaniment to his song. If he dared to howl when Bud was extemporizing, Bud would rebuke him solemnly, explaining that it was not considered polite in the best circles to interrupt a soloist. And an evening was never complete without "Annie Laurie," and "Dixie," with Bondsman's mournful contralto gaming ascendance as the evening progressed.

"That dog bosses me around somethin' scandalous," Bud was wont to remark, as he rose from his labors and prepared for bed. "There I was huntin' around for that chord I lit on the other night and almost findin' it, when he has to howl like a coyote with a sore throat and spile the whole thing. I ought to learned more tunes."

It was almost dusk when Lorry topped the trail that led across the Blue Mesa to Bud's cabin. Gray Leg pricked his ears, and jogged over the wide level, heading straight for the corral. The cabin was dark. Lorry hallooed. A horse in the corral answered, nickering shrilly. Lorry found some loose gramma grass in the stable and threw it to the horse. If this was Shoop's place, Shoop would not be gone long, or he'd have turned the horse to graze on the open mesa.

Lorry entered and lighted the lamp. He gazed with astonishment at the piano. But that could wait. He was hungry. In a few minutes he had a fire going, plates laid for two, had made coffee and cut bacon. He was mixing the dough for hot biscuit when he heard some one ride up. He stepped to the door. A bulky figure was pulling a saddle from a horse. Lorry called a greeting.

"Just a minute, friend," came from the darkness.

Lorry stepped to the kitchen, and put the biscuit pan in the oven. A saddle thumped on the veranda, and Bud Shoop, puffing heavily, strode in. He nodded, filled a basin, and washed. As he polished his bald spot, his glance traveled from the stove to the table, and thence to Lorry, and he nodded approval.

"Looks like you was expectin' comp'ny," he said, smiling.

"Yep. And chuck's about ready."

"So am I," said Bud, rubbing his hands.

"I'm Adams, from Stacey."

"That don't make me mad," said Bud. "How's things over to your town?"

"All right, I guess. Mr. Torrance—"

Bud waved his hand. "Let's eat. Been out since daylight. Them biscuits is just right. Help yourself to the honey."

"There's somebody outside," said Lorry, his arm raised to pass the honey jar.

"That's my dog, Bondsman. He had to size up your layout, and he's through and waitin' to size up you. Reckon he's hungry, too. But business before pleasure is his idea mostly. He's tellin' me to let him in. That there dog bosses me around somethin' scandalous. When did you get in?"

"About sundown."

"Uh-uh. I seen that your horse hadn't grazed out far yet. How do you like this country?"

"Good summer country, all right. Too high for stock in winter."

"Yes. Four feet of snow on the mesa last winter. When you say 'Arizona' to some folks, they don't think of snow so deep a hoss can't get from the woods over there to this cabin." Bud Shoop sighed and rose. "Never mind them dishes. Mornin' 'll do."

"Won't take a minute," said Lorry.

Bud's blue eyes twinkled as he waddled to the living-room. Young Adams was handy around a kitchen. He had laid plates for two, knew how to punch dough, was willing to wash the dishes without a hint, and had fed the horse in the corral.

"He trots right along, like he knew where he was goin'," Bud said to himself. "I like his looks—but that ain't always a sign."

Lorry whistled as he dried the dishes. Bud was seated in a huge armchair when Lorry entered the room. Shoop seemed to pay no attention to Bondsman, who whined and occasionally scratched on the door.

"Funny thing happened this mornin'," said Shoop, settling himself in his chair. "I was ridin' down the ole Milk Ranch Trail when I looked up and seen a bobcat lopin' straight for me. The cat didn't see me, but my hoss stopped, waitin' for me to shoot. Well, that kittycat come right along till I could 'a' almost roped him. Bondsman—that's my dog—never seen him, neither, till I hollered. You ought to seen that cat start back without losin' a jump. I like to fell off the hoss, laughin'. Bondsman he lit out—"

"I'll let him in," said Lorry, moving toward the door.

"—After that cat," continued Shoop, "but the cat never treed, I reckon, for pretty soon back comes Bondsman, lookin' as disgusted as a hen in a rainstorm. 'We're gettin' too old,' I tells Bondsman—"

"Ain't you goin' to let him in?" queried Lorry.

"—We're gettin' too old to chase bobcats just for fun," concluded Shoop. "What was you sayin'?"

"Your dog wants to come in."

"That's right. Now I thought you was listenin' to me."

"I was. But ain't he hungry?"

Shoop chuckled. "Let him in, son."

Lorry opened the door. Bondsman stalked in, sniffed at Lorry's boots, and padded to the kitchen.

"What do you feed him?" said Lorry, hesitating.

"He won't take nothin' from you," said Shoop, heaving himself up. "I've had him since he was a pup. You set down and I'll 'tend to him.

"And I says to him," said Shoop, as he returned to his chair,—"I says, 'Bondsman, that there cat was just passin' the buck to us to see if we was game.' And he ain't got over it yet."

"I've roped 'em," said Lorry—"roped 'em out of a tree."

"Uh-uh. Where'd you learn to rope?"

"At the Starr Ranch. I worked there once."

"Git tired of it?"

"Nope. I had a argument with the foreman."

"Uh-uh. I reckon it ain't hard to pick a fuss with High Chin."

"I wasn't lookin' for a fuss. It was his funeral."

"So I heard; all but the procession."

"And that's why I came up to see you. Mr. Torrance told me to hunt you up."

"He did, eh? Well, now, John sure gets queer idees. I don't need a man round here."

"I was after a job in the Service."

"And he sends you to me. Why, I ain't ever worked a day for the Service."

"I guess he wanted you to look me over," said Lorry, smiling.

"Well, they's lots of time, 'less you're in a hurry."

"If I can't get in the Service, I'll look up a job punchin'," said Lorry. "I got to get somethin'."

Bondsman stalked in, licking his chops. He nuzzled Shoop's hand. Lorry snapped his fingers. Bondsman strode to him. Lorry patted his knee. The big dog crouched and sprang to Lorry's knees, where he sat, studying him quizzically, his head to one side, his keen eyes blinking in the lamplight. Lorry laughed and patted the dog.

"He's trying to get my number," said Lorry.

"He's got it," said Shoop. "You could 'a' snapped your fingers off afore he'd 'a' come nigh you, 'less he wanted to. And while we're talkin' about it, you can tell John Torrance I said to give you a try."

Lorry sat up quickly. "Guess you didn't know that Buck Hardy is lookin' for me," said Lorry. "Mr. Torrance says I got to square myself with Buck afore I get the job."

"He did, eh? Well, speakin' of Buck, how would you like to hear a little talk from a real music-box?"

"Fine!"

Shoop waddled to the piano. "I ain't no reg'lar music sharp," he explained unnecessarily, "but I got a couple of pieces broke to go polite. This here piano is cold-mouthed, and you got to rein her just right or she'll buffalo you. This here piece is 'Annie Laurie.'"

As Bud struck the first note, Bondsman leaped from Lorry's knees and took his place beside the piano. The early dew had just begun to fall when Bondsman joined in. Lorry grinned. The dog and his master were absolutely serious in their efforts. As the tune progressed, Lorry's grin faded, and he sat gazing intently at the huge back of his host.

"Why, he's playin' like he meant it," thought Lorry. "And folks says Bud Shoop was a regular top-hand stem-winder in his day."

Shoop labored at the piano with nervous care. When he turned to Lorry his face was beaded with sweat.

"I rode her clean through to the fence," he said, with a kind of apologetic grin. "How did you like that piece?"

"I always did like them old tunes," replied Lorry. "Give us another."

Shoop's face beamed. "I only got one more that I can get my rope on. But if you can stand it, I can. This here one is 'Dixie.'"

And Bud straightened his broad shoulders, pushed back his sleeves, and waded across the sandy bottoms of Dixie, hitting the high spots with staccato vehemence, as though Dixie had recently suffered from an inundation and he was in a hurry to get to dry land. Bondsman's moody baritone reached up and up with sad persistency.

Lorry was both amused and astonished. Shoop's intensity, his real love for music, was a revelation. Lorry felt like smiling, yet he did not smile. Bud Shoop could not play, but his personality forced its own recognition, even through the absurd medium of an untutored performance on that weird upright piano. Lorry began to realize that there was something more to Bud Shoop than mere bulk.

Bud swung round, puffing. "I got that tune where I can keep her in sight as long as she lopes on the level. But when she takes to jumpin' stumps and makin' them quick turns, I sure have to do some hard ridin' to keep her from losin' herself. Me and Bondsman's been worryin' along behind them two tunes for quite a spell. I reckon I ought to started in younger. But, anyhow, that there piano is right good comp'ny. When I been settin' here alone, nights, and feelin' out her paces, I get so het up and interested that I don't know the fire's out till Bondsman takes to shiverin' and whinin' and tellin' me he'd like to get some sleep afore mornin'."

And Bondsman, now that the music had stopped, stalked to Lorry and eyed him with an expression which said plainly: "It's his weak spot— this music. You will have to overlook it. He's really a rather decent sort of person."

"I got a mechanical player in the bedroom," said Shoop. "And a reg'lar outfit of tunes for dances."

Lorry was tempted to ask to hear it, but changed his mind. "I've heard them players. They're sure good for a dance, but I like real playin' better."

Bud Shoop grinned. "That's the way with Bondsman here. Now he won't open his head to one of them paper tunes. I've tried 'em all on him. You can't tell me a dog ain't got feelin's."

Chapter XV
John and Demijohn

The grass on the high mesa was heavy with dew when Lorry stepped from the cabin next morning. His pony, Gray Leg, stood close to the corral, where Shoop's horses were playfully biting at him over the bars. Lorry unhobbled Gray Leg and turned Shoop's horses out to water. The three ponies trotted to the water-hole, sniffed at the water, and, whirling, raced across the mesa, pitching and kicking in the joy of liberation.

After breakfast Bud and Lorry sat out in the sun, enjoying the slow warmth. The morning air was still keen in the shade. Bondsman lay between them, watching the distant horses.

"He won't let 'em get far into the timber," said Shoop. "He sure saves me a lot of steps, roundin' up them hosses."

"I can whistle Gray Leg to me," said Lorry. "Then the other horses'll come."

Shoop nodded. "What you goin' to do to-day?"

"Me? Well, it's so kind of quiet and big up here I feel like settin' around and takin' it all in. I ain't been in the high country much. 'Course I don't aim to camp on you."

"You're sure welcome," said Shoop heartily. "It gets lonesome up here But if you ain't got no reg'lar plan I was thinkin' of ridin' over to Sheep Crossin'—and mebby on down to Jason."

"Suits me fine!"

Shoop heaved himself up. Lorry whistled shrilly. Gray Leg, across the mesa, raised his head. Lorry whistled again. The pony lowered his head and nipped at the bunch-grass as he moved slowly toward the house. Shoop's horses watched him, and finally decided that they would follow. Gray Leg stopped just out of reach.

"Get in the corral, there!" said Lorry, waving his arm.

The pony shied and trotted into the corral, the other horses following.

Bondsman was not exactly disgruntled, but he might have been happier Shoop had told him to "keep house" until they returned.

"It's a funny thing," said Shoop as he mounted. "Now, if I was to tell that dog he was gettin' too old to ramble with me, he'd feel plumb sick and no account. But when I tell him he's got to do somethin'—like watchin' the house—he thinks it's a reg'lar job. He's gettin' old, but, just like folks, he wants to think he's some use. You can't tell me dogs don't know. Why, I've seen young folks so durned fussy about their grandmas and grandpas, trying to keep 'em from putterin' around, that the old folks just nacherally folded their hands and set down and died, havin' nothin' else to do. And a dog is right proud about bein' able to do somethin'. Bondsman there keeps me so busy thinkin' of how I can keep him busy that I ain't got time to shine my boots. That there dog bosses me around somethin' scandalous."

"That's right," acquiesced Lorry. "I seen a ole mule once that they turned loose from a freight wagon because he was too old to pull his own weight. And that mule just followed the string up and down the hills and across the sand, doin' his best to tell the skinner that he wanted to get back into the harness. He would run alongside the other mules, and try to get back in his old place. They would just naturally kick him, and he'd turn and try to wallop 'em back. Then he'd walk along, with his head hangin' down and his ears floppin', as if he was plumb sick of bein' free and wanted to die. The last day he was too stiff to get on his feet, so me and Jimmy Harp heaved him up while the skinner was gettin' the chains on the other mules. That ole mule was sure wabblin' like a duck, but he come aside his ole place and followed along all day. We was freightin' in to camp, back in the Horseshoe Hills. You know that grade afore you get to the mesa? Well, the ole mule pulled the grade, sweatin' and puffin' like he was pullin' the whole load. And I guess he was, in his mind. Anyhow, he got to the top, and laid down and died. Mules sure like to work. Now a horse would have fanned it."

Shoop nodded. "I never seen a animile too lazy to work if it was only gettin' his grub and exercise. But I've seen a sight of folks too lazy to do that much. Why, some folks is so dog-gone no account they got to git killed afore folks ever knowed they was livin'. Then they's some folks so high-chinned they can't see nothin' but the stars when they'd do tol'able well if they would follow a good hoss or a dog around and learn how to live human. But this ain't gettin' nowhere, and the sun's keepin' right along doin' business."

They rode across the beautiful Blue Mesa, and entered the timberlands, following a ranger trail through the shadowy silences. At the lower level, they came upon another mesa through which wound a mountain stream. And along a stream ran the trail, knee-high in grass on either side.

Far below them lay the plains country, its hazy reaches just visible over the tree-tops. Where the mountain stream merged with a deeper stream the ground was barren and dotted with countless tracks of cattle and sheep. This was Sheep Crossing, a natural pass where the cattlemen and sheepmen drifted their stock from the hills to the winter feeding-grounds of the lower country. It was a checking point for the rangers; the gateway to the hills.

The thin mountain air was hot. The unbridled ponies drank eagerly, and were allowed to graze. The men moved over to the shade of a blue-topped spruce. As Lorry was about to sit down he picked an empty whiskey bottle from the grass, turned the label toward Shoop, and grinned. He tossed the bottle into the edge of the timber.

Shoop rolled a cigarette, and Lorry squatted beside him. Presently Shoop's voice broke the indolent silence of noon: "Just why did you chuck that bottle over there?"

"I don't know. Horse might step on it and cut himself."

"Yes. But you chucked it like you was mad at somethin'. Would you thrun it away if it was full?"

"I don' know. I might 'a' smelt of it to see if it was whiskey or kerosene some herder forgot."

"It's right curious how a fella will smell of a bottle to see what's in it or what's been in it. Most folks does that. I guess you know what whiskey smells like."

"Oh, some; with the boys once or twice. I never did get to like it right well."

Shoop nodded. "I ain't what you'd call a drinkin' man myself, but I started out that way. I been tol'able well lit up at times. But temperance folks what never took a drink can tell you more about whiskey than I can. Now that there empty bottle, a hundred and thirty miles from a whiskey town, kind of set me thinkin'."

Lorry leaned back against the spruce and watched a hawk float in easy circles round the blue emptiness above. He felt physically indolent; at one with the silences. Shoop's voice came to him clearly, but as though from a distance, and as Shoop talked Lorry visualized the theme, forgetting where he was in the vivid picture the old ex-cowboy sketched in the rough dialect of the range.

"I've did some thinkin' in my time, but not enough to keep me awake nights," said Shoop, pushing back his hat. "That there whiskey bottle kind of set me back to where I was about your years and some lively. Long about then I knowed two fellas called 'John' and 'Demijohn.' John was young and a right good cow-hand. Demijohn was old, but he was always dressed up like he was young, and he acted right lively. Some folks thought he was young. They met up at a saloon down along the Santa Fé. They got acquainted, and had a high ole time.

"That evenin', as John was leavin' to go back to the ranch, Demijohn tells him he'll see him later. John remembers that. They met up ag'in. And finally John got to lookin' for Demijohn, and if he didn't show up reg'lar John would set out and chase Demijohn all over the country, afoot and ahorseback, and likin' his comp'ny more every time they met.

"Now, this here Demijohn, who was by rights a city fella, got to takin' to the timber and the mesas, with John followin' him around lively. Ole Demijohn would set in the shade of a tree—no tellin' how he got there—and John would ride up and light down; when mebby Demijohn would start off to town, bein' empty, and John after him like hell wasn't hot enough 'less he sweat runnin'. And that young John would ride clean to town just to say 'How' to that ole hocus. And it come that John got to payin' more attention to Demijohn than he did to punchin' cows. Then come a day when John got sick of chasin' Demijohn all over the range, and he quit.

"But the first thing he knowed, Demijohn was a chasin' him. Every time John rode in and throwed off his saddle there'd be ole Demijohn, settin' in the corner of the corral or under his bunk or out in the box stall, smilin' and waitin'. Finally Demijohn got to followin' John right into the bunk-house, and John tryin' his durndest to keep out of sight.

"One evenin', when John was loafin' in the bunk-house, ole Demijohn crawls up to his bunk and asks him, whisperin', if he ain't most always give John a good time when they met up. John cussed, but 'lowed that Demijohn was right. Then Demijohn took to pullin' at young John's sleeve and askin' him to come to town and have a good time. Pretty soon John gets up and saddles his cayuse and fans it for town. And that time him and Demijohn sure had one whizzer of a time. But come a week later, when John gits back to the ranch, the boss is sore and fires him. Then John gits sore at the boss and at himself and at Demijohn and the whole works. So he saddles up and rides over to town to have it out with Demijohn for losin' a good job. But he couldn't lick Demijohn right there in town nohow. Demijohn was too frequent for him.

"When young John wakes up next mornin' he is layin' under a tree, mighty sick. He sees he is up on the high mesa, but he don' know how he got there; only his pony is grazin' near by, with reins all tromped and the saddle 'way up on his withers. John sets up and rubs his eyes, and there he sees ole Demijohn settin' in the grass chucklin' to hisself, and his back is turned to young John, for he don't care nohow for a fella when he is sick. Ole Demijohn is always feelin' good, no matter how his friends feel. Well, young John thinks a while, and pretty soon he moseys over to a spring and gets a big, cold drink and washes his head, and feels better.

"He never knowed that just plain water tasted so good till that mornin'. Then he sets awhile, smellin' of the clean pine air and listenin' to the wind runnin' loose in the tree-tops and watchin' the clouds driftin' by, white and clean and proud-like. Pretty soon he rares up and walks over to the tree where ole Demijohn sets rockin' up and down and chucklin'. He takes a holt of Demijohn by the shoulder, and he says: 'You darned ole hocus, you, I lost my job, and I'm broke, lopin' around this country with you.'

"'Forget it!' says ole Demijohn. 'Ain't I good comp'ny?'

"'Mebby you be—for some folks,' says young John. 'But not for me. You don't belong up in this here country; you belong back in town, and I reckon you better fan it.'

"Ole Demijohn he laughed. 'You can't run me off the range that easy,' he says.

"'I can't, eh?' says young John, and he pulls his gun and up and busts ole Demijohn over the head. Then, bein' a likely young fella, he shuts his jaw tight and fans it back to the ranch. The fo'man is some surprised to see him come ridin' up, whistlin' like he owned the works. Fellas what's fired mostly looks for work some place else. But young John got the idee that he owed it to hisself to make good where he started as a cow-hand. 'I busted my ole friend Demijohn over the head,' he says to the fo'man. 'We ain't friends no more.'

"The fo'man he grins. 'All right, Jack,' he says. 'But if I see him hangin' round the corrals ag'in, or in the bunk-house, you needn't to wait for me to tell you which way is north.'

"Well, young John had done a good job. 'Course ole Demijohn used to come sneakin' round in the moonlight, once in a spell, botherin' some of the boys, but he stayed clear of young John. And young John he took to ridin' straight and hard and 'tendin' to business. I ain't sayin' he ever got to be president or superintendent of a Sunday School, for this ain't no story-book yarn; but he always held a good job when he wanted it, and he worked for a good boss—which was hisself."

Lorry grinned as he turned to Shoop. "That ole Demijohn never got close enough to me to get busted on the head."

"Them hosses is strayin' down the creek," said Shoop, rising.

They turned and rode north, somewhat to Lorry's surprise. The trail was ragged and steep, and led from the mesa to the cañon bottom of the White River. Before Lorry realized where they were, Jason loomed before them on the mesa below.

"She's a quick trail to town in summer," explained Shoop. "Snow hangs too heavy in the cañon to ride it in winter."

At Jason they tied their horses, and entered the ranger's office. Lorry waited while Shoop talked with Torrance in the private office. Presently Shoop came to the door and gestured to Lorry.

"Mr. Shoop says he thinks you could qualify for the Service," Torrance said. "We will waive the matter of recommendations from the Starr people. But there is one thing I can't do. I can't hire a man who is wanted by the authorities. There's a deputy sheriff in town with a warrant for you. That is strictly your affair. If you can square yourself with the deputy, I'll put you to work."

"I'll go see what he wants," said Lorry.

"He wants you. Understand, you'll only jeopardize your chances by starting a row."

"They won't be a row," said Lorry.

When he returned he was accompanied by the deputy. Lorry took his stand without parley.

"I want to ask you folks a question, and then I'm through," he asserted. "Will you listen to what he says and what I say, and then say who is right?"

"That might not settle it," said Torrance. "But go ahead."

"Then all I got to say is, was I right or wrong when I turned that hobo loose and saved him from gettin' beat up by High Chin and the boys, and mebby strung up, afore they got through?"

"Morally you were right," said Torrance. "But you should have appealed to Sheriff Hardy to guard his prisoner."

"That's all right, Mr. Torrance. But suppose they wasn't time. And suppose,—now Buck's deputy is here to listen to it,—suppose I was to say that Buck is scared to death of High-Chin Bob. Everybody knows it."

The deputy flushed. He knew that Lorry spoke the truth.

Torrance turned to Shoop. "What do you think, Bud?"

Bud coughed and shrugged his heavy shoulders. "Bein' as I'm drug into this, I say the boy did a good job and he's right about Hardy, which you can tell him," he added, turning to the deputy.

"Then that's all I got to say," and Lorry pushed back his hat and rumpled his hair.

The deputy was not there to argue. He had been sent to get Lorry.

"I don't say he ain't right. But how about my job if I ride back to Stacey with nothin' to show for the trip but my expense card?"

"Buck Hardy isn't a fool," said Torrance.

"Oh, hell!" said Lorry, turning to the deputy. "I'll go back with you. I'm sick of jawin' about the right and the wrong and who's to blame. But I want to say in company that I'll go just as far as the county line of this county. You're south of your county. If you can get me across the line, I'll go on to Stacey."

Bud Shoop mopped his face with a bandanna. He was not overhot, but he wanted to hide the grin that spread over his broad countenance. He imagined he could see the deputy just about the time they arrived at the county line, and the mental picture seemed to amuse him.

"The idee is, the kid thinks he's right," said Shoop presently. "Speakin' personal, I never monkey with a man when he thinks he's right—and he is."

"All I got to go by is the law," asserted the deputy. "As for Adams here sayin' I won't run him in, I got orders to do it, and them orders goes."

"Adams has applied for a position in the Service," said Torrance.

"I ain't got anything against Lorry personal," said the deputy.

"Then just you ride back an' tell Buck Hardy that Bud Shoop says he'll stand responsible for Adams keepin' the peace in Jason County, same as I stood responsible for Buck oncet down in the Panhandle. Buck will remember, all right."

"Can't you give me a letter to Buck, explainin' things?" queried the deputy.

Bud glanced at Torrance. "I think we can," said the supervisor.

Lorry stepped to the door with the deputy. There was no personal feeling evident as they shook hands.

"You could tell ma to send down my clothes by stage," said Lorry.

Shoop and Torrance seemed to be enjoying themselves.

"I put in my say," said Bud, "'cause I kind of like the kid. And I reckon I saved that deputy a awful wallopin'. When a fella like young Adams talks pleasant and chokes his hat to death at the same time you can watch out for somethin' to fall."

"Do you think Adams would have had it out with him?"

"He'd 'a' rode along a spell, like he said. Mebby just this side of the county line he'd 'a' told the deputy which way was north. And if the deputy didn't take the hint, I reckon Adams would 'a' lit into him. I knowed Adams's daddy afore he married Annie Adams and went to live in Sonora."

"Then you knew that his father was Jim Waring?"

"I sure did. And I reckon I kep' somebody from gettin' a awful wallopin'. I was a kid oncet myself."

Chapter XVI
Play

The installation of Bud Shoop as supervisor of the White Mountain District was celebrated with an old-fashioned barbecue by the cattlemen and sheepmen leasing on the reserve. While John Torrance had always dealt fairly with them, the natives felt that he was more or less of a theorist in the matter of grazing-leases. Shoop was a practical cowman; one of themselves. Naturally there was some dissatisfaction expressed by disgruntled individuals who envied Shoop's good fortune. But this was overwhelmed by the tide of popular acclaim with which Shoop was hailed as a just administrator of their grazing-rights.

The barbecue was a boisterous success. Although the day of large holdings was past, the event lacked nothing in numbers or enthusiasm. The man who owned a hundred head of cattle was quite as popular as his neighbor who owned perhaps eight hundred or a thousand. Outfits fraternized, ran pony races, roped for prizes, and rode bucking horses, as their predecessors had raced, roped, and "rode 'em" in the days of old.

Lorry, itching to enter the roping contest, was checked by a suggestion from the genial Bud.

"I've heard you was top-hand with a rope. But you're a ranger, by the grace of God and me and John Torrance. Let the boy's play, but don't play with 'em yet. Keep 'em guessin' just how good you are. Let 'em get to know you slow—and solid."

Lorry accepted Bud's advice, and made himself popular with the various outfits by maintaining a silence when questioned as to how he "put High-Chin Bob out of business." The story of that affair had had a wide circulation, and gained interest when it became known that High Chin and his men were present. Their excuse for coming was only legitimate in that a barbecue draws no fine lines of distinction. Any one who has a horse and an appetite is welcome. The Starr riders were from the northern county, but they would have been quite as welcome had they come from Alaska.

Bud Shoop was present in a suit of religiously severe black, his pants outside his boots. He had donned a white shirt and knotted a black silk bandanna round his short neck.

The morning was noisy with pony races, roping contests, and the riding of pitching horses. The events were not tabulated, but evolved through the unwritten law of precedent.

After the noon feast there was talk of a shooting-match. Few of the local men packed guns, and none of them openly. The Starr riders were the only exception. This fact was commented upon by some of the old-timers, who finally accosted Bud with the suggestion that he "show that Starr outfit what a gun was made for." Bud declined.

"I ain't had a gun in my hand, except to clean it, since I quit punchin'," he told them. "And, anyhow, I'm no fancy gun sharp."

"High Chin and his outfit is sure handin' it to us," complained the old-timers. "And you're about the only man here who could show 'em."

"No use provin' it to 'em when they know it," Bud said.

The committee retired and consulted among themselves. Bud was talking with a cattleman when they again accosted him.

"Say, Bud, them Starr boys has cleaned us out on ropin' and racin'. We trimmed 'em on ridin'. Now that makes two to one, and we're askin' you as a old-timer if we're goin' to let them fellas ride north a-tellin' every hay-tosser atween here and Stacey that we're a bunch of jays?"

"Oh, shucks!" was all Bud had to say.

"And that High-Chin Bob says he aims to hang young Adams's scalp on his belt afore he gits through," asserted a townsman.

"I'll set in the game," said Bud.

And he waddled across the street to his office. In a few minutes he came back and mingled with the crowd. The Starr boys were pitching dollars at a mark when Bud and a companion strolled past. High Chin invited Shoop to join in the game. Shoop declined pleasantly.

"Things is runnin' slow," said a Starr man. "Wish I'd 'a' fetched my music along. Mebby I could git somebody to sing me to sleep."

Bud laughed. "Have a good time, boys." And he moved on.

"That was one for you—and yore piano," said his companion.

"Mebby so. We'll let that rest. I'm lookin' for a friend of mine." And Shoop edged along the crowd.

The man that Shoop was looking for was standing alone beneath the shade of an acacia, watching the crowd. He was a tall, heavy man, dark-featured, with a silver-gray beard and brown eyes that seemed to twinkle with amusement even when his lips were grim. The giant sheepman of the south country was known to every one on account of his great physique and his immense holdings in land and sheep. Shoop talked with him for a few minutes. Together they strolled back to the crowd.

The Starr boys were still pitching dollars when Shoop and the sheepman approached.

"Who's top-hand in this game?" queried Shoop genially.

"High Chin—and at any game you got," said a Starr man.

"Well, now!"

"Any game you got."

Shoop gazed about, saw Lorry, and beckoned to him.

"Here's my candidate," said Shoop. "He kep' out of the ropin' so as to give you fellas a chance." And he turned to Lorry. "Give him a whirl," he said, indicating High Chin. "It's worth a couple of dollars just to find out how good he is."

High Chin surveyed the circle of faces, poised a dollar, and threw it. Lorry threw and lost. High Chin pocketed the two dollars. The Starr boys grinned. High Chin threw again. The dollar slid close to the line. Lorry shied his dollar and knocked the other's coin several feet away from the line.

"Try him ag'in," said Shoop.

Lorry tossed again. His dollar dropped on the line. High Chin threw. His coin clinked squarely on Lorry's, but spun off, leaving it undisturbed.

"You break even—at that game," said Shoop. "It was a good shot."

"Folks been sayin' the same of you," said High Chin, turning to the supervisor.

"Oh, folks will talk. They're made that way," chuckled Shoop.

"Well, I got ten bucks that says High Chin can outshoot any hombre in this crowd," said a Starr boy.

"I'm right glad you got it," said Shoop pleasantly.

"Meanin' I stand to lose it, eh?"

"Oh, gosh, no! You're steppin' on your bridle. I was congratulatin' you on your wealth."

"I ain't seen that you been flashin' any money," said the cowboy.

"Nope. That ain't what money's made for. And I never bet on a sure thing. Ain't no fun in that."

The giant sheepman, whose movements were as deliberate as the sun's, slowly reached in his pocket and drew out a leather pouch. He counted out forty dollars in gold-pieces.

"I'll lay it even," he said, his eyes twinkling, "that Bud Shoop can outshoot any man in the crowd."

"I'll take ten of that," said the Starr man.

"And I'll take ten," said another cowboy.

"John," said Shoop, turning to the sheepman, "you're a perpendicular dam' fool."

Word went forth that High-Chin Bob, of the Starr, and Bud Shoop were to shoot a match for a thousand dollars a side, and some of the more enthusiastic believed it. In a few minutes the street was empty of all save the ponies at the hitching-rails.

In a shallow arroyo back of town the excited throng made wagers and talked of wonderful shots made by the principals. High Chin was known as a quick and sure shot. Shoop's reputation was known to fewer of the crowd. The Starr boys backed their foreman to the last cent. A judge was suggested, but declined as being of the locality. Finally the giant sheepman, despite his personal wager, was elected unanimously. He was known to be a man of absolute fairness, and qualified to judge marksmanship. He agreed to serve, with the proviso that the Starr boys or any of High Chin's friends should feel free to question his decisions. The crowd solidified back of the line, where Shoop and High Chin stood waiting for the test.

The marksmen faced two bottles on a rock some thirty paces away. At the word, each was to "go for his gun" and shoot. High Chin carried his gun in the usual holster. Bud Shoop's gun was tucked in the waistband of his pants.

"Go!" said the sheepman.

High Chin's hand flashed to his hip. His gun jumped and spoke. Shoop's wrist turned. Both bottles were shattered on the instant. A tie was declared.

The men were placed with their backs toward the targets—two empty bottles. The sheepman faced them, with his hands behind his back. When he snapped his fingers they were to turn and fire. Many of the onlookers thought this test would leave High Chin a point ahead.

Both men swung and fired at the signal. Again both bottles were shattered. Although a tie was again declared, the crowd cheered for Shoop, realizing his physical handicap. Yet many asserted that High Chin was the faster man, won to this decision by his lightning speed of movement and his easy manner, suggesting a kind of contemptuous indifference to results.

In contrast to High Chin's swift, careless efficiency, Shoop's solid poise and lack of elbow motion showed in strong relief. Their methods were entirely dissimilar. But it was evident to the old-timers that Shoop shot with less effort and waste motion than his lithe competitor. And High Chin was the younger man by twenty years.

Thus far the tests had not been considered difficult. But when the sheepman stepped off ten paces and faced the competitors with a cigar held at arm's length, the chattering of the crowd ceased. High Chin, as guest, was asked to shoot first. He raised his gun. It hung poised for a second. As it jumped in his hand the ash flirted from the end of the cigar. The crowd stamped and cheered. Shoop congratulated High Chin. The crowd hooted and called to Shoop to make good. Even as they called, his hand flashed up. Hardly had the report of his gun startled them to silence when they saw that his hands were empty. A roar of laughter shook the crowd. Some one pointed toward the sheepman. The laughter died down. He held a scant two inches of cigar in his fingers. Then they understood, and were silent again. They gathered round the sheepman. He held up his arms. Shoop's bullet had nipped the cigar in two before they had realized that he intended to shoot.

"You're havin' the luck," said High.

"You're right," said Shoop. "And luck, if she keeps steady gait, is just as good a hoss to ride as they is."

Still, there were those who maintained that Shoop had made a chance hit. But High Chin knew that this was not so. He had met his master at the six-gun game.

Bud Shoop's easy manner had vanished. As solid as a rock, his lips in a straight line, he waited for the next test while High Chin talked and joked with the bystanders.

"You'll shoot when you see something to shoot at," was the sheepman's word. The crowd laughed. He stood behind the marksmen, a tin can in each hand. Both High Chin and Shoop knew what was coming, and Shoop decided to surprise the assemblage. The main issue was not the shooting contest, and if High-Chin Bob had not already seen enough of Shoop's work to satisfy him, the genial Bud intended to clinch the matter right there.

Without warning, the sheepman tossed the cans into the air. Shoop and High Chin shot on the instant. But before High Chin's can touched the ground Shoop shot again. It was faster work than any present had ever seen. A man picked up the cans and brought them to the sheepman. One can had a clean hole in it. The other had two holes through it. Those nearest the marksmen wondered why Shoop had not shot twice at his own can. But the big sheepman knew that Shoop had called High Chin's bluff about "any game going."

Even then the match was a tie so far as precedent demanded. Each man had made a hit on a moving target.

The crowd had ceased to applaud.

"How about a try from the saddle?" suggested High Chin.

"I reckon I look just as fat and foolish settin' in a saddle as anywhere," said Shoop.

The crowd shuffled over to a more open spot, on the mesa. Shoop and High Chin mounted their horses. A tin cracker box was placed on a flat rock out in the open.

The men were to reload and shoot at top speed as they rode past the box. The Starr foreman immediately jumped his pony to a run, and, swaying easily, threw a shot at the box as he approached it, another and another when opposite, and, turning in the saddle, fired his three remaining shots. The box was brought back and inspected. The six shots had all hit.

Shoop, straight and solid as a statue, ran his pony down the course, but held his fire until almost opposite the box. Then six reports rippled out like the drawing of a stick quickly across a picket fence. It was found that the six shots had all hit in one side of the box. The sheepman was asked for a decision. He shook his head and declared the match a draw. And technically it was a draw. Every one seemed satisfied, although there was much discussion among individuals as to the relative merits of the contestants.

As the crowd dispersed and some of them prepared to ride home, two horsemen appeared on the northern road, riding toward town. As they drew nearer Shoop chuckled. Lorry, standing a few paces away, glanced at him.

The supervisor was talking to Bob Brewster. "High, you're the best I ever stacked up against, exceptin' one, and it's right curious that he is just a-ridin' into this powwow. If you want to see what real shootin' is, get him to show you."

"I don't know your friend," said High, eyeing the approaching horsemen, "but he's a beaut if he can outshoot you."

"Outshoot me? Say, High, that hombre ridin' the big buckskin hoss there could make us look about as fast as a couple of fence-posts when it comes to handlin' a gun. And his pardner ain't what you'd call slow."

High Chin's lean face darkened as he recognized Waring riding beside a gaunt, long-legged man whose gray eyes twinkled as he surveyed the little group.

"Pat—and Jim Waring," muttered Shoop. "And us just finished what some would call a ole-time shootin'-bee!"

"Who's your friend?" queried High Chin, although he knew.

"Him? That's Jim Waring, of Sonora. And say, High, I ain't his advertisin' agent, but between you and me he could shoot the fuzz out of your ears and never as much as burn 'em. What I'm tellin' you is first-class life insurance if you ain't took out any. And before you go I just want to pass the word that young Adams is workin' for *me*. Reckon you might be interested, seein' as how he worked for you a spell."

High Chin met Shoop's gaze unblinkingly. He was about to speak when Pat and Waring, rode up and greeted the supervisor. High Chin wheeled his horse and loped back to town. A few minutes later he and his men rode past. To Shoop's genial wave of farewell they returned a whoop that seemed edged with a vague challenge.

Pat, who was watching them, asked Shoop who the man was riding the pinto.

"Why, that's High-Chin Bob Brewster, Starr fo'man. He's kind of a wild bird. I reckon he came over here lookin' for trouble. He's been walkin' around with his wings and tail spread like he was mad at somethin'."

"I thought I knew him," said Pat. And he shrugged his shoulders.

Shoop noticed that Waring was gazing at Pat in a peculiar manner. He attached no significance to this at the time, but later he recalled the fact that there had been trouble between Pat and the Brewster boys some years ago. The Brewsters had then openly threatened to "get Pat if he ever rode north again."

Chapter XVII
Down the Wind

Waring, several miles out from the home shack, on the new range, sat his horse Dexter, watching his men string fence. They ran the barbed wire with a tackle, stringing it taut down the long line of bare posts that twinkled away to dots in the west. Occasionally Waring rode up and tested the wire with his hand. The men worked fast. Waring and Pat had picked their men; three husky boys of the high country who considered stringing fence rather pleasant exercise. There was no recognized foreman. Each knew his work, and Waring had added a foreman's pay to their salaries, dividing it equally among them. Later they would look after the ranch and the cattle.

Twenty thousand acres under fence, with plenty of water, would take care of eight hundred or a thousand head of cattle. And as a provision against a lean winter, Waring had put a mowing-machine in at the eastern end of the range, where the bunch-grass was heavy enough to cut. It would be necessary to winter-feed. Four hundred white-faced Herefords grazed in the autumn sunshine. Riding round and among them leisurely was the Mexican youth, Ramon.

Backed against a butte near the middle of the range was the broad, low-roofed ranch-house. A windmill purred in the light breeze, its lean, flickering shadow aslant the corrals. The buildings looked new and raw in contrast to the huge pile of grayish-green greasewood and scrub cedar gathered from the clearing round them.

In front of the house was a fenced acre, ploughed and harrowed to a dead level. This was to be Pat's garden, wherein he had planned to grow all sorts of green things, including cucumbers. At the moment Pat was standing under the veranda roof, gazing out across the ranch. The old days of petty warfare, long night rides, and untold hardships were past. Next spring his garden would bloom; tiny green tendrils would swell to sturdy vines. Corn-leaves would broaden to waving green blades shot with the rich brown of the ripening ears. Although he had never spoken of it, Pat had dreamed of blue flowers nodding along the garden fence; old-fashioned bachelor's-buttons that would spring up as though by accident. But he would have to warn Waco, the erstwhile tramp, not to mistake them for weeds.

"Peace and plenty," muttered Pat, smiling to himself. "The Book sure knows how to say those things."

The gaunt, grizzled ex-sheriff reached in his vest for a cigar. As he bit the end off and felt for a match, he saw a black speck wavering in the distance. He shaded his eyes with his hand.

"'Tain't a machine," he said. "And it ain't a buckboard. Some puncher lookin' for a job, most likely."

He turned and entered the house. Waco, shaven and in clean shirt and overalls, was "punching dough" in the kitchen.

"Did Jim say when he would ride in?" queried Pat.

"About sundown. I fixed 'em up some chuck this morning. Jim figures they're getting too far out to ride in every noon."

"Well, when you get your bread baked we'll take a whirl at those ditches. How are the supplies holding out?"

"We're short on flour. Got enough to last over till Monday. Plenty bacon and beans and lard."

"All right. We'll hook up to-morrow and drive in."

Waco nodded as he tucked a roll of dough into the pan. Pat watched him for a moment. Waco, despite his many shortcomings, could cook, and, strangely enough, liked to putter round the garden.

Picked up half-starving on the mesa road, near St. Johns, he had been brought to the ranch by Pat, where a month of clean air and industry had reshaped the tramp to something like a man. Both Pat and Waring knew that the hobo was wanted in Stacey. They had agreed to say nothing about the tramp's whereabouts just so long as he made himself useful about the ranch. They would give him a chance. But, familiar with his kind, they were mildly skeptical as to Waco's sincerity of purpose. If he took to drinking, or if Buck Hardy heard of his whereabouts, he would have to go. Meanwhile, he earned his keep. He was a good cook, and a good cook, no matter where or where from, is a power in the land.

As Waco closed the oven door some one hallooed. Pat stepped to the veranda. A cowboy astride a bay pony asked if Waring were around.

"I can take your message," said Pat.

"Well, it's for you, I guess. Letter from Buck Hardy."

"Yes, it's for me," said Pat. "Who sent you?"

"Hardy. Said something about you had a man down here he wanted."

"All right. Stay for chuck?"

"I got to git back. How's things down this way?"

"Running on time. Just tell Buck I'll be over right soon."

"To-day?"

Pat's gray eyes hardened. "Buck tell you to ask me that?"

"Well—no. I was just wonderin'."

"Then keep right on wondering," said Pat. "You got your answer."

The cowboy swung up and rode off. "To hell with him!" he said. "Thinks he can throw a scare into me because he's got a name for killin'. To hell him!"

Pat climbed the hill back of the house and surveyed the glimmering levels.

"Wish Jim would ride in. Funny thing—Hardy sending a Starr boy with word for me. But perhaps the kid was riding this way, anyhow."

Pat shook his head, and climbed slowly down to the house. Waco was busy in the kitchen when he came in.

After the noon meal, Pat again climbed the hill. He seemed worried about something. When he returned he told Waco to hitch the pintos to the buckboard.

"Get your coat," he told Waco. "We're going over to Stacey."

Waco's hands trembled. "Say, boss, if you don't mind—"

"Get your coat. I'll talk to Buck. You needn't to worry. I'll square you with Buck. We can use you here."

Waco did as he was told. They drove out of the yard. Waco leaped down and closed the gate.

The pintos shook themselves into the harness and trotted down the faintly marked new road. The buckboard swayed and jolted. Something rubbed against Waco's hip. He glanced down and saw Pat's gun on the seat between them. Pat said nothing. He was thinking hard. The cowboy messenger's manner had not been natural. The note bore the printed heading of the sheriff's office. Perhaps it was all right. And if it were not, Pat was not the man to back down from a bluff.

Several miles out from the ranch ran the naked posts of the line fence. Pat reined in the ponies and gazed up and down the line. A mile beyond, the ranch road merged with the main-traveled highway running east and west. He spoke to the horses. They broke into a fast trot. Waco, gripping the seat, stared straight ahead. Why had Pat laid that gun on the seat?

A thin, gray veil drifted across the sun. From the northwest a light wind sprang up and ran across the mesa, whipping the bunch-grass. The wind grew heavier, and with it came a fine, dun-colored dust. An hour and the air was thick with a shifting red haze of sand. The sun glowed dimly through the murk.

Waco turned up his coat-collar and shivered. The air was keen. The ponies fought the bit, occasionally breaking into a gallop. Pat braced his feet and held them to a trot. A weird buzzing came down the wind. The ponies reared and took to the ditch as a machine flicked past and drummed away in the distance.

To Waco, rigid and staring, the air seemed filled with a kind of hovering terror, a whining threat of danger that came in bursts of driving sand and dwindled away to harsh whisperings. He stood it as long as he could. Pat had not spoken.

Waco touched his arm. "I got a hunch," he said hoarsely,—"I got a hunch we oughta go back."

Pat nodded. But the ponies swept on down the road, their manes and tails whipping in the wind. Another mile and they slowed down in heavy sand. The buckboard tilted forward as they descended the sharp pitch of an arroyo. Unnoticed, Pat's gun slipped to the floor of the wagon.

In the arroyo the wind seemed to have died away, leaving a startled quietness. It still hung above them, and an occasional gust filled their eyes with grit. Waco drew a deep breath. The ponies tugged through the heavy sand.

Without a sound to warn them a rider appeared close to the front wheel of the buckboard. Waco shrank down in sodden terror. It was the Starr foreman, High-Chin Bob. Waco saw Pat's hand flash to his side, then fumble on the seat.

"I'm payin' the Kid's debt," said High Chin, and, laughing, he threw shot after shot into the defenseless body of his old enemy.

Waco saw Pat slump forward, catch himself, and finally topple from the seat. As the reins slipped from his fingers the ponies lunged up the arroyo. Waco crouched, clutching the foot-rail. A bullet hummed over his head. Gaining the level, the ponies broke into a wild run. The red wind whined as it drove across the mesa. The buckboard lurched sickeningly. A scream of terror wailed down the wind as the buckboard struck a telegraph pole. A blind shock—and for Waco the droning of the wind had ceased.

Dragging the broken traces, the ponies circled the mesa and set off at a gallop toward home. At the side of the road lay the splintered buckboard, wheels up. And Waco, hovering on the edge of the black abyss, dreamed strange dreams.

Waring, riding in with the crew, found the ranch-house deserted and the pinto ponies dragging the shreds of a broken harness, grazing along the fence. Waring sent a man to catch up the team. Ramon cooked supper. The men ate in silence.

After supper Waring changed his clothes, saddled Dex, and packed some food in the saddle-pockets. "I am going out to look for Pat," he told one of his men. "If Waco shows up, keep him here till I get back. Those horses didn't get away from Pat. Here's a signed check. Get what you need and keep on with the work. You're foreman till I get back."

"If there's anything doing—" began the cowboy.

"I don't know. Some one rode in here to-day. It was along about noon that Pat and Waco left. The bread was baked. I'd say they drove to town for grub; only Pat took his gun—without the holster. It looks bad to me. If anything happens to me, just send for Lorry Adams at the Ranger Station."

Waring rode out, looking for tracks. His men watched him until he had disappeared behind a rise. Bender, the new foreman, turned to his fellows.

"I'd hate to be the man that the boss is lookin' for," he said, shaking his head.

"Why, he's lookin' for Pat, ain't he?" queried one of the men.

"That ain't what I mean," said the foreman.

The wind died down suddenly. The sun, just above the horizon, glowed like a disk of burnished copper. The wagon ruts were filled with fine sand. Waring read the trail. The buckboard had traveled briskly. It had stopped at the line. The tracks of the fretting ponies showed that clearly. Alongside the tracks of the ponies were the half-hidden tracks of a single horse. Waring glanced back at the sun, and put Dex to a lope. He swung into the main road, his gaze following the half-obliterated trail of the single horseman. Suddenly he reined up. The horseman had angled away from the road and had ridden north across the open country. He had not gone to Stacey. Waring knew that the horseman had been riding hard. Straight north from where Waring had stopped was the Starr Ranch.

He rode on, his heart heavy with a black premonition. The glowing copper disk was now half-hidden by the western hills.

At the brink of the arroyo he dismounted. He could see nothing distinctly in the gloom of its depths. Stooping, he noted the wagon tracks as he worked on down. His foot struck against something hard. He fumbled and picked Pat's gun from the sand. Every chamber was loaded.

"He didn't have a chance." Waring was startled by his own voice. He thrust the gun in his waistband. The twilight deepened rapidly. Rocks and ridges in the arroyo assumed peculiar shapes like those of men crouching; men prone; men with heads up, listening, watching, waiting. Yet Waring's instinct for hidden danger told him that there was no living thing in the arroyo—unless—Suddenly he sprang forward and dropped to his knees beside a huddled shape near a boulder.

"Pat!" he whispered.

Then he knew; saw it all as clearly as though he had witnessed it— the ambushment in the blinding sandstorm; the terror-stricken Waco; the frightened ponies; the lunging and swaying buckboard. And Pat, left for dead, but who had dragged himself from the roadway in dumb agony.

The dole of light from the sinking sun was gone. Waring's hands came away from the opened shirt shudderingly. He wiped his hands on the sand, and, rising, ran back to Dex. He returned with a whiskey flask. Pat was of tough fiber and tremendous vitality. If the spark were still unquenched, if it could be called back even for a breath, that which Waring knew, yet wanted to confirm beyond all doubt, might be given in a word. He raised Pat's head, and barely tilted the flask. The spirit of the mortally stricken man, perchance loath to leave such a brave hermitage, winged slowly back from the far shore of dreams. In the black pit of the arroyo, where death crouched, waiting, life flamed for an instant.

Waring felt the limp body stir. He took Pat's big, bony hand in his.

"Pat!" he whispered.

A word breathed heavily from the motionless lips. "You, Jim?"

"Yes! For God's sake, Pat, who did this thing?"

"Brewster—Bob. Letter—in my coat."

"I'll get *him*!" said Waring.

"Shake!" exclaimed the dying man, and the grip of his hand was like iron. Waring thought he had gone, and leaned closer. "I'm—kind of tired— Jim. Reckon—I'll—rest."

Waring felt the other's grip relax. He drew his hand from the stiffening fingers. A dull pain burned in his throat. He lighted a match, and found the message that had lured Pat to his death in the other's coat-pocket. He rose and stumbled up the arroyo to his horse.

Halfway back to the ranch, and he met Ramon riding hard. "Ride back," said Waring. "Hook up to the wagon and come to the arroyo."

"Have you found the Señor Pat?"

"Yes. He is dead."

Ramon whirled his pony and pounded away in the darkness.

Out on the highway two long, slender shafts of light slid across the mesa, dipped into an arroyo, and climbed skyward as a machine buzzed up the opposite pitch. The lights straightened again and shot on down the road, swinging stiffly from side to side. Presently they came to a stop. In the soft glow of their double radiance lay a yellow-wheeled buckboard, shattered and twisted round a telegraph pole. The lights moved up slowly and stopped again.

A man jumped from the machine and walked round the buckboard. Beneath it lay a crumpled figure. The driver of the machine ran a quick hand over the neck and arms of Waco, who groaned. The driver lifted him and carried him to the car. Stacey lay some twenty miles behind him. He was bound south. The first town on his way was thirty miles distant. But the roads were good. He glanced back at the huddled figure in the tonneau. The car purred on down the night. The long shafts of light lifted over a rise and disappeared.

In about an hour the car stopped at the town of Grant. Waco was carried from the machine to a room in the hotel, and a doctor was summoned. Waco lay unconscious throughout the night.

In the morning he was questioned briefly. He gave a fictitious name, and mentioned a town he had heard of, but had never been in. His horses had run away with him.

The man who had picked him up drove away next morning. Later the doctor told Waco that through a miracle there were no bones broken, but that he would have to keep to his bed for at least a week. Otherwise he would never recover from the severe shock to his nervous system.

And Waco, recalling the horror of the preceding day, twisted his head round at every footstep in the hall, fearing that Waring had come to question him. He knew that he had done no wrong; in fact, he had told Pat that they had better drive back home. But a sense of shame at his cowardice, and the realization that his word was as water in evidence, that he was but a wastrel, a tramp, burdened him with an aching desire to get away—to hide himself from Waring's eyes, from the eyes of all men.

He kept telling himself that he had done nothing wrong, yet fear shook him until his teeth chattered. What could he have done even had he been courageous? Pat had had no chance.

He suffered with the misery of indecision. Habit inclined him to flee from the scene of the murder. Fear of the law urged him. Three nights after he had been brought to Grant, he dressed and crept down the back stairs, and made his way to the railroad station. Twice he had heard the midnight freight stop and cut out cars on the siding. He hid in the shadows until the freight arrived. He climbed to an empty box-car and waited. Trainmen crunched past on the cinders. A jolt and he was swept away toward the west. He sank into a half sleep as the iron wheels roared and droned beneath him.

Chapter XVIII
A Piece of Paper

In the little desert hotel at Stacey, Mrs. Adams was singing softly to herself as she moved about the dining-room helping Anita clear away the breakfast dishes. Mrs. Adams had heard from Lorry. He had secured a place in the Ranger Service. She was happy. His letter had been filled with enthusiasm for the work and for his chief, Bud Shoop. This in itself was enough to make her happy. She had known Bud in Las Cruces. He was a good man. And then—Jim had settled down. Only last week he had ridden over and told her how they were getting on with the work at the ranch. He had hinted then that he had laid his guns away. Perhaps he had wanted her to know *that* more than anything else. She had kissed him good-bye. His gray eyes had been kind. "Some day, Annie," he had said. Her face flushed as she recalled the moment.

A boot-heel gritted on the walk. She turned. Waring was standing in the doorway. His face was set and hard. Involuntarily she ran to him.

"What is it, Jim? Lorry?"

He shook his head. She saw at once that he was dressed for a long ride and that—an unusual circumstance—a gun swung at his hip. He usually wore a coat and carried his gun in a shoulder holster. But now he was in his shirt-sleeves. A dread oppressed her. He was ready on the instant to fight, but with whom? Her eyes grew big.

"What is it?" she whispered again.

"The Brewster boys got Pat."

"Not—they didn't kill him!"

Waring nodded.

"But, Jim—"

"In the Red Arroyo on the desert road. I found him. I came to tell you."

"And you are going—"

"Yes. I was afraid this would happen. Pat made a mistake."

"But, Jim! The law—the sheriff—you don't have to go."

"No," he said slowly.

"Then why do you go? I thought you would never do that again. I—I—prayed for you, Jim. I prayed for you and Lorry. I asked God to send you back to me with your two hands clean. I told Him you would never kill again. Oh, Jim, I wanted you—here! Don't!" she sobbed.

He put his arm round her shoulders. Stooping, he kissed her.

"You are going?" she asked, and her hands dropped to her sides.

"Yes; I told Pat I would get Brewster. Pat went out with his hand in mine on that word. My God, Annie, do you think I could ride back to the ranch and face the boys or sleep nights with Pat's hand reaching for me in the dark to remind me of my word? Can't you see where I stand? Do you think I could look Lorry in the face when he knew that I sat idle while the man that murdered Pat was riding the country free?"

"Pat was your friend. I am your wife," said Mrs. Adams.

Waring's lips hardened. "Pat's gone. But I'm calling myself his friend yet. And the man that got him is going to know it."

Before she could speak again Waring was gone.

She dropped to a chair and buried her face in her arms. Anita came to her and tried to comfort her. But Mrs. Adams rose and walked to the office doorway. She saw Waring riding down the street. She wanted to call out to him, to call him back. She felt that he was riding to his death. If he would only turn! If he would only wave his hand to show that he cared—But Waring rode on, straight and stern, black hate in his heart, his free hand hollowed as though with an invisible vengeance that was gone as he drew his fingers tense.

He rode north, toward the Starr Ranch. He passed a group of riders drifting some yearlings toward town. A man spoke to him. He did not reply.

And as he rode he heard a voice—the Voice of his desert wanderings, the Voice that had whispered to him from the embers of many a night fire in the Southern solitudes. Yet there, was this difference. That voice had been strangely dispassionate, detached; not the voice of a human being. But now the Voice was that of his friend Pat softly reiterating: "Not this way, Jim."

And Waring cursed. His plan was made. He would suffer no interference. If Brewster were at the Starr Ranch, he would question him first. If he were not, there would be no questioning. Waring determined to trail him. If Brewster had left that part of the country, that would prove his guilt.

Waring knew that Hardy and his men had ridden south, endeavoring to find some clue to the murderer's whereabouts. Waring, guided by almost absolute knowledge, rode in the opposite direction and against a keen instinct that told him High-Chin Bob was not at the ranch. Yet Waring would not overlook the slightest chance. Brewster was of the type that would kill a man in a quarrel and ride home, depending on his nerve and lack of evidence to escape punishment.

The Voice had said, "Not this way, Jim." And Waring knew that it had been the voice of his own instinct. Yet a stubborn purpose held him to his course. There was one chance in a thousand that Bob Brewster was at the ranch and would disclaim all knowledge of the shooting.

Starr was away when Waring arrived. Mrs. Starr made Waring welcome, and told him that her husband would be in that evening. He was out with one of his men running a line for a new fence. The old days of open range were past. And had Mr. Waring heard that Pat had been killed? Buck Hardy was out searching for the murderer. Did Mr. Waring know of a likely foreman? Bob Brewster had left suddenly. Jasper—her husband—was not well: had the rheumatics again. He could hardly walk—and his foreman had left. "Things always happened that way."

Mrs. Starr paused for lack of breath.

"When did Brewster leave, Mrs. Starr?"

"Why, the last Jasper seen of him was Wednesday morning. Jasper is worried. I'm right glad you rode over. He'll be glad to see you."

"Do you mind if I look over the horses in your corral?"

"Goodness, no! I'll have Sammy go with you—"

"Thanks; but I'd rather you said nothing to the boys."

"You don't think that Bob—"

"Mrs. Starr, I wouldn't say so if I knew it. Bob Brewster has friends up here. I'm looking for one of them."

"Goodness, Mr. Waring, I hope you don't think any of our boys was mixed up in that."

"I hope not. Have you seen Tony or Andy Brewster lately?"

"Why, no. I—why, yes! Tony and Andy rode over last Sunday. I remember it was Sunday because Bob was out to the line shack. Tony and Andy hung around for a while, and then rode out to look for Bob."

"Well, I'll step over and look at the horses. You say Jasper will be in this evening?"

"If he ain't too stiff with rheumatics to ride back."

Waring walked round the corrals, looking for a pony lame forward and with half a front shoe gone. Finally he noticed a short-coupled bay that had not moved when he had waved his arm. Waring climbed through the bars and cornered the horse. One front shoe was entirely gone, and the pony limped as Waring turned him loose.

Mrs. Starr was getting supper when Waring returned to the house.

"Any of the boys coming in with Jasper?" he queried.

"Why, nobody except Pete. Pete's been layin' off. He claims his horse stepped in a gopher hole and threw him. Jasper took him along, feelin' like he wanted some one on account of his rheumatics. Jasper gets so stiff ridin' that sometimes he can hardly get on his horse. Mebby you noticed Pete's pony, that chunky bay in the corral—lame forward."

"Yes, I noticed that. But that pony didn't step in a gopher hole. He was ridden down by some one in a hurry to get somewhere. He cast a shoe and went tender on the rocks."

Mrs. Starr stared at Waring.

He shook his head and smiled. "I don't know. I can only guess at it."

"Well, you'll stay for supper—and you can talk to Jasper. He's worried."

"Thank you. And would you mind asking this man Pete in to supper with us?"

"I figured to, him being with Jasper and not feeling right well."

About sundown Starr rode in. Waring helped him from his horse. They shook hands in silence. The old cattleman knew at once why Waring had come, but he had no inkling of what was to follow.

The cowboy, Pete, took care of the horses. A little later he clumped into the house and took a seat in a corner. Waring paid no attention to him, but talked with Starr about the grazing and the weather.

Just before supper Starr introduced Waring.

The cowboy winced at Waring's grip. "Heard tell of you from the boys," he said.

"You want to ride over to our place," said Waring pleasantly. "Pat and I will show you some pretty land under fence."

The cowboy's eyelids flickered. How could this man Waring speak of Pat that way, when he must know that Pat had been killed? Everybody knew that. Why didn't Mrs. Starr or Starr say something? But Starr was limping to the table, and Mrs. Starr was telling them to come and have supper.

In the glow of the hanging lamp, Starr's lined, grizzled features were as unreadable as carved bronze. Waring, at his left, sat directly opposite the cowboy, Pete. The talk drifted from one subject to another, but no one mentioned the killing of Pat. Waring noted the cowboy's lack of appetite.

"I looked over your saddle-stock this afternoon," said Waring. "Noticed you had a bay out there, white blaze on his nose. You don't want to sell that pony, do you?"

"Oh, that's Pete's pony, Baldy," said Mrs. Starr.

Starr glanced at Waring. The horse Baldy was good enough as cow-ponies went, but Waring had not ridden over to buy horses.

"I aim to keep that cayuse," said Pete, swallowing hard.

"But every man has his price,"—and Waring smiled. "I'll make my offer; a hundred, cash."

"Not this evenin'," said the cowboy.

Waring felt in the pocket of his flannel shirt. "I'll go you one better. I'll make it a hundred, cash, and this to boot." And his arm straightened.

Pete started back. Waring's hand was on the table, the fingers closed His fingers slowly opened, and a crumpled piece of paper lay in his palm. The cowboy's lips tightened. His eyes shifted from Waring to Starr, and then back again.

Mrs. Starr, who could not understand the strange silence of the men, breathed hard and wiped her forehead with her apron.

"Read it!" said Waring sharply.

The cowboy took the piece of paper, and, spreading it out, glanced at it hurriedly.

"This ain't for me," he asserted.

"Did you ever see it before?"

"This? No. What have I got to do with the sheriff's office?"

"Pete," said Waring, drawing back his hand, "you had better read that note again."

"Why, I—Pete can't read," said Mrs. Starr. "He can spell out printed reading some, but not writing."

"Then how did you know this paper was from the sheriff's office?" queried Waring.

The cowboy half rose.

"Sit down!" thundered Waring. "Who sent you with a note to Pat last Wednesday?"

"Who said anybody sent me?"

"Don't waste time! I say so. That broken shoe your cayuse cast says so, for I trailed him from my ranch to the line fence. And you have said so yourself. This paper is not from the sheriff's office. It's a tax receipt."

The cowboy's face went white.

"Honest, so help me, Mr. Waring, I didn't know the Brewster boys was after Pat. Bob he give me the paper. Said it was from the sheriff, and I was to give it to Pat if you weren't around."

"And if I happened to be around?"

"I was to wait until you was out with the fence gang—"

"How did you know I would be out with them?"

"Bob Brewster told me you would be."

Waring folded the piece of paper and tore it across.

"Starr," he said, turning to the old cattleman, "you have heard and seen what has happened since we sat down." And Waring turned on the cowboy. "How much did Bob Brewster give you for this work?"

"I was to get fifty dollars if I put it through."

"And you put it through! You knew it was crooked. And you call yourself a man! And you took a letter to Pat that called him out to be shot down by that coyote! Do you know that Pat's gun was loaded when I found it; that he didn't have a chance?"

Waring's face grew suddenly old. He leaned back wearily.

"I wonder just how you feel?" he said presently. "If I had done a trick like that I'd take a gun and blow my brains out. God, I'd rather be where Pat is than have to carry your load the rest of my life! But you're yellow clean through, and Bob Brewster knew it and hired you. Now you will take that lame cayuse and ride north just as quick as you can throw a saddle on him. And when you go,"—and Waring rose and pointed toward the doorway,— "forget the way back to this country."

The cowboy shuffled his feet and picked up his hat. Starr got up stiffly and limped to his room. He came out with a check, which he gave to the cowboy.

Waring pushed back his chair as though to step round the table and follow the cowboy, but he hesitated, and finally sat down.

"I'm sorry it happened this way, Mrs. Starr," he said.

"It's awful! And one of our men!"

"That's not your fault, Mrs. Starr."

Starr fumbled along the clock shelf, found his pipe, and lighted it. He sat down near Waring as Mrs. Starr began to clear away the dishes.

"If I can do anything to help run down that white-livered skunk—"

"You can, Jasper. Just keep it to yourself that I have been here. Pete left of his own accord. I don't want the Brewster boys to know I'm out on their trail."

Starr nodded and glanced at his wife. "I looked to see you kill him," he said, gesturing toward the doorway.

"What! That poor fool? I thought you knew me better, Jasper."

Chapter XIX
The Fight in the Open

Starr was awakened at midnight by the sound of boot-heels on the ranch-house veranda. He lighted a lamp and limped to the door. The lamplight shone on the smooth, young face of a Mexican, whose black sombrero was powdered with dust.

"What do you want?" queried Starr.

"I am look for the Señor Jim. I am Ramon, of his place. From the rancho I ride to Stacey. He is not there. Then I come here."

"And you ain't particular about wakin' folks up to tell 'em, either."

"I would find him," said Ramon simply.

"What's your business with Jim Waring?"

"It is that I am his friend. I know that he is ride looking for the men who killed my patron the Señor Pat. I am Ramon."

"Uh-uh. Well, suppose you are?"

"It is not the suppose. I am. I would find Señor Jim."

"Who said he was here?"

"The señora at the hotel would think that he was here."

Starr scratched his grizzled head. Waring had said nothing about the Mexican. And Starr did not like Mexicans. Moreover, Waring had said to tell no one that he had been at the Starr Ranch.

"I don't know where Jim Waring is," said Starr, and, stepping back, he closed the door.

Ramon strode to his horse and mounted. All gringos were not like the Señor Jim. Many of them hated Mexicans. Ah, well, he would ride back to Stacey. The señora at the cantina was a pleasant woman. She would not shut the door in his face, for she knew who he was. He would ask for a room for the night. In the morning he would search for Señor Jim. He must find him.

Mrs. Adams answered his knock at the hotel door by coming down and letting him in. Ramon saw by the office clock that it was past three. She showed him to a room.

No, the señor had not been at the Starr Rancho. But he would find him.

Ramon tiptoed to the open window, and knelt with his arms on the sill. A falling star streaked the night.

"And I shall as soon find him as I would find that star," he murmured. "Yet to-morrow there will be the sun. And I will ask the Holy Mother to help me. She will not refuse, knowing my heart."

Without undressing, he flung himself on the bed. As he slept he dreamed; a strange, vivid dream of the setting sun and a tiny horseman limned against the gold. The horseman vanished as he rose to follow. If he were only sure that it was the Señor Jim! The dream had said that the señor had ridden into the west. In the morning—

With the dawn Ramon was up. Some one was moving about in the kitchen below. Ramon washed and smoothed his long black hair with his hands. He stepped quietly downstairs. Breakfast was not ready, so he walked to the kitchen and talked with Anita.

To her, who understood him as no gringo could, he told of his quest. She knew nothing of the Señor Jim's whereabouts, save that he had come yesterday and talked with the señora. Anita admired the handsome young Mexican, whose face was so sad save when his quick smile lightened the shadow. And she told him to go back to the ranch and not become entangled in the affairs of the Americanos. It would be much better for him so.

Ramon listened patiently, but shook his head. The Señor Jim had been kind to him; had given him his life down in the Sonora desert. Was Ramon Ortego to forget that?

Mrs. Adams declined to take any money for Ramon's room. He worked for her husband, and it was at Ramon's own expense that he would make the journey in search for him. Instead she had Anita put up a lunch for Ramon.

He thanked her and rode away, taking the western trail across the morning desert.

Thirty miles beyond Stacey, he had news of Waring. A Mexican rancher had seen the gringo pass late in the evening. He rode a big buckskin horse. He was sure it must be the man Ramon sought. There was not another such horse in Arizona.

Ramon rode on next day, inquiring occasionally at a ranch or crossroad store. Once or twice he was told that such a horse and rider had passed many hours ago. At noon he rested and fed his pony. All that afternoon he rode west. Night found him in the village of Downey, where he made further inquiry, but without success.

Next morning he was on the road early, still riding west. No dream had come to guide him, yet the memory of the former dream was keen. If that dream were not true, all dreams were lies and prayer a useless ceremony.

For three days he rode, tracing the Señor Jim from town to town, but never catching up with him. Once he learned that Waring had slept in the same town, but had departed before daybreak. Ramon wondered why no dream had come to tell him of this.

That day he rode hard. There were few towns on his way. He reined in when he came to the fork where the southern highway branches from the Overland Road. The western road led on across the mountains past the great cañon. The other swept south through cattle land and into the rough hills beyond which lay Phoenix and the old Apache Trail. He hailed a buckboard coming down the southern road. The driver had seen nothing of a buckskin horse. Ramon hesitated, closing his eyes. Suddenly in the darkness glared a golden sun, and against it the tiny, black silhouette of a horseman. His dream could not lie.

Day by day the oval of his face grew narrower, until his cheek-bones showed prominently. His lips lost their youthful fullness. Only his eyes were the same; great, velvet-soft black eyes, gently questioning, veiled by no subtlety, and brighter for the deepening black circles beneath them.

The fifth day found him patiently riding west, despite the fact that all trace of Waring had been lost. Questioned, men shook their heads and watched him ride away, his lithe figure upright, but his head bowed as though some blind fate drew him on while his spirit drowsed in stagnant hopelessness.

To all his inquiries that day he received the same answer. Finally, in the high country, he turned and retraced his way.

A week after he had left Stacey he was again at the fork of the highway. The southern road ran, winding, toward a shallow valley. He took this road, peering ahead for a ranch, or habitation of any kind. That afternoon he stopped at a wayside store and bought crackers and canned meat. He questioned the storekeeper. Yes, the storekeeper had seen such a man pass on a big buckskin cayuse several days ago. Ramon thanked him and rode on. He camped just off the road that evening. In the morning he set out again, cheered by a new hope. His dream had not lied; only there should have been another dream to show him the way before he had come to the fork in the road.

That afternoon three men passed him, riding hard. They were in their shirt-sleeves and were heavily armed. Their evident haste caused Ramon to note their passing with some interest. Yet they had thundered past him so fast, and in such a cloud of dust, that he could not see them clearly.

Waring, gaunt as a wolf, unshaven, his hat rimmed with white dust, pulled up in front of the weathered saloon in the town of Criswell on the edge of the desert.

He dismounted and stepped round the hitching-rail. His face was lined and gray. His eyes were red-rimmed and heavy. As he strode toward the saloon door, he staggered and caught himself. Dex shuffled uneasily, knowing that something was wrong with his master.

Waring drew his hand across his eyes, and, entering the saloon, asked for whiskey. As in a dream, he saw men sitting in the back of the place. They leaned on their elbows and talked. He drank and called for more. The loafers in the saloon glanced at each other. Three men had just ridden through town and down into the desert, going over-light for such a journey. And here was the fourth. They glanced at Waring's boots, his belt, his strong shoulders, and his dusty sombrero. Whoever he was, he fitted his clothes. But a man "going in" was a fool to take more than one drink. The three men ahead had not stopped at the saloon. One of them had filled a canteen at the tank near the edge of the town. They had seemed in a great hurry for men of their kind.

Waring wiped his lips and turned. His eyes had grown bright. For an instant he glanced at the men, the brown walls spotted with "Police Gazette" pictures, the barred window at the rear of the room. He drew out his gun, spun the cylinder, and dropped it back into the holster.

The stranger, whoever he was, seemed to be handy with that kind of tool. Well, it was no affair of theirs. The desert had taken care of such affairs in the past, and there was plenty of room for more.

From the saloon doorway they saw Waring ride to the edge of town, dismount, and walk out in the desert in a wide circle. He returned to his horse, and, mounting, rode at right angles to the course the three riders had taken.

One of the men in the doorway spoke. "Thought so," he said with finality.

The others nodded. It was not their affair. The desert would take care of that.

About the middle of the afternoon, Waring rode down a sandy draw that deepened to an arroyo. Near the mouth of the arroyo, where it broke off abruptly to the desert level, he reined up. His horse stood with head lowered, his gaunt sides heaving. Waring patted him.

"Not much longer, old boy," he said affectionately.

With his last burst of strength, the big buckskin had circled the course taken by the three men, urged by Waring's spur and voice. They were heading in a direct line across the level just beyond the end of the arroyo where Waring was concealed. He could not see them, but as usual he watched Dex's ears. The horse would be aware of their nearness without seeing them. And Waring dared not risk the chance of discovery. They must have learned that he was following them, for they had ridden hard these past few days. Evidently they had been unwilling to chance a fight in any of the towns. And, in fact, Waring had once been ahead of them, knowing that they would make for the desert. But that night he had overslept, and they had passed him in the early hours of morning.

Slowly Dex raised his head and sniffed. Waring patted him, afraid that he would nicker. He had dismounted to tighten the cinches when he thought he heard voices in argument. He mounted again. The men must have ridden hard to have made such good time. Again he heard voices. The men were near the mouth of the arroyo. Waring tossed his hat to the ground and dropped his gauntlets beside his hat. Carefully he wiped his sweating hands on his bandanna. Dex threw up his head. His nostrils worked. Waring spoke to him.

A shadow touched the sand at the mouth of the arroyo. Waring leaned forward and drove in the spurs. The big buckskin leaped to a run as he rounded the shoulder of the arroyo.

The three horsemen, who had been riding close together, spread out on the instant. Waring threw a shot at the foremost figure even as High Chin's first shot tore away the front of his shirt. Waring fired again. Tony Brewster, on the ground, emptied his gun as Waring spurred over him. Turning in the saddle as he flashed past High Chin, Waring fired at close range at the other's belt buckle. Out on the levels, Andy Brewster's horse was running with tail tucked down. Waring threw his remaining shot at High Chin, and, spurring Dex, stood in his stirrups as he reloaded his gun.

The rider ahead was rocking in the saddle. He had been hit, although Waring could not recall having shot at him. Suddenly the horse went down, and Andy Brewster pitched to the sand. Waring laughed and reined round on the run, expecting each instant to feel the blunt shock of a bullet. High Chin was still sitting his horse, his gun held muzzle up. Evidently he was not hard hit, or, if he were, he was holding himself for a final shot at Waring. Behind him, almost beneath his horse, his brother Tony had raised himself on his elbow and was fumbling with his empty gun.

Waring rode slowly toward High Chin. High Chin's hand jerked down. Waring's wrist moved in answer. The two reports blended in a blunt, echoless roar. Waring felt a shock that numbed his thigh. High Chin sat stiffly in the saddle, his hand clasping the horn. He turned and gazed down at his brother.

"Thought you got him," said Tony Brewster from the ground. "Sit still and I'll get him from under your horse."

Waring knew now that High Chin was hit hard. The foreman had let his gun slip from his fingers. Waring saw a slight movement just beneath High Chin's horse. A shock lifted him from the saddle, and he dropped to the ground as Tony Brewster fired. But there was no such thing as quit just so long as Waring could see to shoot. Dragging himself to his gun, he shook the sand from its muzzle. He knew that he could not last long. Already flecks of fire danced before his eyes. He bit his lip as he raised himself and drew fine on that black figure beneath High Chin's horse. The gun jumped in his hand. Waring saw the black figure twitch and roll over. Then his sight grew clouded. He tried to brush away the blur that grew and spread. For an instant his eyes cleared. High Chin still sat upright in the saddle. Waring raised his gun and fired quickly. As his hand dropped to the sand, High Chin pitched headlong and lay still.

Then came a soft black veil that hid the glimmering sun and the wide desert reaches.

High Chin, his legs paralyzed by a slug that had torn through his abdomen and lodged in his spine, knew that he had made his last fight. He braced himself on his hands and called to his brother Tony. But his brother did not answer. High Chin's horse had strayed, and was grazing up the arroyo. The stricken man writhed round, feeling no pain, but conscious of a horrible numbness across his back and abdomen.

"When it hits my heart I'm done," he muttered. "Guess I'll go over and keep Tony company."

Inch by inch he dragged himself across the sand. Tony Brewster lay on his back. High Chin touched him; felt of the limp arm, and gazed curiously at the blue-edged hole in his brother's chest. With awful labor that brought a clammy moisture to his face, he managed to drag himself close to his brother and writhe round to a position where he could sit up, braced against the other's body. He gazed out across the desert. It had been a fast fight. Waring was done for. High Chin wondered how long he would last. The sun was near the horizon. It seemed only a few minutes ago that the sun had been directly overhead and he and his brothers had been cursing the heat. It was growing cold. He shivered. A long shadow reached out toward him from the bank of the arroyo. In a few minutes it would touch him. Then would come night and the stars. The numbness was creeping toward his chest. He could not breathe freely. He moved his arms. *They* were alive yet. He opened and closed his fingers, gazing at them curiously. It was a strange thing that a man should die like this; a little at a time, and not suffer much pain. The fading flame of his old recklessness flared up.

"I'm goin' across," he said. "But, by God, I'm takin' Jim Waring with me!"

He glanced toward the buckskin horse that stood so patiently beside that silent figure out there. Waring was done for. High Chin blinked. A long shaft of sunlight spread across the sand, and in the glow High Chin saw that the horse was moving toward him. He stared for a few seconds. Then he screamed horribly.

Waring, his hand gripping the stirrup, was dragging across the sand beside the horse that stepped sideways and carefully as Waring urged him on. Dex worked nearer to High Chin, but so slowly that High Chin thought it was some horrible phantasy sent to awaken fear in his dulled brain. But that dragging figure, white-faced and terrible—that was real! Within a few paces of High Chin, Dex stopped and turned his head to look down at Waring. And Waring, swaying up on his hands, laughed wildly.

"I came over—to tell you—that it was Pat's gun—" He collapsed and lay still.

High Chin sat staring dully at the gunman's uncovered head. The horse sniffed at Waring. High Chin's jaw sagged. He slumped down, and lay back across the body of his brother.

A pathway of lamplight floated out and across the main street of Criswell. A solitary figure lounged at the saloon bar. The sharp barking of a dog broke the desert silence. The lounger gazed at the path of lamplight which framed the bare hitching-rail. His companions of the afternoon had departed to their homes. Again the dog barked shrilly. The saloon-keeper moved to a chair and picked up a rumpled paper.

The lounger, leaning on his elbow, suddenly straightened. He pointed toward the doorway. The saloon-keeper saw the motion from the corner of his eye. He lowered his paper and rose. In the soft radiance a riderless horse stood at the hitching-rail, his big eyes glowing, his ears pricked forward. Across the horse's shoulder was a ragged tear, black against the tawny gold of his coat. The men glanced at each other. It was the horse of the fourth man; the man who had staggered in that afternoon, asked for whiskey, and who had left as buoyantly as though he went to meet a friend.

"They got him," said the saloon-keeper.

"They got him," echoed the other.

Together they moved to the doorway and peered out. The man who had first seen the horse stepped down and tied the reins to the rail. He ran his hand down the horse's shoulder over muscles that quivered as he examined the wound. He glanced at the saddle, the coiled rope, the slackened cinches, and pointed to a black stain on the stirrup leather.

"From the south," he said. "Maguey rope, and that saddle was made in Mexico."

"Mebby he wants water," suggested the saloon-keeper.

"He's had it. Reins are wet where he drug 'em in the tank."

"Wonder who them three fellas was?"

"Don' know. From up north, by their rig. I'm wonderin' who the fourth fella was—and where he is."

"Why, he's out there, stiff'nin' on the sand. They's been a fight. And, believe me, if the others was like him—she was a dandy!"

"I guess it's up to us to do somethin'," suggested the lounger.

"Not to-night, Bill. You don't ketch me ridin' into a flash in the dark before I got time to tell myself I'm a dam' fool. In the mornin', mebby—"

Their heads came up as they heard a horse pounding down the road. A lean pony, black with sweat, jumped to a trembling stop.

A young Mexican swung down and walked stiffly up to Dex.

"Where is Señor Jim?" he queried, breathing hard.

"Don' know, hombre. This his hoss?"

"Si! It is Dex."

'Well, the hoss came in, recent, draggin' the reins."

"Then you have seen him?"

"Seen who? Who are you, anyway?"

"Me, I am Ramon Ortego, of Sonora. The Señor Jim is my friend. I would find him."

"Well, if your friend sports a black Stetson and a dam' bad eye and performs with a short-barreled .45, he rode in this afternoon just about a hour behind three other fellas. They lit out into the dry spot. Reckon you'll find your friend out there, if the coyotes ain't got to him."

Ramon limped to the rail and untied Dex. Then he mounted his own horse.

"Dex," he said softly, riding alongside, "where is the Señor Jim?"

The big buckskin swung his head round and sniffed Ramon's hand. Then he plodded down the street toward the desert. At the tank Ramon let his horse drink. Dex, like a great dog, sniffed the back trail on which he had come, plodding through the night toward the spot where he knew his master to be.

Ramon, burdened with dread and weariness, rode with his hands clasped round the saddle-horn. The Señor Jim, his Señor Jim, had found those whom he sought. He had not come back. Ramon was glad that he had filled the canteen. If the man who had killed his Señor Jim had escaped, he would follow him even as he had followed Waring. And he would find him. "And then I shall kill him," said Ramon simply. "He does not know my face. As I speak to him the Señor Jim's name I shall kill him, and the Señor Jim will know then that I have been faithful."

The big buckskin plodded on across the sand, the empty stirrups swinging. Ramon's gaze lifted to the stars. He smiled wanly.

"I follow him. Wherever he has gone, I follow him, and he will not lose the way."

His bowed head, nodding to the pace of the pony, seemed to reiterate in grotesque assertion his spoken word. Ramon's tired body tingled as Dex strode faster. The horse nickered, and an answering nicker came from the night. His own tired pony struck into a trot. Dex stopped. Ramon slid down, and, stumbling forward, he touched a black bulk that lay on the sand.

Waring, despite his trim build, was a heavy man. Ramon was just able to lift him and lay him across the saddle. A coyote yipped from the brush of the arroyo. As Ramon started back toward town his horse shied at something near the arroyo's entrance. Ramon did not know that the bodies of Tony and Bob Brewster formed that low mound half-hidden by the darkness.

A yellow star, close to the eastern horizon, twinkled faintly and then disappeared. The saloon at Criswell had been closed for the night.

> Next morning the marshal of Criswell sent a messenger to the telegraph office at the junction. There was no railroad entering the Criswell Valley. The messenger bore three telegraph messages; one to Sheriff Hardy, one to Bud Shoop, and one to Mrs. Adams.

Ramon, outside Waring's room in the marshal's house, listened as the local doctor moved about. Presently he heard the doctor ask a question. Waring's voice answered faintly. Ramon stepped from the door and found his way to the stable. Dex, placidly munching alfalfa, turned his head as Ramon came in.

"The Señor Jim is not dead," he told the horse.

And, leaning against Dex, he wept softly, as women weep, with a happiness too great to bear. The big horse nuzzled his shoulder with his velvet-smooth nose, as though he would sympathize. Then he turned to munching alfalfa again in huge content. He had had a weary journey. And though his master had not come to feed him, here was the gentle, low-voiced Ramon, whom he knew as a friend.

Chapter XX
City Folks

Bud Shoop's new duties kept him exceedingly busy. As the days went by he found himself more and more tied to office detail. Fortunately Torrance had left a well-organized corps of rangers, each with his own special work mapped out, work that Shoop understood, with the exception of seeding and planting experiments, which Lundy, the expert, attended to as though the reserve were his own and his life depended upon successful results along his special line.

Shoop had long since given up trying to dictate letters. Instead he wrote what he wished to say on slips of paper which his clerk cast into conventional form. The genial Bud's written directions were brief and to the point.

Among the many letters received was one from a writer of Western stories, applying for a lease upon which to build a summer camp. His daughter's health was none too good, and he wanted to be in the mountains. Shoop studied the letter. He had a vague recollection of having heard of the writer. The request was legitimate. There was no reason for not granting it.

Shoop called in his stenographer. "Ever read any of that fella's books?"

"Who? Bronson? Yes. He writes bang-up Western stories."

"He does, eh? Well, you get hold of one of them stories. I want to read it. I've lived in the West a few minutes myself."

A week later Shoop had made his decision. He returned a shiny, new volume to the clerk.

"I never took to writin' folks reg'lar," he told the clerk. "Mebby I got the wrong idee of 'em. Now I reckon some of them is human, same as you and me. Why, do you know I been through lots of them things he writes about. And, by gollies, when I read that there gun-fight down in Texas, I ketched myself feelin' along my hip, like I was packin' a gun. And when I read about that cowboy's hoss,—the one with the sarko eye and the white legs,—why, I ketched myself feelin' for my ole bandanna to blow my nose. An' I seen dead hosses a-plenty. But you needn't to say nothin' about that in the letter.

Just tell him to mosey over and we'll talk it out. If a man what knows hosses and folks like he does wa'n't raised in the West, he ought to been. Heard anything from Adams?"

"He was in last week. He's up on Baldy. Packed some stuff up to the lookout."

"Uh-uh. Now, the land next to my shack on the Blue ain't a bad place for this here writer. I got the plat, and we can line out the five acres this fella wants from my corner post. But he's comin' in kind of late to build a camp."

"It will be good weather till December," said the clerk.

"Well, you write and tell him to come over. Seen anything of Hardy and his men lately?"

"Not since last Tuesday."

"Uh-uh. They're millin' around like a lot of burros—and gettin' nowhere. But Jim Waring's out after that bunch that got Pat. If I wasn't so hefty, I'd 'a' gone with him. I tell you the man that got Pat ain't goin' to live long to brag on it."

"They say it was the Brewster boys," ventured the stenographer.

"They say lots of things, son. But Jim Waring *knows*. God help the man that shot Pat when Jim Waring meets up with him. And I want to tell you somethin'. Be kind of careful about repeatin' what 'they say' to anybody. You got nothin' to back you up if somebody calls your hand. 'They' ain't goin' to see you through. And you named the Brewster boys. Now, just suppose one of the Brewster boys heard of it and come over askin' you what you meant? I bet you a new hat Jim Waring ain't said Brewster's name to a soul—and he *knows*. I'm goin' over to Stacey. Any mail the stage didn't get?"

"Letter for Mrs. Adams."

"Uh-uh. Lorry writes to his ma like he was her beau—reg'lar and plenty. Funny thing, you can't get a word out of him about wimmin-folk, neither. He ain't that kind of a colt. But I reckon when he sees the gal he wants he'll saddle up and ride out and take her." And Bud chuckled.

Bondsman rapped the floor with his tail. Bondsman never failed to express a sympathetic mood when his master chuckled.

"Now, look at that," said Shoop, grinning. "He knows I'm goin' over to Stacey. He heard me say it. And he says I got to take him along, 'cause he knows I ain't goin' on a hoss. That there dog bosses me around somethin' scandalous."

The stenographer smiled as Shoop waddled from the office with Bondsman at his heels. There was something humorous, almost pathetic, in the gaunt and grizzled Airedale's affection for his rotund master. And Shoop's broad back, with the shoulders stooped slightly and the set stride as he plodded here and there, often made the clerk smile. Yet there was nothing humorous about Shoop's face when he flashed to anger or studied some one who tried to mask a lie, or when he reprimanded his clerk for naming folk that it was hazardous to name.

The typewriter clicked; a fly buzzed on the screen door; a beam of sunlight flickered through the window. The letter ran:—

> Yours of the 4th inst. received and contents noted. In answer would state that Supervisor Shoop would be glad to have you call at your earliest convenience in regard to leasing a camp-site on the White Mountain Reserve.

Essentially a business letter of the correspondence-school type.

But the stenographer was not thinking of style. He was wondering what the girl would be like. There was to be a girl. The writer had said that he wished to build a camp to which he could bring his daughter, who was not strong. The clerk thought that a writer's daughter might be an interesting sort of person. Possibly she was like some of the heroines in the writer's stories. It would be interesting to meet her. He had written a poem once himself. It was about spring, and had been published in the local paper. He wondered if the writer's daughter liked poetry.

In the meantime, Lorry, with two pack-animals and Gray Leg, rode the hills and cañons, attending to the many duties of a ranger.

And as he caught his stride in the work he began to feel that he was his own man. Miles from headquarters, he was often called upon to make a quick decision that required instant and individual judgment. He made mistakes, but never failed to report such mistakes to Shoop. Lorry preferred to give his own version of an affair that he had mishandled rather than to have to explain some other version later. He was no epitome of perfection. He was inclined to be arbitrary when he knew he was in the right. Argument irritated him. He considered his "Yes" or "No" sufficient, without explanation.

He made Shoop's cabin his headquarters, and spent his spare time cording wood. He liked his occupation, and felt rather independent with the comfortable cabin, a good supply of food, a corral and pasture for the ponies, plenty of clear, cold water, and a hundred trails to ride each day from dawn to dark as he should choose. Once unfamiliar with the timber country, he grew to love the twinkling gold of the aspens, the twilight vistas of the spruce and pines, and the mighty sweep of the great purple tides of forest that rolled down from the ranges into a sheer of space that had no boundary save the sky.

He grew a trifle thinner in the high country. The desert tan of his cheeks and throat deepened to a ruddy bronze.

Aside from pride in his work, he took special pride in his equipment, keeping his bits and conchas polished and his leather gear oiled. Reluctantly he discarded his chaps. He found that they hindered him when working on foot. Only when he rode into Jason for supplies did he wear his chaps, a bit of cowboy vanity quite pardonable in his years.

If he ever thought of women at all, it was when he lounged and smoked by the evening fire in the cabin, sometimes recalling "that Eastern girl with the jim-dandy mother." He wondered if they ever thought of him, and he wished that they might know he was now a full-fledged ranger with man-size responsibilities. "And mebby they think I'm ridin' south yet," he would say to himself. "I must have looked like I didn't aim to pull up this side of Texas, from the way I lit out." But, then, women didn't understand such things.

Occasionally he confided something of the kind to the spluttering fire, laughing as he recalled the leg of lamb with which he had waved his hasty farewell.

"And I was scared, all right. But I wasn't so scared I forgot I'd get hungry." Which conclusion seemed to satisfy him.

When he learned that a writer had leased five acres next to Bud's cabin, he was skeptical as to how he would get along with "strangers." He liked elbow-room. Yet, on second thought, it would make no difference to him. He would not be at the cabin often nor long at a time. The evenings were lonely sometimes.

But when camped at the edge of the timber on some mountain meadow, with his ponies grazing in the starlit dusk, when the little, leaping flame of his night fire flung ruddy shadows that danced in giant mimicry in the cavernous arches of the pines; when the faint tinkle of the belled pack-horse rang a faëry cadence in the distance; then there was no such thing as loneliness in his big, outdoor world. Rather, he was content in a solid way. An inner glow of satisfaction because of work well done, a sense of well-being, founded upon perfect physical health and ease, kept him from feeling the need of companionship other than that of his horses. Sometimes he sat late into the night watching the pine gum ooze from a burning log and swell to golden bubbles that puffed into tiny flames and vanished in smoky whisperings. At such times a companion would not have been unwelcome, yet he was content to be alone.

Later, when Lorry heard that the writer was to bring his daughter into the high country, he expressed himself to Shoop's stenographer briefly: "Oh, hell!" Yet the expletive was not offensive, spoken gently and merely emphasizing Lorry's attitude toward things feminine.

While Lorry was away with the pack-horses and a week's riding ahead of him, the writer arrived in Jason, introduced himself and his daughter,—a rather slender girl of perhaps sixteen or eighteen,—and later, accompanied by the genial Bud, rode up to the Blue Mesa and inspected the proposed camp-site. As they rode, Bud discoursed upon the climate, ways of building a log cabin, wild turkeys, cattle, sheep, grazing, fuel, and water, and concluded his discourse with a dissertation upon dogs in general and Airedales in particular. The writer was fond of dogs and knew something about Airedales. This appealed to Shoop even more than had the writer's story of the West.

Arrived at the mesa, tentative lines were run and corners marked. The next day two Mormon youths from Jason started out with a load of lumber and hardware. The evening of the second day following they arrived at the homestead, pitched a tent, and set to work. That night they unloaded the lumber. Next morning they cleared a space for the cabin. By the end of August the camp was finished. The Mormon boys, to whom freighting over the rugged hills was more of a pastime than real work, brought in a few pieces of furniture—iron beds, a stove, cooking-utensils, and the hardware and provisions incidental to the maintenance of a home in the wilderness.

The writer and his daughter rode up from Jason with the final load of supplies. Excitement and fatigue had so overtaxed the girl's slender store of strength that she had to stay in bed for several days. Meanwhile, her father put things in order. The two saddle-horses, purchased under the critical eye of Bud Shoop, showed an inclination to stray back to Jason, so the writer turned them into Lorry's corral each evening, as his own lease was not entirely fenced.

Riding in from his long journey one night, Lorry passed close to the new cabin. It loomed strangely raw and white in the moonlight. He had forgotten that there was to be a camp near his. The surprise rather irritated him. Heretofore he had considered the Blue Mesa was his by a kind of natural right. He wondered how he would like the city folks. They had evidently made themselves at home. Their horses were in his corral.

As he unsaddled Gray Leg, a light flared up in the strange camp. The door opened, and a man came toward him.

"Good-evening," said the writer. "I hope my horses are not in your way."

"Sure not," said Lorry as he loosened a pack-rope.

He took off the packs and lugged them to the veranda. The tired horses rolled, shook themselves, and meandered toward the spring.

"I'm Bronson. My daughter is with me. We are up here for the summer."

"My name is Adams," said Lorry, shaking hands.

"The ranger up here. Yes. Well, I'm glad to meet you, Adams. My daughter and I get along wonderfully, but it will be rather nice to have a neighbor. I heard you ride by, and wanted to explain about my horses."

"That's all right, Mr. Bronson. Just help yourself."

"Thank you. Dorothy—my daughter—has been under the weather for a few days. She'll be up to-morrow, I think. She has been worrying about our using your corral. I told her you would not mind."

"Sure not. She's sick, did you say?"

"Well, over-tired. She is not very strong."

"Lungs?" queried Lorry, and immediately he could have kicked himself for saying it.

"I'm afraid so, Adams. I thought this high country might do her good."

"It's right high for some. Folks got to take it easy at first; 'specially wimmin-folk. I'm right sorry your girl ain't well."

"Thank you. I shouldn't have mentioned it. She is really curious to know how you live, what you do, and, in fact, what a real live ranger looks like. Mr. Shoop told her something about you while we were in Jason. They became great friends while the camp was building. She says she knows all about you, and tries to tease me by keeping it to herself."

"Bud—my boss—is some josher," was all that Lorry could think of to say at the time.

Bronson went back to his cabin. Lorry, entering his camp, lighted the lamp and built a fire. The camp looked cozy and cheerful after a week on the trail.

When he had eaten he sat down to write to his mother. He would tell her all about the new cabin and the city folks. But before he had written more than to express himself "that it was too darned bad a girl had to stay up in the woods without no other wimmin-folks around," he became drowsy. The letter remained unfinished. He would finish it to-morrow. He would smoke awhile and then go to bed.

A healthy young animal himself, he could not understand what sickness meant. And as for lungs—he had forgotten there were such things in a person's make-up. And sick folks couldn't eat "regular grub." It must be pretty tough not to be able to eat heartily. Now, there was that wild turkey he had shot near the Big Spring. He tiptoed to the door. The lights were out in the other cabin. It was closed season for turkey, but then a fellow needed a change from bacon and beans once in a while.

He had hidden the turkey in a gunny-sack which hung from a kitchen rafter. Should he leave it in the sack, hang it from a rafter of their veranda, out of reach of a chance bobcat or coyote, or—it would be much more of a real surprise to hang the big bird in front of their door in all his feathered glory. The sack would spoil the effect.

He took off his boots and walked cautiously to the other cabin. The first person to come out of that cabin next morning would actually bump into the turkey. It would be a good joke.

"And if he's the right kind of a hombre he won't talk about it," thought Lorry as he returned to his camp. "And if he ain't, I am out one fine bird, and I'll know to watch out for him."

Chapter XXI
A Slim Whip of a Girl

When Bronson opened his door to the thin sunlight and the crisp chill of the morning, he chuckled. He had made too many camps in the outlands to be surprised by an unexpected gift of game out of season. His neighbor was a ranger, and all rangers were incidentally game wardens. Bronson believed heartily in the conservation of game, and in this instance he did not intend to let that turkey spoil.

He called to his daughter.

Her brown eyes grew big. "Why, it's a turkey!"

Bronson laughed. "And to-day is Sunday. We'll have a housewarming and invite the ranger to dinner."

"Did he give it to you? Isn't it beautiful! What big wings—and the breast feathers are like little bronze flames! Do wild turkeys really fly?"

"Well, rather. It's a fine sight to see them run to a rim rock and float off across a cañon."

"Did you tell him about our horses? Is he nice? What did he say? But I could never imagine a turkey like that flying. I always think of turkeys as strutting around a farmyard with their heads held back and all puffed out in front. This one is heavy! I can't see how he could even begin to fly."

"They have to get a running start. Then they usually flop along and sail up into a tree. Once they are in a tree, they can float off into space easily. They seem to fly slowly, but they can disappear fast enough. The ranger seems to be a nice chap."

"Did he really give the turkey to us?"

"It was hanging right here when I came out. I can't say that he gave it to us. You see, it is closed season for turkey."

"But we must thank him."

"We will. Let's ask him to dinner. He seems to be a pleasant chap; quite natural. He said we were welcome to keep our horses in his corral. But if you want to have him for a real friendly neighbor, Dorothy, don't mention the word 'turkey.' We'll just roast it, make biscuits and gravy, and ask him to dinner. He will understand."

"Then I am going to keep the wings and tail to put on the wall of my room. How funny, not to thank a person for such a present."

"The supervisor would reprimand him for killing game out of season, if he heard about it."

"But just one turkey?"

"That isn't the idea. If it came to Mr. Shoop that one of his men was breaking the game laws, Mr. Shoop would have to take notice of it. Not that Shoop would care about one of his men killing a turkey to eat, but it would hurt the prestige of the Service. The natives would take advantage of it and help themselves to game."

"Of course, you know all about those matters. But can't I even say 'turkey' when I ask him to have some?"

"Oh," laughed Bronson, "call it chicken. He'll eat just as heartily."

"The ranger is up," said Dorothy. "I can hear him whistling."

"Then let's have breakfast and get this big fellow ready to roast. It will take some time."

An hour later, Lorry, fresh-faced and smiling, knocked on the lintel of their open doorway.

Bronson, in his shirt-sleeves and wearing a diminutive apron to which clung a fluff of turkey feathers, came from the kitchen.

"Good-morning. You'll excuse my daughter. She is busy."

"I just came over to ask how she was."

"Thank you. She is much better. We want you to have dinner with us."

"Thanks. But I got some beans going—"

"But this is chicken, man! And it is Sunday."

Lorry's gray eyes twinkled. "Chickens are right scarce up here. And chicken sure tastes better on Sunday. Was you goin' to turn your stock out with mine?"

"That's so!"

They turned Bronson's horses out, and watched them charge down the mesa toward the three animals grazing lazily in the morning sunshine.

"Your horses will stick with mine," said Lorry. "They won't stray now."

"Did I hear a piano this morning, or did I dream that I heard some one playing?"

"Oh, it was me, foolin' with Bud's piano in there. Bud's got an amazin' music-box. Ever see it?"

"No. I haven't been in your cabin."

"Well, come right along over. This was Bud's camp when he was homesteadin'. Ever see a piano like that?"

Bronson gazed at the carved and battered piano, stepping close to it to inspect the various brands. "It is rather amazing. I didn't know Mr. Shoop was fond of music."

"Well, he can't play reg'lar. But he sure likes to try. You ought to hear him and Bondsman workin' out that 'Annie Laurie' duet. First off, you feel like laughin'. But Bud gets so darned serious you kind of forget he ain't a professional. 'Annie Laurie' ain't no dance tune—and when Bud and the dog get at it, it is right mournful."

"I have seen a few queer things,"—and Bronson laughed,—"but this beats them all."

"You'd be steppin' square on Bud's soul if you was to josh him about that piano," said Lorry.

"I wouldn't. But thank you just the same. You have a neat place here, Adams."

"When you say 'neat' you say it all."

"I detest a fussy camp. One gets enough of that sort of thing in town Is that a Gallup saddle or a Frazier?"

"Frazier."

"I used a Heiser when I was in Mexico. They're all good."

"That's what I say. But there's a hundred cranks to every make of saddle and every rig. You said you were in Mexico?"

"Before I was married. As a young man I worked for some of the mines. I went there from college."

"I reckon you've rambled some." And a new interest lightened Lorry's eyes. Perhaps this man wasn't a "plumb tenderfoot," after all.

"Oh, not so much. I punched cattle down on the Hassayampa and in the Mogollons. Then I drifted up to Alaska. But I always came back to Arizona. New Mexico is mighty interesting, and so is Colorado.

California is really the most wonderful State of all, but somehow I can't keep away from Arizona."

"Shake! I never been out of Arizona, except when I was a kid, but she's the State for me."

A shadow flickered in the doorway. Lorry turned to gaze at a delicate slip of a girl, whose big brown eyes expressed both humor and trepidation.

"My daughter Dorothy, Mr. Adams. This is our neighbor, Dorothy."

"I'm right glad to meet you, miss."

And Lorry's strong fingers closed on her slender hand. To his robust sense of the physical she appealed as something exceedingly fragile and beautiful, with her delicate, clear coloring and her softly glowing eyes. What a little hand! And what a slender arm! And yet Lorry thought her arm pretty in its rounded slenderness. He smiled as he saw a turkey feather fluttering on her shoulder.

"Looks like that chicken was gettin' the best of you," he said, smiling.

"That's just it," she agreed, nothing abashed. "Father, you'll have to help."

"You'll excuse us, won't you? We'll finish our visit at dinner."

Lorry had reports to make out. He dragged a chair to the table. That man Bronson was all right. Let's see—the thirtieth—looked stockier in daylight. Had a good grip, too, and a clear, level eye. One mattock missing in the lookout cabin—and the girl; such a slender whip of a girl! Just like a young willow, but not a bit like an invalid. Buckley reports that his man will have the sheep across the reservation by the fourth of the month. Her father had said she was not over-strong. And her eyes! Lorry had seen little fawns with eyes like that—big, questioning eyes, startled rather than afraid.

"Reckon everything she sees up here is just amazin' her at every jump. I'll bet she's happy, even if she *has* got lungs. Now, a fella couldn't help but to like a girl like that. She would made a dandy sister, and a fella would just about do anything in the world for such a sister. And she wouldn't have to ask, at that. He would just naturally want to do things for her, because— well, because he couldn't help feeling that way. Funny how some wimmin made a man feel like he wanted to just about worship them, and not because they did anything except be just themselves. Now, there was that Mrs. Weston. She was a jim-dandy woman—but she was different. She always seemed to know just what she was going to say and do. And Mrs. Weston's girl, Alice. Reckon I'd scrap with her right frequent. She was still—"

Dog-gone it! Where was he drifting to? Sylvestre's sheep were five days crossing the reserve. Smith reported a small fire north of the lookout. The Ainslee boys put the fire out. It hadn't done any great damage.

Lorry sat back and chewed the lead pencil. As he gazed out of the window across the noon mesa a faint fragrance was wafted through the doorway. He sniffed and grinned. It was the warm flavor of wild turkey, a flavor that suggested crispness, with juicy white meat beneath. Lorry jumped up and grabbed a pail as he left the cabin. On his way back from the spring, Bronson waved to him. Lorry nodded. And presently he presented himself at Bronson's cabin, his face glowing, his flannel shirt neatly brushed, and a dark-blue silk bandanna knotted gracefully at his throat.

"This is the princess," said Bronson, gesturing toward his daughter "And here is the feast."

"And it was a piano," continued Bronson as they sat down.

"Really? 'Way up here?"

"My daughter plays a little," explained Bronson.

"Well, you're sure welcome to use that piano any time. If I'm gone, the door is unlocked just the same."

"Thank you, Mr. Adams, I only play to amuse myself now."

Lorry fancied there was a note of regret in her last word. He glanced at her. She was gazing wistfully out of the window. It hurt him to see that tinge of hopelessness on her young face.

"This here chicken is fine!" he asserted.

The girl's eyes were turned to him. She smiled and glanced roguishly at her father. Lorry laughed outright.

"What is the joke?" she demanded.

"Nothin'; only my plate is empty, Miss Bronson."

Bronson grabbed up carving-knife and fork. "Great Caesar! I must have been dreaming. I *was* dreaming. I was recalling a turkey hunt down in Virginia with Colonel Stillwell and his man Plato. Plato was a good caller— but we didn't get a turkey. Now, this is as tender as—as it ought to be. A little more gravy? And as we came home, the colonel, who was of the real mint-julep type, proposed as a joke that Plato see what he could do toward getting some kind of bird for dinner that night. And when Plato lifted the covers, sure enough there was a fine, fat roast chicken. The colonel, who lived in town and did not keep chickens, asked Plato how much he had paid for it. Plato almost dropped the cover. 'Mars' George,' he said with real solicitude in his voice,' is you sick?' And speaking of turkeys—"

"Who was speaking of turkeys?" asked Dorothy.

"Why, I think this chicken is superior to any domestic turkey I ever tasted," concluded Bronson.

"Was you ever in politics?" queried Lorry. And they all laughed heartily.

After dinner Lorry asked for an apron.

Dorothy shook her finger at him. "It's nice of you—but you don't mean it."

"Now, ma wouldn't 'a' said that, miss. She'd 'a' just tied one of her aprons on me and turned me loose on the dishes. I used to help her like that when I was a kid. Ma runs the hotel at Stacey."

"Why, didn't we stop there for dinner?" asked Dorothy.

"Yes, indeed. All right, Adams, I'll wash 'em and you can dry 'em, and Dorothy can rest."

"It's a right smilin' little apron," commented Lorry as Dorothy handed it to him.

"And you do look funny! My, I didn't know you were so big! I'll have to get a pin."

"I reckon it's the apron looks funny," said Lorry.

"I made it," she said, teasing him.

"Then that's why it is so pretty," said Lorry gravely.

Dorothy decided to change the subject. "I think you should let me wash the dishes, father."

"You cooked the dinner, Peter Pan."

"Then I'll go over and try the piano. May I?"

"If you'll play for us when we come over, Miss Bronson."

Bronson and Lorry sat on the veranda and smoked. Dorothy was playing a sprightly melody. She ceased to play, and presently the sweet old tune "Annie Laurie" came to them. Lorry, with cigarette poised in his fingers, hummed the words to himself. Bronson was watching him curiously. The melody came to an end. Lorry sighed.

"Sounds like that ole piano was just singin' its heart out all by itself," he said. "I wish Bud could hear that."

Almost immediately came the sprightly notes of "Anitra's Dance."

"And that's these here woods—and the water prancin' down the rocks, and a slim kind of a girl dancin' in the sunshine and then runnin' away to hide in the woods again." And Lorry laughed softly at his own conceit.

"Do you know the tune?" queried Bronson.

"Nope. I was just makin' that up."

"That's just Dorothy," said Bronson.

Lorry turned and gazed at him. And without knowing how it came about, Lorry understood that there had been another Dorothy who had played and sung and danced in the sunshine. And that this sprightly, slender girl was a bud of that vanished flower, a bud whose unfolding Bronson watched with such deep solicitude.

Chapter XXII
A Tune for Uncle Bud

Lorry had ridden to Jason, delivered his reports to the office, and received instructions to ride to the southern line of the reservation. He would be out many days. He had brought down a pack-horse, and he returned to camp late that night with provisions and some mail for the Bronsons.

The next day he delayed starting until Dorothy had appeared. Bronson told him frankly that he was sorry to see him go, especially for such a length of time.

"But I'm glad," said Dorothy.

Lorry stared at her. Her face was grave, but there was a twinkle of mischief in her eyes. She laughed.

"Because it will be such fun welcoming you home again."

"Oh, I thought it might be that piano—"

"Now I shan't touch it!" she pouted, making a deliberate face at him.

He laughed. She did such unexpected things, did them so unaffectedly Bronson put his arms about her shoulders.

"We're keeping Mr. Adams, Peter Pan. He is anxious to be off. He has been ready for quite a while and I think he has been waiting till you appeared so that he could say good-bye."

"Are you anxious to be off?" she queried.

"Yes, ma'am. It's twenty miles over the ridge to good grass and water."

"Why, twenty miles isn't so far!"

"They's considerable up and down in them twenty miles, Miss Bronson Now, it wouldn't be so far for a turkey. He could fly most of the way. But a horse is different, and I'm packin' a right fair jag of stuff."

"Well, good-bye, ranger man. Good-bye, Gray Leg,—and you two poor horses that have to carry the packs. Don't stay away all winter."

Lorry swung up and started the pack-horses. At the edge of the timber he turned and waved his hat. Dorothy and her father answered with a hearty Good-bye that echoed through the slumbering wood lands.

One of Bronson's horses raised his head and nickered. "Chinook is saying 'Adios,' too. Isn't the air good? And we're right on top of the world. There is Jason, and there is St. Johns, and 'way over there ought to be the railroad, but I can't see it."

Bronson smiled down at her.

She reached up and pinched his cheek. "Let's stay here forever, daddy."

"We'll see how my girl is by September. And next year, if you want to come back—"

"Come back! Why, I don't want to go away—ever!"

"But the snow, Peter Pan."

"I forgot that. We'd be frozen in tight, shouldn't we?"

"I'm afraid we should. Shall we look at the mail? Then I'll have to go to work."

"Mr. Adams thinks quite a lot of his horses, doesn't he?" she queried.

"He has to. He depends on them, and they depend on him. He has to take good care of them."

"I shouldn't like it a bit if I thought he took care of them just because he had to."

"Oh, Adams is all right, Peter. I have noticed one or two things about him."

"Well, I have noticed that he has a tremendous appetite," laughed Dorothy.

"And you're going to have, before we leave here, Peter Pan."

"Then you'd better hurry and get that story written. I want a new saddle and, oh, lots of things!"

Bronson patted her hand as she walked with him to the cabin. He sat down to his typewriter, and she came out with a book.

She glanced up occasionally to watch the ponies grazing on the mesa. She was deeply absorbed in her story when some one called to her. She jumped up, dropping her book.

Bud Shoop was sitting his horse a few paces away, smiling. He had ridden up quietly to surprise her.

"A right lovely mornin', Miss Bronson. I reckon your daddy is busy."

"Here I am," said Bronson, striding out and shaking hands with the supervisor. "Won't you come in?"

"About that lease," said Shoop, dismounting. "If you got time to talk business."

"Most certainly. Dorothy will excuse us."

"Is Adams gone?"

"He left this morning."

"Uh-uh. Here, Bondsman, quit botherin' the young lady."

"He isn't bothering. I know what he wants." And she ran to the kitchen.

Shoop's face grew grave. "I didn't want to scare the little lady, Bronson, but Lorry's father—Jim Waring—has been shot up bad over to Criswell. He went in after that Brewster outfit that killed Pat. I reckon he got 'em—but I ain't heard."

"Adams's father!"

"Yes, Jim Waring. Here comes the little missy. I'll tell you later. Now Bondsman is sure happy."

And Bud forced a smile as Dorothy gave the dog a pan of something that looked suspiciously like bones and shreds of turkey meat.

A little later Bud found excuse to call Bronson aside to show him a good place to fence-in the corral. Dorothy was playing with Bondsman.

"Jim's been shot up bad. I was goin' to tell you that Annie Adams, over to Stacey, is his wife. She left him when they was livin' down in Mexico. Lorry is their boy. Now, Jim is as straight as a ruler; I don't know just why she left him. But let that rest. I got a telegram from the marshal of Criswell. Reads like Jim was livin', but livin' mighty clost to the edge. Now, if I was to send word to Lorry he'd just nacherally buckle on a gun and go after them Brewster boys, if they's any of 'em left. He might listen to me if I could talk to him. Writin' is no good. And I ain't rigged up to follow him across the ridge. It's bad country over there. I reckon I better leave word with you. If he gets word of the shootin' while he's out there, he'll just up and cut across the hills to Criswell a-smokin'. But if he gets this far back he's like to come through Jason—and I can cool him down, mebby."

"He ought to know; if his father is—"

"That's just it. But I'm thinkin' of the boy. Jim Waring's lived a big chunk of his life. But they ain't no use of the kid gettin' shot up. It figures fifty that I ought to get word to him, and fifty that I ought to keep him out of trouble—"

"I didn't know he was that kind of a chap: that is, that he would go out after those men—"

"He's Jim Waring's boy," said Bud.

"It's too bad. I heard of that other killing."

"Yes. And I've a darned good mind to fly over to Criswell myself. I knowed Pat better than I did Jim. But I can't ride like I used to. But"—and the supervisor sighed heavily—"I reckon I'll go just the same."

"I'll give your message to Adams, Mr. Shoop."

"All right. And tell him I want to see him. How's the little lady these days?"

"She seems to be much stronger, and she is in love with the hills and cañons."

"I'm right glad of that. Kind of wish I was up here myself. Why, already they're houndin' me down there to go into politics. I guess they want to get me out of this job, 'cause I can't hear crooked money jingle. My hands feels sticky ever' time I think of politics. And even if a fella's hands ain't sticky— politics money is. Why, it's like to stick to his feet if he ain't right careful where he walks!"

"I wish you would stay to dinner, Mr. Shoop."

"So I'll set and talk my fool notions—and you with a writin' machine handy? Thanks, but I reckon I'll light a shuck for Jason. See my piano?"

"Yes, indeed. Dorothy was trying it a few nights ago."

"Then she can play. Missy," and he called to Dorothy, who was having an extravagant romp with Bondsman, "could you play a tune for your Uncle Bud?"

"Of course." And she came to them.

They walked to the cabin. Bondsman did not follow. He had had a hard play, and was willing to rest.

Dorothy drew up the piano stool and touched the keys. Bud sank into his big chair. Bronson stood in the doorway. By some happy chance Dorothy played Bud's beloved "Annie Laurie."

When she had finished, Bud blew his nose sonorously. "I know that tune," he said, gazing at Dorothy in a sort of huge wonderment. "But I never knowed all that you made it say."

He rose and shuffled to the doorway, stopping abruptly as he saw Bondsman. Could it be possible that Bondsman had not recognized his own tune? Bud shook his head. There was something wrong somewhere. Bondsman had not offered to come in and accompany the pianist. He must have been asleep. But Bondsman had not been asleep. He rose and padded to Shoop's horse, where he stood, a statue of rugged patience, waiting for Shoop to start back toward home.

"Now, look at that!" exclaimed Bud. "He's tellin' me if I want to get back to Jason in time to catch the stage to-morrow mornin' I got to hustle. That there dog bosses me around somethin' scandalous."

When Shoop had gone, Dorothy turned to her father. "Mr. Shoop didn't ask me to play very much. He seemed in a hurry."

"That's all right, Peter Pan. He liked your playing. But he has a very important matter to attend to."

"He's really just delicious, isn't he?"

"If you like that word, Peter. He is big and sincere and kind."

"Oh, so were some of the saints for that matter," said Dorothy, making a humorous mouth at her father.

Chapter XXIII
Like One Who Sleeps

Bondsman sat in the doorway of the supervisor's office, gazing dejectedly at the store across the street. He knew that his master had gone to St. Johns and would go to Stacey. He had been told all about that, and had followed Shoop to the automobile stage, where it stood, sand-scarred, muddy, and ragged as to tires, in front of the post-office. Bondsman had watched the driver rope the lean mail bags to the running-board, crank up the sturdy old road warrior of the desert, and step in beside the supervisor. There had been no other passengers. And while Shoop had told Bondsman that he would be away some little time, Bondsman would have known it without the telling. His master had worn a coat—a black coat—and a new black Stetson. Moreover, he had donned a white shirt and a narrow hint of a collar with a black "shoe-string" necktie. If Bondsman had lacked any further proof of his master's intention to journey far, the canvas telescope suitcase would have been conclusive evidence.

The dog sat in the doorway of the office, oblivious to the clerk's friendly assurances that his master would return poco tiempo. Bondsman was not deceived by this kindly attempt to soothe his loneliness.

Toward evening the up-stage buzzed into town. Bondsman trotted over to it, watched a rancher and his wife alight, sniffed at them incuriously, and trotted back to the office. That settled it. His master would be away indefinitely.

When the clerk locked up that evening, Bondsman had disappeared.

As Bronson stepped from his cabin the following morning he was startled to see the big Airedale leap from the veranda of Shoop's cabin and bound toward him. Then he understood. The camp had been Bondsman's home. The supervisor had gone to Criswell. Evidently the dog preferred the lonely freedom of the Blue Mesa to the monotonous confines of town.

Bronson called to his daughter. "We have a visitor this morning, Dorothy."

"Why, it's Bondsman! Where is Mr. Shoop?"

"Most natural question. Mr. Shoop had to leave Jason on business Bondsman couldn't go, so he trotted up here to pay us a visit."

"He's hungry. I know it. Come, Bondsman."

From that moment he attached himself to Dorothy, following her about that day and the next and the next. But when night came he invariably trotted over to Shoop's cabin and slept on the veranda. Dorothy wondered why he would not sleep at their camp.

"He's very friendly," she told her father. "He will play and chase sticks and growl, and pretend to bite when I tickle him, but he does it all with a kind of mental reservation. Yesterday, when we were having our regular frolic after breakfast, he stopped suddenly and stood looking out across the mesa, and it was only my pony, just coming from the edge of the woods. Bondsman tries to be polite, but he is really just passing the time while he is waiting for Mr. Shoop."

"You don't feel flattered, perhaps. But don't you admire him all the more for it?"

"I believe I do. Poor Bondsman! It's just like being a social pet, isn't it? Have to appear happy whether you are or not."

Bondsman knew that she proffered sympathy, and he licked her hand lazily, gazing up at her with bright, unreadable eyes.

Bud Shoop wasted no time in Stacey. He puffed into the hotel, indecision behind him and a definite object in view.

"No use talkin'," he said to Mrs. Adams. "We got to go and take care of Jim. I couldn't get word to Lorry. No tellin' where to locate him just now. Mebby it's just as well. They's a train west along about midnight. Now, you get somebody to stay here till we get back—"

"But, Mr. Shoop! I can't leave like this. I haven't a thing ready. Anita can't manage alone."

"Well, if that's all, I admire to say that I'll set right down and run this here hotel myself till you get back. But it ain't right, your travelin' down there alone. We used to be right good friends, Annie. Do you reckon I'd tell you to go see Jim if it wa'n't right? If he ever needed you, it's right now. If he's goin' to get well, your bein' there'll help him a pow'ful sight. And if he ain't, you ought to be there, anyhow."

"I know it, Bud. I wish Lorry was here."

"I don't. I'm mighty glad he's out there where he is. What do you think he'd do if he knowed Jim was shot up?"

"He would go to his father—"

"Uh-uh?"

"And—"

"Go ahead. You wa'n't born yesterday."

"He would listen to me," she concluded weakly.

"Yep. But only while you was talkin'. That boy is your boy all right, but he's got a lot of Jim Waring under his hide. And if you want to keep that there hide from gettin' shot full of holes by a no-account outlaw, you'll just pack up and come along."

Bud wiped his forehead, and puffed. This sort of thing was not exactly in his line.

"Here's the point, Annie," he continued. "If I get there afore Lorry, and you're there, he won't get into trouble. Mebby you could hold him with your hand on the bridle, but he's runnin' loose right where he is. Can't you get some lady in town to run the place?"

"I don't know. I'll see."

Bud heaved a sigh. It was noticeably warmer in Stacey than at Jason.

Bud's reasoning, while rough, had appealed to Mrs. Adams. She felt that she ought to go. She had only needed some such impetus to send her straight to Waring. The town marshal's telegram had stunned her. She knew that her husband had followed the Brewsters, but she had not anticipated the awful result of his quest. In former times he had always come back to her, taking up the routine of their home life quietly. But this time he had not come back. If only he had listened to her! And deep in her heart she felt that old jealousy for the lure which had so often called him from her to ride the grim trails of his profession. But this time he had not come back. She would go to him, and never leave him again.

Anita thought she knew of a woman who would take charge of the hotel during Mrs. Adams's absence. Without waiting for an assurance of this, Bud purchased tickets, sent a letter to his clerk, and spent half an hour in the barber shop.

"Somebody dead?" queried the barber as Bud settled himself in the chair.

"Not that I heard of. Why?"

"Oh, nothing, Mr. Shoop. I seen that you was dressed in black and had on a black tie—"

Later, as Bud surveyed himself in the glass, trying ineffectually to dodge the barber's persistent whisk-broom, he decided that he did look a bit funereal. And when he appeared at the supper table that evening he wore an ambitious four-in-hand tie of red and yellow. There was going to be no funeral or anything that looked like it, if he knew it.

Aboard the midnight train he made Mrs. Adams comfortable in the chair car. It was but a few hours' run to The Junction. He went to the smoker, took off his coat, and lit a cigar. Around him men sprawled in all sorts of awkward attitudes, sleeping or trying to sleep. He had heard nothing further about Waring's fight with the Brewsters. They might still be at large. But he doubted it. If they were—Shoop recalled the friendly shooting contest with High-Chin Bob. If High Chin were riding the country, doubtless he would be headed south. But if he should happen to cross Shoop's trail by accident—Bud shook his head. He would not look for trouble, but if it came his way it would bump into something solid.

Shoop had buckled on his gun before leaving Jason. His position as supervisor made him automatically a deputy sheriff. But had he been nothing more than a citizen homesteader, his aim would have been quite as sincere.

It was nearly daylight when they arrived at The Junction. Shoop accompanied Mrs. Adams to a hotel. After breakfast he went out to get a buck-board and team. Criswell was not on the line of the railroad.

They arrived in Criswell that evening, and were directed to the marshal's house, where Ramon met them.

"How's Jim?" was Shoop's immediate query.

"The Señor Jim is like one who sleeps," said Ramon.

Mrs. Adams grasped Shoop's arm.

"He wakens only when the doctor is come. He has spoken your name, señora."

The marshal's wife, a thin, worried-looking woman, apologized for the untidy condition of her home, the reason for which she wished to make obvious. She was of the type which Shoop designated to himself as "vinegar and salt."

"Reckon I better go in first, Annie?"

"No." And Mrs. Adams opened the door indicated by the other woman.

Shoop caught a glimpse of a white face. The door closed softly. Shoop turned to Ramon.

"Let's go take a smoke, eh?"

Ramon led the way down the street and on out toward the desert. At the edge of town, he paused and pointed across the spaces.

"It was out there, señor. I found him. The others were not found until the morning. I did not know that they were there."

"The others? How many?"

"Three. One will live, but he will never ride again. The others, High of the Chin and his brother, were buried by the marshal. None came to claim them."

"Were you in it?"

"No, señor. It was alone that Señor Jim fought them. He followed them out there alone. I come and I ask where he is gone. I find him that night. I do not know that he is alive."

"What became of his horse?"

"Dex he come back with no one on him. It is then that I tell Dex to find for me the Señor Jim."

"And he trailed back to where Jim went down, eh? Uh-uh! I got a dog myself."

"Will the Señor Jim ride again?" queried Ramon.

"I dunno, boy, I dunno. But if you and me and the doc and the señora—and mebby God—get busy, why, mebby he'll stand a chance. How many times was he hit?"

"Two times they shot him."

"Two, eh? Well, speakin' from experience, they was three mighty fast guns ag'in' him. Say five shots in each gun, which is fifteen. And he had to reload, most-like, for he can empty a gun quicker than you can think. Fifteen to five for a starter, and comin' at him from three ways to once. And he got the whole three of 'em! Do you know what that means, boy? But shucks! I'm forgettin' times has changed. How they been usin' you down here?"

"I am sleep in the hay by Dex."

"Uh-uh. Let that rest. Mebby it's a good thing, anyhow. Got any money?"

"No, señor. I have use all."

"Where d' you eat?"

"I have buy the can and the crackers at the store."

"Can and crackers, eh? Bet you ain't had a square meal for a week. But we'll fix that. Here, go 'long and buy some chuck till I get organized."

"Gracias, señor. But I can pray better when I do not eat so much."

"Good Lord! But, that's some idee! Well, if wishin' and hopin' and such is prayin', I reckon Jim'll pull through. I reckon it's up to the missus now."

"Lorry is not come?"

"Nope. Couldn't get to him. When does the mail go out of this bone-hill?"

"I do not know. To-morrow or perhaps the next day."

"Uh-uh. Well, you get somethin' to eat, and then throw a saddle on Dex and I'll give you a couple of letters to take to The Junction. And, come to think, you might as well keep right on fannin' it for Stacey and home. They can use you over to the ranch. The missus and me'll take care of Señor Jim."

"I take the letter," said Ramon, "but I am come back. I am with the Señor Jim where he goes."

"Oh, very well, amigo. Might as well give a duck a bar of soap and ask him to take a bath as to tell you to leave Jim. Such is wastin' talk."

Chapter XXIV
The Genial Bud

"And just as soon as he can be moved, his wife aims to take him over to Stacey."

So Bud told the Marshal of Criswell, who, for want of better accommodations, had his office in the rear of the general store.

The marshal, a gaunt individual with a watery blue eye and a soiled goatee, shook his head. "The law is the law," he stated sententiously.

"And a gun's a gun," said Shoop. "But what evidence you got that Jim Waring killed Bob Brewster and his brother Tony?"

"All I need, pardner. When I thought Andy Brewster was goin' to pass over, I took his antimortim. But he's livin'. And he is bound over to appear ag'in' Waring. What you say about the killin' over by Stacey ain't got nothin' to do with this here case. I got no orders to hold Andy Brewster, but I'm holdin' him for evidence. And I'm holdin' Waring for premeditated contempt and shootin' to death of said Bob Brewster and his brother Tony. And I got said gun what did it."

"So you pinched Jim's gun, eh? And when he couldn't lift a finger or say a word to stop you. Do you want to know what would happen if you was to try to get a holt of said gun if Jim Waring was on his two feet? Well, Jim Waring would pull said trigger, and Criswell would bury said city marshal."

"The law is the law. This town's payin' me to do my duty, and I'm goin' to do it."

"Speakin' in general, how much do you owe the town so far?"

"Look-a-here! You can't run no whizzer like that on me. I've heard tell of you, Mr. Shoop. No dinky little ole forest ranger can come cantelopin' round here tellin' me my business!"

"Mebby I'm dinky, and mebby, I'm old, but your eyesight wants fixin' if you callin' me little, old hoss. An' I ain't tryin' to tell you your business.

I'm tellin' you mine, which is that Jim Waring goes to Stacey just the first minute he can put his foot in a buck-board. And he's goin' peaceful. I got a gun on me that says so."

"The law is the law. I can run you in for packin' concealed weapons, Mr Shoop."

"Run me in!" chuckled Shoop. "Nope. You'd spile the door. But let me tell you. A supervisor is a deputy sheriff—and that goes anywhere they's a American flag. I don't see none here, but I reckon Criswell is in America. What's the use of your actin' like a goat just because you got chin whiskers? I'm tellin' you Jim Waring done a good job when he beefed them coyotes."

The marshal's pale-blue eyes blinked at the allusion to the goat. "Now, don't you get pussonel, neighbor. The law is the law, and they ain't no use you talkin'."

Bud's lips tightened. The marshal's reiterated reference to the law was becoming irksome. He would be decidedly impersonal henceforth.

"I seen a pair of walkin' overalls once, hitched to a two-bit shirt with a chewin'-tobacco tag on it. All that held that there fella together was his suspenders. I don't recollec' whether he just had goat whiskers or chewed tobacco, but somebody who had been liquorin' up told him he looked like the Emperor Maximilian. And you know what happened to Maxy."

"That's all right, neighbor. But mebby when I put in my bill for board of said prisoner and feed for his hoss and one Mexican, mebby you'll quit talkin' so much, 'less you got friends where you can borrow money."

"Your bill will be paid. Don't you worry about that. What I want to know is: Does Jim Waring leave town peaceful, or have I got to hang around here till he gets well enough to travel, and then show you? I got somethin' else to do besides set on a cracker barrel and swap lies with my friends."

"You can stay or you can go, but the law is the law—"

"And a goat is a goat. All right, hombre, I'll stay."

"As I was sayin'," continued the marshal, ignoring the deepening color of Shoop's face, "you can stay. You're too durned fat to move around safe, anyhow. You might bust."

Shoop smiled. He had stirred the musty marshal to a show of feeling. The marshal, who had keyed himself up to make the thrust, was disappointed. He made that mistake, common to his kind, of imagining that he could continue that sort of thing with impunity.

"You come prancin' into this town with a strange woman, sayin' that she is the wife of the defendant. Can you tell me how her name is Adams and his'n is Waring?"

"I can!" And with a motion so swift that the marshal had no time to help himself, Bud Shoop seized the other's goatee and yanked him from the cracker barrel. "I got a job for you," said Shoop, grinning until his teeth showed.

And without further argument on his part, he led the marshal through the store and up the street to his own house. The marshal back-paddled and struggled, but he had to follow his chin.

Mrs. Adams answered Bud's knock. Bud jerked the marshal to his knees.

"Apologize to this lady—quick!"

"Why, Mr. Shoop!"

"Yes, it's me, Annie. Talk up, you pizen lizard!"

"But, Bud, you're hurting him!"

"Well, I didn't aim to feed him ice-cream. Talk up, you Gila monster— and talk quick!"

"I apologize," mumbled the marshal.

Bud released him and wiped his hand on his trousers.

"Sticky!" he muttered.

The marshal shook his fist at Bud. "You're under arrest for disturbin' the peace. You're under arrest!"

"What does it mean?" queried Mrs. Adams.

"Nothin' what he ain't swallowed, Annie. Gosh 'mighty, but I wasted a lot of steam on that there walkin' clothes-rack! The blamed horn toad says he's holdin' Jim for shootin' the Brewsters."

"But he can't," said Mrs. Adams. "Wait a minute; I'll be right out. Sit down, Bud. You are tired out and nervous."

Bud sat down heavily. "Gosh! I never come so clost to pullin' a gun in my life. If he was a man, I reckon I'd 'a' done it. What makes me mad is that I let him get *me* mad."

When Mrs. Adams came out to the porch she had a vest in her hand. Inside the vest was pinned the little, round badge of a United States marshal.

Bud seized the vest, and without waiting to listen to her he plodded down the street and marched into the general store, where the town marshal was talking to a group of curious natives.

"Can you read?" said Bud, and without waiting for an answer shoved the little silver badge under the marshal's nose. "The law is the law," said Bud. "And that there vest belongs to Jim Waring."

Bud had regained his genial smile. He was too full of the happy discovery to remain silent.

"Gentlemen," he said, assuming a manner, "did your honorable peace officer here tell you what he said about the wife of the man who is layin' wounded and helpless in his own house? And did your honorable peace officer tell you-all that it is her money that is payin' for the board and doctorin' of Tony Brewster, likewise layin' wounded and helpless in your midst? And did your honorable peace officer tell you that Jim Waring is goin' to leave comfortable and peaceful just as soon as the A'mighty and the doc'll turn him loose? Well, I seen he was talkin' to you, and I figured he might 'a' been tellin' you these things, but I wa'n't sure. Was you-all thinkin' of stoppin' me? Such doin's! Why, when I was a kid I used to ride into towns like this frequent, turn 'em bottom side up, spank 'em, and send 'em bawlin' to their—to their city marshal, and I ain't dead yet. Now, I come peaceful and payin' my way, but if they's any one here got any objections to how I wear my vest or eat my pie, why, he can just oil up his objection, load her, and see that she pulls easy and shoots straight. I ain't no charity organization, but I'm handin' you some first-class life insurance free."

That afternoon Buck Hardy arrived, accompanied by a deputy. Andy Brewster again made deposition that without cause Waring had attacked and killed his brothers. Hardy had a long consultation with Shoop, and later notified Brewster that he was under arrest as an accomplice in the murder of Pat and for aiding the murderer to escape. While circumstantial evidence pointed directly toward the Brewsters, who had threatened openly from time to time to "get" Pat, there was valuable evidence missing in Waco, who, it was almost certain, had been an eye-witness of the tragedy. Waco had been traced to the town of Grant, at which place Hardy and his men had lost the trail. The demolished buckboard had been found by the roadside. Hardy had tracked the automobile to Grant.

Shoop suggested that Waco might have taken a freight out of town. Despite Hardy's argument that Waco had nothing to fear so far as the murder was concerned, Shoop realized that the tramp had been afraid to face the law and had left that part of the country.

Such men were born cowards, irresolute, weak, and treacherous even to their own infrequent moments of indecision. There was no question but that Waring had acted within the law in killing the Brewsters. Bob Brewster had fired at him at sight. But the fact that one of the brothers survived to testify against Waring opened up a question that would have to be answered in court. Shoop offered the opinion that possibly Andy Brewster, the youngest of the brothers, was not directly implicated in the murder, only taking sides with his brother Bob when he learned that he was a fugitive. In such a premise it was not unnatural that his bitterness toward Waring should take the angle that it did. And it would be difficult to prove that Andy Brewster was guilty of more than aiding his brother to escape.

The sheriff and Shoop talked the matter over, with the result that Hardy dispatched a telegram from The Junction to all the Southern cities to keep a sharp watch for Waco.

Next morning Shoop left for Jason with Hardy and his deputy.

Several days later Waring was taken to The Junction by Mrs. Adams and Ramon, where Ramon left them waiting for the east-bound. The Mexican rode the big buckskin. He had instructions to return to the ranch.

Late that evening, Waring was assisted from the train to the hotel at Stacey. He was given Lorry's old room. It would be many weeks before he would be strong enough to walk again.

For the first time in his life Waring relinquished the initiative. His wife planned for the future, and Waring only asserted himself when she took it for granted that the hotel would be his permanent home.

"There's the ranch, Annie," he told her. "I can't give that up."

"And you can't go back there till I let you," she asserted, smiling.

"I'll get Lorry to talk to you about that. I'm thinking of making him an offer of partnership. He may want to set up for himself some day. I married young."

"I'd like to see the girl that's good enough for my Lorry."

Waring smiled. "Or good enough to call you 'mother.'"

"Jim, you're trying to plague me."

"But you will some day. There's always some girl. And Lorry is a pretty live boy. He isn't going to ride a lone trail forever."

Mrs. Adams affected an indifference that she by no means felt.

"You're a lot better to-day, Jim."

"And that's all your fault, Annie."

She left the room, closing the door slowly. In her own room at the end of the hall, she glanced at herself in the glass. A rosy face and dark-brown eyes smiled back at her.

But there were many things to attend to downstairs. She had been away more than a week. And there was evidence of her absence in every room in the place.

Chapter XXV
The Little Fires

With the coming of winter the Blue Mesa reclaimed its primordial solitude. Mount Baldy's smooth, glittering roundness topped a world that swept down in long waves of dark blue frosted with silver; the serried minarets of spruce and pine bulked close and sprinkled with snow. Blanketed in white, the upland mesas lay like great, tideless lakes, silent and desolate from green-edged shore to shore. The shadowy caverns of the timberlands, touched here and there with a ray of sunlight, thrilled to the creeping fingers of the cold. Tough fibers of the stiff-ranked pines parted with a crackling groan, as though unable to bear silently the reiterant stabbing of the frost needles. The frozen gum of the black spruce glowed like frosted topaz. The naked whips of the quaking asp were brittle traceries against the hard blue of the sky.

Below the rounded shoulders of the peaks ran an incessant whispering as thin swirls of powdered snow spun down the wind and sifted through the moving branches below.

The tawny lynx and the mist-gray mountain lion hunted along snow-banked ranger trails. The blue grouse sat stiff and close to the tree-trunk, while gray squirrels with quaintly tufted ears peered curiously at sinuous forms that nosed from side to side of the hidden trail below.

The two cabins of the Blue Mesa, hooded in white, thrust their lean stovepipes skyward through two feet of snow. The corrals were shallow fortifications, banked breast-high. The silence seemed not the silence of slumber, but that of a tense waiting, as though the whole winter world yearned for the warmth of spring.

No creak of saddle or plod of hoof broke the bleak stillness, save when some wandering Apache hunted the wild turkey or the deer, knowing that winter had locked the trails to his ancient heritage; that the white man's law of boundaries was void until the snows were thin upon the highest peaks.

Thirty miles north of this white isolation the low country glowed in a sun that made golden the far buttes and sparkled on the clay-red waters of the Little Colorado. Four thousand feet below the hills cattle drifted across the open lands.

Across the ranges, to the south, the barren sands lay shimmering in a blur of summer heat waves; the winter desert, beautiful in its golden lights and purple, changing shadows. And in that Southern desert, where the old Apache Trail melts into the made roads of ranchland and town, Bronson toiled at his writing. And Dorothy, less slender, more sprightly, growing stronger in the clean, clear air and the sun, dreamed of her "ranger man" and the blue hills of her autumn wonderland. With the warmth of summer around her, the lizards on the rocks, and the chaparral still green, she could hardly realize that the Blue Mesa could be desolate, white, and cold. As yet she had not lived long enough in the desert to love it as she loved the wooded hills, where to her each tree was a companion and each whisper of the wind a song.

She often wondered what Lorry was doing, and whether Bondsman would come to visit her when they returned to their cabin on the mesa. She often recalled, with a kind of happy wonderment, Bondsman's singular visit and how he had left suddenly one morning, heedless of her coaxing. The big Airedale had appeared in Jason the day after Bud Shoop had returned from Criswell. That Bondsman should know, miles from the town, that his master had returned was a mystery to her. She had read of such happenings; her father had written of them. But to know them for the very truth! That was, indeed, the magic, and her mountains were towering citadels of the true Romance.

Long before Bronson ventured to return to his mountain camp, Lorry was riding the hill trails again as spring loosened the upland snows and filled the cañons and arroyos with a red turbulence of waters bearing driftwood and dead leaves. With a companion ranger he mended trail and rode along the telephone lines, searching for sagging wires; made notes of fresh down timber and the effect of the snow-fed torrents on the major trails.

Each day the air grew warmer. Tiny green shoots appeared in the rusty tangle of last season's mesa grasses. Imperceptibly the dull-hued mesas became fresh carpeted with green across which the wind bore a subtly soft fragrance of sun-warmed spruce and pine.

To Lorry the coming of the Bronsons was like the return of old friends. Although he had known them but a short summer season, isolation had brought them all close together. Their reunion was celebrated with an old-fashioned dinner of roast beef and potatoes, hot biscuit and honey, an apple pie that would have made a New England farmer dream of his ancestors, and the inevitable coffee of the high country.

And Dorothy had so much to tell him of the wonderful winter desert; the old Mexican who looked after their horses, and his wife who cooked for them. Of sunshine and sandstorms, the ruins of ancient pueblos in which they discovered fragments of pottery, arrowheads, beads, and trinkets, of the lean, bronzed cowboys of the South, of the cattle and sheep, until in her enthusiasm she forgot that Lorry had always known of these things. And Lorry, gravely attentive, listened without interrupting her until she asked why he was so silent.

"Because I'm right happy, miss, to see you lookin' so spry
and pretty I'm thinkin' Arizona has been kind of a heaven
for you."

"And you?" she queried, laughing.

"Well, it wasn't the heat that would make me call it what it was up here last winter. I rode up once while you was gone. Gray Leg could just make it to the cabin. It wasn't so bad in the timber. But comin' across the mesa the cinchas sure scraped snow."

"Right here on our mesa?"

"Right here, miss. From the edge of the timber over there to this side it was four feet deep on the level."

"And now," she said, gesturing toward the wavering grasses. "But why did you risk it?"

Lorry laughed. He had not considered it a risk. "You remember that book you lent me. Well, I left it in my cabin. There was one piece that kep' botherin' me. I couldn't recollect the last part about those 'Little Fires.' I was plumb worried tryin' to remember them verses. When I got it, I sure learned that piece from the jump to the finish."

"The 'Little Fires'? I'm glad you like it. I do.

"'From East to West they're burning in tower and forge
and home,
And on beyond the outlands, across the ocean foam;
On mountain crest and mesa, on land and sea and height,
The little fires along the trail that twinkle down the night.'

"And about the sheep-herder; do you remember how—

"'The Andalusian herder rolls a smoke and points the way,
As he murmurs, "Caliente," "San Clemente," "Santa Fé,"
Till the very names are music, waking memoried desires,

And we turn and foot it down the trail to find the little fires.
Adventuring! Adventuring! And, oh, the sights to see!
And little fires along the trail that wink at you and me.'"

"That's it! But I couldn't say it like that. But I know some of them little fires."

"We must make one some day. Won't it be fun!"

"It sure is when a fella ain't hustlin' to get grub. That poem sounds better after grub, at night, when the stars are shinin' and the horses grazin' and mebby the pack-horse bell jinglin' 'way off somewhere. Then one of them little fires is sure friendly."

"Have you been reading this winter?"

"Oh, some. Mostly forestry and about the war. Bud was tellin' me to read up on forestry. He's goin' to put me over west—and a bigger job this summer."

"You mean—to stay?"

"About as much as I stay anywhere."

Dorothy pouted. She had thought that the Blue Mesa and the timberlands were more beautiful than ever that spring, but to think that the neighboring cabin would be vacant all summer! No cheery whistling and no wood smoke curling from the chimney and no blithe voice talking to the ponies. No jolly "Good-mornin', miss, and the day is sure startin' out proud to see you." Well, Dorothy had considered Mr. Shoop a friend. She would have a very serious talk with Mr. Shoop when she saw him.

She had read of Waring's fight in the desert and of his slow recovery, and that Waring was Lorry's father; matters that she could not speak of to Lorry, but the knowledge of them lent a kind of romance to her ranger man. At times she studied Lorry, endeavoring to find in him some trace of his father's qualities. She had not met Waring, but she imagined much from what she had heard and read. And could Lorry, who had such kind gray eyes and such a pleasant face, deliberately go out and kill men as his father had done? Why should men kill each other? The world was so beautiful, and there was so much to live for.

Although the trail across the great forest terraces below was open clear up to the Blue Mesa, the trails on the northern side of the range were still impassable. The lookout man would not occupy his lonely cabin on Mount Baldy for several weeks to come, and Lorry's work kept him within a moderate radius of the home camp.

Several times Dorothy and her father rode with Lorry, spending the day searching for new vistas while he mended trail or repaired the telephone line that ran from Mount Baldy to the main office. Frequently they would have their evening meal in Bronson's camp, after which Lorry always asked them to his cabin, where Dorothy would play for them while they smoked contentedly in front of the log fire. To Dorothy it seemed that they had always lived in a cabin on the Blue Mesa and that Lorry had always been their neighbor, whom it was a joy to tease because he never showed impatience, and whose attitude toward her was that of a brother.

And without realizing it, Lorry grew to love the sprightly, slender Dorothy with a wholesome, boyish affection. When she was well, he was happy. When she became over-tired, and was obliged to stay in her room, he was miserable, blaming himself for suggesting some expedition that had been too much for her strength, so often buoyed above its natural level by enthusiasm. At such times he would blame himself roundly. And if there seemed no cause for her depression, he warred silently with the power that stooped to harm so frail a creature. His own physical freedom knew no such check. He could not quite understand sickness, save when it came through some obvious physical injury.

Bronson was glad that there was a Lorry; both as a companion to himself and as a tower of strength to Dorothy. Her depression vanished in the young ranger's presence. It was a case of the thoroughbred endeavoring to live up to the thoroughbred standard. And Bronson considered anything thoroughbred that was true to type. Yet the writer had known men physically inconsequent who possessed a fine strain of courage, loyalty, honor. The shell might be misshapen, malformed, and yet the spirit burn high and clear. And Bronson reasoned that there was a divinity of blood, despite the patents of democracy.

Bronson found that he had to go to Jason for supplies. Dorothy asked to go with him. Bronson hesitated. It was a long ride, although Dorothy had made it upon occasion. She teased prettily. Lorry was away. She wasn't afraid to stay alone, but she would be lonesome. If she kissed him three times, one right on top of the other, would he let her come? Bronson gave in to this argument. They would ride slowly, and stay a day longer in Jason to rest.

When they arrived at Jason, Dorothy immediately went to bed. She wanted to be at her best on the following day. She was going to talk with Mr. Shoop. It was a very serious matter.

And next morning she excused herself while her father bought supplies. She called at the supervisor's office. Bud Shoop beamed. She was so alert, so vivacious, and so charming in her quick slenderness. The genial Bud placed a chair for her with grandiloquent courtesy.

"I'm going to ask a terrible favor," she began, crossing her legs and clasping her knee.

"I'm pow'ful scared," said Bud.

"I don't want favors that way. I want you to like me, and then I will tell you."

"My goodness, missy! Like you! Who said I didn't?"

"No one. But you have ordered Lorry Adams to close up his camp and go over to work right near the Apache Reservation."

"I sure did."

"Well, Mr. Shoop, I don't like Apaches."

"You got comp'ny, missy. But what's that got to do with Lorry?"

"Oh, I suppose he doesn't care. But what do you think his *mother* would say to you if he—well, if he got *scalped*?"

A slow grin spread across Bud's broad face. Dorothy looked solemn disapproval. "I can't help it," he said as he shook all over. Two tears welled in the corner of his eyes and trickled down his cheeks. "I can't help it, missy. I ain't laughin' at you. But Lorry gettin' scalped! Why, here you been livin' up here, not five miles from the Apache line, and I ain't heard you tell of bein' scared of Injuns. And you ain't no bigger than a minute at that."

"That's just it! Suppose the Apaches did come over the line? What could we do if Lorry were gone?"

"Well, you might repo't their trespassin' to me. And I reckon your daddy might have somethin' to say to 'em. He's been around some."

"Oh, I suppose so. But there is a lot of work to do in Lorry's district, I noticed, coming down. The trails are in very bad condition."

"I know it. But he's worth more to the Service doin' bigger work. I got a young college man wished onto me that can mend trails."

"Will he live at Lorry's cabin?"

"No. He'll head in from here. I ain't givin' the use of my cabin and my piano to everybody."

Dorothy's eyes twinkled. "If Lorry were away some one might steal your piano."

"Now, see here, missy; you're joshin' your Uncle Bud. Do you know that you're tryin' to bribe a Gov'ment officer? That means a pow'ful big penalty if I was to repo't to Washington."

Dorothy wrinkled her nose. "I don't care if you do! You'd get what-for, too."

"Well, I'll tell you, missy. Let's ask Bondsman about this here hocus Are you willin' to stand by what he says?"

"Oh, that's not fair! He's *your* dog."

"But he's plumb square in his jedgments, missy. Now, I'll tell you. We'll call him in and say nothin'. Then you ask him if he thinks I ought to put Lorry Adams over west or leave him to my camp this summer. Now, if Bondsman wiggles that stub tail of his, it means, 'yes.' If he don't wiggle his tail, he says, 'no,'—huh?"

"Of course he'll wiggle his tail. He always does when I talk to him."

"Then suppose I do the talkin'?"

"Oh, you can make him do just as you wish. But all right, Mr. Shoop And you will really let Bondsman decide?"

"'Tain't accordin' to rules, but seein' it's you—"

Bud called to the big Airedale. Bondsman trotted in, nosed Dorothy's hand, and looked up at his master.

"Come 'ere!" commanded Shoop brusquely. "Stand right there! Now, quit tryin' to guess what's goin' on and listen to the boss. Accordin' to your jedgment, which is plumb solid, do I put Lorry to work over on the line this summer?"

Bondsman cocked his ears, blinked, and a slight quiver began at his shoulders, which would undoubtedly accentuate to the affirmative when it reached his tail.

"Rats!" cried Dorothy.

The Airedale grew rigid, and his spike of a tail cocked up straight and stiff.

Bud Shoop waved his hands helplessly. "I might 'a' knowed it! A lady can always get a man steppin' on his own foot when he tries to walk around a argument with her. You done bribed me and corrupted Bondsman. But I'm stayin' right by what I said."

Dorothy jumped up and took Bud's big hand in her slender ones. "You're just lovely to us!" And her brown eyes glowed softly.

Bud coughed. His shirt-collar seemed tight. He tugged at it, and coughed again.

"Missy," he said, leaning forward and patting her hand,—"missy, I would send Lorry plumb to—to—Phoenix and tell the Service to go find him, just to see them brown eyes of yours lookin' at me like that. But don't you say nothin' about this here committee meetin' to nobody. I reckon you played a trick on me for teasin' you. So you think Lorry is a right smart hombre, eh?"

"Oh," indifferently, "he's rather nice at times. He's company for father."

"Then I reckon you set a whole lot of store by your daddy. Now, I wonder if I was a young, bow-legged cow-puncher with kind of curly hair and lookin' fierce and noble, and they was a gal whose daddy was plumb lonesome for company, and I was to get notice from the boss that I was to vamose the diggin's and go to work,—now, I wonder who'd ride twenty miles of trail to talk up for me?"

"Why, I would!"

"You got everything off of me but my watch," laughed Bud. "I reckon you'll let me keep that?"

"Is it a good watch?" she asked, and her eyes sparkled with a great idea.

"Tol'able. Cost a dollar. I lost my old watch in Criswell. I reckon the city marshal got it when I wa'n't lookin'."

"Well, you may keep it—for a while yet. When are you coming up to visit us?"

"Just as soon as I can, missy. Here's your daddy. I want to talk to him a minute."

Three weeks later, when the wheels of the local stage were beginning to throw a fine dust, instead of mud, as they whirred from St. Johns to Jason, Bud Shoop received a tiny flat package addressed in an unfamiliar hand. He laid it aside until he had read the mail. Then he opened it. In a nest of cotton batting gleamed a plain gold watch. A thin watch, reflecting something aristocratic in its well-proportioned simplicity. As he examined it his genial face expressed a sort of childish wonderment. There was no card to show from where it had come. He opened the back of the case, and read a brief inscription.

"And the little lady would be sendin' this to me! And it's that slim and smooth; nothin' fancy, but a reg'lar thoroughbred, just like her."

He laid the watch carefully on his desk, and sat for a while gazing out of the window. It was the first time in his life that a woman had made him a present. Turning to replace the watch in the box, he saw something glitter in the cotton. He pulled out a layer of batting, and discovered a plain gold chain of strong, serviceable pattern.

That afternoon, as Bud came from luncheon at the hotel, a townsman accosted him in the street. During their chat the townsman commented upon the watch-chain. Bud drew the watch from his pocket and exhibited it proudly.

"Just a little present from a lady friend. And her name is inside the cover, along with mine."

"A lady friend, eh? Now, I thought it was politics mebby?"

"Nope. Strictly pussonel."

"Well, Bud, you want to watch out."

"If you're meanin' that for a joke," retorted Bud, "it's that kind of a joke what's foundered in its front laigs and can't do nothin' but walk around itself. I got the same almanac over to my office."

Chapter XXVI
Idle Noon

The occasional raw winds of spring softened to the warm calm of summer. The horses had shed their winter coats, and grew sleek and fat on the lush grasses of the mesa. The mesa stream cleared from a ropy red to a sparkling thread of silver banked with vivid green. If infrequent thunderstorms left a haze in the cañons, it soon vanished in the light air.

Bronson found it difficult to keep Dorothy from over-exerting herself. They arose at daybreak and went to bed at dusk, save when Lorry came for an after-dinner chat or when he prevailed upon Dorothy to play for them in his cabin. On such occasions she would entertain them with old melodies played softly as they smoked and listened, the lamp unlighted and the door wide open to the stars.

One evening, when Dorothy had ceased to play for them, Lorry mentioned that he was to leave on the following day for an indefinite time. There had been some trouble about a new outfit that was grazing cattle far to the south. Shoop had already sent word to the foreman, who had ignored the message. Lorry had been deputized to see the man and have an understanding with him. The complaint had been brought to Shoop by one of the Apache police that some cowboys had been grazing stock and killing game on the Indian reservation.

Dorothy realized that Lorry might be away for some time. She would miss him. And that night she asked her father if she might not invite a girl friend up for the summer. They were established. And Dorothy was much stronger and able to attend to the housekeeping. Bronson was quite willing. He realized that he was busy most of the time, writing. He was not much of a companion except at the table. So Dorothy wrote to her friend, who was in Los Angeles and had already planned to drive East when the roads became passable.

Lorry was roping the packs next morning when Dorothy appeared in her new silver-gray corduroy riding-habit—a surprise that she had kept for an occasion. She was proud of the well-tailored coat and breeches, the snug-fitting black boots, and the small, new Stetson. Her gray silk waist was brightened by a narrow four-in-hand of rich blue, and her tiny gauntlets of soft gray buckskin were stitched with blue silk.

She looked like some slender, young exquisite who had stepped from the stage of an old play as she stood smoothing the fingers of her gloves and smiling across at Lorry. He said nothing, but stared at her. She was disappointed. She wanted him to tell her that he liked her new things, she had spent so much time and thought on them. But there he stood, the pack-rope slack in his hand, staring stupidly.

She nodded, and waved her hand.

"It's me," she called. "Good-morning!"

Lorry managed to stammer a greeting. He felt as though she were some strange person that looked like Dorothy, but like a new Dorothy of such exquisite attitude and grace and so altogether charming that he could do nothing but wonder how the transformation had come about. He had always thought her pretty. But now she was more than that. She was alluring; she was the girl he loved from the brim of her gray Stetson to the toe of her tiny boot.

"Would you catch my pony for me?"

Lorry flushed. Of course she wanted Chinook. He swung up on Gray Leg and spurred across the mesa. His heart was pounding hard. He rode with a dash and a swing as he rounded up the ponies. As he caught up her horse he happened to think of his own faded shirt and overalls. He was wearing the essentially proper clothing for his work. For the first time he realized the potency of carefully chosen attire. As he rode back with the pastured pony trailing behind him, he felt peculiarly ashamed of himself for feeling ashamed of his clothing. Silently he saddled Chinook, accepted her thanks silently, and strode to his cabin. When he reappeared he was wearing a new shirt, his blue silk bandanna, and his silver-studded chaps. He would cache those chaps at his first camp out, and get them when he returned.

Bronson came to the doorway.

Dorothy put her finger to her lips. "Lorry is stunned, I think. Do I look as spiff as all that?"

"Like a slim young cavalier; very dashing and wonderful, Peter Pan."

"Not a bit like Dorothy?"

"Well, the least bit; but more like Peter Pan."

"I was getting tired of being just Dorothy. That was all very well when I wasn't able to ride and camp and do all sorts of adventures.

"And that isn't all," she continued. "I weigh twelve pounds more than I did last summer. Mr. Shoop weighed me on the store scales. I wanted to weigh him. He made an awful pun, but he wouldn't budge."

Bronson nodded. "I wouldn't ride farther than the Big Spring, Peter It's getting hot now."

"All right, daddy. I wish that horrid old story was finished. You never ride with me."

"You'll have some one to ride with you when Alice comes."

"Yes; but Alice is only a girl."

Bronson laughed, and she scolded him with her eyes. Just then Lorry appeared.

Bronson stooped and kissed her. "And don't ride too far," he cautioned.

Lorry drove the pack-animals toward Bronson's cabin. He dismounted to tighten the cinch on Chinook's saddle.

The little cavalcade moved out across the mesa. Dorothy rode behind the pack-animals, who knew their work too well to need a lead-rope. It was *her* adventure. At the Big Spring, she would graciously allow Lorry to take charge of the expedition.

Lorry, riding behind her, turned as they entered the forest, and waved farewell to Bronson.

To ride the high trails of the Arizona hills is in itself an unadulterated joy. To ride these wooded uplands, eight thousand feet above the world, with a sprightly Peter Pan clad in silver-gray corduroys and chatting happily, is an enchantment. In such companionship, when the morning sunlight dapples the dun forest carpet with pools of gold, when vista after vista unfolds beneath the high arches of the rusty-brown giants of the woodlands; when somewhere above there is the open sky and the marching sun, the twilight underworld of the green-roofed caverns is a magic land.

The ponies plodded slowly upward, to turn and plod up the next angle of the trail, without loitering and without haste. When Dorothy checked her pony to gaze at some new vista, the pack-animals rested, waiting for the word to go on again. Lorry, awakened to a new charm in Dorothy, rode in a silence that needed no interpreter.

At a bend in the trail, Dorothy reined up. "Oh, I just noticed! You are wearing your chaps this morning."

Lorry flushed, and turned to tie a saddle-string that was already quite secure.

Dorothy nodded to herself and spoke to the horses. They strained on up a steeper pitch, pausing occasionally to rest.

Lorry seemed to have regained his old manner. Her mention of the chaps had wakened him to everyday affairs. After all, she was only a girl; not yet eighteen, her father had said. "Just a kid," Lorry had thought; "but mighty pretty in those city clothes." He imagined that some women he had seen would look like heck in such a riding-coat and breeches. But Dorothy looked like a kind of stylish boy-girl, slim and yet not quite as slender as she had appeared in her ordinary clothes. Lorry could not help associating her appearance with a thoroughbred he had once seen; a dark-bay colt, satin smooth and as graceful as a flame. He had all but worshiped that horse. Even as he knew horses, through that colt he had seen perfection; his ideal of something beautiful beyond words.

From his pondering, Lorry arrived at a conclusion having nothing to do with ideals. He would buy a new suit of clothes the first time he went to Phoenix. It would be a trim suit of corduroy and a dark-green flannel shirt, like the suit and shirt worn by Lundy, the forestry expert.

At the base of a great gray shoulder of granite, the Big Spring spread in its natural rocky bowl which grew shallower toward the edges. Below the spring in the black mud softened by the overflow were the tracks of wild turkey and the occasional print of a lynx pad. The bush had been cleared from around the spring, and the ashes of an old camp-fire marked the spot where Lorry had often "bushed over-night" on his way to the cabin.

Lorry dismounted and tied the pack-horses. He explained that they were still a little too close to home to be trusted untied.

Dorothy decided that she was hungry, although they had been but two hours on the trail. Could they have a real camp-fire and make coffee?

"Yes, ma'am; right quick."

"Lorry, don't say 'yes, ma'am.' I—it's nice of you, but just say 'Dorothy.'"

"Yes, ma'am."

Dorothy's brown eyes twinkled.

Lorry gazed at her, wondering why she smiled.

"Yes, ma'am," she said stiffly, as though to a superior whom she feared.

Lorry grinned. She was always doing something sprightly, either making him laugh or laughing at him, talking to the horses, planning some little surprise for their occasional dinners in the Bronson cabin, quoting some fragment of poetry from an outland song,—she called these songs "outlandish," and had explained her delight in teasing her father with "outlandish" adjectives; whistling in answer to the birds, and amusing herself and her "men-folks" in a thousand ways as spontaneous as they were delightful.

With an armful of firewood, Lorry returned to the spring. The ponies nodded in the heat of noon. Dorothy, spreading their modest luncheon on a bright new Navajo blanket, seemed daintier than ever against the background of the forest. They made coffee and ate the sandwiches she had prepared. After luncheon Lorry smoked, leaning back against the granite rock, his hat off, and his legs crossed in lazy content.

"If it could only be like this forever," sighed Dorothy.

Lorry promptly shook his head. "We'd get hungry after a spell."

"Men are always hungry. And you've just eaten."

"But I could listen to a poem," he said, and he winked at a tree-trunk.

"It's really too warm even to speak of 'The Little Fires,' isn't it? Oh, I know! Do you remember the camp we made?"

"Where?"

"Oh, silly!"

"Well, I ain't had time to remember this one yet—and this is the first for us."

"Lorry, you're awfully practical."

"I got to be."

"And I don't believe you know a poem when you see one."

"I reckon you're right. But I can tell one when I hear it."

"Very well, then. Shut your eyes tight and listen:—

"'Do you remember the camp we made as we nooned on the mesa floor,
    Where the grass rolled down like a running sea in the wind—and the world our own?
You laughed as you sat in the cedar shade and said 't was the ocean shore
    Of an island lost in a wizardry of dreams, for ourselves alone.

"'Our ponies grazed in the idle noon, unsaddled, at ease, and slow;
    The ranges dim were a faëryland; blue hills in a haze of

gray.
Hands clasped on knee, you hummed a tune, a melody
light and low;
    And do you remember the venture planned in jest—for
your heart was gay?'"

Dorothy paused. "You may open your eyes. That's all."

"Well, it's noon," said Lorry, "and there are the ponies, and the hills are over there. Won't you say the rest of it?"

"Oh, the rest of it is about a venture planned that never came true. It couldn't, even in a poem. But I'll tell you about it some day."

"I could listen right now."

Dorothy shook her head. "I am afraid it would spoil our real adventure. But if I were a boy—wouldn't it be fun! We would ride and camp in the hills at night and find all the little fires along the trail—"

"We'd make our own," said Lorry.

"Of course, Mr. Practical Man."

"Well, I can't help bein' like I am. But sometimes I get lazy and sit and look at the hills and the cañons and mesas down below, and wonder what's the good of hustlin'. But somehow I got to quit loafin' after a spell—and go right to hustlin' again. It's a sure good way to get rested up; just to sit down and forget everything but the big world rollin' down to the edge of nothin'. It makes a fella's kickin' and complainin' look kind of small and ornery."

"I never heard you complain, Lorry."

"Huh! You ain't been along with me when I been right up against it and mebby had to sweat my way out of some darned box cañon or make a ride through some down timber at night. I've said some lovely things them times."

"Oh, I get cross. But, then, I'm a girl. Men shouldn't get cross."

"I reckon you're right. The sun's comin' through that pine there
Gettin' too hot?"

"No, I love it. But I must go. I'll just ride down to the cabin and unsaddle Chinook and say 'Hello' to father—and that's the end of our adventure."

"Won't those city folks be comin' in soon?"

"Yes. And Alice Weston is lovely. I know you'll like her."

"Alice who, did you say?"

"Weston. Alice and her mother are touring overland from Los Angeles. I know you will admire Alice."

"Mebby. If she's as pretty as you."

"Oh, fudge! You like my new suit. And Alice isn't like me at all. She is nearly as tall as you, and big and strong and really pretty. Bud Shoop told me I wasn't bigger than a minute."

"A minute is a whole lot sometimes," said Lorry.

"You're not so practical as you were, are you?"

"More. I meant that."

Dorothy rose and began to roll the Navajo blanket.

Lorry stepped up and took it from her. "Roll it long and let it hang down. Then it won't bother you gettin' on or off your horse. That's the way the Indians roll 'em."

He jerked the tie-strings tight. "Well, I reckon I'll be goin'," he said, holding out his hand.

"Good-bye, ranger man."

"Good-bye, Dorothy."

Her slender hand was warm in his. She looked up at him, smiling. He had never looked at her that way before. She hoped so much that he would say nothing to spoil the happiness of their idle noon.

"Lorry, we're great friends, aren't we?"

"You bet. And I'd do most anything to make you happy."

"But you don't have to do anything to make me happy. I *am* happy. Aren't you?"

"I aim to be. But what makes you ask?"

"Oh, you looked so solemn a minute ago. We'll be just friends always, won't we?"

"Just friends," he echoed, "always."

Her brown eyes grew big as he stooped and kissed her. She had not expected that he would do that.

"Oh, I thought you liked me!" she said, clasping her hands.

Lorry bit his lips, and the hot flush died from his face.

"But I didn't know that you cared—like that! I really don't mind because you kissed me good-bye—if it was just good-bye and nothing else." And she smiled a little timidly.

"I—I reckon I was wrong," he said, "for I was tryin' not to kiss you. If you say the word, I'll ride back with you and tell your father. I ain't ashamed of it—only if you say it was wrong."

Dorothy had recovered herself. A twinkle of fun danced in her eyes. "I can't scold you now. You're going away. But when you get back—" And she shook her finger at him and tried to look very grave, which made him smile.

"Then I'll keep right on ridin' south," he said.

"But you'd get lonesome and come back to your hills. I know! And it's awfully hot in the desert."

"Would you be wantin' me to come back?"

"Of course. Father would miss you."

"And that would make you unhappy—him bein' lonesome, so I reckon I'll come back."

"I shall be very busy entertaining my guests," she told him with a charming tilt of her chin. And she straightway swung to the saddle.

Lorry started the pack-horses up the hill and mounted Gray Leg. She sat watching him as he rode sideways gazing back at her.

As he turned to follow the pack-horses up the next ascent she called to him:—

"Perhaps I won't scold you when you come back."

He laughed, and flung up his arm in farewell. Dorothy reined Chinook round, and rode slowly down through the silent woodlands.

Her father came out and took her horse. She told him of their most wonderful camp at the Big Spring. Bronson smiled.

"And Lorry kissed me good-bye," she concluded. "Wasn't it silly of him?"

Bronson glanced at her quickly. "Do you really care for Lorry, Peter Pan?"

"Heaps! He's the nicest boy I ever met. Why shouldn't I?"

"There's no reason in the world why you shouldn't. But I thought you two were just friends."

"Why, that's what I said to Lorry. Don't look so mournful, daddy. You didn't think for a minute that I'd *marry* him, did you?"

"Of course not. What would I do without you?"

Chapter XXVII
Waco

The tramp Waco, drifting south through Prescott, fell in with a quartet of his kind camped along the railroad track. He stumbled down the embankment and "sat in" beside their night fire. He was hungry. He had no money, and he had tramped all that day. They were eating bread and canned peaches, and had coffee simmering in a pail. They asked no questions until he had eaten. Then the usual talk began.

The hobos cursed the country, its people, the railroad, work and the lack of it, the administration, and themselves. Waco did not agree with everything they said, but he wished to tramp with them until something better offered. So he fell in with their humor, but made the mistake of cursing the trainmen's union. A brakeman had kicked him off a freight car just outside of Prescott.

One of the hobos checked Waco sharply.

"We ain't here to listen to your cussin' any union," he said. "And seem' you're so mouthy, just show your card."

"Left it over to the White House," said Waco.

"That don't go. You got your three letters?"

"Sure! W.B.Y. Catch onto that?"

"No. And this ain't no josh."

"Why, W.B.Y. is for 'What's bitin' you?' Know the answer?"

"If you can't show your I.W.W., you can beat it," said the tramp.

"Tryin' to kid me?"

"Not so as your mother would notice. Got your card?"

Waco finally realized that they meant business. "No, I ain't got no I.W.W. card. I'm a bo, same as you fellas. What's bitin' you, anyway?"

"Let's give him the third, fellas."

Waco jumped to his feet and backed away. The leader of the group hesitated wisely, because Waco had a gun in his hand.

"So that's your game, eh? Collectin' internal revenue. Well, we're union men. You better sift along." And the leader sat down.

"I've a dam' good mind to sift you," said Waco, backing toward the embankment. "Got to have a card to travel with a lousy bunch like you, eh?"

He climbed to the top of the embankment, and, turning, ran down the track. Things were in a fine state when a guy couldn't roll in with a bunch of willies without showing a card. Workmen often tramped the country looking for work. But hobos forming a union and calling themselves workmen! Even Waco could not digest that.

But he had learned a lesson, and the next group that he overtook treading the cinders were more genial. One of them gave him some bread and cold meat. They tramped until nightfall. That evening Waco industriously "lifted" a chicken from a convenient hencoop. The hen was old and tough and most probably a grandmother of many years' setting, but she was a welcome contribution to their evening meal. While they ate Waco asked them if they belonged to the I.W.W. They did to a man. He had lost his card. Where could he get a renewal? From headquarters, of course. But he had been given his card up in Portland; he had cooked in a lumber camp. In that case he would have to see the "boss" at Phoenix.

There were three men in the party besides Waco. One of them claimed to be a carpenter, another an ex-railroad man, and the third an iron moulder. Waco, to keep up appearances, said that he was a cook; that he had lost his job in the Northern camps on account of trouble between the independent lumbermen and the I.W.W. It happened that there had been some trouble of that kind recently, so his word was taken at its face value.

In Phoenix, he was directed to the "headquarters," a disreputable lounging-room in an abandoned store on the outskirts of the town. There were papers and magazines scattered about; socialistic journals and many newspapers printed in German, Russian, and Italian. The place smelled of stale tobacco smoke and unwashed clothing. But the organization evidently had money. No one seemed to want for food, tobacco, or whiskey.

The "boss," a sharp-featured young man, aggressive and apparently educated, asked Waco some questions which the tramp answered lamely. The boss, eager for recruits of Waco's stamp, nevertheless demurred until Waco reiterated the statement that he could cook, was a good cook and had earned good money.

"I'll give you a renewal of your card. What was the number?" queried the boss.

"Thirteen," said Waco, grinning.

"Well, we may be able to use you. We want cooks at Sterling."

"All right. Nothin' doin' here, anyway."

The boss smiled to himself. He knew that Waco had never belonged to the I.W.W., but if the impending strike at the Sterling smelter became a reality a good cook would do much to hold the I.W.W. camp together. Any tool that could be used was not overlooked by the boss. He was paid to hire men for a purpose.

In groups of from ten to thirty the scattered aggregation made its way to Sterling and mingled with the workmen after hours. A sinister restlessness grew and spread insidiously among the smelter hands. Men laid off before pay-day and were seen drunk in the streets. Others appeared at the smelter in a like condition. They seemed to have money with which to pay for drinks and cigars. The heads of the different departments of the smelter became worried. Local papers began to make mention of an impending strike when no such word had as yet come to the smelter operators. Outside papers took it up. Surmises were many and various. Few of the papers dared charge the origin of the disturbances to the I.W.W. The law had not been infringed upon, yet lawlessness was everywhere, conniving in dark corners, boasting openly on the street, setting men's brains afire with whiskey, playing upon the ignorance of the foreign element, and defying the intelligence of Americans who strove to forfend the threatened calamity.

The straight union workmen were divided in sentiment. Some of them voted to work; others voted loudly to throw in with the I.W.W., and among these were many foreigners—Swedes, Hungarians, Germans, Poles, Italians; the usual and undesirable agglomeration to be found in a smelter town.

Left to themselves, they would have continued to work. They were in reality the cheaper tools of the trouble-makers. There were fewer and keener tools to be used, and these were selected and turned against their employers by that irresistible potency, gold; gold that came from no one knew where, and came in abundance. Finally open threats of a strike were made. Circulars were distributed throughout town over-night, cleverly misstating conditions. A grain of truth was dissolved in the slaver of anarchy into a hundred lies.

Waco, installed in the main I.W.W. camp just outside the town, cooked early and late, and received a good wage for his services. More men appeared, coming casually from nowhere and taking up their abode with the disturbers.

A week before the strike began, a committee from the union met with a committee of townsmen and representatives of the smelter interests. The argument was long and inconclusive. Aside from this, a special committee of townsmen, headed by the mayor, interviewed the I.W.W. leaders.

Arriving at no definite understanding, the citizens finally threatened to deport the trouble-makers in a body. The I.W.W. members laughed at them. Socialism, in which many of the better class of workmen believed sincerely, began to take on the red tinge of anarchy. A notable advocate of arbitration, a foreman in the smelter, was found one morning beaten into unconsciousness. And no union man had done this thing, for the foreman was popular with the union, to a man. The mayor received an anonymous letter threatening his life. A similar letter was received by the chief of police. And some few politicians who had won to prominence through questionable methods were threatened with exposure if they did not side with the strikers.

Conditions became deplorable. The papers dared not print everything they knew for fear of political enmity. And they were not able to print many things transpiring in that festering underworld for lack of definite knowledge, even had they dared.

Noon of an August day the strikers walked out. Mob rule threatened Sterling. Women dared no longer send their children to school or to the grocery stores for food. They hardly dared go themselves. A striker was shot by a companion in a saloon brawl. The killing was immediately charged to a corporation detective, and our noble press made much of the incident before it found out the truth.

Shortly after this a number of citizens representing the business backbone of the town met quietly and drafted a letter to a score of citizens whom they thought might be trusted. That was Saturday evening. On Sunday night there were nearly a hundred men in town who had been reached by the citizens' committee. They elected a sub-committee of twelve, with the sheriff as chairman. Driven to desperation by intolerable conditions, they decided to administer swift and conclusive justice themselves. To send for troops would be an admission that the town of Sterling could not handle her own community.

It became whispered among the I.W.W. that "The Hundred" had organized. Leaders of the strikers laughed at these rumors, telling the men that the day of the vigilante was past.

On the following Wednesday a rabid leader of the disturbers, not a union man, but a man who had never done a day's work in his life, mounted a table on a street corner and addressed the crowd which quickly swelled to a mob. Members of "The Hundred," sprinkled thinly throughout the mob, listened until the speaker had finished. Among other things, he had made a statement about the National Government which should have turned the mob to a tribunal of prompt justice and hanged him. But many of the men were drunk, and all were inflamed with the poison of the hour. When the man on the table continued to slander the Government, and finally named a name, there was silence. A few of the better class of workmen edged out of the crowd. The scattered members of "The Hundred" stayed on to the last word.

Next morning this speaker was found dead, hanging from a bridge a little way out of town. Not a few of the strikers were startled to a sense of broad justice in his death, and yet such a hanging was an outrage to any community. One sin did not blot out another. And the loyal "Hundred" realized too late that they had put a potent weapon in the hands of their enemies.

A secret meeting was called by "The Hundred." Wires were commandeered and messages sent to several towns in the northern part of the State to men known personally by members of "The Hundred" as fearless and loyal to American institutions. Already the mob had begun rioting, but, meeting with no resistance, it contented itself with insulting those whom they knew were not sympathizers. Stores were closed, and were straightway broken into and looted. Drunkenness and street fights were so common as to evoke no comment.

Two days later a small band of cowboys rode into town. They were followed throughout the day by other riders, singly and in small groups. It became noised about the I.W.W. camp that professional gunmen were being hired by the authorities; were coming in on horseback and on the trains. That night the roadbed of the railroad was dynamited on both sides of town. "The Hundred" immediately dispatched automobiles with armed guards to meet the trains.

Later, strangers were seen in town; quiet men who carried themselves coolly, said nothing, and paid no attention to catcalls and insults. It was rumored that troops had been sent for. Meanwhile, the town seethed with anarchy and drunkenness. But, as must ever be the case, anarchy was slowly weaving a rope with which to hang itself.

Up in the second story of the court-house a broad-shouldered, heavy-jawed man sat at a flat-topped desk with a clerk beside him. The clerk wrote names in a book. In front of the clerk was a cigar-box filled with numbered brass checks. The rows of chairs from the desk to the front windows were pretty well filled with men, lean, hard-muscled men of the ranges in the majority. The room was quiet save for an occasional word from the big man at the desk. The clerk drew a check from the cigar-box. A man stepped up to the desk, gave his name, age, occupation, and address, received the numbered check, and went to his seat. The clerk drew another check.

A fat, broad-shouldered man waddled up, smiling.

"Why, hello, Bud!" said the heavy-jawed man, rising and shaking hands. "I didn't expect to see you. Wired you thinking you might send one or two men from your county."

"I got 'em with me," said Bud.

"Number thirty-seven," said the clerk.

Bud stuffed the check in his vest pocket. He would receive ten dollars a day while in the employ of "The Hundred." He would be known and addressed while on duty as number thirty-seven. "The Hundred" were not advertising the names of their supporters for future use by the I.W.W.

Bud's name and address were entered in a notebook. He waddled back to his seat.

"Cow-punch," said someone behind him.

Bud turned and grinned. "You seen my laigs," he retorted.

"Number thirty-eight."

Lorry came forward and received his check.

"You're pretty young," said the man at the desk. Lorry flushed, but made no answer.

"Number thirty-nine."

The giant sheepman of the high country strode up, nodded, and took his check.

"Stacey County is well represented," said the man at the desk.

When the clerk had finished entering the names, there were forty-eight numbers in his book. The man at the desk rose.

"Men," he said grimly, "you know what you are here for. If you haven't got guns, you will be outfitted downstairs. Some folks think that this trouble is only local. It isn't. It is national. Providence seems to have passed the buck to us to stop it. We are here to prove that we can. Last night our flag— our country's flag—was torn from the halyards above this building and trampled in the dust of the street. Sit still and don't make a noise. We're not doing business that way. If there are any married men here, they had better take their horses and ride home. This community does not assume responsibility for any man's life. You are volunteers. There are four ex-Rangers among you. They will tell you what to do. But I'm going to tell you one thing first; don't shoot high or low when you have to shoot. Draw plumb center, and don't quit as long as you can feel to pull a trigger. For any man that isn't outfitted there's a rifle and fifty rounds of soft-nosed ammunition downstairs."

The heavy-shouldered man sat down and pulled the notebook toward him The men rose and filed quietly downstairs.

As they gathered in the street and gazed up at the naked halyards, a shot dropped one of them in his tracks. An eagle-faced cowman whipped out his gun. With the report came the tinkle of breaking glass from a window diagonally opposite. Feet clattered down the stairs of the building, and a woman ran into the street, screaming and calling out that a man had been murdered.

"Reckon I got him," said the cowman. "Boys, I guess she's started."

The men ran for their horses. As they mounted and assembled, the heavy-shouldered man appeared astride a big bay horse.

"We're going to clean house," he stated. "And we start right here."

Chapter XXVIII
A Squared Account

The housecleaning began at the building diagonally opposite the assembled posse. In a squalid room upstairs they found the man who had fired upon them. He was dead. Papers found upon him disclosed his identity as an I.W.W. leader. He had evidently rented the room across from the court-house that he might watch the movements of "The Hundred." A cheap, inaccurate revolver was found beside him. Possibly he had fired, thinking to momentarily disorganize the posse; that they would not know from where the shot had come until he had had time to make his escape and warn his fellows.

The posse moved from building to building. Each tenement, private rooming-house, and shack was entered and searched. Union men who chanced to be at home were warned that any man seen on the street that day was in danger of being killed. Several members of the I.W.W. were routed out in different parts of the town and taken to the jail.

Saloons were ordered to close. Saloon-keepers who argued their right to keep open were promptly arrested. An I.W.W. agitator, defying the posse, was handcuffed, loaded into a machine, and taken out of town. Groups of strikers gathered at the street corners and jeered the armed posse. One group, cornered in a side street, showed fight.

"We'll burn your dam' town!" cried a voice.

The sheriff swung from his horse and shouldered through the crowd. As he did so, a light-haired, weasel-faced youth, with a cigarette dangling from the corner of his loose mouth, backed away. The sheriff followed and pressed him against a building.

"I know you!" said the sheriff. "You never made or spent an honest dollar in this town. Boys," he continued, turning to the strikers, "are you proud of this skunk who wants to burn your town?"

A workman laughed.

"You said it!" asserted the sheriff. "When somebody tells you what he is, you laugh. Why don't you laugh at him when he's telling you of the buildings he has dynamited and how many deaths he is responsible for? Did he ever sweat alongside of any of you doing a day's work? Do you know him? Does he know anything about your work or conditions? Not a damned thing! Just think it over. And, boys, remember he is paid easy money to get you into trouble. Who pays him? Is there any decent American paying him to do that sort of thing? Stop and think about it."

The weasel-faced youth raised his arm and pointed at the sheriff. "Who pays you to shoot down women and kids?" he snarled.

"I'm taking orders from the Governor of this State."

"To hell with the Governor! And there's where he'll wake up one of these fine days."

"Because he's enforcing the law and trying to keep the flag from being insulted by whelps like you, eh?"

"We'll show you what's law! And we'll show you the right kind of a flag—"

"Boys, are you going to stand for this kind of talk?" And the sheriff's heavy face quivered with anger. "I'd admire to kill you!" he said, turning on the youth. "But that wouldn't do any good."

The agitator was taken to the jail. Later it was rumored that a machine had left the jail that night with three men in it. Two of them were armed guards. The third was a weasel-faced youth. He was never heard of again.

As the cavalcade moved on down the street, workmen gathered on street corners and in upper rooms and discussed the situation. The strike had got beyond their control. Many of them were for sending a delegation to the I.W.W. camp demanding that they disband and leave. Others were silent, and still others voted loudly to "fight to a finish."

Out beyond the edge of town lay the I.W.W. camp, a conglomeration of board shacks hastily erected, brush-covered hovels, and tents. Not counting the scattered members in town, there were at least two hundred of the malcontents loafing in camp. When the sheriff's posse appeared it was met by a deputation. But there was no parley.

"We'll give you till sundown to clear out," said the sheriff and, turning, he and his men rode back to the court-house.

That evening sentinels were posted at the street corners within hail of each other. In a vacant lot back of the court-house the horses of the posse were corralled under guard. The town was quiet. Occasionally a figure crossed the street; some shawl-hooded striker's wife or some workman heedless of the sheriff's warning.

Lorry happened to be posted on a corner of the court-house square. Across the street another sentinel paced back and forth, occasionally pausing to talk with Lorry.

This sentinel was halfway up the block when a figure appeared from the shadow between two buildings. The sentinel challenged.

"A friend," said the figure. "I was lookin' for young Adams."

"What do you want with him?"

"It's private. Know where I can find him?"

"He's across the street there. Who are you, anyway?"

"That's my business. He knows me."

"This guy wants to talk to you," called the sentinel.

Lorry stepped across the street. He stopped suddenly as he discovered the man to be Waco, the tramp.

"Is it all right?" asked the sentinel, addressing Lorry.

"I guess so. What do you want?"

"It's about Jim Waring," said Waco. "I seen you when the sheriff rode up to our camp. I seen by the papers that Jim Waring was your father. I wanted to tell you that it was High-Chin Bob what killed Pat. I was in the buckboard with Pat when he done it. The horses went crazy at the shootin' and ditched me. When I come to I was in Grant."

"Why didn't you stay and tell what you knew? Nobody would 'a' hurt you."

"I was takin' no chance of the third, and twenty years."

"What you doin' in this town?"

"Cookin' for the camp. But I can't hold that job long. My whole left side is goin' flooey. The boss give me hallelujah to-day for bein' slow. I'm sick of the job."

"Well, you ought to be. Suppose you come over to the sheriff and tell him what you know about the killin' of Pat."

"Nope; I was scared you would say that. I'm tellin' *you* because you done me a good turn onct. I guess that lets me out."

"Not if I make you sit in."

"You can make me sit in all right. But you can't make me talk. Show me a cop and I freeze. I ain't takin' no chances."

"You're takin' bigger chances right now."

"Bigger'n you know, kid. Listen! You and Jim Waring and Pat used me white. I'm sore at that I.W.W. bunch, but I dassent make a break. They'd get me. But listen! If the boys knowed I was tellin' you this they'd cut me in two. Two trucks just came into camp from up north. Them trucks was loaded to the guards. Every man in camp's got a automatic and fifty rounds. And they was settin' up a machine gun when I slipped through and beat it, lookin' for you. You better fan it out of this while you got the chanct."

"Did they send you over to push that bluff—or are you talkin' straight?"

"S' help me! It's the bleedin' truth!"

"Well, I'm thankin' you. But get goin' afore I change my mind."

"Would you shake with a bum?" queried Waco.

"Why—all right. You're tryin' to play square, I reckon. Wait a minute! Are you willin' to put in writin' that you seen High-Chin Bob kill Pat? I got a pencil and a envelope on me. Will you put it down right here, and me to call my friend and witness your name?"

"You tryin' to pinch me?"

"That ain't my style."

"All right. I'll put it down."

And in the flickering rays of the arc light Waco scribbled on the back of the envelope and signed his name. Lorry's companion read the scrawl and handed it back to Lorry. Waco humped his shoulders and shuffled away.

"Why didn't you nail him?" queried the other.

"I don't know. Mebby because he was trustin' me."

Shortly afterward Lorry and his companion were relieved from duty. Lorry immediately reported to the sheriff, who heard him without interrupting, dismissed him, and turned to the committee, who held night session discussing the situation.

"They've called our bluff," he said, twisting his cigar round in his lips.

A ballot was taken. The vote was eleven to one for immediate action. The ballot was secret, but the member who had voted against action rose and tendered his resignation.

"It would be plain murder if we were to shoot up their camp. It would place us on their level."

Just before daybreak a guard stationed two blocks west of the court-house noticed a flare of light in the windows of a building opposite. He glanced toward the east. The dim, ruddy glow in the windows was not that of dawn. He ran to the building and tried to open the door to the stairway. As he wrenched at the door a subdued soft roar swelled and grew louder. Turning, he ran to the next corner, calling to the guard. The alarm of fire was relayed to the court-house.

Meanwhile the two cowboys ran back to the building and hammered on the door. Some one in an upstairs room screamed. Suddenly the door gave inward. A woman carrying a cheap gilt clock pushed past them and sank in a heap on the sidewalk. The guards heard some one running down the street. One of them tied a handkerchief over his face and groped his way up the narrow stairs. The hall above was thick with smoke. A door sprang open, and a man carrying a baby and dragging a woman by the hand bumped into the guard, cursed, and stumbled toward the stairway.

The cowboy ran from door to door down the long, narrow hall, calling to the inmates. In one room he found a lamp burning on a dresser and two children asleep. He dragged them from bed and carried them to the stairway. From below came the surge and snap of flames. He held his breath and descended the stairs. A crowd of half-clothed workmen had gathered. Among them he saw several of the guards.

"Who belongs to these kids?" he cried.

A woman ran up. "She's here," she said, pointing to the woman with the gilt clock, who still lay on the sidewalk. A man was trying to revive her. The cowboy noticed that the unconscious woman still gripped the gilt clock.

He called to a guard. Together they dashed up the stairs and ran from room to room. Toward the back of the building they found a woman insanely gathering together a few cheap trinkets and stuffing them into a pillow-case. She was trying to work a gilt-framed lithograph into the pillow-case when they seized her and led her toward the stairway. She fought and cursed and begged them to let her go back and get her things. A burst of flame swept up the stairway. The cowboys turned and ran back along the hall. One of them kicked a window out. The other tied a sheet under the woman's arms and together they lowered her to the ground.

Suddenly the floor midway down the hall sank softly in a fountain of flame and sparks.

"Reckon we jump," said one of the cowboys.

Lowering himself from the rear window, he dropped. His companion followed. They limped to the front of the building. A crowd massed in the street, heedless of the danger that threatened as a section of roof curled like a piece of paper, writhed, and dropped to the sidewalk.

A group of guards appeared with a hose-reel. They coupled to a hydrant. A thin stream gurgled from the hose and subsided. The sheriff ran to the steps of a building and called to the crowd.

"Your friends," he cried, "have cut the water-main. There is no water."

The mass groaned and swayed back and forth.

From up the street came a cry—the call of a range rider. A score of cowboys tried to force the crowd back from the burning building.

"Look out for the front!" cried the guards. "She's coming!"

The crowd surged back. The front of that flaming shell quivered, curved, and crashed to the street.

The sheriff called to his men. An old Texas Ranger touched his arm "There's somethin' doin' up yonder, Cap."

"Keep the boys together," ordered the sheriff; "This fire was started to draw us out. Tell the boys to get their horses."

Dawn was breaking when the cowboys gathered in the vacant lot and mounted their horses. In the clear light they could see a mob in the distance; a mob that moved from the east toward the court-house. The sheriff dispatched a man to wire for troops, divided his force in halves, and, leading one contingent, he rode toward the oncoming mob. The other half of the posse, led by an old Ranger, swung round to a back street and halted.

The shadows of the buildings grew shorter. A cowboy on a restive pony asked what they were waiting for. Some one laughed.

The old Ranger turned in his saddle. "It's a right lovely mornin'," he remarked impersonally, tugging at his silver-gray mustache.

Suddenly the waiting riders stiffened in their saddles. A ripple of shots sounded, followed by the shrill cowboy yell. Still the old Ranger sat his horse, coolly surveying his men.

"Don't we get a look-in?" queried a cowboy.

"Poco tiempo," said the Ranger softly.

The sheriff bunched his men as he approached the invaders. Within fifty yards of their front he halted and held up his hand. Massed in a solid wall from curb to curb, the I.W.W. jeered and shouted as he tried to speak. A parley was impossible. The vagrants were most of them drunk.

The sheriff turned to the man nearest him.

"Tell the boys that we'll go through, turn, and ride back. Tell them not to fire a shot until we turn."

As he gathered his horse under him, the sheriff's arm dropped. The shrill "Yip! Yip!" of the range rose above the thunder of hoofs as twenty ponies jumped to a run. The living thunder-bolt tore through the mass. The staccato crack of guns sounded sharply above the deeper roar of the mob. The ragged pathway closed again as the riders swung round, bunched, and launched at the mass from the rear. Those who had turned to face the second charge were crowded back as the cowboys, with guns going, ate into the yelling crowd. The mob turned, and like a great, black wave swept down the street and into the court-house square.

The cowboys raced past, and reined in a block below the court-house. As they paused to reload, a riderless horse, badly wounded, plunged among them. A cowboy caught the horse and shot it. Another rider, gripping his shirt above his abdomen, writhed and groaned, begging piteously for some one to kill him. Before they could get him off his horse he spurred out, and, pulling his carbine from the scabbard, charged into the mob, in the square. With the lever going like lightning, he bored into the mob, fired his last shot in the face of a man that had caught his horse's bridle, and sank to the ground. Shattered and torn he lay, a red pulp that the mob trampled into the dust.

The upper windows of the court-house filled with figures. An irregular fire drove the cowboys to the shelter of a side street. In the wide doorway of the court-house several men crouched behind a blue-steel tripod. Those still in the square crowded past and into the building. Behind the stone pillars of the entrance, guarded by a machine gun, the crazy mob cheered drunkenly and defied the guards to dislodge them.

From a building opposite came a single shot, and the group round the machine gun lifted one of their fellows and carried him back into the building. Again came the peremptory snarl of a carbine, and another figure sank in the doorway. The machine gun was dragged back. Its muzzle still commanded the square, but its operators were now shielded by an angle of the entrance.

Back on the side street, the old ex-Ranger had difficulty in restraining his men. They knew by the number of shots fired that some of their companions had gone down.

The sheriff was about to call for volunteers to capture the machine gun when a white handkerchief fluttered from an upper window of the court-house. Almost immediately a man appeared on the court-house steps, alone and indicating by his gestures that he wished to parley with the guard. The sheriff dismounted and stepped forward.

One of his men checked him. "That's a trap, John. They want to get you, special. Don't you try it."

"It's up to me," said the sheriff, and shaking off the other's hand he strode across the square.

At the foot of the steps he met the man. The guard saw them converse for a brief minute; saw the sheriff shake his fist in the other's face and turn to walk back. As he turned, a shot from an upper window dropped him in his stride.

The cowboys yelled and charged across the square. The machine gun stuttered and sprayed a fury of slugs that cut down horses and riders. A cowboy, his horse shot from under him, sprang up the steps and dragged the machine gun into the open. A rain of slugs from the upper windows struck him down. His companions carried him back to cover. The machine gun stood in the square, no longer a menace, yet no one dared approach it from either side.

When the old Ranger, who had orders to hold his men in reserve, heard that the sheriff had been shot down under a flag of truce, he shook his head.

"Three men could 'a' stopped that gun as easy as twenty, and saved more hosses. Who wants to take a little pasear after that gun?"

Several of his men volunteered.

"I only need two," he said, smiling. "I call by guess. Number twenty-six, number thirty-eight, and number three."

The last was his own number.

In the wide hallway and massed on the court-house stairs the mob was calling out to recover the gun. Beyond control of their leaders, crazed with drink and killing, they surged forward, quarreling, and shoved from behind by those above.

"We're ridin'," said the old Ranger.

With a man on each side of him he charged across the square.

Waco, peering from behind a stone column in the entrance, saw that Lorry was one of the riders. Lorry's lips were drawn tight. His face was pale, but his gun arm swung up and down with the regularity of a machine as he threw shot after shot into the black tide that welled from the court-house doorway. A man near Waco pulled an automatic and leveled it. Waco swung his arm and brained the man with an empty whiskey bottle. He threw the bottle at another of his fellows, and, stumbling down the steps, called to Lorry. The three riders paused for an instant as Waco ran forward.

The riders had won almost to the gun when Waco stooped and jerked it round and poured a withering volley into the close-packed doorway.

Back in the side street the leader of the cowboys addressed his men.

"We'll leave the horses here," he said. "Tex went after that gun, and I reckon he's got it. We'll clean up afoot."

But the I.W.W. had had enough. Their leaders had told them that with the machine gun they could clean up the town, capture the court-house, and make their own terms. They had captured the court-house, but they were themselves trapped. One of their own number had planned that treachery. And they knew that those lean, bronzed men out there would shoot them down from room to room as mercilessly as they would kill coyotes.

They surrendered, shuffling out and down the slippery stone steps. Each man dropped his gun in the little pile that grew and grew until the old Ranger shook his head, pondering. That men of this kind should have access to arms and ammunition of the latest military type—and a machine gun. What was behind it all? He tried to reason it out in his old-fashioned way even as the trembling horde filed past, cordoned by grim, silent cowboys.

The vagrants were escorted out of town in a body. Fearful of the hate of the guard, of treachery among themselves and of the townsfolk in other places, they tramped across the hills, followed closely by the stern-visaged riders. Several miles north of Sterling they disbanded.

When a company of infantrymen arrived in Sterling they found several cowboys sluicing down the court-house steps with water hauled laboriously from the river.

The captain stated that he would take charge of things, and suggested that the cowboys take a rest.

"That's all right, Cap," said a puncher, pointing toward the naked flagstaff. "But we-all would admire to see the Stars and Stripes floatin' up there afore we drift."

"I'll have the flag run up," said the captain.

"That's all right, Cap. But you don't sabe the idee. These here steps got to be *clean* afore that flag goes up."

"And they's some good in bein' fat," said Bud Shoop as he met Lorry next morning. "The army doc just put a plaster on my arm where one of them automatic pills nicked me. Now, if I'd been lean like you—"

"Did you see Waco?" queried Lorry.

"Waco? What's ailin' you, son?"

"Nothin'. It was Waco went down, workin' that machine gun against his own crowd. I didn't sabe that at first."

"Him? Didn't know he was in town."

"I didn't, either, till last night. He sneaked in to tell me about the killin' of Pat. Next I seen him was when he brained a fella that was shootin' at me. Then somehow he got to the gun—and you know the rest."

"Looks like he was crazy," suggested Shoop.

"I don' know about that. I got to him before he cashed in. He pawed around like he couldn't see. I asked what I could do. He kind of braced up then. 'That you, kid?' he says. 'They didn't get you?' I told him no. 'Then I reckon we're square,' he says. I thought he was gone, but he reached out his hand. Seems he couldn't see. 'Would you mind shakin' hands with a bum?' he says. I did. And then he let go my hand. He was done."

"H'm! And him! But you can't always tell. Sometimes it takes a bullet placed just right, and sometimes religion, and sometimes a woman to make a man show what's in him. I reckon Waco done you a good turn that journey. But ain't it hard luck when a fella waits till he's got to cross over afore he shows white?"

"He must 'a' had a hunch he was goin' to get his," said Lorry. "Or he wouldn't chanced sneakin' into town last night. When do we go north?"

"To-morrow. The doc says the sheriff will pull through. He sure ought to get the benefit of the big doubt. There's a man that God A'mighty took some trouble in makin'."

"Well, I'm mighty glad it's over. I don't want any more like this. I come through all right, but this ain't fightin'; it's plumb killin' and murder."

"And both sides thinks so," said Bud. "And lemme tell you; you can read your eyes out about peace and equality and fraternity, but they's goin' to be killin' in this here world just as long as they's fools willin' to listen to other fools talk. And they's always goin' to be some fools."

"You ain't strong on socialism, eh, Bud?"

"Socialism? You mean when all men is born fools and equal? Not this mawnin', son. I got all I can do figurin' out my own trail."

Chapter XXIX
Bud's Conscience

Those riders who had come from the northern part of the State to Sterling were given transportation for themselves and their horses to The Junction. From there they rode to their respective homes. Among them were Bud Shoop, the giant sheepman, and Lorry, who seemed more anxious than did Shoop to stop at Stacey on their way to the reserve.

"Your maw don't know you been to Sterling," Shoop said as they rode toward Stacey.

"But she won't care, now we're back again. She'll find out some time."

"I'm willin' to wait," said Bud. "I got you into that hocus. But I had no more idee than a cat that we'd bump into what we did. They was a time when a outfit like ours could 'a' kep' peace in a town by just bein' there. Things are changin'—fast. If the Gov'ment don't do somethin' about allowin' the scum of this country to get hold of guns and ca'tridges wholesale, they's goin' to be a whole lot of extra book-keepin' for the recordin' angel. I tell you what, son, allowin' that I seen enough killin' in my time so as just seein' it don't set too hard on my chest, that mess down to Sterling made me plumb sick to my stummick. I'm wonderin' what would 'a' happened if Sterling hadn't made that fight and the I.W.W. had run loose. It ain't what we did. That had to be did. But it's the idee that decent folks, livin' under the American flag, has got to shoot their way back to the law, like we done."

"Mebby the law ain't right," suggested Lorry.

"Don't you get that idee, son. The law is all right. Mebby it ain't handled right sometimes."

"But what can anybody do about it?"

"Trouble is that folks who want to do the right thing ain't always got the say. Or mebby if they have got the say they leave it to the other fella.

"What did the folks in Arizona do long back in eighty, when the sheep disease got bad. First off they doctored up the sick sheep, tryin' to save 'em. That didn't work, so they took to killin' 'em to save the good sheep. But the disease had got into the blood of some of the good sheep. Then some of the big sheepmen got busy. Arizona made a law that no stock was to be shipped into any of her territory without bein' inspected. That helped some. But inspectors is human, and some sick sheep got by.

"Then one day a fella that had some brains got up in the State House and spoke for the shuttin' out of all stock until the disease was stomped out. You see, that disease didn't start in this here country. But who downed that fella? Why, the sheepmen themselves. It would hurt their business. And the funny part of it is them sheepmen was willin' enough to ship sick sheep anywhere they could sell 'em. But some States was wise. California, she put a inspection tax of twenty-five dollars on every carload of stock enterin' her State—or on one animal; didn't make no difference. That inspection tax had to be paid by the shipper of the stock, as I said, whether he shipped one head or a hundred. And the stock had to be inspected before loadin'."

"You mean immigrants?" queried Lorry.

"The same. The gate is open too wide. If I had the handlin' of them gates I would shut 'em for ten years and kind of let what we got settle down and get acquainted. But the man hirin' cheap labor wouldn't. He'll take anything that will work cheap, and the country pays the difference, like we done down to Sterling."

"You mean there can't be cheap labor?"

"The same. Somebody's got to pay."

"Well, Sterling paid," said Lorry, "if a man's life is worth anything."

"Yes, she paid. And the worst part of the whole business is that the men what paid didn't owe anything to the smelter or to them others. They just made a present of their lives to this here country. And the country ain't goin' to even say 'thanks.'"

"You're pretty sore about it, aren't you, Bud?"

"I be. And if you had my years you'd be likewise. But what's worryin' me right now is I'm wonderin' what your maw'll say to me when she finds out."

"You can say we been south on business."

"Yes," grunted Bud, "and I got the receipt right here on my left wing."

"Hurtin' you much?"

"Just enough to let me know I'm livin' and ain't ridin' through hell shootin' down a lot of pore, drunk fools that's tryin' to run the oven. And them kind would kick if they was ridin' in hell on a free pass and their hotel bills paid. But over there is the hills, and we can thank God A'mighty for the high trails and the open country. I ain't got the smell of that town out of my nose yet."

When they arrived at Stacey, Lorry learned that his father had recently gone to the ranch. After supper that evening, Mrs. Adams mentioned the strike. The papers printed columns of the awful details; outrages and killings beyond the thought of possibility. And Mrs. Adams spoke of the curious circumstance that the men who put down the lawlessness were unnamed; that all that could be learned of them was that there were ranchers and cowmen who were known by number alone.

"And I'm glad that you didn't go riding off down there," she said to Lorry. "The paper says men from all over the State volunteered."

"So am I," said Shoop promptly. "I was readin' about that strike when we was over to The Junction. Lorry and me been over that way on business. I seen that that young fella, number thirty-eight, was one of the men who went after that machine gun."

"How do you know that he was a young man?" queried Mrs. Adams.

"Why—er—only a young fella would act that foolish, I reckon. You say Jim is feelin' spry ag'in?"

"Oh, much better! He's lame yet. But he can ride."

"That's good."

"And did you see that the paper says men are volunteering to go to France? I wonder what will happen next?"

"I dunno," said Shoop gravely. "I been thinkin' about that."

"Well, I hope Lorry won't think that he has to go. Some of the boys in town are talking about it."

"It's in the air," said Shoop.

"And his father will need him now. Could you spare him, if Jim finds he can't get along alone?"

"I don't know," laughed Bud. "I reckon I need somebody to look after them campers up to my old place."

"Oh, I forgot to tell you; the folks that were here last summer stopped by on their way to Jason. Mrs. Weston and her girl. They said they were going to visit Mr. Bronson."

"H'm! Then I reckon I got to keep Lorry. Don't know what three females would do with just Bronson for comp'ny. He's a-tickin' at that writin' machine of his most all day, and sometimes nights. It must be like livin' in a cave."

"But Dorothy hasn't," said Lorry.

"That's right! My, but that little gal has built up wonderful since she's been up there! Did you see my watch?"

"Why, no!"

"Some style to that!" And Shoop displayed the new watch with pride. "And here's the name of the lady what give it to me."

Lorry's mother examined the watch, and handed it to Lorry, to whom the news of the gift was a surprise.

"But she didn't give him a watch," said Shoop, chuckling.

Up in their room that night, Lorry helped Bud out of his coat. Shoop's arm was stiff and sore.

"And your mother would think it was a mighty queer business, if she knowed this," said Bud, "or who that number thirty-eight was down there."

"You sure made a good bluff, Bud."

"Mebby. But I was scared to death. When I was talkin' about Sterling so free and easy, and your maw mighty near ketched me that time, my arm was itchin' like hell-fire, and I dassen scratch it. I never knowed a fella's conscience could get to workin' around his system like that. Now, if it was my laig, I could 'a' scratched it with my other foot under the table. Say, but you sure showed red in your face when your maw said them Weston folks was up to the camp."

"Oh, I don't know."

"Well, I do. Here, hook onto your Uncle Bud's boot. I'm set: go ahead and pull. You can't do nothin' but shake the buildin'. Say, what does Bronson call his gal 'Peter Pan' for?"

"Why, it's a kind of foreign name," flashed Lorry. "And it sounds all right when you say it right. You said it like the 'pan' was settin' a mile off."

"Well, you needn't to get mad."

Chapter XXX
In the Hills

Lorry's return to the mountains was somewhat of a disappointment to his expectations. Dorothy had greeted him quite casually and naturally enough, in that she knew nothing of his recent venture. He was again introduced to Mrs. Weston and her daughter. For the first time Dorothy heard of the automobile accident and Lorry's share in the subsequent proceedings. She asked Lorry why he had not told her that he knew the Westons. He had no reply save "Oh, I don't know," which rather piqued Dorothy. He was usually definite and frank.

The Westons occupied Bronson's cabin with Dorothy. Bronson pitched a tent, moved his belongings into it, and declared himself, jokingly, free from Dorothy's immediate tyranny.

Dorothy, busy in the kitchen, asked her father to invite Lorry to dinner that evening. Through a sort of youthful perverseness not unmixed with bucolic pride, Lorry declined the invitation. He would be busy making ready for another trip in the hills. He had already planned his own evening meal. He appreciated the invitation, but they could get along without him. These excuses satisfied Bronson. Lorry's real reason for declining was that Dorothy had not invited him in person. He knew it, and felt ashamed of himself. What reason had he to expect her to invite him personally, except that she had almost invariably done so heretofore? And back of this was the subtle jealousy of caste. The Westons were "her kind of folks." He was not really one of them. Boyishly he fancied that he would do as a companion when there was no one else available. He was very much in love with Dorothy and did not realize it.

And Dorothy was disappointed in him. She had wanted the Westons to know what a really fine fellow he was.

Alice Weston at once recalled Lorry's attitude toward her on a former occasion when he had been tacitly invited to go with them to the Horseshoe Hills and he had stayed at the hotel. She told Dorothy that Mr. Adams was not to be taken too seriously. After all, he was nothing more than a boy, and perhaps he would feel better, having declined to risk possible embarrassment at their table.

Dorothy was inwardly furious on the instant, but she checked herself. What did Alice Weston know about Lorry? Well, Alice knew that he was a good-looking young savage who seemed quite satisfied with himself. She thought that possibly she could tame him if she cared to try. Dorothy, with feminine graciousness, dared Alice to invite Lorry to the dinner. Alice was to know nothing of his having declined an earlier invitation. Greatly to Dorothy's surprise, Alice Weston accepted the challenge.

She waited until just before the dinner hour. Lorry was mending a pack-saddle when she came to his cabin. He dropped his work and stood up.

"I have been thinking about that tramp you arrested," she began. "And I think you were right in what you did."

"Yes, ma'am," stammered Lorry.

Her manner had been especially gracious.

"And I didn't have a chance to say good-bye—that time"—and she smiled—"when you rode off waving your scarf—"

"It was a leg of lamb," corrected Lorry.

"Well, you waved it very gracefully. What big, strong arms! They don't look so big when your sleeves are down."

Lorry promptly rolled down his sleeves. He felt that he had to do something.

"And there is so much to talk about I hardly know where to begin. Oh, yes! Thank you so much for repairing our car."

"That was nothin'."

"It meant a great deal to us. Is that your horse—the one standing alone over there?"

"Yes, ma'am. That's Gray Leg."

"I remember him. I couldn't ever forget that morning—but I don't want to hinder your work. I see you are mending something."

"Just fittin' a new pad to this pack-saddle. I was figurin' to light out to-morrow."

"So soon? That's too bad. But, then, we can visit at dinner this evening. Dorothy said she expected you. I believe it is almost ready."

"I don't know, Miss Weston. It's like this—"

"And I know Mr. Bronson meant to ask you. He has been quite busy Perhaps he forgot."

"He—"

"So I am here as ambassador. Will I do?"

"Why, sure! But—"

"And mother would be so disappointed if you didn't come. So should I, especially as you are leaving to-morrow. What is it they say in Mexico, 'Adios'? I must run back."

She proffered her hand gracefully. Lorry shook hands with her. She gave his fingers a little, lingering squeeze that set his pulses racing. She was a mighty pretty girl.

"We shall expect you," she called, halfway to the cabin.

And she sure could change a fellow's mind for him without half trying. She hadn't given him a chance to refuse her invitation. She just knew that he was coming to supper. And so did he.

Alice Weston held Lorry's attention from the beginning, as she had intended. She was gowned in some pale-green material touched here and there with a film of lace. Lorry was fascinated by her full, rounded arms, her beautifully strong wrists, and by the way in which she had arranged her heavy, dark hair. In the daylight that afternoon he had noticed that her eyes were blue. He had thought them brown. But they were the color of wood violets untouched by the sun. While she lacked the positive outdoor coloring of Dorothy, her complexion was radiant with youth and health. Lorry felt subdued, disinclined to talk despite Dorothy's obvious attempts to be entertaining. He realized that Dorothy was being exceedingly nice to him, although he knew that she was a little high-strung and nervous that evening.

After dinner Bronson and Lorry smoked out on the veranda. When the others came out, Bronson suggested that they have some music. Lorry promptly invited them to his cabin.

"Alice plays wonderfully," said Dorothy.

Bronson, talking with Mrs. Weston, enjoyed himself. He had been isolated so long that news from the "outside" interested him.

Lorry, gravely attentive to the playing, happened to glance up. Dorothy was gazing at him with a most peculiar expression. He flushed. He had not realized that he had been staring at Alice Weston; at her round, white throat and graceful arms. But just then she ceased playing.

"Have you any music that you would like?" she asked Lorry.

"There's some here. I don't know what it's like. Some songs and dances the boys fetched up for Bud."

"What fun!" said Alice. "And what an assortment! Shall we try this?"

And she began to play a flimsy tune printed on a flimsy sheet that doubled and slid to the keys. Lorry jumped up, spread it out, and stood holding a corner of it while she played. Close to her, he was sensible of a desire to caress her hair, to kiss her vivid lips as she glanced up at him and smiled. He had no idea then that she was deliberately enthralling him with every grace she possessed.

The fact that she rather liked him made her subtleties all the more potent. It flattered her to see the frank admiration in his gray eyes. She knew he was anything but "soft," which made the game all the more alluring. He was to leave soon—to-morrow. Meanwhile, she determined that he should remember her.

Late that evening Bronson and the others said good-night. Alice, not Dorothy, asked Lorry when he was to leave. His "some time to-morrow" sounded unnaturally indefinite.

He was standing in the doorway of his camp as the others entered Bronson's cabin. Alice Weston was the last to enter. For an instant she stood in the lamplight that floated through the doorway, looking back toward him. Impulsively he waved good-night. Her attitude had seemed to call for it. He saw her fingers flash to her lips. She tilted her chin and threw him a kiss.

"Dog-gone the luck!" he growled as he entered his cabin. And with the brief expletive he condemned his disloyalty to the sprightly, slender Dorothy; the Peter Pan of the Blue Mesa; the dream girl of that idle noon at the Big Spring. The other girl—well, she was just playing with him.

In view of Lorry's training and natural carefulness it was especially significant that he decided next day that he had forgotten to lay in enough supplies for his journey south. He would ride to Jason and pack in what he needed. He had a fair excuse. Bronson had recently borrowed some of his canned provisions. He was well on his way to Jason that morning before the others had arisen.

He was back at the camp shortly after nine that night. As he passed Bronson's cabin he saw a light in the window. Mrs. Weston was talking with Dorothy. Lorry had hoped to catch a glimpse of Alice Weston. He had been hoping all that day that he would see her again before he left. Perhaps she was asleep.

As he passed the corral a greeting came from the darkness:—

"Good-evening! I thought you had gone."

"I—I didn't see you," he stammered.

Alice Weston laughed softly. "Oh, I was just out here looking at the stars. It's cooler out here. Then you changed your mind about going?"

"Nope. I had to go to Jason for grub. I'm going to-morrow."

"Oh, I see! We thought you had gone."

"Got a headache?" queried Lorry.

Her voice had been so unnaturally low, almost sad.

"No. I just wanted to be alone."

Lorry fumbled in his pockets. "I got the mail," he stated.

"I'll give it to Mr. Bronson."

Lorry leaned down and gave her the packet of letters and papers.

"Good-bye. I won't see you in the mornin'"

"We'll miss you."

"Honest?"

"Of course!" And she gave him her hand.

He drew his foot from the stirrup. "Put your foot in there," he said, still holding her hand.

"But why?"

"'Cause I'm goin' to ride off with you, like in books." He laughed, but his laughter was tense and unnatural.

It was dark. The stars shone faintly. The air was soft with a subtle fragrance; the fragrance of sun-warmed pine that the night had stolen from the slumbering woodlands. She slipped her foot in the wide stirrup. Half laughing, she allowed him to draw her up. She felt the hard strength of his arm, and was thrilled. She had not meant to do anything like this.

"You been playin' with me," he told her, whispering, "and I take my pay."

She turned her face away, but he found her lips and crushed her to him.

"Oh!" she whispered as he kissed her again and again.

Slowly his arm relaxed. White-faced and trembling, she slid to the ground and stood looking up at him.

"I hate you!" she said.

"No, you don't," said Lorry quite cheerfully.

And he reached out his hand as though to take her hand again.

She stood still, making no effort to avoid him. Then—"No, please!" she begged.

Lorry sat for a moment looking down at her. There had been no make-believe on her part when he held her in his arms. He knew that. And now? She had said that she hated him. Perhaps she did for having made her do that which she had never dreamed of doing. But he told himself that he could stand a whole lot of that kind of hate. And did he really care for her? Could a girl give what she had given and forget on the morrow? He would never forget.

She had told herself that he should have reason to remember her.

After he had gone she stood gazing across the starlit mesa. She heard Lorry whistling cheerily as he unsaddled his pony. A falling star flamed and faded across the night.

Chapter XXXI
In the Pines

Alice Weston pleaded headache next morning. She did not get up until noon. Meanwhile Dorothy came, bringing hot coffee and toast.

"Does it really hurt?" queried Dorothy. "Or is it one of those headaches that is always going to hurt, but never does?"

Alicesmiledandsippedhercoffee."Oh,it'snotbad.Iwanttorest
Perhaps it's the altitude."

"Perhaps," said Dorothy. "I'm sorry, Alice."

They chatted awhile. Suddenly Alice thought of the letters Lorry had given her. She had carried them to her room, and had forgotten them.

"Mr. Adams left some mail with me last night. I happened to be outside when he rode past."

"Why, I thought he had gone!"

"He said he had to go to Jason for something or other. He left early this morning, I think."

Dorothy glanced at the mail. "All for daddy—except this circular. H'm! 'Intelligent clothing for Intelligent People.' Isn't that awful? How in the world do such firms get one's address when one lives 'way up here in the sky. Do you ever get advertisements like this?"

"Oh, yes; heaps of them."

"Well, *your* gowns are beautiful," sighed Dorothy.

"You are a darling," said Alice, caressing Dorothy's cheek.

"So are you, dear." And Dorothy kissed her. "And you coaxed Lorry to come to dinner, after all! I don't know what made him so grumpy, though. I would have been sorry if he hadn't come to dinner, even if he was grumpy."

"Do you like him?" queried Alice.

"Of course; he has been so nice to us. Don't you?"

Alice's lips trembled. Suddenly she hid her face in her hands and burst into tears.

"Why, Alice, what *is* the matter?"

"Nothing," she sobbed. "I'm just tired—of everything."

"It must be the altitude," said Dorothy gravely. "Father says it does make some persons nervous. Just rest, Allie, and I'll come in again."

Without telling her father anything further than that she was going for a ride, Dorothy saddled Chinook.

Dorothy was exceedingly trustful, but she was not at all stupid. She thought she understood Alice's headache. And while Dorothy did not dream that her friend cared anything for Lorry, she was not so sure that Lorry did not care for Alice. Perhaps he had said something to her. Perhaps they had become rather well acquainted in Stacey last summer.

Dorothy rode toward the Big Spring. She had no definite object in view other than to be alone. She was hurt by Lorry's incomprehensible manner of leaving. What had she done to cause him to act so strangely? And why had he refused her invitation and accepted it again through Alice? "But I'll never, never let him know that I care about that," she thought. "And when he comes back everything will be all right again."

Just before she reached the Big Spring her pony nickered. She imagined she could see a horse standing back of the trees round the spring. Some ranger returning to Jason or some cattle outfit from the south was camped at the spring. But when Chinook nickered again and the other pony answered, she knew at once that Lorry was there. Why had he stopped at the spring? He had started early enough to have made a camp farther on.

Lorry saw her coming, and busied himself adjusting one of the packs. As she rode up he turned and took off his hat. His face was flushed. His eyes did not meet hers as she greeted him.

"I didn't look for you to ride up here," he said lamely.

"And I didn't expect to find you here," she said as she dismounted. She walked straight to him. "Lorry, what is the matter? You're not like my ranger man at all! Are you in trouble?"

Her question, so frank and sincere, and the deep solicitude in her troubled eyes hurt him, and yet he was glad to feel that hot pain in his throat. He knew now that he cared for her more than for any living being; beyond all thought of passion or of selfishness. She looked and seemed like a beautiful boy, with all the frankness of true comradeship in her attitude and manner. And she was troubled because of him—and not for herself. Lorry thought of the other girl. He had taken his pay. His lips burned dry as he recalled that moment when he had held her in his arms.

Dorothy saw the dull pain in his eyes, a sort of dumb pleading for forgiveness for something he had done; she could not imagine what. He dropped to his knee, and taking her slender hand in his kissed her fingers.

"Don't be silly," she said, yet her free hand caressed his hair. "What is it, ranger man?"

"I been a regular dam' fool, Dorothy."

"But, Lorry! You know—if there is anything, anything in the world that I can do—Please, *please* don't cry. If you were to do that I think I should die. I couldn't stand it. You make me afraid. What is it? Surely it is not—Alice?"

He crushed her fingers. Suddenly he stood up and stepped back. The sunlight shone on his bared head. He looked very boyish as he shrugged his shoulders as though to free himself from an invisible hand that oppressed and irritated him. His sense of fair play in so far as Alice Weston was concerned would not allow him to actually regret that affair. To him that had been a sort of conquest. But shame and repentance for having been disloyal to Dorothy were stamped so clearly upon his features that she understood. She knew what he was about to say, and checked him.

"Don't tell me," she said gently. "You have told me. I know Alice is attractive; she can't help that. If you care for her—"

"Care for her! She was playin' with me. When I found out that—"

Dorothy caught her breath. Her eyes grew big. She had not thought that Alice Weston—But then that did not matter now. Lorry was so abjectly sorry about something or other. He felt her hand on his sleeve. She was smiling. "You're just a great big, silly boy, ranger man. I'm really years older than you. Please don't tell me anything. I don't want to know. I just want you to be happy."

"Happy? And you say that!"

"Of course!"

"Well, mebby I could be happy if you was to set to and walk all over me."

"Oh, but that wouldn't do any good. Tell me why you stopped here at the spring. You didn't expect to meet any one, did you?"

"I—stopped here—because we camped here that time."

"Well, Lorry, it's really foolish of you to feel so badly when there's nothing the matter. If you wanted to kiss Alice and she let you—why, that isn't wrong. A boy kissed me once when I was going to school in the East. I just boxed his ears and laughed at him. It is only when you act grumpy or feel badly that I worry about you. I just want to be your little mother then — and try to help you."

"You make me feel like I wasn't fit to ever touch your hand again," he told her.

"But you mustn't feel that way," she said cheerily. "I want you to be brave and strong and happy; just as you were that day we camped here. And you will, won't you?"

"Yes, ma'am. I'm takin' orders from you."

"But you mustn't wait for me to tell you. Just be yourself, and then I know you will never be ashamed of anything you do. I must go now. Good-bye, Lorry."

She gave her hand, and he drew her to him. But she turned her face away as he bent his head above her.

"No; not now, Lorry. I—can't. Please don't."

"I—guess you're right. I reckon you showed me just where I stand. Yes, you're plumb right about it, Dorothy. But I'm comin' back—"

"I'll wait for you," she said softly.

He turned briskly to the ponies. The pack-horses plodded up the trail as he mounted Gray Leg and rode over to her.

She reached up and patted Gray Leg's nose. "Good-bye, everybody!" she chirruped. And she kissed Gray Leg's nose.

Back in the ranges, far from the Big Spring, Lorry made his camp that night. As he hobbled the horses he talked to them affectionately after his manner when alone with them.

"And you, you old trail-hitter," he said to Gray Leg, "I reckon you think you're some ladies' man, don't you? Well, you got a right to be proud. Step along there, and 'tend to your grazin' and don't go to rubbin' noses with the other horses. You're a fool if you do."

Chapter XXXII
Politics

The week following Lorry's departure the Westons left for the East. As for Dorothy, she confessed to herself that she was not sorry. While Alice had been unusually nice to every one, Dorothy felt that Alice was forcing herself to appear natural and happy. Mrs. Weston knew this, and wondered what the cause could be. Mrs. Weston had found Dorothy delightful and Bronson interesting, but she had been so long in the West that its novelty had worn thin. She did not regret it when they shipped their machine from Stacey and took the Overland for New York.

A few days after they had gone, Bud Shoop rode up to the Blue Mesa. It was evident that he wanted to talk with Bronson, so Dorothy coaxed Bondsman to her favorite tree, and sat stroking his shaggy head as she read from a new book that Shoop had brought with the mail.

The genial Bud was in a fix. Perhaps Bronson, who had been a newspaper man and knew something about politics, could help him out. Bronson disclaimed any special keenness of political intelligence, but said he would be glad to do anything he could for Shoop.

"It's like this," Bud began, seating himself on the edge of the veranda; "John Torrance, who was supervisor before you came in, got me this job and put it up to me to stick. Now, I like John, and I figure John ain't scared of me. But here's where I lose the trail. A ole friend, the biggest shipper of sheep in this State, goes and gets it into his head that they's a State Senator over there drawin' down pay that ought to come to me. Recollec', I said he was a sheepman—and I been for the longhorns all my days. And he's got the nerve to tell me that all the sheepmen in this here county are strong for me if I run for the job. If I didn't know him like I know this here right hand, I would say he was gettin' hardenin' of the brain in his ole aige. But he's a long ways from havin' his head examined yet.

"Then along comes a representative of the Cattlemen's Association and says they want me to run for State Senator. Then along comes a committee of hay-tossers from up around St. Johns and says, polite, that they are waitin' my pleasure in the matter of framin' up their ticket for senatorial candidate from this mesa country. They say that the present encumbrance in the senatorial chair is such a dog-gone thief that he steals from hisself just to keep in practice. I don't say so. 'Course, if I can get to a chair that looks big and easy, without stompin' on anybody—why, I'm like to set down. But if I can't, I figure to set where I be.

"Now, this here war talk is gettin' folks excited. And ridin' excitement down the trail of politics is like tryin' to ride white lightnin' bareback. It's like to leave you so your friends can't tell what you looked like. And somebody that ain't got brains enough to plug the hole in a watch-key has been talkin' around that Bud Shoop is a fighter, with a record for gettin' what he goes after. And that this same Bud Shoop is as honest as the day is long. Now, I've seen some mighty short days when I was tradin' hosses. And then this here stingin' lizard goes to work and digs up my deputy number over to Sterling and sets the papers to printin' as how it was me, with the help of a few parties whose names are of no special int'rest, settled that strike."

"So you were at Sterling?"

"Uh-uh. Between you and me, I was. And it wa'n't what you'd call a girl's school for boys, neither. But that's done. What I'm gettin' at is: If I resign here, after givin' my word to Torrance to stick, it looks like I been playin' with one hand under the table. The papers will lie like hell boostin' me, and if I don't lie like hell, boostin' myself, folks'll think I'm a liar, anyhow. Now, takin' such folks one at a time, out back of the store, mebby, where they ain't no wimmin-folks, I reckon I could make 'em think different. But I can't lick the county. I ain't no angel. I never found that tellin' the truth kep' me awake nights. And I sleep pretty good. Now, I writ to Torrance, tellin' him just how things was headed. What do you think he writ back?"

"Why, he told you to go ahead and win, didn't he?"

"Yep. And he said that it was apparent that the State needed my services more than the Service did. That's somethin' like a train with a engine on each end. You don't know which way it's headed."

"I'd take it as a sincere compliment."

"Well, I did swell up some. Then I says to myself: 'Bud, you ain't no fancy office man, and even if you are doin' good work here, you can't put it in writin' for them big bugs at Washington.' Mebby John is so dog-gone busy—like the fella with both bands full and his suspenders broke—- that he'd be glad to get behind 'most anything to get shut of me."

"I think you're mistaken. You know you can't keep a born politician out of politics."

"Meanin' me?"

"You're the type."

"By gravy, Bronson! I never seen you hidin' your watch when I come up to visit you before."

"See here, Shoop. Why don't you write to Torrance and ask him point-blank if he has had a hand in getting you nominated for Senator? Torrance is a big man in his line, and he probably knows what he is doing."

Shoop grinned. "You win the pot!" he exclaimed. "That's just what I been thinkin' right along. I kind of wanted somebody who wasn't interested in this deal to say it. Well, I reckon I bothered you long enough. You got your alfalfa to—I—you got your writin' to do. But they's one thing. If I get roped in and got to run, and some new supervisor comes botherin' around up here, puttin' some ranger in my camp that ain't like Lorry, all you got to do is to move over into my cabin and tell 'em to keep off the grass. That there four hundred and eighty is mine. I homesteaded it, and I got the papers. It ain't on the reserve."

"I thought it was."

"So do some yet. Nope. I'm just east of the reservation line; outside the reserve. I aimed to know what I was doin' when I homesteaded that piece of sky farm."

"And yet you took exception to my calling you a born politician."

Shoop chuckled. "Speakin' personal, I been thinkin' about that job of State Senator for quite a spell. Now, I reckon you got sense enough not to get mad when I tell you that I just been tryin' out a little speech I framed up for my constituents. Just a kind of little alfalfa-seed talk. Outside of ijuts and Mexicans, it's about what I aim to hand to the voters of this here district, puttin' it up to them that I was roped into this hocus and been settin' back on the rope right along. And that's a fact. But you got to rub some folks' noses in a fact afore they can even smell it."

"And you have the nerve to tell me that you framed up all that stuff to get my sympathy? Shoop, you are wasting time in Arizona. Go East. And forgive me for falling for your most natural appeal."

The genial Bud chuckled and wiped his eyes. "But it's true from the start to the wire."

"I must congratulate you." And, "Dorothy!" called Bronson. "Come and shake hands with our next Senator from the mesa country."

"Really?" exclaimed Dorothy. "But we will lose our supervisor. Still, I think Mr. Shoop will make a lovely Senator. You are just the right size—and—everything."

"I reckon you're right, missy. Half of the game is lookin' the part afore election. The other half is not sayin' too much after election. If any man gets a promise out of me afore election, it'll have to be did with a stump-puller."

"But we won't see you any more," said Dorothy. "You will be so busy and so important. Senator Shoop will speak here. And Senator Shoop will speak there. And—let me see! Oh, yes! The Senate adjourned after a stormy session in which the Senator from Mesa County, supported by an intelligent majority, passed his bill for the appropriation of twenty thousand dollars to build a road from Jason to the Blue Mesa. What fun!"

Bud polished his bald head. "Now, I reckon that ain't such a joke. We'll build a road plumb through to the old Apache Trail and ketch them tourists goin' into Phoenix."

"You see," said Dorothy, turning to her father, "I know something about politics. I read the local papers. Mr. Shoop's name is in every one of them. I read that article about the Sterling strike. I have been wondering—"

Shoop immediately called attention to Bondsman, who was gently tugging at the supervisor's pants leg.

"Now, look at that! Do you know what he's tellin' me? He's tellin' me I got a piano in that there cabin and we ain't had a duet for quite a spell. That there dog bosses me around somethin' scandalous."

Bondsman slipped from beneath Dorothy's hand as she stooped to pat him He trotted to Shoop's cabin, and stood looking up at the door.

"Would you be playin' 'Annie Laurie' for us?" queried Shoop.

Dorothy played for them, unaccompanied by Bondsman. Shoop shook his head. Either the tune had lost its charm for the Airedale or else Dorothy's interpretation differed from Bud's own.

"Thanks, missy," said Shoop when she had finished playing. "Guess I'll be movin' along."

"Oh, no! You'll stay to-night. I'll play for you. Make him stay, father."

"I wish you would, Shoop. I'd like to talk with you about the election."

"Well, now, that's right neighborly of you folks. I was aimin' to ride back this evening. But I reckon we'll stay. Bondsman and me ain't so spry as we was."

After supper Dorothy played for them again, with no light except the dancing red shadows from the pine logs that flamed in the fireplace.

Shoop thanked her. "I'll be livin' in town,"—and he sighed heavily,—"where my kind of piano-playin' would bring the law on me, most-like. Now, that ole piano is hacked up some outside, but she's got all her innards yet and her heart's right. If you would be takin' it as a kind of birthday present, it's yours."

"You don't mean *me*?"

"I sure do."

"But I couldn't accept such a big present. And then, when we go away this winter—"

"Listen to your Uncle Bud, missy. A little lady give me a watch onct. 'T wa'n't a big watch, but it was a big thing. 'Cause why? 'Cause that little lady was the first lady to give me a present in my life. I was raised up by men-folks. My mammy she wa'n't there long after I come. Reckon that's why I never was much of a hand with wimmin-folks. I wa'n't used to 'em. And I don't care how old and ornery a man is; the first time he gets a present from a gal, it kind of hits him where he breathes. And if it don't make him feel warm inside and mighty proud of bein' who he is, why, it's because he's so dog-gone old he can't think. I ain't tellin' no secret when I say that the little lady put her name in that watch alongside of mine. And her name bein' there is what makes that present a big thing—bigger than any piano that was ever built.

"Why, just a spell ago I was settin' in my office, madder'n a cat what had tore his Sunday pants, 'cause at twelve o'clock I was goin' over to the saloon to fire that young ranger, Lusk, for gettin' drunk. I pulled out this here watch, and I says to myself: 'Bud, it was clost around twelve o'clock by a young fella's watch onct when he was filled up on liquor and rampin' round town when he ought to been to work. And it was the ole foreman's gal that begged that boy's job back for him, askin' her daddy to give him another chanct.' And the boy he come through all right. I know—for I owned the watch. And so I give Lusk another chanct."

Dorothy stepped to Shoop's chair, and, stooping quickly, kissed his cheek. Bondsman, not to be outdone, leaped jealously into Bud's lap and licked the supervisor's face. Shoop spluttered, and thrust Bondsman down.

"Things is comin' too fast!" he cried, wiping his face. "I was just goin' to say something when that dog just up and took the words right out of my mouth. Oh, yes! I was just wishin' I owned a piano factory."

Chapter XXXIII
The Fires of Home

Bud Shoop read the newspaper notice twice before he realized fully its import. The Adams House at Stacey was for sale. "Then Jim and Annie's patched it up," he soliloquized. And the genial Bud did not refer to the Adams House.

Because his master seemed pleased, Bondsman waited to hear the rest of it with head cocked sideways and tail at a stiff angle.

"That's all they is to it," said Shoop.

Bondsman lay down and yawned. He was growing old. It was only Bud's voice that could key the big Airedale up to his earlier alertness. The office was quiet. The clerk had gone out for his noon meal. The fall sunshine slanted lazily through the front-office windows. The room was warm, but there was a tang of autumn in the air. Shoop glanced at the paper again. He became absorbed in an article proposing conscription. He shook his head and muttered to himself. He turned the page, and glanced at the livestock reports, the copper market, railroad stocks, and passed on to an article having to do with local politics.

Bondsman, who constituted himself the guard of Shoop's leisure, rapped the floor with his tail. Shoop glanced over the top of his paper as light footsteps sounded in the outer office. Dorothy tapped on the lintel and stepped in. Shoop crumpled the paper and rose. Bondsman was at her side as she shook hands with the supervisor.

"My new saddle came," she said, patting Bondsman. "And father's latest book. Why don't you cheer?"

"Goodness, missy! I started cheerin' inside the minute I seen you. Now, I reckon you just had to have that new saddle."

"It's at the store. Father is over there talking politics and war with Mr. Handley."

"Then you just set down and tell your Uncle Bud the news while you're waitin'."

"But I am not *waiting*. I am visiting *you*. And I told you the news."

"And to think a new saddle could make your eyes shine like that! Ain't you 'shamed to fool your Uncle Bud?"

"I haven't—if you say you know I have."

"'Course. Most any little gal can get the best of me."

"Well, because you are so curious—Lorry is back."

"I reckoned that was it."

"He rode part-way down with us. He has gone to see his father."

"And forgot to repo't here first."

"No. He gave me the reports to give to you. Here they are. One of Mr. Waring's men, that young Mexican, rode up to the mesa last week and left word that Lorry's father wanted to see him."

"I aim to know about that," chuckled Shoop. And he smoothed out the paper and pointed to the Adams House sale notice.

"The Adams House for sale? Why—"

"Jim and Annie—that's Jim Waring and Mrs. Waring now—are goin' to run the ranch. I'm mighty glad."

"Oh, I see! And Lorry is really Laurence Waring?"

"You bet! And I reckon Lorry'll be fo'man of that ranch one of these days. Cattle is sky-high and goin' up. I don't blame him."

"He didn't say a word about that to me."

"'Course not. He's not one to say anything till he's plumb sure."

"He might have said *something*" asserted Dorothy.

"Didn't he?" chuckled Shoop.

Dorothy's face grew rosy. "Your master is very inquisitive," she told Bondsman.

"And your little missy is right beautiful this mawnin'," said Shoop. "Now, if I was a bow-legged young cow-puncher with curly hair, and looked fierce and noble and could make a gal's eyes shine like stars in the evenin', I reckon I wouldn't be sittin' here signin' letters."

"He *isn't* bow-legged!" flashed Dorothy. She was very definite about that. "And he's not a cowboy. He is a ranger."

"My goodness! I done put my foot in a gopher hole that shake. I sure am standin' on my head, waitin' for somebody to set me up straight ag'in. You ain't mad at your Uncle Bud, be you?"

Dorothy tossed her head, but her eyes twinkled, and suddenly she laughed. "You know I like you—heaps! You're just jealous."

"Reckon you said it! But I only got one ear laid back yet. Wait till I see that boy."

"Oh, pshaw! You can't help being nice to him."

"And I got comp'ny."

"But really I want to talk seriously, if you will let me. Lorry has been talking about enlisting. He didn't say that he was going to enlist, but he has been talking about it so much. Do you think he will?"

"Well, now, missy that's a right peart question. I know if I was his age I'd go. Most any fella that can read would. I been readin' the papers for two years, and b'ilin' inside. I reckon Lorry's just woke up to what's goin' on. We been kind of slow wakin' up out here. Folks livin' off in this neck of the woods gets to thinkin' that the sun rises on their east-line fence and sets on their west line. It takes somethin' strong to make 'em recollec' the sun's got a bigger job'n that. But I admire to say that when them kind of folks gets started onct they's nothin' ever built that'll stop 'em. If I get elected I aim to tell some folks over to the State House about this here war. And I'm goin' to start by talkin' about what we got to set straight right here to home first. They can *feel* what's goin' on to home. It ain't all print. And they got to feel what's goin' on over there afore they do anything."

"It's all too terrible to talk about," said Dorothy. "But we must do our share, if only to keep our self-respect, mustn't we?"

"You said it—providin' we got any self-respect to keep."

"But why don't our young men volunteer. They are not cowards."

"It ain't that. Suppose you ask Lorry why."

"I shouldn't want to know him if he didn't go," said Dorothy.

"Missy, I'm lovin' you for sayin' that! If all the mothers and sisters and sweethearts was like that, they wouldn't be no conscription. But they ain't. I'm no hand at understandin' wimmin-folks, but I know the mother of a strappin' young fella in this town that says she would sooner see her boy dead in her front yard than for him to go off and fight for foreigners. She don't know what this country's got to fight for pretty quick or she wouldn't talk like that. And she ain't the only one. Now, when wimmin talks that way, what do you expect of men? I reckon the big trouble is that most folks got to see somethin' to fight afore they get goin'. Fightin' for a principle looks just like poundin' air to some folks. I don't believe in shootin' in the dark. How come, I've plugged a rattlesnake by just shootin' at the sound when he was coiled down where I couldn't see him. But this ain't no kind of talk for you to listen to, missy."

"I—you won't say that I spoke of Lorry?"

"Bless your heart, no! And he'll figure it out hisself. But don't you get disap'inted if he don't go right away. It's mighty easy to set back and say 'Go!' to the other fella; and listen to the band and cheer the flag. It makes a fella feel so durned patriotic he is like to forget he ain't doin' nothin' hisself.

"Now, missy, suppose you was a sprightin' kind of a boy 'bout nineteen or twenty, and mebby some gal thought you was good-lookin' enough to talk to after church on a Sunday; and suppose you had rustled like a little nigger when you was a kid, helpin' your ma wash dishes in a hotel and chop wood and sweep out and pack heavy valises for tourists and fill the lamps and run to the store for groceries and milk a cow every night and mornin'.

"And say you growed up without breakin' your laig and went to punchin' cattle and earnin' your own money, and then mebby you got a job in the Ranger Service, ridin' the high trails and livin' free and independent; and suppose a mighty pretty gal was to come along and kind of let you take a shine to her, and you was doin' your plumb durndest to put by a little money, aimin' to trot in double harness some day; and then suppose your daddy was to offer you a half-interest in a growin' cattle business, where you could be your own boss and put by a couple of thousand a year. And you only nineteen or twenty.

"Suppose you had been doin' all that when along comes word from 'way off somewhere that folks was killin' each other and it was up to you to stop 'em. Wouldn't you do some hard thinkin' afore you jumped into your fightin' clothes?"

"But this war means more than that."

"It sure does. But some of us ain't got the idee yet. 'Course all you got to do to some folks is to say 'Fight' and they come a-runnin'. And some of that kind make mighty good soldier boys. But the fella I'm leavin' alone is the one what cinches up slow afore he climbs into the saddle. When he goes into a fight it's like his day's work, and he don't waste no talk or elbow action when he's workin'."

"I wish I were a man!"

"Well, some of us is right glad you ain't. A good woman can do just as much for this country right now as any man. And I don't mean by dressin' up in fancy clothes and givin' dances and shellin' out mebby four per cent of the gate receipts to buy a ambulance with her name on it.

"And I don't mean by payin' ten dollars for a outfit of gold-plated knittin'-needles to make two-bit socks for the boys. What I mean is that a good woman does her best work to home; mebby just by sayin' the right word, or mebby by keepin' still or by smilin' cheerful when her heart is breakin' account of her man goin' to war.

"You can say all you like about patriotism, but patriotism ain't just marchin' off to fight for your country. It's usin' your neighbors and your country right every day in the week, includin' Sunday. Some folks think patriotism is buildin' a big bonfire once a year and lettin' her blaze up. But the real thing is keepin' your own little fire a-goin' steady, right here where you live. And it's thinkin' of that little fire to home that makes the best soldier.

"He's got a big job to do. He's goin' to get it done so he can go back to that there home and find the little fire a-burning bright. What do some of our boys do fightin' alongside of them Frenchmen and under the French flag, when they get wounded and get a furlough? Set around and wait to go back to fightin'? I reckon not. Some of 'em pack up and come four, five thousand miles just to see their folks for mebby two, three days. And when they see them little fires to home a-burnin' bright, why, they say: 'This here is what we're fighting for.' And they go back, askin' God A'mighty to keep 'em facin' straight to the front till the job is done."

Dorothy, her chin in her hand, gazed at Bud. She had never known him to be so intense, so earnest.

"Oh, I know it is so!" she cried. "But what can I do? I have only a little money in the bank, and father makes just enough to keep us comfortable. You see, we spent such lots of money for those horrid old doctors in the East, who didn't do me a bit of good."

"You been doin' your share just gettin' well and strong, which is savin' money. But seein' you asked me, you can do a whole lot if Lorry was to say anything to you about goin'. And you know how better'n I can tell you or your daddy or anybody."

"But Lorry must do as he thinks best. We—we are not engaged."

"'Course. And it ain't no time for a young fella to get engaged to a gal and tie up her feelin's and march off with her heart in his pocket. Mebby some day she's goin' to want it back ag'in, when he ain't livin' to fetch it back to her. I see, by the Eastern papers Torrance has been sendin' me, that some young fellas is marryin' just afore they go to jine the Frenchmen on the front. Now, what are some of them gals goin' to do if their boys don't come back? Or mebby come back crippled for life? Some of them gals is goin' to pay a mighty high price for just a few days of bein' married. It riles me to think of it."

"I hadn't thought of it—as you do," said Dorothy.

"Well, I hope you'll forgive your Uncle Bud for ragin' and rampin' around like this. I can't talk what's in my heart to folks around here. They're mostly narrow-gauge. I reckon I said enough. Let's go look at that new saddle."

"Isn't it strange," said Dorothy, "that I couldn't talk with father like this? He'd be nice, of course, but he would be thinking of just me."

"I reckon he would. And mebby some of Lorry."

"If Lorry should ask me about his going—"

"Just you tell him that you think one volunteer is worth four conscripts any time and any place. And if that ain't a hint to him they's somethin' wrong with his ears."

Shoop rose and plodded out after Dorothy. Bondsman trailed lazily behind. Because Shoop had not picked up his hat the big dog knew that his master's errand, whatever it was, would be brief. Yet Bondsman followed, stopping to yawn and stretch the stiffness of age from his shaggy legs. There was really no sense in trotting across the street with his master just to trot back again in a few minutes. But Bondsman's unwavering loyalty to his master's every mood and every movement had become such a matter of course that the fine example was lost in the monotony of repetition.

A dog's loyalty is so often taken for granted that it ceases to be noticeable until in an unlooked-for hazard it shines forth in some act of quick heroism or tireless faithfulness worthy of a greater tribute than has yet been written.

Bondsman was a good soldier.

Chapter XXXIV
Young Life

Ramon was busy that afternoon transferring mattresses and blankets from the ranch-house to the new, low-roofed bunk-house that Waring had built. Ramon fitted up three beds—one for the cook, one for an old range-rider that Waring had hired when his men had left to enlist, and one for himself.

The partitions of the ranch-house had been taken down, the interior rearranged, and the large living-room furnished in a plain, comfortable way.

As Ramon worked he sang softly. He was happy. The señora was coming to live with them, and perhaps Señor Jim's son. Señor Jim had been more active of late. His lameness was not so bad as it had been. It was true the Señor Jim did not often smile, but his eyes were kindly.

Ramon worked rapidly. There was much to do in the other house. The bale of Navajo blankets was still unopened. Perhaps the Señor Jim would help to arrange them in the big room with the stone fireplace. The señora would not arrive until to-morrow, but then the home must be made ready, that she would find it beautiful. And Ramon, accustomed to the meagerly furnished adobes of old Mexico, thought that the ranch-house was beautiful indeed.

Waring ate with the men in the new bunk-house that evening. After supper he went over to the larger building and sat alone in the living-room, gazing out of the western window. His wounds ached, and in the memory of almost forgotten trails he grew young again. Again in Old Mexico, the land he loved, he saw the blue crest of the Sierras rise as in a dream, and below the ranges a tiny Mexican village of adobe huts gold in the setting sun. Between him and the village lay the outlands, ever mysterious, ever calling to him. Across the desert ran a thin trail to the village. And down the trail the light feet of Romance ran swiftly as he followed. He could even recall the positions of the different adobes; the strings of chiles dark red in the twilight; the old black-shawled señora who had spoken a guttural word of greeting as he had ridden up.

Back in Sonora men had said, "Waring has made his last ride." They had told each other that a white man was a fool to go alone into that country. Perhaps he had been a fool. But the thrill of those early days, when he rode alone and free and men sang of him from Sonora to the Sweetgrass Hills! And on that occasion he had found the fugitive he sought, yet he had ridden back to Sonora alone. He had never forgotten the face of the young Mexican woman who had pleaded with him to let her lover go. Her eyes were big and velvet black. Her mouth was the mouth of a Madonna.

Waring had told her that it was useless to plead. He remembered how her eyes had grown dull and sullen at his word. He told her that he was simply doing his duty. She had turned on him like a panther, her little knife glittering in the dusk as she drove it at his breast. The Mexican lover had jerked free and was running toward the foothills. Waring recalled his first surprise at the wiry strength of her wrist as he had twisted the knife from her. If the Mexican lover had not turned and shot at him—The black figure of the Mexican had dropped just where the road entered the foothills. The light had almost gone. The vague bulk of the Sierras wavered. Outlines vanished, leaving a sense of something gigantic, invisible, that slumbered in the night. The stars were big and softly brilliant as he had ridden north.

The old wound in his shoulder ached. The Mexican had made a good shot—for a Mexican.

Out on the Arizona mesa, against the half disk of gold, was the black silhouette of a horseman. Waring stepped to the doorway. Ramon was seated just outside the door, smoking a cigarette. The southern stars were almost visible. Each star seemed to have found its place, and yet no star could be seen.

"It is Lorry," said Ramon. "He has ridden far."

Waring smiled. Fifty miles had not been considered a big day's ride in his time. *In his time!* But his day was past. The goddess he had followed had left him older than his years, crippled, unable to ride more than a few hours at a time; had left him fettered to the monotony of the far mesa levels and the changeless hills. Was this his punishment, or simply a black trick of fate, that the tang of life had evaporated, leaving a stagnant pool wherein he gazed to meet the blurred reflection of a face weary with waiting for—what end?

Unused to physical inactivity, Waring had grown somber of mind these latter days. Despite the promise of more comfortable years, he had never felt more lonely. With the coming of Lorry the old order would change. Young blood, new life would have its way.

The sound of pattering hoofs grew louder. Waring heard the old familiar, "Hi! Yippy! Yip!" of the range rider. Young blood? New life? It was his own blood, his own life reincarnate in the cheery rider that swung down and grasped his hand. Nothing had changed. Life was going on as it always had.

"Hello, dad! How's the leg?"

Waring smiled in the dusk. "Pretty fair, Lorry. You didn't waste any time getting here."

"Well, not much. I rode down with Bronson and Dorothy."

"Do you call her 'Dorothy'?"

"Ever since she calls me 'Lorry.'"

"Had anything to eat?"

"Nope. I cut across. How's mother?"

"She will be here to-morrow. We have been getting things ready. Let Ramon take your horse—"

"Thanks. I'll fix him in two shakes."

And in two shakes bridle and saddle were off, and Gray Leg was rolling in the corral.

While Lorry ate, Ramon laid a fire in the big stone fireplace. Alter supper Lorry and his father sat gazing at the flames. Lorry knew why he had been sent for, but waited for his father to speak.

Presently Waring turned to him. "I sent for you because I need some one to help. And your mother wants you here. I won't urge you, but I can offer you Pat's share in the ranch. I bought his share last week. You'll have a working interest besides that. You know something about cattle. Think it over."

"That's a dandy offer," said Lorry. "I'm right obliged, dad. But there's something else. You put your proposition straight, and I'm going to put mine straight. Now, if you was in my boots, and she liked you enough, would you marry her?"

"You haven't told me who she is."

"Why—Dorothy Bronson. I thought you knew."

Waring smiled. "You're pretty young, Lorry."

"But you married young, dad."

"Yes. And I married the best woman in the world. But I can't say that I made your mother happy."

"I guess ma never cared for anybody but you," said Lorry.

"It isn't just the caring for a person, Lorry."

"Well, I thought it was. But I reckon you know. And Dorothy is the prettiest and lovin'est kind of a girl *you* ever seen. I was wishin' you was acquainted."

"I should like to meet her. Are you sure she is your kind of girl, Lorry? Now, wait a minute; I know how you feel. A girl can be good-looking and mighty nice and think a lot of a man, and yet not be the right girl for him."

"But how is he goin' to find that out?"

"If he must find out—by marrying her."

"Then I aim to find out, if she is willin'. But I wanted to tell you—because you made me that offer. I was askin' your advice because you been through a lot."

"I wish I could advise you. But you're a man grown, so far as taking care of yourself is concerned. And when a man thinks of getting married he isn't looking for advice against it. Why don't you wait a year or two?"

"Well, mebbe I got to. Because—well, I didn't ask Dorothy yet. Then there's somethin' else. A lot of the fellas up in the high country have enlisted in the regulars, and some have gone over to Canada to join the Foreign Legion. Now, I don't want to be the last hombre on this mesa to go."

"There has been no call for men by the Nation."

"But it's comin', dad. Any fella can see that. I kind of hate to wait till Uncle Sam says I got to go. I don't like going that way."

"What do you think your mother will say?"

"Gosh! I know! That's why I wanted to talk to you first. If I'm goin', I want to know it so I can say to her that I *am* goin' and not that I aim to go."

"Well, you will have to decide that."

"Well, I'm goin' to—before ma comes. Dog-gone it! You know how it is tryin' to explain things to a woman. Wimmin don't understand them kind of things."

"I don't know about that, Lorry."

Lorry nodded. "I tell you, dad—you kind of set a pace for me. And I figure I don't want folks to say: 'There goes Jim Waring's boy.' If they're goin' to say anything, I want it to be: 'There goes Lorry Waring.'"

Waring knew that kind of pride if he knew anything. He was proud of his son. And Waring's most difficult task was to keep from influencing him in any way. He wanted the boy to feel free to do as he thought best.

"You were in that fight at Sterling," said Waring, gesturing toward the south.

"But that was different," said Lorry. "Them coyotes was pluggin' at us, and we just nacherally had to let 'em have it. And besides we was workin' for the law."

"I understand there wasn't any law in Sterling About that time."

"Well, we made some," asserted Lorry.

"And that's just what this war means. It's being fought to make law."

"Then I'm for the law every time, big or little. I seen enough of that other thing."

"Think it over, Lorry. Remember, you're free to do as you want to. I have made my offer. Then there is your mother—and the girl. It looks as though you had your hands full."

"You bet! Business and war and—and Dorothy is a right big order. I'm gettin' a headache thinkin' of it!"

Waring rose. "I'm going to turn in. I have to live pretty close to the clock these days."

"See you in the mornin'," said Lorry, giving his hand. "Good-night, dad."

"Good-night, boy."

Chapter XXXV
The High Trail

Black-edged against the silvery light of early dawn the rim of the world lay dotted with far buttes and faint ranges fading into the spaces of the north and south. The light deepened and spread to a great crimson pool, tideless round the bases of magic citadels and mighty towers. Golden minarets thrust their slender, fiery shafts athwart the wide pathway of the ascending sun. The ruddy glow palpitated like a live ember naked to the wind. The nearer buttes grew boldly beautiful. Slowly their molten outlines hardened to rigid bronze. Like ancient castles of some forgotten land, isolated in the vast mesa, empty of life, they seemed to await the coming of a host that would reshape their fallen arches and their wind-worn towers to old-time splendor, and perfect their imageries.

But the marching sun knew no such sentiment. Pitilessly he pierced their enchanted walls, discovering their pretense, burning away their shadowy glory, baring them for what they were—masses of jumbled rock and splintered spires; rain-gutted wraiths of clay, volcanic rock, the tumbled malpais and the tufa of the land.

Black shadows shifted. That which had been the high-arched entrance to a mighty fortress was now a shallow hollow in a hill. Here and there on the western slope of the mounds cattle grazed in the chill morning air. Enchantments of the dawn reshaped themselves to local landmarks.

From his window Lorry could discern the distant peak of Mount Baldy glimmering above the purple sea of forest. Not far below the peak lay the viewless level of the Blue Mesa. The trail ran just below that patch of quaking asp.

The hills had never seemed so beautiful, nor had the still mesas, carpeted with the brown stubble of the close-cropped bunch-grass.

Arizona was his country—his home. And yet he had heard folk say that Arizona was a desert, But then such folk had been interested chiefly in guide-posts of the highways or the Overland dining-car menu.

And he had been offered a fair holding in this land—twenty thousand acres under fence on a long-term lease; a half-interest in the cattle and their increase. He would be his own man, with a voice in the management and sale of the stock. A year or two and he could afford to marry—if Dorothy would have him. He thought she would. And to keep in good health she must always live in the West. What better land than Arizona, on the high mesa where the air was clean and clear; where the keen August rains refreshed the sunburned grasses; where the light snows of winter fell but to vanish in the retrieving sun? If Dorothy loved this land, why should she leave it? Surely health meant more to her than the streets and homes of the East?

And Lorry had asked nothing of fortune save a chance to make good. And fortune had been more than kind to him. He realized that it was through no deliberate effort of his own that he had acquired the opportunity which offered. Why not take advantage of it? It would give him prestige with Bronson. A good living, a good home for her. Such luck didn't come to a man's door every day.

He had slept soundly that night, despite his intent to reason with himself. It was morning, and he had made no decision—or so he thought. There was the question of enlisting. Many of his friends had already gone. Older men were now riding the ranges. Even the clerk in the general store at Stacey's had volunteered. And Lorry had considered him anything but physically competent to "make a fight." But it wasn't all in making a fight. It was setting an example of loyalty and unselfishness to those fellows who needed such an impulse to stir them to action. Lorry thought clearly. And because he thought clearly and for himself, he realized that he, as an individual soldier in the Great War, would amount to little; but he knew that his going would affect others; that the mere news of his having gone would react as a sort of endless chain reaching to no one knew what sequestered home.

And this, he argued, was his real value: the spirit ever more potent than the flesh. Why, he had heard men joke about this war! It was a long way from home. What difference did it make to them if those people over there were being starved, outraged, murdered? That was their own lookout. Friends of his had said that they were willing to fight to a finish if America were threatened with invasion, but that could never happen. America was the biggest and richest country in the world. She attended to her own business and asked nothing but that the other nations do likewise.

And those countries over there were attending to their own business. If our ships were blown up, it was our own fault. We had been warned.

Anyway, the men who owned those ships were out to make money and willing to take a chance. It wasn't our business to mix in. We had troubles enough at home. As Lorry pondered the shallow truths a great light came to him. *"Troubles enough at home,"* that was it! America had already been invaded, yet men slumbered in fancied security. He had been at Sterling —

Lorry could hear Ramon stirring about in the kitchen. The rhythmically muffled sound suggested the mixing of flapjacks. Lorry could smell the thin, appetizing fragrance of coffee.

With characteristic abruptness, he made his decision, but with no spoken word, no gesture, no emotion. He saw a long day's work before him. He would tackle it like a workman.

And immediately he felt buoyantly himself again. The matter was settled.

He washed vigorously. The cold water brought a ruddy glow to his face He whistled as he strode to the kitchen. He slapped the gentle-eyed Ramon on the shoulder. Pancake batter hissed as it slopped over on the stove.

"Cheer up, amigo!" he cried! "Had a good look at the sun this mornin'?"

"No, señor. I have made the breakfast, si."

"Well, she's out there, shinin' right down on Arizona."

"The señora?" queried Ramon, puzzled.

"No; the sun. Don't a mornin' like this make you feel like jumpin' clean out of your boots and over the fence?"

"Not until I have made the flapcake, Señor Lorry."

"Well, go the limit. Guess I'll roust out dad."

Bud Shoop scowled, perspired, and swore. Bondsman, close to Shoop's chair, blinked and lay very still. His master was evidently beyond any proffer of sympathy or advice. Yet he had had no argument with any one lately. And he had eaten a good breakfast. Bondsman knew that. Whatever the trouble might be, his master had not consulted him about it. It was evidently a matter that dogs could not understand, and hence, very grave. Bondsman licked his chops nervously. He wanted to go out and lie in the sunshine, but he could not do that while his master suffered such tribulation of soul. His place was close to his master now, if ever.

Around Shoop were scattered pieces of paper; bits of letters written and torn up.

"It's a dam' sight worse resignin' than makin' out my application—and that was bad enough," growled Shoop. "But I got to do this personal. This here pen is like a rabbit gone loco. Now, here I set like a bag of beans, tryin' to tell John Torrance why I'm quittin' this here job without makin' him think I'm glad to quit—which I am, and I ain't. It's like tryin' to split a flea's ear with a axe; it can't be did without mashin' the flea. Now, if John was here I could tell him in three jumps. The man that invented writin' must 'a' been tongue-tied or had sore throat some time when he wanted to talk awful bad. My langwidge ain't broke to pull no city rig—or no hearse. She's got to have the road and plenty room to sidestep.

"Now, how would I say it if John were here? Would I start off with 'Dear John' or 'Dear Old Friend'? I reckon not. I'd just say: 'John, I'm goin' to quit. I tried to do by you what I said I would. I got a chanct to bust into the State House, and I got a good reason for bustin' in. I been nominated for Senator, and I got to live up to the name. I'm a-goin' to run for Senator—and mebby I'll keep on when I get started, and end up somewhere in Mexico. I can't jine the reg'lars account of my physical expansibility and my aige, so I got to do my fightin' to home. I'm willin' to stick by this job if you say the word. Mebby some folks would be dissap'inted, but I can stand that if they can. What do you reckon I better do?'

"Now, that's what I'd say if John was here. Why in tarnation can't I say it on paper? Lemme see."

Bud filled a sheet with his large, outdoor script. When he had finished, he tucked the letter in an envelope hurriedly. He might reconsider his attempt if he re-read the letter.

He was carefully directing the envelope when Lorry strode in.

"'Bout time you showed up," said Shoop.

Lorry dropped his hat on the floor and pulled up a chair. He was a bit nervous. Preamble would make him more so. He spoke up quickly.

"Bud, I want to resign."

"Uh-uh. You tired of this job?"

"Nope; I like it."

"Want more pay?"

"No; I get all I'm worth."

"Ain't you feelin' well?"

"Bully! I'm going to enlist."

"Might 'a' knowed it," said Bud, leaning back and gazing at the newly addressed envelope on his desk. "Got your reports all in?"

"Yes, sir."

"Well, seem' you're quittin' for the best reason I know, I'm right glad. You done your work like I expected. Your mother knows you're goin' to jine the army?"

"I told her yesterday. I've been at the ranch."

"Uh-uh. How's your dad?"

"He ain't so spry. But he is better."

"Uh-uh. That young Mexican stayin' at the ranch with him?"

"You couldn't chase Ramon away with a gun."

"Uh-uh. Well, Lorry, I just been sweatin' out a letter tellin' John Torrance that I've quit. I'm goin' to run for State Senator."

"I knew they would land you. Everybody knew it."

"So we're both leavin' the Service. And we're leavin' a mighty good job; mebby not such big pay, but a man's job, that has been the makin' of some no-account boys. For no fella can work for the Service without settin' up and ridin' straight. Now, when I was a young buster chasin' cow-tails over the country I kind of thought the Forestry Service was a joke. It ain't. It's a mighty big thing. You're leaving it with a clean record. Mebby some day you'll want to get back in it. Were you goin' on up?"

"I figured to straighten up things at the cabin."

"All right. When you come down you can get your check. Give my regards to Bronson and the little missy."

"You bet I will!"

Bud rose and proffered his hand. Lorry, rather embarrassed, shook hands and turned to go. "See you later," he said.

"I was going over to Stacey," said Shoop. "Mebby I'll be out when you get back. But your check'll be here all right. You sure look like you was walkin' on sunshine this mawnin'. Gosh, what a whoopin' fine place this here world is when you are young—and—kind of slim! Now, Bondsman and me—we was young onct. When it comes to bein' young or State Senator—you can have the politics and give me back my ridin' legs. You're ridin' the High Trail these days.

"If I could just set a hoss onct, with twenty years under my hide, and look down on this here country, and the sage a-smellin' like it used to and the sunshine a-creepin' across my back easy and warm, with a sniff of the timber comin' down the mawnin' breeze; and 'way off the cattle a-lookin' no bigger'n flies on a office map—why, I wouldn't trade that there seat in the saddle for a million in gold. But I reckon I would 'a' done it, them days. Sometimes I set back and say 'Arizona' just to myself. I'm a-lovin' that name. Accordin' to law, I'm livin' single, and if I ain't married to Arizona, she's my best gal, speakin' general. 'Course, a little lady give me a watch onct. And say, boy, if she sets a lot of store by you—why, you—why, git out of this here office afore I make a dam' fool of myself!"

And the genial Bud waved his arm, blustering and swearing heartily.

Bondsman leaped up. A ridge of hair rose along his neck. For some unknown reason his master had ordered Lorry to leave the office—and at once. But Lorry was gone, and Bud was patting the big Airedale. It was all right. Nothing was going to happen. And wasn't it about time for the stage to arrive?

Bondsman trotted to the doorway, gazed up and down the street, and came back to Shoop. The stage had arrived, and Bondsman was telling Shoop so by the manner in which he waited for his master to follow him into the sunlight. Bud grinned.

"You're tellin' me the stage is in—and I got a letter to send."

Bud picked up his hat. Bondsman had already preceded him to the doorway, and stood waiting. His attitude expressed the extreme patience of age, but that the matter should be attended to without unreasonable delay. Shoop sighed heavily.

"That there dog bosses me around somethin' scandalous."

Halfway across the Blue Mesa, Dorothy met her ranger man. She had been watching the trail. Lorry dismounted and walked with her to the cabin. Bronson was glad to see him. They chatted for a while. Lorry would have spoken of his father's offer—of his plans, of many things he wished Bronson to know, yet he could not speak of these things until he had talked with Dorothy. He would see Bronson again. Meanwhile—

A little later Lorry went to his cabin to take stock of the implements and make his final report. He swept the cabin, picked up the loose odds and ends, closed the battered piano gently, and sat down to think.

He had made his decision, and yet—he had seen Dorothy again; touched her hand, talked with her, and watched her brown eyes while he talked. The Great War seemed very far away. And here he was at home. This was his country. But he had set his face toward the High Trail. He could not turn back.

Dorothy stood in the doorway, her finger at her lips. Bronson was busy writing. Lorry rose and stepped out. He stooped and lifted her to Gray Leg. She sat sideways in the saddle as he led the pony across the mesa to the veritable rim of the world.

Far below lay the open country, veiled by the soft haze of distance. He gave her his hand, and she slipped to the ground and stood beside him. For the first time the tremendous sweep of space appalled her. She drew close to him and touched his arm.

"What is it, Lorry?"

"You said—once—that you would wait for me."

"Yes. And now you are here, I'll never be lonesome again."

"Were you lonesome?"

"A little. I had never really waited—like that—before."

He frowned and gazed into the distances. It had been easy to decide—when alone. Then he faced her, his gray eyes clear and untroubled.

"I'm going to enlist," he said simply.

She had hoped that he would. She wanted to think that of him. And yet, now that he had spoken, now that he was actually going—Her eyes grew big. She wanted to say that she was glad. Her lips trembled.

He held out his arms. She felt their warm strength round her. On the instant she thought of begging him not to go. But his eyes were shining with a high purpose, that shamed her momentary indecision. She pressed her cheek to his.

"I will wait for you," she whispered, and her face was wet with tears of happiness.

She was no longer the little mother and he her boy, for in that moment he became to her the man strength of the race, his arms her refuge and his eyes her courage for the coming years.